DERAILED

DERAILED

A DETECTIVE RAVN THRILLER

MICHAEL KATZ KREFELD

Translated from Danish by Lindy Falk van Rooyen

Cover design by Podium Publishing

ISBN: 978-1-0394-3331-1

Published in 2023 by Podium Publishing, ULC
www.podiumaudio.com

DERAILED

“Always the same theme
But can’t you see
We’ve got everything going on.
Every time you go away
You take a piece of me with you.”

Daryl Hall

PROLOGUE

Stockholm, 2013

In the glow of the rising sun, the seagulls shrieked at each other over the scrapyard near Hjulsta. At the far end of the yard, a battered bulldozer was forging its way southwards. A thick black billow of smoke spewed exhaust fumes into the clear frosty sky. The bulldozer's driver, Anton, was wearing a winter coat with the scrapyard's green logo on his breast pocket and a padded leather cap pulled well down over his ears. He was sipping coffee from a thermos cup as he stared bleary-eyed through the windscreen, and he listened to the pop music that was blaring from his radio. But something on the massive heap of scrap engines and spare parts caught his eye and sharpened his focus. He took his foot off the accelerator and put the thermos cup on the instrument panel. Once the bulldozer had come to a halt, he got down from his cabin perch and walked over to the junk heap. His gaze followed its incline to the tip, where an emaciated naked woman was standing with her back facing him, as if looking out over the scrapyard. Anton took off one of his woollen mittens, fished his mobile phone out of his breast pocket, and quickly punched in a number.

The anorexic woman was planted in scrap metal up to her knees, as if to make sure that she wouldn't blow away in the stiff breeze. Her skin was pulled taut over her bones and painted with lime, which gave her body the appearance of marble. Even her eyeballs were chalk-white, and she stared over the rolling hills of junk metal, as if she were a Roman statue of a goddess.

"Hi, it's Anton," the driver said. "I've found another one."

"Found what?" his boss said in a sour voice.

"One of the white angels."

"Are you sure?"

"I'm looking right at her as we speak. She looks exactly like the others . . . What do you want me to do?"

A deep sigh sounded on the end of the line. "I guess we'll have to call the police . . . again."

1

Copenhagen, 16 October 2010

The old auto repair warehouse was deserted. In the dark, only the hum of the generator in the corner broke the desolate silence. A faint glow of blue came from the grease pit, which cut through the centre of the building. A portable spotlight lay in the bottom of the pit. Next to it on the filthy floor, a naked woman crouched in the foetal position. Her body was badly beaten and there were large bruises on her arms and legs, and her long blonde hair had clumps of dried blood from the open wound at her right temple. There were red lashing marks along her back and buttocks, as if she had been whipped.

Masja opened her eyes and stared into the sharp fluorescent light. She gasped for breath. Fear and adrenaline surged in her body once more. Every muscle tensed and her throat constricted with thirst. Slowly, she tried to get up, but the pain in her abdomen stopped her. She had no idea how she had ended up in this stinking hole. Her body ached and she could not think straight. She tried to get up again, and this time, supporting herself against the cold cement wall beside her, she managed to get to her knees. The temperature in the deserted warehouse was close to freezing point and she was shivering with cold. About two metres in front of her, she saw a small bundle of clothing. A red silk dress, a G-string, and a pair of mocha-coloured leather boots. She recognised them. They belonged to her. Someone must have undressed her, she realised. But she had no recollection of the details.

Suddenly, a loud noise came from the other side of the hall. Masja got to her feet slowly. A draught of night air entered the building, a momentary relief from the nauseating stench of oil and grease. Masja stood on her tiptoes, and just managed to peer over the edge of the grease pit. A group of people approached the pit. Two broad figures were pushing and shoving three slim ones, who were jostled between them. The broad figures ordered the slim ones to take the steps into the pit.

Masja grabbed her bundle of clothing and tried to cover herself with the dress. The slim figures were three girls about her own age. They could not have been more than eighteen or twenty years old. They appeared to be Slavic or Eastern European girls, she guessed. The one lagging at the back swayed on her feet, clearly under the influence of something or other. The other two girls clutched onto each other, crying and praying at once. Masja recognised their prayer; it was one of the Orthodox religious verses that she knew from her youth. And she could understand parts of the exchange between the two girls. They were speaking Russian.

"We're going to die here," cried the younger of the two girls.

Masja tried to say something, but her voice was gone.

Her throat ached when she tried again. "Who are y-you . . . ?" she stuttered. "Where are we?"

The two girls took no notice of her, simply clung to each other. Masja cast a look over her shoulder, but she could no longer see the two men who had brought the girls down. Taking the gap, she pulled on her bloody dress, pushed past the girls, and headed for the stairs. *I have to get away from here! Now!* she thought.

In that moment, she heard the outer door of the hall open again, and five men entered the building. The fluorescent pipes that ran along the edge of the grease pit lit up. Masja froze like a deer in headlights. She tried to shield her eyes with her hands, but the light was coming from all sides. Instinctively, she stumbled back to the other girls. The five men loomed above them. As if dragons in a fantasy, their breath formed huge clouds of condensation before their mouths. Masja could hear one of them speak in Russian. She could not understand the other voices, but she guessed that it was Albanian or Serbian, something like that.

"That one!" a voice bellowed out of the dark. "We've worked that one over good and proper already!"

She recognised the voice. The hoarse rasp he had when he spoke or panted. He was the one who had egged the others on when they raped her, and he was the one who used the belt on her. "Help, help me, Igor . . ."

Masja collapsed on the cold cement ground.

2

Two days earlier

Ragnar Bertelsen sat on the hotel bed, watching the news on the little TV that hung on the opposite wall. He was in his mid-fifties with thinning hair on his head, which was a stark contrast to the bushy mane on his chest and back. A towel with a Radisson logo was wrapped tightly around his middle in a vain attempt to hide the size of his large gut. Ragnar sipped his glass of prosecco. "That is a-ma-zing," he said in Norwegian, staring at the newscast. "Absolutely amazing!"

The bathroom door opened and Masja came into the room. Her naked hips and pert breasts shone from the body lotion that she had just applied after her bath. Ragnar was momentarily distracted by Masja's butt as she bent over to pick up her black G-string from the floor. "This is unbelievable."

Masja turned round, and Ragnar quickly averted his gaze.

"What's that?" Masja said, slipping on the G-string.

"Those miners from Chile! They've been trapped in a mine for more than two months, and now they have finally been rescued. Isn't that incredible?"

He pointed at the screen with his glass. CNN was broadcasting live, pixelated pictures from the mine where the miners, rescue workers and the president of their country were posing for the camera.

"And they were all trapped down there, you say?"

Ragnar frowned. "No, just the ones with the sunglasses. The story has been on the news all autumn. Didn't you hear about it?"

"I don't watch TV. I prefer to read."

"Really?" Ragnar cast her a sceptical glance. "I would never have guessed."

Masja shrugged as she wriggled into her wine-red dress. "Why are they wearing sunglasses?"

"Because their eyes are not used to daylight, which is much too bright for them after such a long time underground. They would damage their eyes if they didn't wear sunglasses."

"Huh. My boyfriend has exactly the same sunglasses. He's crazy about them. Oakley Radar. Before, he used to swear by M Frame and Jawbone. They cost a packet, but it's worth every penny, he says."

Ragnar wasn't sure what she was talking about, but he nodded politely before returning his attention to the screen.

Masja found her black clutch bag on the little oval table in front of the panorama window, and for a moment, she enjoyed the view of the city from the sixteenth floor. The traffic over Langebro towards the Copenhagen Town Hall had increased. On the Christianshavn side, the golden tower of the Church of Our Saviour glinted in the afternoon sun. Igor had invited her up there on their first date three months ago, but unfortunately the tower had been closed that day. And he didn't mention it again. Come to think of it, it had been a while since they'd done something together. But he'd promised her that they'd go out for sushi when she got off work. That felt a bit like a date.

Masja turned and headed for the door. "See you around, love," she said to her client.

Ragnar got up from the bed. "Can I tempt the young lady with a glass of bubbly before she goes?"

"No, thanks, sweetheart. Maybe next time," she said, already at the door.

"So, I can call you again?"

"Of course, sweetheart, you were super cute."

Ragnar came over and gallantly opened the door for her. "And you were . . . fantastic," he said with a smile that showed how much he meant it. "A last kiss goodbye?"

"On the cheek," she said prettily, presenting it to him.

Ragnar kissed her gently. "See you, Karina," he said, watching her walk down the corridor.

Masja pushed the elevator button. The doors opened and she cast Ragnar a little smile over her shoulder before stepping inside.

On the way down she counted the money that her client had given Karina for the ride. "Karina" was her professional name. It sounded sufficiently Danish to hide her Lithuanian roots, even though the clients really couldn't care less where she came from as long as she delivered the goods. And that Karina did, to whoever would pay the 1,700-kroner-plus per hour for an escort. All the "teddy bears" and other losers who waited around in hotels. Unlike Masja. *She* had a boyfriend.

His name was Igor, and he was waiting for her downstairs in the lobby.

3

The parking lot in front of the Copenhagen Radisson Hotel was almost empty. In her high heels, Masja struggled to keep up with Igor's long strides back to the car. Igor had grown up in Saint Petersburg, but he was strutting across the parking lot as if he were a hip-hop gangster from California. Flexing his muscles, shades perched on his forehead, he pitched and rolled on his trainers as he walked, a style directly imported from MTV rather than a tough childhood in a ghetto.

"Fuck, my throat's bone-dry," Igor said, glancing over his shoulder at Masja. He had his mobile phone up to his ear, waiting for his call to be answered. "These days, I don't get anything to eat but peanuts," he added, jerking his thumb at the hotel bar where he had been waiting for her.

"Sweetheart, I've told you so many times that you don't need to drive me to work."

"Who else is going to look after you, baby?"

"I can take care of myself. The teddy bears are harmless."

"I hate those fuckers. You're much too good for them."

A voice came on the other end of the line and Igor's attention immediately reverted to the phone. He presented himself in Russian, said yes, thank you, he was ready and grateful for their trust and the chance to join the game tonight. Masja was surprised to hear the humble ring of his voice. Humility was very rare for Igor.

He fished the car keys out of the pocket of his black leather jacket, tipped his Oakleys in place, and pressed the button, immediately prompting a crisp beep from the black BMW 320i with polished eighteen-inch hubcaps gleaming in the parking lot right in front of them. Igor ended his conversation and got into the driver's seat.

"Who was that?" Masja asked as she slammed her door closed.

"No one. It's just business," he muttered, and leaned over to open the glove compartment. Reaching inside, he took out a Wunder-Baum from the pile and replaced the used one hanging from the rear-view mirror.

Masja couldn't stand the synthetic smell of "green apple." She pinched her nose. "There's something I have been thinking about . . . with regards to . . . business."

"Yeah?" Igor said distractedly as he punched another number into his phone and started the car.

"I want to give it up. I don't want to do this anymore. I want to find something else."

"Really? Why?"

"But . . . I thought you'd be happy. You don't like me . . . what I'm doing," she said with a little pout on her lips.

Igor shrugged and transferred the phone to his other ear, still waiting for the person to pick up. "I don't want to interfere with your decisions. I understand you. I understand that you want to make money. I don't judge, you know that, baby. It's your call."

"Money isn't everything. We can get by with less."

A scornful laugh escaped from Igor's lips. "Money is *everything* in this world. If you don't have it, you're nothing. Without it, folks piss all over you. Believe me. *Hej*, Janusz, what's up, man?" he said into the receiver. "You'll never guess . . . I'm in! The old man is gonna let me play. It's gonna be wild!"

As he steered the car down Amager Boulevard towards Christianshavn, Igor told Janusz about the poker game that was happening that night. It would take place at Kaminsky's, in the back room that was known as the King's Suite. Only the best of the best were invited to their table, the big-time players. Kaminsky had no time for lightweights who just arsed around, juggling their chips, and tonight's game was set with the old guard from the Balkans, men with big money, even bigger balls, and lousy poker faces. Igor laughed. He told Janusz that he'd been busting his chops for months to get an invitation, so he could show Kaminsky that he had what it took to win and secure the old man his 28 precent commission on the profit. "You can bet your fucking arse I'm a player, my man!"

Masja gave him a look when he finally put the phone away. Igor smiled at her sweetly.

"You're going to play tonight?" she said.

"Yeah, baby. It's a great opportunity."

"But we are going out for dinner. Sushi. You promised."

Igor took a deep breath. "This is a big chance for me, baby."

"But you promised."

The traffic lights ahead changed to red, and Igor braked sharply. He twisted his torso towards her and took off his Oakleys. His soft brown eyes were like molten pots of chocolate, and he gave her a look of absolute adoration. He gave her that look the first day they met, Masja remembered. That look made her knees weak. "You know that you are the most important thing in my life, baby."

"We had a date," Masja said disapprovingly. Her lips pouted again.

"I'll make it up to you, I promise, but I can't let this chance pass me by."

"But I've cancelled a lot of things for our sake."

"But baby, I'm doing this for *us*. This is a very important game. I'm going to sit at the table with those rich old teddy bears, who are ripe for the plucking. One of us still has to earn money, right?" he said with that beguiling smile of his, turning up the charm.

"We'll celebrate big time tomorrow. I promise."

"I don't want to celebrate. I just want us to be together," she said sulkily.

"Me too, baby. Me too." He took her chin in his hand, gently made her look up, and kissed her on the lips. The goatee and slim moustache outlining his mouth tickled her lips.

The lights had turned green, and the car behind them tooted impatiently. Igor ignored it and kept kissing her, caressing Masja's cheek all the while.

His fingers reeked of "green apple," but in that moment, Masja couldn't have cared less.

4

It was 3:30 a.m. and the four men in the back room at Kaminsky's had been playing Texas hold 'em for over five hours. The pile of chips had shifted back and forth evenly between the players, but now a clear pattern was emerging. The largest pile stood in front of Igor and Lucian, a fat middle-aged Serbian man who was dressed in camouflage trousers with a Hawaiian shirt. It was only a matter of time before the other two players, Milan and Rastko, would be annihilated. The King's Suite reeked of sweat, cigarette smoke, and the beetroot soup that Kaminsky was lovingly stirring in a pot in the small tea kitchen just behind the card table. If you lost at his table, he gave you a bowl of beetroot soup. A meagre comfort. Welcome to Kaminsky's.

Loud cheers could be heard from the front room, where the other guests were watching a football game from the East European league on TV. Kaminsky's guests came to his place to see sport, play cards, drink, and, not least, take care of their mutual business. As a rule, the kind of deals that did not tolerate the scrutiny of daylight. Most of the guests came from the old guard of countries neighbouring the Caucasus: Belarus, Ukraine, the Baltics. As such, Kaminsky's club, which presented itself on the street as a closed-down hairdressers on Colbjørnsensgade just behind Copenhagen Central Station, was nicknamed Little Soviet. But the name could also have something to do with the fact that Kaminsky's moustache and unpredictable temperament gave him an uncanny likeness to Stalin in the latter years of his rule.

Milan dried his sweaty hands on his shirt before pushing the last of his chips into the pot, which stood in the middle of the table. He glanced at the beetroot soup involuntarily, as if he already knew that this would be his last hand. "How about the story of those Chilean miners who got rescued from that mine collapse?"

Rastko, who was sitting opposite Milan, scratched his bushy grey-speckled beard and yawned. "They must be really horny after two months in that hole, unless of course they're all fags and have been fucking each other all this time."

Milan laughed and leaned back in his chair. "Are you in, Igor?"

Igor nodded and raised his hand by 500 euros. And he saw the twitch at the corner of Lucian's eye at once. It was faint, but he *did* see it. *This hand will be mine, regardless of the size of Lucian's raise,* he thought triumphantly. It was a hard-core game, much better than he'd expected. As the game progressed, and his pile of chips grew, Igor had often been tempted to turn his head to catch a hint of acknowledgement in Kaminsky's eye, but he had restrained himself.

"I heard that both the mistress *and* the wife of one of the miners were waiting for him. Can you imagine how much shit he was in?" Milan laughed raucously. His entire body jiggled with every snort of laughter.

"Yeah, he probably wished he could go back down the shaft immediately," replied Rastko, cackling along with Milan.

Lucian folded and tossed his cards down in front of him. "Are we here to play cards or gaggle like hens at a tea party?"

Igor turned over his cards, showing the others his two nines, which, together with the community cards on the table, was more than enough to tip the scales in his favour. He leaned forward and raked the chips into his own pile.

Rastko and Milan were relegated to the soup pot. Only Igor and Lucian were left at the table. They played for another hour, without the chips shifting ownership significantly. Igor was only 1,000 euros ahead of Lucian, which was not enough to force his hand. Even though the winnings in front of him were impressive, the situation irked Igor. Lucian was tiring, worn thin by the long hours at the table and endless glasses of slivovitz. And he was bleary-eyed from all those Drina cigarettes that he'd been chain-smoking from the moment he sat down. Frankly, the guy was starting to look like an easy victim. Till now, he'd been able to keep himself sufficiently awake so as not to fall into any of the traps that Igor had laid for him along the way.

As soon as the next round was dealt, Igor could see that Lucian had received something that he could use. With two jacks already on the table, it was not difficult to figure out that he had one of the kings in his hand. Lucian raised the stakes and pushed half of his chips to the middle of the table: 10,000 euros. Igor wasn't about to get his balls in a knot about Lucian's jacks; he knew that he was holding both the Queen of Hearts and the Queen of Spades. "I see your ten and raise you ten thousand." With outstretched arms, Igor shoved his chips into the centre of the table. One pile toppled onto the other and scattered over the surface.

"Stop tossing your chips around, boy," snapped Lucian.

"They're *my* chips, and I'll do with them whatever the hell I want," Igor shot back, deliberately trying to get a rise out of his opponent. And he wasn't disappointed. When Igor played his river card, which was the King of Clubs, Lucian pushed the remainder of his chips into the pot. Then he took out his wallet and started hauling out bills. "I'll bloody well raise the stakes so I can watch you fall flat on your puppy-dog face!"

A hush fell over the room. Igor turned around and looked at Kaminsky. The old man had stopped stirring his pot on the stove. Everyone knew that you never laid cold cash, or anything of value for that matter, on his table. Everyone knew better than to expose Kaminsky to that kind of embarrassment, should the cops—against all odds—decide to pitch up for a visit.

Kaminsky rubbed his moustache and watched Igor, who was already smiling victoriously. "See that you finish your game," the old man said. Then he returned to stirring his blood-red soup.

Igor turned back around to Lucian, who sat watching him with his arms crossed over his chest.

"You keep twiddling your chips—as long as you still have them," Lucian told Igor triumphantly.

Igor shoved the remainder of his chips to the centre of the table. Lucian couldn't bluff him; he didn't have any kings and he knew it.

Lucian picked up the jacks, the same jacks supporting his raise in the first instance. The same jacks that would not be worth shit against Igor's ladies. *This was almost too easy*, Igor thought. Even with Kaminsky's cut, there was more money on the table than he had ever dreamt of winning. Enough to trade in on a new car, enough to buy a new flat-screen—fuck that, he could buy an *entire* new flat instead.

"You're only halfway up on your raise," Lucian pointed out.

"The rest is only a telephone call away," Igor said, leaning his elbows on the table. "I don't go throwing money around like a child on the town with daddy's wallet. But I'm good for whatever you've got in your moleskin," Igor said mockingly, nodding at Lucian's worn leather wallet.

Lucian lifted his bleary eyes. Beyond Igor's shoulder, he noticed that Kaminsky was giving him a hard stare. "All right," he said gruffly. "I believe you. What've you got?"

Igor grinned. "That king didn't help you," he said, poking a finger at the card that lay on the table between them. "Least of all when you're collecting jacks. Gentlemen, may I introduce you to my ladies?" he said, turning over his cards. "Together with her sister on the table, they make for a fine threesome, don't you think?"

Lucian focused his gaze on the cards and nodded with an impressed expression on his face. Then he dried his sweaty forehead with the back of his hand and leaned towards his cards. "You know, you were right about that jack. It was good to get hold of him," he said, flipping his card to show his Jack of Clubs. "And in the company of his father, the King of Clubs, ten of Clubs, and the nine on the table, these lads can perform miracles," he added with a nasty smile on his lips. "Do you know the odds of a royal straight flush?"

"But of course," Igor replied with a smile. "One to six hundred thousand, or thereabouts. Not the best odds, in fact."

Lucian nodded and picked up his card. "Which must make me one of the luckiest men in the world. Luckier than those goddamned miners who everyone keeps gabbing on about."

Igor shrugged. "We'll see."

"Yes, we'll see," Lucian repeated, turning over his card.

In an instant, Igor's world crashed. Everything around him seemed to drop away, except for that Queen of Spades, which shot a blinding light into his face. He could not tear his eyes away from it. He couldn't breathe and felt his throat constrict, as if he had a noose around his neck. He thought he was going to die, right then and there, or maybe he just hoped that he would. At that moment, death would come as a salvation.

"Good thing your mouth is open, my friend, because it's time to eat your soup," said Lucian.

The other two Serbians came to the table. Looked down at the cards. "I'll be damned," said Milan. "What a hand. What a game. This one's made for the history books. How much money is in the pot?" His eyes skimmed over the chips and the pile of banknotes strewn on top. Then he smiled at Lucian. "Respect, man. You've just won thirty thousand euros." He clapped Igor on the shoulder. "And you, my pal, have to make the most expensive call you've ever made."

"I-I—" Igor stammered. He tried to smile, but he couldn't breathe, let alone pretend to be cool. "I . . . seem to have spoken too soon."

"What do you mean?"

He looked at Lucian. "Of course I have some of the money—of course I do—but I . . ." He raised his palms helplessly, desperately hoping for some kind of understanding.

The three Serbians pinned him with an ice-cold stare. "Are you saying that you cannot pay?" Lucian said through gritted teeth.

"No, no, I can pay . . . most of it, but . . ."

"'Most of it' is not good enough," said Milan.

"Not good enough at all," said Rastko.

"Perhaps you would prefer a Serbian manicure?" Lucian put his hand into his pocket and brought out a pair of rusty pruning shears, which he slapped down on the table. "It will be pretty hard for you to play poker without any fingers."

Igor stared at the shears in panic. He scraped back his chair and tried to jump to his feet, but Milan moved surprisingly quickly and pushed him back down onto his seat. "Not so fast, pal."

"Put that away," Kaminsky's voice said behind them. The old man slowly put down the soup ladle. Then he turned down the gas on the stove. Then he calmly made his way over to the table. "Put it down, I said. Right now."

Lucian stared up at Kaminsky, who stared right back. After a moment's hesitation, Lucian reluctantly put the shears back into his pocket. "I just want the money that I have earned, nothing else."

"Igor will get you your money. You can trust him, else he wouldn't be sitting at my table. Understood?"

"Yes, of course, Kaminsky," said Lucian without looking up. He crossed his arms over his chest. "Forgive my outburst. I intended you no disrespect, you know that. How much do you have, boy?"

Igor stared at the floor. "About forty thousand—in Danish kroner."

Lucian raised an eyebrow at Milan. He shook his head. "That's nowhere near enough," he said.

"You have twenty-four hours, or else . . . snip, snip," said Lucian, raising a hand and demonstrating his promise with the index and middle finger of his right hand.

5

Christianshavn, 2013

It was Friday night and The Sea Otter, an old pub next to the canal in the Christianshavn Quarter, was packed. It had become a "hip" place to be once more. "Every Time You Go Away" was blaring from the jukebox. At The Sea Otter you could get a beer for 20 kroner, listen to the golden oldies on the jukebox, roll the dice for the next round, or simply mind your own damn business and kiss your girl in a corner in peace, and as Daryl Hall crooned the last lines of his song, one more time, Thomas Ravnsholdt got up from his barstool. He swayed on his feet and signalled to Johnson behind the bar that he'd like another "set." Ravn drank Jim Beam shots in a glass with Carlsberg Hof from the bottle.

"Don't you think you've had enough, Ravn?" Johnson muttered.

"I haven't even got started," Thomas slurred.

Johnson raised his eyebrows at Thomas but took the order and fixed him another round. Just turned fifty, Johnson was a man with the body of an ox but for the tattoos that ran all the way down his bulky arms. You couldn't see what they represented, the tattoos, because he'd had them done way back when he was just a conscripted sailor boy on Her Majesty the Queen's royal yacht, *Dannebrog*.

Thomas was weaving his way through the crowd, aiming for the jukebox—an old Wurlitzer, which had stood in that corner in the pub for as long as he could remember. While he rummaged through his jacket pockets for coins, he looked at the photographs that hung on the wall above the jukebox. Signed black-and-white portraits of legendary artists and musicians who had visited The Sea Otter over the years: Gasolin', Lone Kellermann, Clausen & Petersen, Kim Larsen, and Thomas's personal favourite, Mr. DT—wearing black nail polish, a hat to match, and a white tuxedo.

Thomas inserted a 5-kroner coin into the slot. He didn't have to look at the buttons because he knew exactly what he wanted to hear: F-5. *Take it away, Daryl*, and the Wurlitzer did not disappoint. The familiar sound of the metronome and the distorted electric organ cranked the song in motion. Behind him, a couple of guests jeered and yelled at him to put on something else. Thomas ignored them and shuffled back to his barstool.

"Hey, you, sailor boy!" a voice shouted as he was about to sit down.

Thomas half-turned and cast a glance over his shoulder. At the table behind him sat a muscular biker dude in yellow shades and a T-shirt that looked three sizes too small for him. "We've heard that song more than enough times, understood?"

"But it's a classshic," slurred Thomas.

"That doesn't make it any better. It's still moffie-music." Snorts of laughter came from the dude's two comrades sharing his table. Wearing matching leather vests with a logo on the back, each clutched their respective dice cups.

"So call me a 'moffie,' but there still hasn't been a better song written since."

"I think I prefer the other one, the original version," said a middle-aged woman in a tweed suit at the bar counter. She had a bush of wiry grey hair that sprang out of her head in all directions, as if she'd stuck her fingers in a plug.

Thomas turned and smiled at the woman who was propping up the bar counter at the opposite end to his. "My dear Victoria, this *is* the original version: Daryl Hall wrote and recorded the song in 1980—five years *before* Paul Young made it famous. With all due respect to Paul, he's not in the same league as Daryl," he said, and took up his seat again.

Victoria threw back her head and exhaled a cloud of smoke up to the ceiling. "If you say so, my friend. I still prefer the other one."

"Each to their own, Victoria," Thomas said with a shrug. "We live in a free country."

Johnson stole a glance at the biker dudes as he set the Hof down on the counter. "Ravn, don't you think it's time to get back to your nest?"

Thomas shook his head and picked up his shot glass. "Not voluntarily, my friend."

He downed the shot of Jim Beam and chased with the Hof. Five minutes later, Daryl Hall had reached the final chorus line, and as if on cue, Thomas slid off his barstool, made his way over to the Wurlitzer, and fumbled for coins in his pockets.

The biker with the yellow shades looked up from his dice cup and caught sight of Thomas.

"No fucking way!" he fumed. He pushed to his feet and elbowed his way through the crowd till he was standing right in Thomas's face. "You've played that song for the last time," he said, and shoved Thomas aside. He deposited his own coin in the slot, and moments later the jukebox responded with the sound of AC/DC's "Highway to Hell." The biker turned on his heel and punched a victorious fist in the air as he sauntered back to his mates, who were nodding enthusiastically to the AC/DC beat.

Thomas was still in the corner, swaying on his feet. He tried to focus on the pictures in front of him, gave up, and simply began turning his pockets inside out, then laid his find on top of the jukebox, one coin after another. By the time he was done ransacking his clothing, a modest bounty of 5- and 10-kroner coins was piled next to his battered mobile phone and a crumpled, laminated police badge. He reckoned he had enough money for fifteen songs: "Every Time You Go Away" fifteen times. *Take it away, Daryl. This is going to be an excellent evening.*

Thomas stumbled back to his barstool and ordered a new round for himself and a vermouth for Victoria, who raised her glass gratefully and called him an angel. Moments later, the electric organ chimed, and Daryl dutifully took it away.

All at once, a ruckus broke out behind Thomas. The biker dudes had had enough.

"That's fucking it!" Yellow Shades was on his feet and charging to the jukebox in a second. Without taking a beat, he bent down and flexed every muscle in his body, seriously jeopardising the confines of his T-shirt as he lifted the Wurlitzer and unceremoniously dropped it again. The jukebox tilted, whimpered, and went *shtum*. The cheerful vibe in the pub continued regardless, the chatter so loud that only those guests who were in the immediate vicinity of the jukebox noticed its demise. Johnson looked up from the bar and merely watched in silence as the biker made his way back to his table. But as he came past, Thomas slid off his barstool. He looked up at the bloke standing in front of him. He was at least one and a half heads taller than Thomas.

"You owe me seventy-five kroner for that stunt you just pulled," he said quietly.

"Is that so?!" the biker growled.

Victoria appeared at Thomas's side and laid a hand on his shoulder. "Maybe you should let this one go, Ravn?" She turned to the biker and gave him a cold smile. "Why don't we all mind our own business?"

"Not a chance," Thomas said, shaking his head. "I put seventy-five kroner in the jukebox. You killed it. Ergo, you owe me seventy-five kroner."

The biker looked Victoria up and down, then returned his gaze to Thomas. "Maybe you should listen to your lezzie girlfriend here before you get hurt?"

"Victoria is not a lesbian. She just really likes tweed," Thomas mumbled.

"I still think she looks like a lezzie."

Victoria narrowed her eyes at the biker. "For a bloke with boobs, you're surprisingly obsessed with other people's sexuality," she said.

The biker bloke's jaw dropped. He gaped at Victoria and Thomas in turn.

Thomas crossed his arms over his chest. "Come to think of it, Victoria, I think this guy owes you an apology as well, not to mention Daryl, for rudely interrupting his song. So, who would you like to apologise to first?"

"Are you fucking brain dead?" the biker spat.

"Possibly. But you still owe me seventy-five kroner, and an apology to Daryl and Victoria."

"Niller!" one of the biker's mates yelled from their table behind them.

"What?!" Yellow Shades snapped, turning his head.

"That guy's a copper," he said, nodding at Thomas with a worried expression on his face. "Maybe you should just let it go, man."

Niller tipped his yellow shades down his nose and peered over the rim at Thomas. "You've got to be joking! This ol' prick?" he said, jerking his thumb at Thomas.

His pal nodded. "Last summer, he busted me and Rune outside Christiania with a brick of Marok."

Niller turned and stared at Thomas, utterly incredulous. He crossed his arms over his chest. "Is that true? You a copper?"

"Regardless of what I am, you still owe me seventy-five kroner and an apology to Victoria and Daryl."

"Are you?!" Niller yelled in his face. Then his arms fell to his sides, both fists clenched.

"He's on leave though," Victoria explained, "so you won't be thrown in a cell *today*." She gulped down the last of her vermouth with satisfaction.

"On leave? Really?" A grim smile came to Niller's lips. Then he took a swing with his right arm.

Thomas retracted his head a couple of centimetres and just managed to avoid getting Niller's fist in his face. He followed up with a left hook, which Thomas dodged while jabbing his elbow against the biker's temple. Usually, a blow from Thomas's elbow would have sent anyone to the floor, but given his drunken state, his aim was a bit off and he merely grazed the target as a result. Even so, the biker lost his shades, which were sent flying across the room. Thomas watched their trajectory in fascination, as if they were a winged insect passing over the heads of the guests at the counter. The thought was absurd and brought a smile to his lips, till he felt the sharp blow of a fist in his solar plexus. Followed by a second clean shot on his cheek. The latter knocked Thomas to the floor. His vision blurred and he was only vaguely aware of the feet of the people who intervened and kept Niller from stomping on his head. Then he passed out cold.

Ten minutes later, Thomas was sitting on the kerb outside The Sea Otter, a dishcloth filled with ice pressed against his swollen chin. The three biker dudes were a little further down the road, yelling insults at Johnson and a posse of regular customers who were gathered by the door.

Eduardo was squatting down next to Thomas, regarding him with concern through his thick glasses. "Bloody hell, Ravn, what were you thinking?" he said with the lilt of a Spanish accent. *"Eres stupida?"*

Thomas shook his head. It hurt like hell, and he instantly regretted the movement. "Did the arsehole apologise? Did he?!"

"Yes, of course he did, Ravn, with his fist. Five times, in fact," Eduardo replied, raking a hand through his curly dark hair.

Thomas shrugged. "Well, that's all I asked for," he mumbled. "But he still owes me seventy-five kroner."

A blonde girl tugged on Eduardo's arm and told him that she'd like to get back inside, where it was warm. "Are you going to be okay?" asked Eduardo.

Thomas nodded, sending another shot of pain into his brain. Not long after, he heard the remainder of the guests at the door go back into the pub. He rose to his feet unsteadily. "The next round is on me," he said, making for the door. But Johnson put a hand on his chest and took the dishcloth from him.

"Go home, Ravn."

"What do you mean?"

Johnson made no reply, simply regarded him evenly.

"Not even one for the road?"

Johnson stood his ground in silence.

All things considered, Thomas was mindful of keeping a safe distance from the edge of the canal. He stuck to the pavement, deliberately avoiding the raised cobbles. He knew that many a drunkard had been tripped up by them before, landed in the harbour, and drowned.

It was closing time, and there was a jolly atmosphere in the pubs all along the canal. On Christianshavn Square, folks jostled for taxis to take them over Langebro Bridge to the nightclubs in the Copenhagen city. Luckily, he only needed to get to the other side of the street, but he was too drunk to judge the distance between the cars that rushed past.

A honking horn warned him that he was about to get run over, and he stumbled across the second lane as fast as he could.

When he reached the other end of the square, he continued down Dronningensgade towards the old city wall, which flanked the residential block where he lived. He fumbled in his pocket for the keys. Throwing his head back, he looked up to the top floor. The living room lights were still on. He took the stairs, arrived in front of the door, and was about to put his keys in the keyhole, but the buzzer against the wall distracted him: *Thomas Ravnsholdt & Eva Kilde* the little square of paper taped above it said. Written in Eva's handwriting. Thomas turned on his heel and went back down the stairs.

Thomas walked down Sofiegade, which led him back to the canal. In the dark, he could just make out the boats that were tethered at the end of the street, including his own, which had a short mast and a jib sail with a radar at the top. The radar didn't actually work, nor had he ever raised the sail, but the mast distinguished his boat from the others, and generally served as a useful target in his drunken attempts to find his way home.

He wobbled from the quay onto the aft deck. He knew that one of the hatch covers was missing, and he tread around the hole carefully, picking his way towards the cabin of his old Grand Banks. He yanked on the door, which was hanging on its hinges. He swore an oath. *I really ought to get it fixed one day*, he thought.

A clammy smell of damp and the leftovers in the pizza boxes that were piled on the moth-bitten sofa greeted him as he stepped inside. He continued past the kitchenette and down the steps that led down to the V-bunk in the sleeping quarters. He threw himself onto the mattress and closed his eyes, listening to the rain, which had just begun to drum on the hatch pane just above him. He knew that it was only a matter of minutes before the worn canvas over his cabin would start to leak, pissing down rain onto his feet. He knew that he ought to get up and find a bucket to put at the foot-end of his bunk. But he couldn't face getting up, and right now, getting his toes wet was the least of his problems.

6

15 October 2010

Masja was sitting on the black leather sofa, a duvet wrapped around her. Lajka, her chihuahua, was snuggled in her lap as she tried to read the latest volume of *The Witch Dragon's Daughter*, a fantasy series that she followed religiously. It was after 10 a.m. and she still had not heard from Igor. For once, she couldn't concentrate on her book. Then she heard his key in the front door, and Igor's voice as he came into the hallway.

Lajka jumped up and started to bark loudly. Masja hushed up the dog. She tried to discern who Igor was talking to on the phone, but all she could make out was that Igor said that he had to sell his car. That didn't make any sense. Igor loved that car—he'd even given it a nickname.

Igor walked into the living room. Without looking in her direction, he shrugged off his leather jacket, cradling his mobile phone to his ear. "Fuck you, Janusz, we both know that Lola is worth more than that. You're taking advantage of the situation."

Igor ended the call and threw the phone onto their marble dining table. His face was pale as a sheet, and he had black rings under his eyes. Masja could smell him from the sofa. She wrinkled her nose and shuddered. Stale alcohol and sweat reminded her of the worst kind of clients. Lajka kept barking, even though she tried to shut her up. "Where have you been all night?" Masja asked.

Igor raised his hand. "Not now, Masja. Tell me, how much cash have we got?" Instead of waiting for an answer, he flipped over their black leather armchair.

"What the hell are you doing?!"

Igor didn't reply but found what he was looking for: the thick white envelope that was hidden between the seat of the chair and its springs.

"That is *my* money. Keep your paws off it," Masja snapped angrily.

Igor ignored her. "I need to borrow some," he said. "I'm flat broke."

"What about the five thousand kroner that you already owe me?"

He shot her a glance. "You live here for free, am I right?"

"Gee, thanks, Igor," she said sarcastically.

He tore open the envelope and started counting the notes. "Nineteen thousand. Is that really all you've got?"

Masja's body was shaking with rage now. "First you stay away all night, without a word, and then you come home and steal my money! Have you lost your fucking mind?!"

"It's just a loan, Masja. Are you sure you don't have any more?" He tossed the envelope and stuck the wad of notes into the front of his jeans.

"No, you've taken all I have. Satisfied?" she yelled back.

Lajka cowered, hopped off her lap, and took cover under the coffee table.

Igor covered his face with one hand. "What about your mother? Can we borrow money from her?"

Masja sat up on the sofa. "My mother?!"

"Yes, for fuck's sake. How much can we get from her?"

Masja snorted in disbelief. "You've got to be really desperate, Igor. My mother doesn't earn shit. She's a cleaning lady, you know that. *I* am the one who sends *her* money every month, remember?"

"Okay, okay," he said. "Have you got any appointments today? Any clients?"

"Fuck you, Igor. Fuck you for asking me that!"

"I'm sorry, baby, but I'm desperate." He looked at her with an expression of utter defeat in his eyes. "So do you have any or not?"

Masja was on the verge of tears. Damned him for being such an idiot. "Didn't you hear what I said yesterday? I don't want to do this anymore. Don't you understand?!"

Igor came over to the sofa and sat down beside her. "Yes, of course I do. But that's a long-term goal. And this is happening right now."

"How much have you lost?"

"Too much," Igor said, bowing his head. "Much too much."Masja had an urge to stroke his hair, but before she could do so, Igor jumped to his feet again. He picked up his phone from the marble table and redialled Janusz's number. "Lola is yours for forty. But I must have the money today." Then he hung up and turned around to face Masja.

She felt sorry for him. With his hands hanging loosely by his sides, Igor looked like a wet dog. He looked just like Lajka after they'd come home from a walk in the rain. "Come here, sweetheart, let's cuddle for a bit."

"Later," Igor said. "I need to make a phone call." With that, he turned on his heel and went into the bedroom with his phone. The door closed behind him.

Masja leaned back into the sofa and called to Lajka. The dog returned to her lap, made herself comfortable, licking Masja's fingers with a whimper, but she rapped the dog on the snout. She *hated* it when the dog licked her. *Poor Igor*, she thought. He was such a fool—he always believed that there was an easy way out. They had to get out of this rut, do something else, she thought. Even if they wouldn't have much money. Even though she might end up like her mother—scrubbing floors for the rich bloody Danes, all those snobby bitches who thought they were better than her. But what else could she do? And what could Igor do, other than drive stolen cars up to Poland and gamble away his money?

Igor returned to the living room and sat down next to her again.

"Did you get it sorted out?"

Igor was breathing heavily. "I need to ask you a massive favour."

"What is it?" she said, already wary.

"The guy I owe money to has made a suggestion," Igor said, keeping his eyes fixed on the floor.

"What kind of suggestion?"

"Guess for yourself."

Masja pinched her eyes shut. "What are you saying, Igor? Do you really think so little of me? Do you?"

"No, baby, of course not," he said, choking back the tears.

"This is *your* problem, Igor, not mine. You can go fuck him yourself."

"You don't understand how bad it is, baby." He looked up at her as the tears rolled down his cheeks. "They'll cut off my fingers if I don't pay."

"Really?" she said, incredulous, glancing at her own newly manicured nails. "Well, at least then you won't be able to gamble anymore." Too late, she realised that his arm was in the air and the slap hit her hard in the face. Masja screamed and put a hand to her cheek.

Lajka squealed and fled under the coffee table again.

"I'm sorry, I'm sorry, I'm sorry," Igor said. Weeping bitterly, he buried his head in her lap.

Masja screamed and yelled at him, pummelling her fists against his back, neck, and head.

Igor did nothing to protect himself. He just sobbed and let her hit him.

Finally, all Masja's strength was spent, and she started to cry as well.

7

It was seven thirty in the evening and Masja was standing in front of the mirror in the bathroom. She drew a thin line around her plump red lips. She was wearing her favourite wine-red silk dress with a pair of mocha-brown soft leather boots. Igor was standing in the bathroom doorway, smoking as he watched her apply her make-up. "I'm sorry, baby, really I am."

Masja did not reply. She gave her hair a final layer of spray and checked that she didn't have any lipstick on her teeth. Then she turned to Igor. "Shouldn't we get going?"

They drove down Torvegade, past the old city wall around Christiania, and continued down Vermlandsgade. Dusk had fallen, and apart from the occasional taxi heading north to the airport, there were hardly any other cars on the road. "I promise that everything will be better after this," said Igor, shooting a glance in her direction. "I'm going to stop playing, get out of this shitty game, I promise you that, baby. From now on, it's just going to be the two of us."

He rested a hand on her thigh. Masja removed it.

"I understand that you're angry," said Igor. "I'm a piece of shit, an idiot, a swine . . ."

"Could you just shut your mouth, please?"

"Of course, sweetheart, I understand. But just so you know . . ."

Igor hesitated and looked at Masja again. She avoided his eyes and looked out the side window.

"From now on, we'll do it your way," Igor went on. "We'll be a little family—with a baby and everything, just like you wanted. I'll find a job. A real job. There are many things I can do, just you wait and see . . ."

"Can you please stop talking now?"

Igor did as she asked. He took the lane to Amager and turned off at Yderlandsvej, where the auto dealers and bus companies were lined one after the other. Masja's gaze lingered on a row of colourful double-decker buses. They were sightseeing buses for the tourists in the summer, but now they were parked under the roof next to a large, abandoned warehouse. Many years ago, just after they arrived in Denmark, she and her mother had taken a sightseeing trip in one of those buses. Her mother was ecstatic, but she had been desperate to pee about an hour in and had barely been able to enjoy the ride. This place was so far removed from the five-star hotels she was used to—far removed from just about everything, she reflected—and she was beginning to regret agreeing to come out here.

"So, here we are," said Igor, turning into a dark parking lot. In front of them lay an abandoned auto warehouse. Multiple window panes of the warehouse were broken. The crumbling façade was defaced with graffiti.

"I'll give him half an hour. Not a second more," Masja said as she got out of the car.

They crossed the parking lot and came to a tall blue gate. The rank stench of oil filled their nostrils when they entered the warehouse. Masja involuntarily pinched her nose between her forefinger and thumb and concentrated on breathing through her mouth. In a haze of tobacco smoke, at the far end of the massive hall sat four middle-aged men around a little table.

Masja walked along the edge of the long grease pit, which extended down the centre of the building, and walked directly up to the men at the table. They were drinking vodka and canned beers. Igor noticed that they'd probably just kept drinking after he left Kaminsky's in the early hours of that morning.

Lucian half-turned on his stool and gave Igor a cold glance before allowing his gaze to rest on Masja. He wiped his mouth. "So, you've returned with your girlfriend for me?" he said, blowing a column of smoke up to the ceiling. "We'll see if that's enough."

The men around the table leered at Masja and laughed among themselves. Then Lucian came unsteadily to his feet. "She's a pretty whore, I'll give you that, Igor. A lovely little bitch. You've been a lucky man."

Masja narrowed her eyes. "Why don't we keep things friendly?"

"Why?" said Lucian, staring at her. "That's what you are, after all: a whore. You make your living fucking men. The only question is: Are you good at it?" he said, gyrating his hips suggestively.

More laughter and lewd remarks came from the men behind him.

"I don't need this bullshit," Masja said, and turned to face Igor. "We're leaving—right now!"

"Where do you think you're going?" Lucian grabbed her by the hair and yanked her back.

Masja screamed and tried to break free of his grasp. She looked imploringly at Igor, but to her surprise, he started backing away from her.

"Take your clothes off, missy, or do you need help?" Lucian said, clawing at her dress.

Masja kicked out helplessly, unable to wrench out of his grasp. She stared at Igor desperately, but he was already on his way to the door. "Help me, Igor, help me, please!"

Igor shook his head and cast his eyes to the floor. "I'm sorry, baby . . . I had to do it . . . I didn't have a choice . . . I'm sorry . . ."

Lucian's large hands were around Masja's neck, squeezing, and she could barely breathe. He pulled her dress over her head roughly. She could smell him and feel him. Feel his sticky shirt against her naked skin as he pressed into her from behind. Feel the large bulge in his pants.

"There's nothing I look forward to more than teaching whores like you a good lesson," he panted in her ear.

Masja screamed for Igor as he closed the door behind him.

Igor staggered over the parking lot towards his BMW. When he reached the car, he doubled over and was sick all over the fender and his spanking-new white Adidas trainers. He heard steps approaching on the gravel behind him. He wiped the vomit from his mouth and turned around.

Kaminsky gave him a cold look. "There was nothing else you could do. A man's honour is all he has. A man pays what he owes."

"I know that," said Igor.

"I'm surprised you managed to convince her to come out to this hole." He glanced up at the abandoned building. "She must trust you very much. Love you, even."

Igor opened the car door and got in behind the wheel.

Kaminsky leaned one hand on the roof of the car and looked evenly at Igor. "At least Lucian had the decency to let you keep the car, Igor. Drive safely," he said, closing Igor's door for him softly, and then he banged his fist on the roof twice in farewell.

8

Christianshavn, 2013

The constant barking added to the blows of a hammer that seemed to be in his head, and it was impossible to get away from the sound. Thomas opened his eyes. Daylight pierced through the hatch window over his head, driving the pain deep into the back of his eye sockets. "Bloody hell," he mumbled. The moment his master spoke, Møffe jumped up onto the bed. The aging English bulldog licked him greedily on the face, and Thomas tried in vain to push him away.

"Your dog spent the night at my place," Eduardo's voice said from somewhere above him on the aft deck.

Thomas tried to get up, but the hammer in his head forced him flat on his back again. Apparently, Møffe interpreted this as an invitation and began to lick his face again. Thomas managed to push the slobbering dog off his face, scratching Møffe behind the ear instead till he lay beside him with a satisfied grunt.

"Your dog took a dump in my cockpit."

"Rather in yours than in mine," mumbled Thomas.

"Sorry, what did you say?" Eduardo said, and moments later his curly head appeared in the doorway of Thomas's sleeping quarters at the bow.

"I said: I'm sorry to hear that."

"Do you have any coffee?"

Thomas raised one hand in the air and waved at an indefinable spot in the direction of the kitchenette. Eduardo resigned himself to searching through various drawers and cupboards, banging doors and drawers as he went. At least the noise finally got Thomas out of bed. He felt the nausea rise immediately. His body folded in half involuntarily. He'd have to be quick, make a run for it. Gritting his teeth, Thomas flung open the door to his tiny onboard bathroom but remembered too late that the toilet was blocked. His stomach contracted into a knot, and Thomas knew only too well that he had two, maybe three seconds to get out. He lurched past Eduardo in the kitchenette, flung himself through the open cabin door, and just managed to reach the railings before he spewed the sour remains of the last twenty-four hours of booze over the side. The deck pitched underneath him, and his head felt as if it were about to explode, one lightning bolt after another striking him between the eyes.

He heard voices coming from the canal. Looking up slowly, he saw a boat filled with Japanese tourists, a couple of whom were cheerfully filming his misery for posterity on their hand-held Sonys. He turned his back on them and collapsed unceremoniously face down onto the deck. Eduardo came up to check on him. Thomas rolled onto his back and grimaced at his friend. "I didn't realise that the tourist season had opened," he said.

"Pretty sure they sail all year, Ravn."

"Is that so?"

Thomas brought a hand up to his face. His cheek was tender and swollen. "Jesus, I'm all banged up. I must have tripped and fallen down last night." Eduardo nodded without further comment.

"See ya around, Eduardo!" A girl's voice came from Eduardo's ketch, which was berthed in front of Thomas's Grand Banks. Eduardo turned his head and blew a kiss to the blonde who was standing on the roof of his cabin. "I'll call you, sweetheart," said Eduardo. The girl hopped up to the quay and bent down to unlock her bicycle, which was parked next to the canal.

"Who the hell was that?" Thomas mumbled.

"Malene? . . . Maria? . . . Anna!" Eduardo said with a smile. "We met at The Sea Otter last night." He waved to the girl as she cycled on her way.

"Malene-Maria-Anna, huh. That's an unusual name," Thomas remarked drily.

"Well, she's an unusual girl," said Eduardo.

Ten minutes later, Thomas had found his jar of Nescafé and made two cups of instant coffee. They took their mugs onto the mini flybridge over the cabin with an aerial view of all harbour tours and sundry tourists snapping pictures for posterity.

Eduardo sipped his coffee and pulled a face. "A bit stingy with your beans this morning, aren't you, my friend?"

"All the better to spot them," Thomas quipped, taking a slurp of his watered-down coffee. That was pretty sharp, considering his current state, he thought with satisfaction.

Eduardo silently contemplated the puff of condensation he exhaled in the cool air. "I'm worried about you, Ravn."

"No need for that," Thomas said curtly. "I'm fine now. Absolutely fine."

"I'm not talking about your hangover. I mean in general."

"My health in general has never been better."

Eduardo arched his eyebrows and looked Thomas in the eye. "When are you going back?"

"Back? What do you mean? To Station City?"

Eduardo nodded.

"I don't know. It's not something I think about on a daily basis."

"But they can't keep you suspended forever. You have your rights."

Thomas leaned back in his seat and hitched his feet onto the opposite bench. "I'm not suspended; I've been sent on leave. 'Sick leave,' so help me God."

"But for how long?"

"Until they think I'm cured," he said with an ironic smile.

"But do they want you to come back?"

Thomas frowned. "What is this? An interview? Can't you wait for that until you get behind your desk at that news rag of yours?"

"Sorry, I didn't mean to pry."

Thomas's body was shivering. Whether it was due to the hangover or the cool morning breeze, he couldn't say.

Eduardo smiled. “I think it would do you good to get back to work. You were a good cop. You *are* a good cop. Take it from a member of the press corps,” he added, tossing the remainder of the coffee over the railing.

“Which doesn’t mean shit if your work is quashed from above,” Thomas replied.

“Did they actually stop you from investigating?”

Thomas shrugged. “I wasn’t assigned to the case. They kept me away as long as they could, and when they couldn’t keep me out any longer, they sent me on leave.” He smiled bitterly.

“How long has it been?”

“Since I’ve been on leave?”

“No, since . . . it happened.”

“Almost a year.”

“Rough year.”

“Yeah. Rough.”

Eduardo got up from the bench and headed for the ladder. He turned, backed down two rungs, then looked up at Thomas. “It’s a helluva case, Ravn. The kind that cannot be solved.”

“I know,” Thomas said.

“Perhaps it’s time to move on . . . from everything.”

“I know.”

9

Strängnäs, October 1979

The dark cornfield was deserted. The first rays of morning light filtered through the blanket of mist that had settled over the landscape, the trees beyond merely dim shadows, all but swallowed in the thick fog. Erik was crouched on a green bench in the watchtower with his father and Johan Edel, one of his father's hunting buddies. He had just turned ten, and this was the first time that his father had brought him along on a hunt. For more than two hours they had been waiting in their hideout for the beaters and their dogs to chase the buck across the field. It was so cold that Erik's hands were shaking, and he could barely hold the binoculars to his eyes.

"Are you cold, Erik?" said his father in a low voice.

Bertil was in his late fifties. He had big bags under his eyes and a bulbous red nose that suggested he drank more than his health could tolerate.

"N-no, I'm g-g-good," Erik said, doing his best not to drop the binoculars.

Bertil lowered his rifle, a fine Winchester Magnum with a polished walnut shaft, and patted Erik on the head. "If you want, you can slap your arms to warm up," he said. "I always do that when I'm cold." Bertil demonstrated how.

With obvious annoyance, Johan Edel's ice-blue eyes glanced at Bertil. "Cut that out," he said in a nasal voice. "You're going to scare away the animals."

Johan was in his mid-thirties. He had a muscular build and light blond hair that he habitually slicked back, which gave him the air of an English lord, Erik thought.

Bertil smiled apologetically, but before he could reply they heard the sound of dogs howling in the woods on the other side of the field.

"Can you see anything?" Bertil asked Erik.

Erik scanned the field, but the fog limited visibility to a few hundred yards, and he shook his head.

"Let me take a look," said Johan, grabbing the binoculars out of the boy's hands.

"They'll come past soon enough," said Bertil, cocking his rifle.

They could hear the yapping of the dogs coming closer.

"They're two hundred metres out!" said Johan, pointing into the mist.

Erik and his father gazed over the field, but with the naked eye, it was still impossible to see anything through the fog.

Johan returned the binoculars to Erik and looked up at the tree crowns above them. There was a light breeze agitating the outermost branches, and Johan adjusted the aim of his slender Beretta by a single click accordingly. "Are you sure that you want to shoot first?" he asked Bertil.

Bertil nodded. "Considering the sum that I paid for joining this hunt, I think that would be reasonable."

"But of course," said Johan. "I was just making sure that you were comfortable taking the first shot," he explained. He disengaged the safety catch of his Beretta and put it to his chin.

Bertil followed suit. He peered over the field through the binoculars. The first wild buck emerged from the mist. Then a young doe, shaking her head as she slowed down. Moments later, two more bucks came into their sights. The bucks moved cautiously on the edge of the field, but the barking of the hunting dogs scared them out of the cover of the woods. Bertil followed the swift flight of the smallest buck in his scope.

"What are you waiting for?" snarled Johan as the prey approached their hideout rapidly.

Bertil steadied the rifle against his shoulder and held his breath.

"Shoot now!"

Bertil pulled the trigger. The shot exploded in the confined space, making Erik start in fright and cover his ears with his hands.

The bucks picked up speed, the first one jumping clean over the wall, followed by the next. Another shot thundered, and the doe bringing up the rear faltered in mid-leap, tumbled, hit the ground, and stayed down.

"Did you hit it?" asked Bertil.

"Of course I did," said Johan, smiling for the first time since the beginning of the hunt.

Erik looked down at the doe, whose legs were twitching. "It's trying to run away," he said, pointing.

Johan got to his feet. "No, kid. God knows that animal isn't going anywhere."

"It's just the nerves, death throes," explained Bertil. "She's already dead."

"So she doesn't feel anything?" said Erik tremulously.

"I doubt that very much," said Bertil.

Soon after, they took the path into the open field to inspect their kill.

That evening, after darkness had fallen and everything was all over, the eight hunters gathered in front of a black-varnished hut that served as a hunting cabin. Erik stood beside his father, staring wide-eyed at the parade of dead animals that were lined in a row on the ground before the glow of a bonfire. There were five bucks in total, and a single fox, which Johan had shot just before sundown. The hunt master, a young man with a scrawny blond moustache, was making a note of who had shot what. When he came over to Bertil and raised his eyebrows questioningly, Erik ducked his head.

"I'm afraid it's a close-but-no-cigar for me," Bertil remarked cheerfully. "I had him in my sights, but he got away," he added, feigning an aim with an air rifle.

"In that case, I'll note a fat zero next to your name," said the hunt master. "Just like the last three hunts."

Bertil shrugged indifferently.

"Participation in our hunting party is a much-sought-after privilege, Bertil," said the hunt master sternly. "We have rules and standards to meet. We only have space for the best in our company," he added with a serious expression on his face.

Bertil smiled calmly. "Or those who can pay the highest price."

The other hunters laughed.

"Fair enough," said the hunt master, joining in the laughter. "I'll let you get away with a warning this time."

"I'm curious how you manage to survive the Stockholm Exchange with that sterling hunting instinct of yours, Bertil," said Johan sardonically.

More guffaws came from the hunting party.

"I get by," said Bertil. "Patience is the virtue of the old and wise." He smiled at the other huntsmen, all of whom were well-heeled stockbrokers like himself, albeit significantly younger.

"Come along, Erik," Bertil said, taking his son's hand and tipping his hat goodnight to the other gentlemen.

Bertil and Erik got into his father's shiny new black Mercedes SEL and strapped on their seat belts.

"Are you tired, Erik?" Bertil asked as the V8 engine growled to life.

Erik shook his head gloomily. They were driving along the dark main road in the direction of Stockholm. There was scant traffic on the road at that time of night. The rain began to fall, and the windscreen wipers whipped the water away methodically as the downpour increased. Bertil put on his brights, which lit up the trees on either side of the road.

"Did you know that you can catch a deer with the strength of light alone?" Bertil cast a glance at his son, who made no effort to reply, just sat in his seat, staring at his muddy boots. "It's true. If a buck were to step out onto the road right now, the lights would paralyse it and we would hit it head-on."

"Then at least we would have something to take home," Erik said quietly.

Bertil laughed softly. "Ah, I see. Is that what's bothering you?" He reached out and ruffled Erik's hair. "We'll get one next time. Just wait and see."

Erik shrugged his hand off. "But you never hit anything, Papa. The others said so."

"The others say a lot of things. You shouldn't listen to them." Bertil unbuttoned his oilskin coat and pulled a silver flask out of his inside pocket. He screwed off the lid with two fingers and took a generous slurp of brandy. "Don't you worry about them, my boy."

"But they laughed at you, Papa."

"What does that matter?"

"Also Johan," Erik said, turning to stare out of his window.

"We laugh at each other, but there's nothing wrong or mean about it," Bertil said, downing the rest of the brandy and returning the empty flask to his pocket. "You cannot let something like that bother you, understood?"

"Yes, Papa."

They had reached the exit for Mälarhöjden, and Bertil turned off the motorway. They drove through the suburb in silence till they stopped in their driveway.

10

October 2010

Masja stared at the man who had taken a seat at the foot of her bed. He was swinging on the chair in front of the tiny desk in her room. He was wearing a black leather jacket, dark trousers, clunky boots, and a massive gold wristwatch. Hublot or Bulgari, she guessed, which would cost 150,000 to 200,000 kroner at least. The man's jet-black hair was slicked back, his eyes like raisins, and his goatee meticulously groomed. He said nothing, but a smile tugged at the corners of his full mouth, as if he had just delivered a witty remark. And yet, he seemed expectant, rather than ominous or mean.

Masja's head felt light, but her body was strangely numb, as if she were on Valium. Someone had drugged her good and solid, she thought. Only fragments of the last twenty-four hours remained. She remembered that she and another girl were hauled out of the grease pit. The other girl was screaming and given a beating. And there was something about a car. A long drive. Kilometre after kilometre. Above her, motorway lights—like angels hovering in the sky. She looked down at herself and noticed that she was wearing a pastel-blue jumpsuit and a pink T-shirt, which was at least three sizes too big, and it reeked of someone else's perfume, someone else's stale sweat. She looked round the small room. The faded green pattern of the wallpaper reminded her of her grandmother's living room in Daugai.

Masja had no idea where she was. Her throat was bone-dry. She swallowed hard a couple of times. The man smiled and pointed helpfully to the bedside table, where she saw a full glass standing next to a jug of water. She reached for the glass and drank greedily, immediately poured herself another glass, and downed that one as well.

Masja wiped her mouth with the back of her hand. "Who are you? Where am I?"

The man did not reply, simply kept staring at her with that half-smile on his lips.

"Answer me," she rasped.

The man rubbed his goatee, twirling the tuft dangling from his chin between the forefinger and thumb of his left hand. She noticed a large gold signet ring on his little finger. A red stone that glared at her, as if an evil eye.

"Do you think I'm afraid of you?" she spat at him, trying to make her voice sound hard and even. She sat up straight in the bed. "Just you wait till I get out of here. I'll call for the cops, do you understand?!" she yelled.

The man leaned forward and dropped the chair back onto all four of its legs.

"No one is keeping you here, *Masja*," he said in what sounded like a Slavic accent. "You can go if you want to," he added matter-of-factly, pointing at the door. "You can go to . . . the police. But what good would that do?"

"I can report you, lay charges against you for . . ."

The man shrugged. "Good luck with that, girl. Tell me, Masja, have the cops ever helped you before? Do you have a good relationship with them?"

She looked away. "How do you know my name? Did fucking Igor give you my name?!"

"Your name is in your passport," he said, patting his jacket pocket as if he had it right there. "Fucking Igor' gave it to me," he said with his eerie smile.

"Give it back to me, right now," she said, "and I want my clothing and my bag and my money. You're going to get my things for me, right now."

Masja tried to stand up, but her head was spinning. She looked at the glass on the table. Perhaps they'd put something in the water? "Who the hell are you?"

The man leaned towards her and lowered his voice. "You certainly ask a lot of questions," he said. "Allow me to answer some of them. My name is Slavros. I saved you from a very unpleasant situation. From horrible people. Animals who don't have any manners, no morals," he said, tilting his head to one side thoughtfully. "One does not mistreat women—especially not women who are as beautiful as you are."

"Where am I?"

"At my place," he answered, without further specification.

"And you will let me go, just like that?"

The man shrugged and smiled at her again. "But of course . . . you can go right now. But that won't change our predicament."

"And what predicament is that?"

"Your debt to me."

She snorted. "*You* owe *me* my passport and my money. It is Igor who owes you money, not me! Why don't you get hold of him?"

Slavros rubbed his palms, which made a rasping sound. "That is no longer the situation we are in. Your boyfriend Igor—who is not much better than that pig, Lucian—sold you to me in order to settle a gambling debt of forty thousand euros. As unjust as this may sound, Igor has settled *his* debt. I bought your freedom for half that sum. It's a good deal for all parties involved, considering the size of the original debt. Irrespective of whether you walk out that door now or go to the police—or travel to the other side of the world or the moon, for that matter—you are still indebted to me to the tune of twenty thousand euros, and we need to come to some kind of arrangement to settle your debt."

"But Igor is the one who—"

"Forget Igor," Slavros said, looking at her coldly. "Igor is no longer relevant. He is outside the equation. Masja, you have to start thinking about yourself now. You have to look at your options. Find yourself new allies, people who want to help you. Protect you. And believe me when I say that you need all the protection you can get . . ."

"And I suppose you are the one who is responsible for that protection?"

Slavros breathed in deeply. "I could let the debt go back to Lucian, of course. Or I could send it on to others—those who are worse than him. There are other places you could go which are beyond your imagination, places that make that grease pit I found you in look like a palace. And the men who go there make Lucian and his friends look like saints."

He gave her a sympathetic look. "But . . . I don't want to do that. I think you have suffered enough. I want to help you get out of your predicament. But you need to show me some cooperation. You need to use your head, Masja, do you understand?"

"What do you want me to do?"

"The one thing that you are good at doing. The thing you do to earn your living."

Masja dropped her gaze.

"There is no need to be ashamed, my girl. In this world, there are only two kinds of people: those who survive, and those who are victimised. Fighters and fuck-ups. Look me in the eye, Masja."

Masja met his gaze.

"You and I are the same, Masja. We do what we have to do in order to survive. You made your choice a long time ago. You wanted to make something out of your life, and you decided not to 'make do' with less. You don't want to die poor," he said, knitting his bushy eyebrows. "This entire episode with Igor, with Lucian and his friends, is merely a bump in the road. It is nothing in relation to the big picture, the large design for which you have already paved the way."

Masja shook her head, feeling the pressure of tears at the back of her eyes. "You don't know what they did to me . . ."

"And you don't know what *I* have suffered. I could show you a body covered in scars from all the wars that I have fought in my life—in Chechnya, the Balkans, and here. We are survivors, you and I, Masja. We do what we must to reach our goals."

"So what is the plan? What is the goal?" she said, staring vacantly before her.

"The same goal that everyone else hungers for . . . money . . . because money buys you freedom. The freedom to control your own life. No more, no less."

He dipped his hand into his pocket, and for a brief, naïve moment, she thought he was going to give her back her passport. Instead, he handed her a small notebook and a pencil. "I am not a monster, Masja. I am a businessman. And I want you to think of yourself in the same way, that you will become a successful businesswoman. I'm guessing that you probably haven't saved any money, perhaps a couple of thousand? The rest you spent on useless shit—Gucci and Prada. You have to start saving. Make goals for your life."

"I *did* have a goal . . . before this happened."

He shook his head. "No, Masja, you had *dreams*. That is not the same thing. Every idiot can dream, but only a select few know how to realise them. I want you to keep a record, draw up a balance sheet like a proper businesswoman. I will tell you the price of things, and you will keep tabs on the debt you still owe me. You are a beautiful girl, Masja. You are young. And you have value. In my club, that is the only thing that counts."

"Your club?"

"Yes. You will work here. My place is a luxury establishment. Good clients. High security. No one will hurt you. We are one big family, where everyone takes care of each other. That is how it is here." He glanced down at the hands folded in his lap and nodded. "Yes, that is exactly how it is."

"For how long?"

"What do you mean?"

"How long do I have to work here?"

He looked at her soberly. "Hmm . . . I reckon a year, perhaps a little less, perhaps a little longer. There are daily expenses, of course, over and above the twenty thousand euros that you already owe me. Nothing is gratis, you understand?" he said, pointing at the notebook. "Be meticulous with your accounts, so you can see when you have settled your debt. Afterwards, we will draw up a plan for the future. Believe me, I want to help you, Masja. I want to help you make a good life for yourself. I want to help you attain your freedom."

Slavros stood up and extended his hand. It felt awkward, but she took it and shook it firmly. It felt hard and sinewy. She followed him to the door with her eyes. Outside, a young man was waiting. One of his men. A typical Yugo-gangster bloke: bald, black windbreaker, and army boots. Slavros left and the gangster locked the door behind his boss.

Masja was not stupid. No matter what Slavros said, no matter what spin he put on her situation, she knew that she was his prisoner—just like she had been in that hellish grease pit.

She curled her legs up under her and hugged her knees. In spite of herself, she began to cry.

11

Christianshavn, 2013

F-5. The button on the old Wurlitzer lit up for him. Thomas fished a 5-kroner coin from his pocket as Daryl Hall completed his last verse, but he was too drunk to judge the distance between his hand and the slot. The coin slipped through his fingers and landed on the floor. He swayed on his feet, leaned against the jukebox as he bent over, and tried to find it in front of his feet. At last, he found it.

"Ravn, I swear to God, if you play that song again, I'm going to remove it from the playlist for good."

Thomas turned around to face Johnson, who was busy stacking clean beer glasses on the shelf behind the bar. "Wha-da-ya mean?"

"What I mean should be perfectly clear—even to you."

Thomas cast his arms out to the side, almost throwing himself off balance in the process. "But you and I are the only bloody ones left," he said.

"Exactly. And I don't want to hear another peep from Daryl. Play a different song or go home. Take your pick."

"Hell, I was just trying to give the place a little class."

"In that case, you could start by taking a shower."

Thomas dropped the 5-kroner coin again. He looked down but gave up trying to look for it. Then he shuffled back to his barstool. "Hit me again."

Johnson reached for the Jim Beam bottle. "Okay. But this is your last round, *comprende*?"

"Geez, you're starting to sound just like Eduardo."

* * *

Much later, when Thomas had finally made it home, he stood in the road and squinted up at the apartment block. It was raining harder now and stung his face. He brushed over his beard and slicked back his hair. It was getting much too long, he realised absently. He stood staring up at their window for a moment, then took a seat on the wet steps in front of the main entrance. His clothing was drenched anyhow, and he no longer registered the rain. He patted down his thin jacket, looking for his mobile phone. Finally, he found it in his trousers, and rang up his home number. Seconds later, the answering machine came on the other end; it was Eva's voice, at once melodic and matter-of-fact, relaying a standard greeting: *Hej, you have reached . . . sorry we can't come to the phone right now . . . please leave a message after the beep . . .*

Thomas held the phone to his ear long after the monotone, and simply listened to his own breathing in the receiver. He looked up at the top floor again. The lights in the living rooms facing the road were still burning. A click came on the line as the answering machine automatically turned off. He slipped his phone back in his pocket, finally got to his feet, and headed back to the boat.

When he opened the cabin door, Møffe hopped down from the sofa and came over to greet him. He slobbered on Thomas's hands, wagging his entire backside. Thomas bent down and patted his dog. He could hear the rain leaking through the hatch in the bedroom and swore out loud, remembering that the mattress was right underneath and would be soaked through by now. *The sofa it is*, he thought. He made for the sofa, intent on removing the pizza boxes and empty bottles piled on top, but when he got within a metre, he saw that Møffe had shat right in the middle of it all. "Bloody hell, Møffe!"

He looked round for something to clean up the mess. Møffe grunted indifferently and snuggled up on the blanket in his nook under the control panel. Thomas failed to find the toilet paper in the dark and gave up the idea of sleeping on the sofa. He grabbed the neck of the bottle of Danish bitters on the kitchen table and took a seat in the plastic chair by the railing of the aft deck instead. Not long after, Møffe padded over to him and plopped himself down at Thomas's feet with a sympathetic whimper. The dog squinted up at him, cock-eyed, with massive jowls and a protruding underbite.

"Jesus Christ, you're an ugly fucking dog, Møffe." Taking the brute up onto his lap, Thomas threw back his head, put the bitters to his mouth, and drank. When the bottle was empty, he put it down by his feet and buried his face in Møffe's wet coat.

Up on the quay, life was slowly beginning to stir as people woke up to their morning routines.

"Thomas Ravnsholdt! . . . Ravnsholdt!"

Thomas reluctantly opened his eyes. Somewhere beyond the bank of fog in his brain, he sensed that someone was yelling at him from the quay above. The sun was out, and instead of the rain, a grey blanket of mist had settled over the water. His body ached from being slouched in the hard plastic chair for hours. "Ravnsholdt?" the voice above him said again.

Thomas twisted around in his chair and stared up at the quay. High above him, he recognised the quay master, Preben Larsen. Preben, a stocky little man in his mid-fifties, had a face as round as a ball. And you could see him coming a mile off in those cut-off jeans, heelless black clogs, and blue Burmeister & Wain windbreaker that he wore every single day, come summer, wind, rain, or hail.

Thomas smiled with supreme effort, raised two fingers to his brow, and greeted the quay master with a mock salute. "Preben."

It was clear that the quay master was working himself up for a lecture, the subject of which Thomas could already guess. "I am still waiting for a payment from you, Ravnsholdt. Things cannot go on like this."

"Yup, I'll get the money to you today. I'm sorry, I forgot. I've had a lot going on," Thomas said.

Preben frowned. "We are trying to market the canal as an attractive area, Ravnsholdt," he said, looking at Thomas's boat with disgust. "You need to do something about this mess."

"Who is 'we'?"

"I have also received complaints from other boat owners that you habitually relieve yourself in the canal, which is strictly against regulations."

"Who has complained?"

"It does not help matters that every time you hook up to the power supply on the quay, you manage to short-circuit the electrical system," he added, pointing to the fuse box on the quay. "This causes great inconvenience to the other boat owners."

"Yes, I'll take care of that," said Thomas. He got to his feet unsteadily, knowing only too well that the hangover was going to hit him with a vengeance in just a minute or two.

"Your boat is also leaking oil," said Preben, waving his index finger energetically at the shiny pool that had gathered on the surface of the water. "Your boat is a floating environmental catastrophe."

"Look, I know that *Bianca* has seen better days, but she'll be back to her old form, just as soon as I . . . as soon as . . ." His hangover loomed large, making him forget what he wanted to say. "She just needs a little paint here and there," he said at last.

"A paint job alone is not going to do it. Your boat is about to sink, Ravnsholdt. It's a hazard for the harbour—and the tourists," Preben added, casting his chin in the direction of the harbour tour that sailed past in that moment, as if on cue. "And the rest of us."

"Sink?" Indignant, Thomas took a step towards Preben. "My boat cannot sink. *Bianca* is a Grand Banks—one of the most renowned boats ever built. Burmese timber all round, handmade in . . . in . . . Burma."

Preben sighed and rolled his eyes. "For Pete's sake, Ravnsholdt. I don't want to be a dick about this, but if you don't clean up your act and pay your harbour dues, I'll have your boat towed from the canal," he said, staring at the tips of his clogs. "I'm aware of your . . . your situation, of course. So I'm going to give you a few more days' grace to sort things out."

"My . . . situation?" Thomas narrowed his eyes. "Mind your own business, Preben. Here, I'll give you the money right now," he said, digging a few 100-kroner notes out of his hip pocket. "How much do I owe you?"

"I can't accept cash. I sent you a proper invoice in the post."

Thomas put the notes back into his pocket, turned around, and returned to his plastic chair. Soon after, he heard the sound of Preben's clogs retreating over the cobblestones.

Thomas stared over the canal. There was no getting around it; he had to pay his goddamned harbour dues. Preben was not a man to make empty threats. He knew that other boat owners had been evicted for lesser transgressions than failure to pay their harbour dues. If he lost *Bianca* and his berth on the canal, he wouldn't have anything left to live for.

Thomas had bought *Bianca* twelve years ago for 450,000 kroner from an old geezer named Volmer. He had to take a huge loan against his flat, and he was still paying the instalments on the loan. Volmer, who finally drank himself to death a couple of years ago, had been an institution among boat owners on Christianshavn canal. When he wasn't at The Sea Otter or one of the other pubs along the quay, Volmer travelled all over the European waterways. He had sailed all the way to the Mediterranean and spent the winter in one of the harbours down there. It had been Thomas's dream to follow Volmer's example. He was going to take leave and head off to exotic destinations such as Gibraltar, Corsica, or Piraeus. He imagined dropping anchor in deserted bays and sleeping under the stars. But the dreams never became reality. Work at Station City had prevented him from taking the trip, and *Bianca* had suffered under his failure to maintain her properly. Even so, there had been good times on the boat—on the Øresund and here in the canal—good moments that he and Eva had enjoyed together.

So no, he simply could not get around it. He would have to go up to the flat and look for the quay master's bloody invoice.

12

Mälarhöjden, October 1979

Lena tried to suppress her laughter. Her plush red lips kissed the telephone receiver, leaving a fine outline of lipstick on its black acrylic surface. She had turned thirty-two in the summer, and the diamond-set tennis bracelet that sparkled on her left wrist every time she coiffed her blonde curls was an extravagant birthday gift from her husband, Bertil. Her tight minidress had a mint-green tone that enhanced her fair skin.

"Stop nagging me," Lena said, feigning annoyance. A little smile came to her lips. "No, I can't tell you now . . . because . . . just because," she said, idly twirling the telephone line around her index finger. "No, no, Bertil is not here, but . . ." She leaned forward on the chaise longue and looked across the double living room to the TV at the far end. "Erik is here," she added in a hushed voice.

On the floor in front of the rosewood TV cabinet, Erik sat on an oriental carpet, staring at the black-and-white cowboy series that he watched religiously every Sunday afternoon. Week after week, Hopalong Cassidy and his faithful steed Topper saved the American settlers from wild Indians and bloodthirsty bandits. The series was filmed in the 1950s and the characters were stereotypical, making it easy for him to follow the plot in English, and his father had once bought him a shiny toy Colt, just like the one his hero owned. The pistol was his most treasured possession.

Erik dipped an oatmeal cookie into the hot cup of milk that stood in front of him on the carpet. He loved the sensations in his mouth when the warm, squishy cookie dissolved on his tongue. At the other end of the far living room, his mother laughed out loud into the phone. He was tempted to turn up the volume, but if he did, she would yell at him and make him turn it down, which would disturb him even more. Besides, Hopalong Cassidy had already caught Buck the cattle thief, who reminded him of Johan Edel, and Erik knew that the episode would be ending soon anyway, so he savoured the last few precious minutes that he had to himself.

Suddenly, the door into the hallway opened and his father stepped into the TV room. He was wearing a strange leather apron that shielded his white shirt and grey flannel suit trousers. Erik had never seen his father in this strange get-up before, and he wondered what he needed it for.

"What are you watching?" asked Bertil, heading for the open fireplace to warm his hands.

"*Hopalong Cassidy*," mumbled Erik, keeping his eyes trained on the screen.

Bertil took the fire poker from the stand next to the fireplace and stoked the coals.

"I suppose he will survive?"

"Of course he will."

"If you know how it ends, why are you watching?"

Erik didn't reply. His father's comments disturbed him even more than his mother's laughter, and now there were only a few minutes left of this week's episode.

"I said, why are you watching?" Bertil returned the poker to its stand.

"Because it's interesting," said Erik, visibly miffed about the constant interruptions from his parents. On the screen, Hopalong Cassidy had just put Buck behind bars and locked the cell door firmly behind him with a huge bunch of keys on a metal ring, and the forlorn thief threw himself onto his bunk with a heavy sigh of resignation.

Bertil came to stand behind his son. "If you come with me, I'll show you something that is far more interesting than that old cowboy film."

"Can't I just watch to the end, please?"

"Is that you, Bertil?" Lena's voice rang out from the other living room.

"Yes, dear, it's me," said Bertil. He noticed that she had the telephone receiver pressed to her chest. "Who are you talking to, my love?" he asked.

"What?" Lena looked at Bertil in confusion as if she had forgotten she still had the phone in her hand. "It's my . . . my mother. I'm talking to Mama."

"Ah, then do send her my love."

Lena didn't reply but settled back into the chaise longue, out of sight.

Bertil switched the TV off. Erik was about to complain, but his father raised his hand, which instantly made the boy shut his mouth.

"Come with me," said Bertil. "I want to show you something in the cellar."

"Show me?" said Erik, getting to his feet.

Bertil nodded. "Yes, it's time."

Erik gaped at his father. The cellar was forbidden territory, strictly off-limits, his father's holy ground and refuge in the evenings when he came home from work in Stockholm. Sometimes, he spent half the night down there. His father called it his "haven," without any explanation as to what he spent his time doing down there. Erik had never heard his mother ask his father what it was—or complain about it, for that matter—which was remarkable in itself because his mother complained about almost everything else that Papa did.

The dark steps creaked under Erik's feet as he slowly took to the steep wooden stairs that led down into the cellar. When he heard his father slide the bolt in the door behind them, Erik could feel his heart hammering in his chest. It was very dark, and a strange smell filled his nostrils. Some kind of chemical substance, he guessed, similar to the cleaning agent the maid used in the bathroom, but there was also a pungent and sweet aroma in the air, similar to the smell that hit him in the face whenever they stepped into G. Nilsson Liv's, Stockholm's best butchers, which he and his father frequented every Saturday morning. Erik hesitated halfway down the stairs and turned around to look up at his father.

"Go on then, Erik, what are you waiting for?" said Bertil irritably.

Erik did as he was told in silence, till he reached the bottom of the stairs, where the glowing light switch blinked like an evil red eye. "What are we going to do down here?" he asked.

"Keep going," said Bertil impatiently.

"Shall I turn on the light?"

"Yes, that would be wise."

Erik's hands felt along the wall, found the switch, and flipped it. One after another, the fluorescent neon pipes in the ceiling flickered on. Erik shielded his eyes, momentarily blinded by the sharp light after the near-complete darkness.

"I've wanted to share this with you for a long time," Bertil said, his voice emerging from the glare. "I was waiting for you to be old enough to appreciate it."

Erik's gaze wandered along the entire length of the low-ceilinged room. The sight was at once frightening and fascinating, which drew him deeper into the spectacle. Along the wall stood several rows of small tableaux, which were mounted on pedestals carved out of dark wood. Each tableau represented animals in the wild, surrounded by fake grass and leaves, as if they were still alive in the forest.

"Your mother doesn't care to have these upstairs, but I think they work just fine down here in the cellar, don't you think?"

Dumbstruck by a rust-red squirrel that was perched on a branch eating a hazelnut it held between its claws, Erik did not respond. The squirrel appeared so real that Erik involuntarily held his breath, lest he scare it away. Spellbound, he continued down the row of animals: a partridge hiding in the reeds; a hare fleeing over stones beside a river; a badger at the entrance to his hole, which it defended with teeth bared; a buzzard with outstretched wings, taking flight with a mouse clutched in its talons. Each tableau captured a moment that was mimicked to perfection. Moments that would be impossible to approach undisturbed in nature were displayed right in front of his eyes.

Erik continued down the row and saw even more wonderful scenes—animals that he had never seen before: a black raven with a marten's head; a badger with the horns of a deer; an owl with a hare's body; and a black grass snake with dove wings and a rat's feet. "Where . . . where did you get these?" asked Erik in amazement.

"I made them," said Bertil.

Erik turned to see if his father was teasing him. "No . . . seriously?"

"Absolutely. It's called taxidermy—a very exciting hobby of mine. Come with me," said Bertil, showing Erik to his workbench near the wall at the far end of the cellar. Erik stared at the table that was filled with various kinds of tools . . . test tubes containing weird-coloured liquids . . . tall glass jars that held fine mohair brushes that shone in the bright light bearing down from the ceiling . . . tanned animal hides . . . and deer antlers lined on the shelves above . . .

It was a magical place.

"Do you recognise this one?" Bertil asked, pointing at a fox fur spread out on the workbench.

"No. Where did it come from?"

"It's the fox that Johan shot on the hunt. As a rule, I buy what the other hunters shoot—whatever they don't want to keep for themselves, that is."

"But how? *How* do you get them to look alive again? That one over there is just an empty hide."

Bertil laughed. Then he reached down and brought out two moulds from a large drawer and carefully placed them on his work surface. Both the moulds had the form of a fox: the first, in a sitting position, and the second was standing upright with its mouth open wide. The bare, muscular surface of the animals gave them the appearance of prey that had just been skinned.

"Once you have obtained the hide and tanned it properly," said Bertil, "you mount it onto one of these moulds, a meticulous process that requires great precision and hundreds of measurements." He brought a little toolbox and a vernier calliper down from a shelf on the wall. "These are our most important tools, and they require highly skilled and careful handling to create a realistic expression."

Erik looked at the row of shiny tools in the box. Ran his fingers over their cool metal, which brought to mind what his father had said in the car after the hunt. There was more than one way to capture an animal: You could stop it in its tracks with a bullet, or you could catch it in the headlights of your car. And now his father had showed him another method, and his father's craft made the silly hunters' parade of dead wild animals—something that he had admired so much before—seem vulgar and disgusting.

"Watch out with that!" said Bertil, snatching the large syringe that Erik had taken out of the box. Bertil put the syringe away in a drawer, at a safe distance from Erik. "This is not a toy, Erik. Some of these things are very dangerous. You can hurt yourself if you're not careful."

"I'm sorry, I didn't know."

"That syringe is more dangerous than the sharpest scalpel. It's filled with hydrochloric acid."

"What do you use it for?"

"To corrode the brain in the animal's cranium," Bertil said, as if he were trying to scare him. But Erik could not be scared away. On the contrary, he was utterly fascinated.

"Can you teach me how, Papa?"

"Perhaps," said Bertil with a shrug. "Or, to be more precise, I can teach you the technique, but that will only take you halfway."

"What do you mean?"

"A skilled taxidermist, even an amateur like myself, must—like every other artist—possess the ability to create, the skill to find a moment of significance, and capture life in the instant it attains perfection."

Erik nodded in awe. He was still grappling to understand that all these beings in the cellar came from his father's own hand—*his* father, who everyone else laughed at, who his mother always yelled at, who came home exhausted and silent from work every night. It was beyond his comprehension that his father could create such a wonder. All at once, Erik was determined to master this craft himself.

"It's not a matter of just stitching Mikkel-the-Fox onto a mould," said Bertil, lifting the fox hide's legs. "First, you have to consider: What captures the best time in this little fox's life? When did he come close to a state of perfection? What was his very own moment of greatness? Or rather, his fleeting moment of happiness—if a fox is capable of experiencing such a thing." Bertil let the fox legs drop onto the table again. "So, what do you think, Erik? Which moment should we *re*create?"

Erik shook his head. "I . . . I don't know."

"Think about it. When was this little guy the greatest fox he could be?"

"I really don't know. I haven't seen so many foxes—only when they are in flight, or dead."

"Not his finest hour, eh?" his father said with a frown.

Erik cast his eyes at the ground. He was ashamed that he couldn't think of a better scenario for the fox—something that would make his father proud, something that could ensure that he would have free access to the cellar and the animals down here, not to mention all the wonderful tools . . . At that moment, he would gladly have traded every single toy—even his Colt—for the privilege to be down here.

"Perhaps we should depict the fox hunting his prey?" Bertil suggested, trying to help. "Flat on his stomach, stalking a chicken, his mouth watering, bloodthirst shining in his eyes?"

Bertil took out a new mould that represented a fox in a kneeling position, its head lowered.

Erik nodded enthusiastically.

"Or perhaps we should make him drink from a stream, serene in the first light of dawn," suggested Bertil.

"That could also work."

"Or in a mating dance in the field, his back arched, and his tail raised in the air."

Bertil picked up the bushy tail and waved it to make his point.

Erik laughed. "Yes, or sleeping in his hole." The words flew out of his mouth, and he regretted them instantly.

Bertil nodded. "You know, that's not a half-bad idea."

"It isn't?"

"Sleeping on the sly. With one eye open. A fox-sleep. Is that what you mean?" asked Bertil. Excited now, he ducked under the workbench and took out a different mould. In this one, the fox's body was curled around itself. Bertil lifted the head in an attentive pose.

"No," said Erik, pushing the head back down. "His head should be tucked against his body, as if he were sleeping peacefully. As if he were dreaming of all the things he had experienced that day—and all the things that he will do tomorrow."

"Interesting," said Bertil. "What else is the fox dreaming about?"

Erik lowered his voice. "That he is safe here, deep underground, where no one can see or hear him. *Here* he can be himself. In peace. Away from everyone else."

His father was looking at him intently.

Erik cast his eyes down again.

"I'm glad I brought you down here, Erik," said Bertil, stroking his son's head. "I think you could be good at this."

"Really?"

His father kissed him on the forehead. "Yes. Really, really good."

13

29 November 2010

29 November 2010. DAY 33. More than 400 to go. I am Masja. I am twenty-two years old, and I have come to hell. This is my diary. It is *mine*. Do you understand? It is written for no one else. Just for me. I know I am not a writer. I know it will never be as good as *The Witch Dragon's Daughter*. I am only writing this to help me. To survive. So I can bear to be alive. To remind myself that I am still alive. My mother, my dear *mumija*, said that I could have been a teacher if I wanted to. She told me that I was a smart girl. But I said: "Why would anyone accept peanuts for taking care of other people's brats?" That was then. Now I would take care of brats for free.

I am not a teacher.

I am nothing.

Masja began writing a diary. It started a few days after Slavros gave her the notebook that was supposed to be her balance sheet, a record of business that lists the prices for services rendered and tracks her debt to Slavros. But after the first day in Slavros's club, she no longer needed to keep tabs on the price list because her body remembered every single one. Her body knew instinctively what every service performed was worth.

Masja led her bull up the winding staircase. "Bulls" are what they called the clients at Key Club, irrespective of their physical or financial resources. Her hand disappeared in his fist, but she could feel the cool metal of his gold wedding band against her fingers. From the bar downstairs, Joe Cocker's "You Can Leave Your Hat On" accompanied the girls pole-dancing on the stage. The bull was drunk and almost tripped over the top step with its deep-red carpet. Masja prevented him from falling on his face and guided him down the narrow corridor. Officially, the rooms along this corridor were the employees' private quarters; unofficially, they constituted the city's largest brothel. The strip club itself was a third-rate establishment which was as weary-worn as the girls who danced on the stage. It was a sordid money-making machine driven by the principle of maximum profit in the shortest possible amount of time, whether the bulls stayed at the bar to drink the lukewarm beer or went upstairs to fuck a girl. The clientele consisted of a hotchpotch of handymen, students, businessmen, and the obligatory parade of drunken bachelor party guests. According to the tourist guide—even the one available at the city tourist information desk—Key Club was listed as a "strip club," but everyone knew that the girls at the club weren't there just to dance; everyone knew what was for sale, and that there were no boundaries to what could be bought, as long as you paid the asking price to Slavros and his men.

Masja opened her door and pulled the bull inside. It was here that she served them. Here that she slept. Here that she lived her life. The room had no windows, just a bed, a wardrobe and a small table in the corner, where she put on her make-up. It was smaller than the room she once had at home with her mother on Burmeistersgade in Christianshavn. Masja had tried to mask the sour smell coming from the mattress by spraying perfume over the bed, but this had just intensified the stench, making the room stink like a cat litter box. With time, she had got used to the smell in the "bridal suite," which was hers, the best room on offer in Key Club. Slavros had personally escorted Izabella, one of the older girls, to a room at the end of the hall and given Masja the rights to this exclusive space. Not out of consideration to her, of course. It was a practical arrangement. The bulls preferred the "new" girls, and Slavros did his best to provide whatever trappings of style that his club once had.

Karina stood naked in front of the bull and pulled his shirt over his head. While she unbuttoned his trousers, his hands fumbled with her breasts and groped between her legs. When he sat down, wearing nothing but a pair of black socks, he started calling her names: "whore" and much worse. In a harsh whisper, the bull told her what perverse things he was going to do to her—mostly to excite himself—while Karina valiantly tried to get the drunk hard. She was only partially successful with the latter, so she rolled him onto his back and straddled him. After two failed attempts, she started to ride him. The bull grunted and fell into her rhythm. Karina looked down at him. His face looked like a priest's as he stood behind a podium, or rather, the caricature of a priest: pale and swollen, his bushy eyebrows in stark contrast to his receding hairline, his hair so thin it clung to his skull.

In the first few days after Masja came to the club, all the bulls looked like Igor: Igor as a fat man; Igor as an old man; Igor as a Pakistani man; Igor as a sadist. But in a very short time, his features became blurred by that of the bulls. Or maybe she had deliberately supplanted his face and put it all behind her—just as Slavros had said she should.

Karina moaned loudly because she knew that this is what bulls liked. And this one was no different. He started moving faster beneath her. Called her names. Asked if her if his dick was the biggest one she had ever had inside her.

"Oh yes, the biggest dick I have ever had," Karina said as her gaze wandered along the wall to the familiar stain next to the radiator in the corner. But the bull reached up and put one hand around her throat. "Look at me when I take you!"

"Stop," she choked out. The bull tightened his grip, and she couldn't breathe.

Masja tried to free herself, beating against his meaty forearms, but he was too strong. His eyes hardened, and a smile curled up the corners of his narrow lips. "Yes," he said, "that's good. This is how I like it. This is what I want."

Masja was gasping for breath now. She tried to scratch his face, but she couldn't reach. She tried to dismount, wrestle her body off him, but it was as if her desperate struggles only turned him on more. Pearls of sweat dampened his upper lip as he held her fast. Then he started to laugh and arched his body higher, writhing against hers in a bucking ride.

Black spots danced before Masja's eyes, the room spun, and she knew she was going to suffocate, but then she heard the sound of his roar as he finally came with a spray of spittle in her face. The bull's body jerked and went slack, loosening the grip on her throat. Masja fell onto the mattress beside him, gasping for breath. She registered the cold sensation of his damp skin against hers and flinched, moving as far away from him as possible.

Once the bull had put on his clothes and buttoned up his trousers, he looked down at Masja with a cheerful smile on his face. "Don't cry now," he said. "It wasn't *that* bad."

He extracted a crumpled banknote from his trouser pocket and threw it at her. "You were good. I'll ask for you again next time."

After the bull had closed the door behind him, Masja clutched the note in her fist.

She heard a hollow clank on the radiator in the corner. A signal from the bar downstairs that the next bull was on his way up. Times were good at Key Club. Word was out that a new girl had arrived.

The next morning, when the last bull had gone and she could hear the bartender cleaning up in the club downstairs, Masja brought out her diary and wrote everything down. This was the only way she could calm down and get a little sleep, how she kept her demons from eating her brain alive. Her throat still hurt after the near strangulation last night. But in 411 days she would be free—if one of the psychopath bulls at Key Club didn't kill her first. That risk was always there.

I am Masja. I am nothing.

14

Christianshavn, 2013

After half a day's indecision, Thomas had finally resolved to fetch the invoice from Preben so he could pay his harbour dues. Even though the prospect of having a shower and collecting some clean clothes was appealing, he dreaded the thought of going home.

Thomas put Møffe on his lead. The dog grunted, less than pleased about being hauled onto dry land. Thomas looked back at his boat. Yep, Preben was right: *Bianca* was in serious need of repair, but at least she was *his*. He was the captain of his own sinking ship. Thomas pulled on the lead, and Møffe reluctantly followed in his heels up Sofiegade. Møffe whined when they got to the front steps, and Thomas fumbled for the keys to the main door of the complex. "I know, ol' friend," Thomas muttered under his breath, "this isn't easy for either one of us."

At last, Thomas managed to unlock the door and made his way up the stairs. When he reached the fourth-floor landing, the door in front of him opened and his neighbour stuck her head out.

"Good day, Kitty," Thomas said to the elderly lady at the door. She had blue hair and thick reading glasses. A few seconds passed, as if she didn't recognise him.

"Thomas? It . . . it's been a long time," Kitty said.

Thomas nodded, pulling on Møffe's leash and eager to keep moving.

"I thought you'd moved out," said Kitty.

"No, no, not entirely. I've just been away for a while . . . on a trip," he said, trying to smile.

"It's so sad," Kitty said, stepping out onto the landing and clearly intent upon engaging him in conversation.

"Yes, it is," said Thomas. "It was good to see you, Kitty," he added, and fled up the final flight of stairs to the fifth floor. Standing in front of his door, he was relieved to hear Kitty retreat into her flat, and he fished for his keys.

Around the keyhole and doorhandle, the forensics team's rust-red aluminium powder, which is used to look for fingerprints, was still visible. He also yanked a stump of black-and-yellow tape off the doorframe and put it in his pocket. A pile of letters and advertisements on the mat just inside the door obstructed the entrance. It had been three months. He stared at the stack of official, window-enveloped mail among the colourful printed materials, bent down and fished out the letter from the harbour authorities. Mission accomplished.

His pulse was beating hard in his neck, and he bitterly regretted his decision to come up. *No reason to hang around*, he thought. He would have to skip the shower. Besides, the clothes he was wearing were almost dry now. And what he really needed was a drink. Perhaps two.

He caught sight of Eva's wellington boots standing on an open newspaper in the entrance, a pair of Ilse Jacobsens. When she came home with them, he'd made fun of her. *What the hell do you need designer wellingtons for?!* But Eva just ignored him. She broke them in around the flat till she got blisters on her toes. He glanced up at the row of hooks on the wall. One of her expensive handbags. *God, Eva really loved her handbags.*

Thomas stuffed the invoice from the quay master into his pocket. The door to the living room was ajar and light cut into the entrance. He gave the door a nudge and stuck his head inside. The room looked the same as always. A Montana bookcase with his DVD collection and Eva's books. Karnov's Law Collection, seven or eight crime novels and a stack of self-help books. A dining room table from Ilva Furniture Store, the TV screen in the corner, a pale Alcantara leather sofa. The blue painting hung just above it. Eva bought that painting for 15,000 kroner from a now-deceased but brilliant artist whose name he could never remember.

This had been their home. With a view of the canal, a light, peaceful, and happy home. Till that night he came home from the night shift.

Eva lay in the middle of the shattered glass table. The back of her head was smashed in. The candlestick that lay next to her on the floor was smeared with her blood. He was much too late, but he held her cold and stiff body in his arms, screaming out his pain. She had been dead for hours. It all seemed so unreal, as if he had been caught in a bad film in which he played the starring role.

Standing in the doorway, he could see the dark stain her blood made on the wooden floor. He spent hours and hours trying to scrub it clean . . . He couldn't stand being in the flat another second. He turned on his heel, bent down to collect Møffe in his arms, and staggered blindly out of there—out the door, down five flights of stairs—just as he had three months ago, the day he heard that the investigation into her death had been closed for lack of evidence. Eva's death was relegated to the mountain of unsolved cases at Station City. There were no more leads, no more suspects to go after.

There was a sour smell of vomit right next to him. Thomas had no idea who had thrown up, or when it might have happened, and he couldn't have cared less.

He was persona non grata in The Sea Otter and had resorted to the dive that lay just behind Christiania. He had never been there before, and he had no clue what it was called. After Johnson had refused to serve him another round, he had staggered around aimlessly in Christianshavn until he found this place by chance. Johnson had refused to serve him another drink because he said he was too drunk. *But wasn't getting drunk the whole point of going to a pub?* he fumed silently. *What kind of a proprietor can survive with that lousy attitude?* Besides, he was not nearly drunk enough. Granted, it was becoming a challenge, but he could still stand and, more importantly, he was still sober enough to remember the trip he'd taken up to his flat earlier that day.

He signalled to the barkeep for another round. Emptied his glass. Ordered another round. At long last, it began to help. Voices and sounds began to fade into the background, and sleep and oblivion crept up on him instead. Thomas wedged himself into the corner between the bar counter and the wall and closed his eyes. He thought of ordering one more round, made to signal to the barkeep, but annoyingly his arm would not respond accordingly. He dozed for a while, till someone prodded him hard on the shoulder.

"Hey, it's the musical genius."

Thomas opened his eyes. A very big guy standing in front of him was having a word with an equally beefy fellow two chairs away, apparently a pal of his. The second guy was wearing an ugly pair of sunglasses with yellow shades. He had a vague feeling that he'd seen those two somewhere before.

"You've lost your way, shithead," the second fatso with the ugly shades said.

"What?" said Thomas. The guy was right in his face and Thomas struggled to focus.

"There's no music here. Apart from the kind I make," Fatso said. The next moment he grabbed Thomas by the throat and pushed him up against the wall. "Your friends can't save you this time."

Thomas had no idea what this guy was talking about. All he knew was that this was not going to end well. "I don't know who you are . . . and I don't give a damn. Why don't you have a drink on my tab?" Thomas waved the bartender over.

"I think I'll pass this time, pal." The guy's forehead was millimetres from the bridge of Thomas's nose. "I'd rather take the next dance with you."

"You know, you have really bad breath," mumbled Thomas. "Did you just throw up by any chance?"

"What did you say?!"

Thomas hammered his fist into the bloke's kidneys in reply.

The fat man yowled and loosened his grip. He would piss blood tomorrow.

Thomas tried to slip past, but Fatso's pal was all over him and shoved him back up against the wall. Then the two men laid into him. Literally, bashed his head into the wall. They beat the shit out of him, good and solid, and he hit the floor like a sack. At last, the memories faded and he couldn't feel anything. *Keep it up, boys*, he thought, *I can still remember her face*. Then he was lights-out.

Thomas woke up with a vague sense of wet cobblestones against his cheek. The smell of the sea water from the canal. The screech of seagulls above. It was early morning, and the sun had just peeked over the horizon. He could feel someone rummaging in his pockets. Apparently, they didn't find anything of value, because they left him alone. A little while later, he tried to get up. His body ached and he could barely see because of the swelling in his face. He managed to get onto all fours and crawled the few metres between him and the bulwark. He felt for the groundwater tap, which he used to haul himself into a more-or-less upright position. Then he opened the tap and stuck his head under the stream of water.

Thomas had no idea how he had got himself down to the canal, whether they had thrown him out, or he had simply crawled all the whole way home. Nor did he know what else had happened that night. But he clearly remembered the trip to his flat. He could also remember exactly how he had found Eva that night.

He would've liked to say that she had looked peaceful as an angel. But the truth was that the horror she had experienced in the fight for her life had marred her face. He would never forget the sight of it. And he dearly wished that Fatso and his friend had finished the job.

15

It was four thirty in the afternoon and Thomas was sitting on the aft deck of *Bianca* with his legs resting on the chair opposite him. Eduardo came cycling past on the quay above. He rang his bell once and casually greeted him with a "hi." Thomas half-turned in his seat and greeted him in kind, apart from the swollen right eye and the clumps of dried blood that was matted in his hair.

"Jesus, what the hell happened to you?!" asked Eduardo, getting off his bike.

"It was the harbour bus," said Thomas. "It ran me over," he said, gesticulating in that general direction.

Eduardo hopped down onto the deck and looked at his friend. "*Madre mía*. You ought to go to the hospital, Ravn. Did you break anything?"

"Just a molar."

"Does it hurt?"

"What do you think?"

Eduardo opened his leather satchel, rummaged through his papers and found a vial of painkillers, which he handed to Thomas.

"Are you doping yourself up at the office?" said Thomas. He screwed off the lid, shook four pills into his palm and gulped them down with a mouthful of the cold coffee in his mug.

"Tell me, are there still days of the week when you *don't* drink?"

"I'm not counting the days."

Eduardo leaned against the railing and stared at him. "It's time you changed course, skipper. Those pills aren't going to work in the long run."

"You've said that before."

"And I'm happy to say it one more time. What are you going to do about it, Ravn? Do you want to end up like those guys up there?" He pointed to the bench where two bums had settled down with their various plastic bags assembled around their feet.

Thomas glanced up at the bench. "Why not? They look pretty happy to me."

"Cut it out, Thomas. Try to be serious for once in your life. You look worse than your wreck of a boat—which, I believe, will soon be Christianshavn canal history if you don't pull yourself together."

Thomas nodded and dropped his gaze to his lap, breathing heavily. "I went up to our flat yesterday."

"Okay." Eduardo raised his eyebrows. "Maybe it would be a good idea to move back in?"

Thomas snorted. "Yeah, brilliant idea. Apart from the fact that I ran out of there in a cold sweat. I lasted less than five minutes." He stared at the cup in his lap. "Nothing much has changed."

Eduardo pushed away from the railing. "It takes time, Ravn. I could go with you next time if you like."

"If only *I* had been the one to come home first," Thomas said, staring into his mug. "If I hadn't been on the night shift . . . she would still be alive."

"You can't keep blaming yourself."

"A fucking house thief, a nobody. Did you know that he killed her with the silver candlestick that we bought at Casa for eighteen hundred kroner?"

Eduardo nodded. "Yes, you . . ."

"Eva loved that candlestick. Personally, I'd never seen anything so ugly, but we bought it for her sake."

"Yes, you told me," Eduardo said quietly. "It's a terrible case, Ravn, on all accounts."

"An unsolved case," he replied. "I couldn't even do *that* for her." Thomas got to his feet, feeling the nausea immediately, and he realised that Fatso 1 and 2 had beaten him up much worse than he'd like to admit. He slipped past Eduardo and clambered up onto the quay.

"Where are you going?"

"The Sea Otter. Want to join me?"

"It's too early for me. Besides, I have plans."

"A date?"

Eduardo shrugged. "I think it's just sex."

Thomas nodded in reply, then turned on his heel. He made his way down the quay, past the two bums who sat on their bench bickering like an old married couple.

Apart from Victoria propping up her end of the bar with a newspaper and a coffee, and two young folks flirting over the billiards table, there were no other guests at The Sea Otter at this hour. Thomas nodded in greeting to Victoria, who sent a few rings of smoke into the air to underscore her reply. "You look like seven days of rain," she said in her raspy voice.

"I choose to take that as a compliment," Thomas said, taking his seat. "Where is Johnson?" He looked around the empty bar. Victoria shrugged and sipped her coffee.

As if on cue, Johnson appeared in the doorway of the back room, hauling the beer cylinder into its spot under the counter. "Right on time," said Thomas.

Johnson made no reply as he concentrated on attaching the cylinder to its tap. Once he was done preparing the entire contraption, he straightened up and gave Thomas the once-over. "Rough night? Again?"

Thomas shrugged. "I'm afraid you'll have to put the first round on my tab." He slapped his empty pockets to signify that he was out of money.

"Isn't it about time that you pulled yourself together?" Johnson said.

"Yup, probably," said Thomas, drumming his fingers on the counter. "Let's not let that one be idle now," he said, nodding at the beer tap.

Johnson crossed his arms over his chest. "If you don't have any cash, you'll have to work for it."

"Are you kidding me?" Thomas shook his head. "I'm not bloody well going to tend your bar."

Johnson snorted. "You think I'd give you that kind of responsibility? This is a respectable business, and you know it."

Thomas nodded nonchalantly. "Are you going to pour me a beer or not?" Johnson was really starting to get on his nerves.

"As I said: You have to earn it."

Thomas fixed his eyes on the counter and considered his options. First, he knew that he had stashed some money on his boat—if only he could remember where. Second, he knew he had a debit card in the flat. If he couldn't face doing it himself, he could ask Eduardo to go and fetch it. But neither of these options solved his immediate problem. *Goddammit my throat is dry as a desert*, he thought, giving Johnson a thin smile. He was going to remember this stunt of his—and pay the bastard back with interest. "All right, I'm listening. What would you like me to do?"

"Just a little police work."

In spite of himself, Thomas smiled. "For a moment there, I thought you were going to ask me to wash your dishes out back."

"No, not at all."

"What then? Has somebody got their fingers caught in the till? Borrowed a crate of empty beer bottles without your permission?"

Johnson shook his head. "No, it's about a missing person."

"So call the relevant authorities."

"No, not my style. *You* are the one I need for the case."

"I'm on leave, as you know. And now I'm really, really thirsty. Do you mind?" Thomas gave the beer tap in front of him a friendly pat.

"This is important, Ravn."

Thomas took a sharp intake of breath and bit his lip. "I know the feeling. It was important to me, too, when fourteen men from Station City searched for Eva's murderer, but you know what? They came up with zero," he said, touching his thumb and forefinger together in a fat O. He shut his eyes. "Are you going to pour me a beer now, Johnson, or do I have to go somewhere else?"

Johnson fixed his eyes on Thomas while he took a clean glass from above the bar, tilted it in under the tap, which sputtered, and finally filled it with a nice and cool dark beer. Johnson put the glass in front of him. Thomas reached out for it immediately, but Johnson held onto it and looked him in the eye. "I have someone who comes in to clean the place a couple of times a week. Her name is Nadja. She's a nice lady from Lithuania. She came to Denmark about ten or twelve years ago with her daughter and her husband, who is now deceased."

"And?"

"And, about two years ago, her daughter disappeared. No one has heard from the girl since."

"How old is she?" Thomas asked, pulling the glass towards him.

Johnson let him have it. "About twenty years old."

Thomas took a sip of beer. Foam moustached his upper lip. "Why hasn't her mother reported the girl missing before?"

"Nadja didn't dare go to the police. She's never had a good experience with the authorities, neither here, nor in Lithuania. They had some problems."

"What kind of problems?"

Johnson shook his head. "What do I know? Teenage problems?"

"I would also run away if I had to clean up this place." Thomas snorted.

"The daughter didn't clean houses. Her mother does. Nadja is my cleaning lady. Are you listening to me, Ravn?"

"Of course I'm listening," Thomas said, putting the half-empty glass down on the counter. "But what do you want me to do about it? She's probably found a boyfriend and run off with him somewhere, or maybe she's gone back to Lithuania."

Thomas downed the rest of his beer in one gulp.

"No, Nadja has looked everywhere for her. The girl has disappeared. So, can you ask around?"

"Ask around? What do you mean?"

"Yes. I mean at the Station. I can give you her details. Maybe her name pops up in the system. It would mean so much to Nadja. She needs to know what happened to her daughter."

"Again, listen up: I—AM—ON—LEAVE," Thomas said, spelling it out.

Johnson removed the empty glass from the counter. "You're an arsehole, Ravn, do you know that?"

Thomas slid off his barstool. "I think I'll find myself another place with a more cheerful atmosphere." He nodded at Johnson and made for the door.

"What if it were *your* daughter who had disappeared without a trace?"

Thomas stopped in his tracks, turned around slowly to face Johnson. "*My* daughter? I don't have a daughter. And do you know *why*? Because Eva and I didn't get that far. Because some loser smashed the back of her head with a candlestick. Hell, it was probably some two-bit crook from the Baltics who'd skipped the country. That was the only potential lead the entire investigation by Station City produced. So tell me: Why should I help one of their own runaways?"

"No, why would you?" said Johnson sourly. "That's not *your* style to help people less fortunate than you. It was *Eva's* style. She knew how to help others. Isn't that right?"

"Don't you dare mention Eva."

"Why not? It's true, Ravn. Eva had a heart of gold. You, on the other hand, spend your time crying into your beer glass."

Thomas stepped back from the counter. "Always a pleasure to come by for a lecture from the local bartender. By the way, your beer is warm as piss," he said in parting, spun on his heel and walked out the door.

Thomas headed down Sankt Annæ Gade and continued past Café Wilders. When he reached the corner of Wildersgade, he caught sight of the Eifel Bar, which lay a little further down the road. Depending on who was behind the bar, he might be able to score a beer, he reckoned. As he made his way to the Eifel Bar, he considered how he could pay Johnson back.

16

December 2010

Report from the bridal suite. DAY 67. I am Masja. I am still here. I am still alive. Izabella hates me because Slavros moved her out of this room, which used to be hers. I do my best to avoid Iza. I keep my distance. That girl is a witch—like a Dark One from Midgard in *The Witch Dragon's Daughter.* I keep my door locked because I am afraid that Iza will kill me when Slavros and the others are not around.

There are so many stories about Iza. She is the oldest among us, and she has been at the club the longest. Iza is short for Izabella, her hooker name. We all have hooker names. Artist names that we hide behind. It makes the humiliation somewhat easier to bear.

I hate the bulls more than I fear them, even though I know that they can do whatever they want to me. I know that they are here to destroy us, piece by piece, so they can feel better about themselves. Feel powerful. The only person I am really afraid of is Iza. Especially when she is high on coke. I have never seen eyes as wild as hers.

Once, I saw Iza rip the hair out of another girl's head—it left a bare patch on her skull! The girl had to tie up her hair to hide the bald patch from Slavros. Because no one snitches! Another time, I saw Iza threaten a girl with a pair of scissors—she damn near gouged her eyes out!!! Just because Iza thought she had stolen her eyeliner!!! Another girl told me that Iza poured caustic soda over the breasts of a rival while she was asleep, because she had stolen one of Iza's bulls. They say that the girl's breasts looked like mouldy raisins afterwards—it hurts just to think about it!

I have lost a lot of money and many bulls to Iza. I do not dare get on her wrong side. If she sits down at my table when I am talking to a bull, I find an excuse to leave. I hope that she will soon settle her debt to Slavros, so I will be free of her. My own debt is piling up. I do not live here for free. More and more debts—and no HOPE of settling them!

It was a Wednesday evening and business at Key Club was slow. Tina Turner's "Private Dancer" accompanied Iza's gyrations on the pole. She was wearing a corset that was too tight for her voluptuous body and it gaped at the back. Iza was too high to move gracefully, but the four bulls at the stage were lapping up her performance. When she freed her full breasts from the corset in her final dance, a scattering of applause sounded from the bulls, and more banknotes were deposited in Iza's G-string.

Masja was sitting in a corner booth with Lulu, a Polish girl with a squint and lips as broad as tractor tyres. She was keeping half an eye on Iza while they entertained three law students who were dressed in expensive designer clothing. Platinum cards and big banknotes; daddy's boys out on the town with daddy's credit cards. They reminded Masja of the life she once had. A life where the worst thing that could happen to you was boredom. The boys spoke in an affected manner and laughed uproariously at the dumbest jokes. They were obviously on a "slum cruise" on the streets where you could see how the dregs of society lived, perhaps even get a taste of "the real life" in the process and experience something exciting, which they could brag about to their privileged friends afterwards. Masja knew that she was a part of it, their rite of passage into manhood. But the Platinum boys paid well. They had already spent thousands of kroner at the bar for Swedish *lättöl* and private lap dancers. Masja had done the math in her head; she and Lulu could easily earn 5,000 each from these lads. But what she dreaded most, as she laughed on cue at their weak jokes, was that Iza would come over to their table and steal them. Luckily—for now—Iza was too busy working the pole, reeling in the bulls who were seated in front of the stage.

Masja ran her hand along the inner thigh of one of the boys. "Why don't we go upstairs, honey?" she said, wetting her lips.

But the boys were in no hurry. First, they wanted to finish their beers and chase their drinks with a little more snow. "You girls like snow for your nose?" asked the oldest one, smoothing back his long hair.

"I luv tha' snow," said Lulu in her thick Polish accent.

The boys laughed hysterically. Their "slum cruise" was turning into a blast, and ten minutes later their party continued in the men's room, sharing eight lines of coke, which was served on a toilet lid. The boys were ecstatic. Trying their luck, they said that the coke should be payment enough, but Masja and Lulu stood their ground. They laughed off the boys' juvenile tricks and gave them a taste of what awaited them upstairs—just as soon as they had paid the requisite price to Slavros.

Masja could feel the coke rush bubbling under her skin, warming her soul. *Yeah, everything is gonna be just fine*, she thought. There would be a life after Key Club, she told herself. No need to be afraid. Not even Iza could touch her.

The party in the men's room agreed to have another round at the bar before they all went upstairs together.

The minute they came out of the men's room, Masja caught sight of Iza. She was no longer dancing on stage. It was worse: Iza had sat herself down in a booth next to theirs with an elderly bull who was wearing a stained polo shirt and a pair of black clogs. It was Harald, one of Iza's regular clients. Harald ran a small taxi business with ten cars and about as many Pakistani drivers in his employ. Iza poured him a drink and stroked his beer belly, but Harald seemed irritable this evening and removed Iza's hand.

The drinks arrived at their own booth, and one of the drunken boys poured Masja's beer for her. Half of it landed on the floor, which suited Masja just fine. Iza glanced over to their table and gave the boys an inviting smile. Then her cold gaze rested on Masja. When their eyes met, Iza jerked her head almost imperceptibly. Masja understood her signal, but she swallowed the spit in her mouth and remained seated.

Iza's eyes turned to stone, and she repeated the gesture. This time, the movement of her head was more pronounced. Beyond any possibility of misunderstanding. Masja felt utterly alone. The coke rush was gone, taking her false courage along with it. She had no choice; she dare not defy Iza.

Masja was about to make her excuses and get lost as Iza expected, when Tabitha, a girl from Nigeria who habitually flashed a gap between her ivory front teeth in her ebony face, came sauntering past Iza's table. Harald reached out for her and said something to her that Masja could not hear.

Tabitha had told Masja that she was eighteen, but she seemed much younger. She was not particularly smart, either. Tabitha didn't understand much of the Scandinavian languages, usually replying with the word *okay* to whatever you said to her. The other girls made fun of her, stole her things and tricked her out of bulls and drugs. As a result, Tabitha was left with the dregs of the clientele, those who stank or were bat crazy.

Harald waved an arm, indicating that Tabitha should join their table. *Don't be so fucking stupid, Tabitha*, thought Masja. But Tabitha took a seat beside Harald and Iza. The smile she got from the latter as she sat down was pure poison.

"Wasn't there something you wanted to show me upstairs?" one of the boys whispered in Masja's ear.

"Absolutely," said Masja with a smile, and let the bull calf help her slide out of their booth.

It was mid-morning, but the coke binge with the Platinum boys kept Masja wide awake. She would have loved to get some sleep. Not even the Valium she'd taken afterwards in an attempt to calm her mind had helped. For a change, all was still in her room, no shitty music from downstairs, no moaning from the rooms next door. The quiet was liberating. And it had been a profitable night. She had scored 1,500 kroner in tips, and she could pay 4,500 kroner against her debt in total. All things considered, a relatively easy night, if something like that existed at Key Club. Now she desperately needed to go to the toilet but didn't feel like walking all the way to the end of the corridor to the bathroom. When she couldn't hold it anymore, Masja reluctantly got out of bed and put on a pair of panties.

As she approached the toilets at the end of the hall, she noticed a strange smell. The door to the toilets was ajar and she stopped just outside, listening to voices mumbling something inside. As soon as she opened the door, someone grabbed her arm and pulled her inside. The door was quickly shut behind her.

A group of girls were gathered in front of the cubicles. Tabitha was on the floor, face down, with two girls on either side, pinning down her arms and legs. Iza was straddled over her back, an iron held in one hand and a cigarette in the other. Tabitha's buttocks had deep triangular burn marks from the red-hot iron.

"What the . . . what are you doing?" said Masja.

"Isn't it obvious?" said Iza, looking at Masja with those wild eyes of hers.

"We're training the bitch," Iza added. "Teaching her that when you steal, you get punished."

"You are . . . hurting her."

Iza shrugged. "And? It's not my fault the black girl's fucking stupid enough to steal what is mine." She narrowed her eyes. "What about you . . . ?" Iza pointed the iron at Masja. "*You* are the one who stole my room. How are we going to make you pay for *that*?"

"Burn the bitch, Iza," a girl behind Masja said.

"I didn't have a say in the matter, Iza," said Masja. "You know that I asked Slavros to give me another room so that you could move back into the bridal suite."

Iza took a drag from her cigarette. "But you are still there. In *my* room. You have to pay me back. So what did the boys give you last night?"

"A thousand."

"Is that all? I would have thought it was more!"

Masja shook her head. "That was all the cash they had; the rest they gave to Slavros. You can have what they gave me."

"Of course I can have it," said Iza. She turned to Tabitha. "You never paid anything. You people think that everything in life is free, that you can come to this country and steal from the rest of us who work our arses off." She studied Tabitha's face. "You know, you're not as ugly as I first thought. You remind me of a doll I had as a child. The only Black doll in all of Romania. I loved that doll; it was my most treasured possession. Nothing in the world was better than that tiny little doll. Do you hear me, Tabitha?" Iza said, stroking the Nigerian girl's tear-stained cheek.

"O . . . kay," Tabitha choked through the panties that were stuffed in her mouth.

"One day, I took the doll and threw it in the fire. I'm not sure why because I loved that doll. I guess I was curious to see what would happen. And do you know what the flames did to it?" she said, taking a long drag on her cigarette and blowing the smoke into Tabitha's face. "The features of my little darling melted. Her cheeks, face, and entire head became smooth as a baby's bottom. You've never seen anything so smooth, Tabitha. Never." Iza smiled and brought the iron closer to Tabitha's face.

Tabitha tried to wrestle her arms out of their grasp, but the two other girls kept her pinned to the floor. When the tip of the iron was right in front of her nose, Tabitha started to squeal in horror.

"Stop!" Masja yelled.

The other girls turned to stare at Masja in surprise.

Iza jumped up and took a step towards her. "You know what, perhaps I remembered it wrong. Perhaps my most prized possession was a blonde whore-doll—just like you! Hold her down!" Iza commanded.

Two girls standing on either side of Masja grabbed hold of her arms.

Iza shoved Masja against the nearest wall and lifted the iron inches from her face.

"You don't really want to do that," Masja said, trying not to sound as terrified as she was.

"Oh no? What makes you so sure about that?"

"You don't want to damage Slavros's property. If we can't work anymore, and he finds out that you are responsible, you will have to make up our debts. Tabitha's and mine. You'll never get away with it."

"Maybe I think burning you would be worth the price."

The next moment the door opened, and Lulu stuck her head into the room. "Slavros is on his way up!" she said in a harsh whisper. Iza put the iron away and pushed Masja aside. The girls holding Tabitha let go and dashed out the door with the rest of the group. For a moment, Masja stood her ground. Tabitha quickly removed the panties from her mouth. Instinctively, Masja grabbed a towel and covered Tabitha's thighs and buttocks. Then she helped her into the nearest cubicle and closed the door on her.

"What are you doing in here?"

Masja turned around and looked into the face of Slavros. Two of his crew-cut goons were standing just behind him.

"I couldn't sleep. I needed the toilet."

"Is there something wrong? Are you sick down there?" Slavros asked, pointing at her crotch.

Masja shook her head. "Not at all. I take care of myself."

Slavros raised his chin and sniffed the air. "What is that strange smell?"

"I'm not sure. It smells like . . . burnt hair, maybe? I think some of the girls tried out some extensions this evening. It usually smells a bit when you apply them," Masja improvised.

Slavros looked at her suspiciously. "You would tell me if there is something wrong, yes? If there are things happening that I should know about?"

"Of course, Slavros. You can count on me."

"Thank you. I appreciate that. You had a good night last night, Karina. You made good money for us. Keep it up."

As soon as Slavros had gone, Masja opened the cubicle door. Tabitha was shivering, biting her fist to stop herself from making a sound, tears streaming down her face.

"You have to be more careful," Masja said. "For God's sake, you've got to start using your head, or you won't survive another day, Tabitha!" Masja said.

"Okay," Tabitha said.

No. Nothing is okay. You have to *think*. You have to do what you are told and see that you get this over with as soon as possible, do you understand me, Tabitha?

I tried to tell her, but she just cried and cried. I gave her a Valium to calm her down. It was my last one! I helped her, like Tusnad in *The Witch Dragon's Daughter* would have helped her friends who were expelled from Midgard. I knew the pill was nowhere near enough to dull Tabitha's pain. But I felt sorry for her. I had a guilty conscience. I'm not sure why. It wasn't my fault.

Iza is a fucking psychopath. The other girls just tag along for the ride. They are no better than she is. This is far from over. The fewer bulls there are between us, the more bitter the rivalry becomes. And it's almost Christmas. I want bulls for Christmas. Truckloads of them. So I can get away from here. Before we kill each other.

THERE IS NO MERCY.

17

Christianshavn, 2013

A few days after the disagreement with Johnson, Thomas decided to pay Victoria a visit at her second-hand bookstore on the corner of Dronningensgade and Mikkel Vibes Gade. He flipped through the crime books sale on the stand on the pavement before taking the three steps down into the little shop. It was nice and warm inside, with bookcases from floor to ceiling, every shelf packed beyond capacity, worn books stacked every which way that space on the shelves allowed. Charlie Parker's "Summertime" came from the gramophone that was placed on a desk in one corner. Victoria's *Antikvariat* smelt of freshly ground coffee, dusty books and her signature home-rolled Petterøes tobacco.

Thomas sidestepped the bookcase packed with travel guides and headed for the open rack of second-hand CDs, which extended along an entire end wall. He flipped through them alphabetically and soon found what he was looking for. "Bingo," he said under his breath, triumphantly holding up the *Hall & Oates: The Essential* CD, a compilation of hits over the last thirty years. Satisfied, he made a beeline for Victoria's cash desk in the back corner of the shop.

"Ravn," she said in greeting with a home-rolled Petterøes dangling from the corner of her mouth and a pair of cheap, rectangular reading glasses balanced on the tip of her nose. Victoria was the only woman Thomas knew who was never seen in anything other than a tweed suit and black lace-up boots, as if she'd just stepped out of a Charles Dickens novel.

"What do you want for this CD?" Thomas asked, holding it up.

Victoria squinted at him. "Seventy kroner."

"Seventy kroner?" he repeated, aghast. "It's used. You do know that, right?"

Victoria glanced at the CD compilation, then levelled her gaze on Thomas. "It's a double album."

"I only need one of the discs. In fact: one track from one CD, to be precise. I'll give you thirty."

Victoria hooked her thumbs into her braces and regarded Thomas patiently through her thick lenses. "I sell neither half a book, nor single tracks."

"But seventy is a tourist price."

"So leave the album to them," she said, holding out her hand for the CD.

Thomas swiftly removed it from her reach and popped it in his pocket. "All right, then. Put it on my tab."

"I don't sell on . . ."

". . . credit, I know," said Thomas, already on his way to the door.

"Bring *kanelsnegle* with you next time—the real thing from Lagkagehuset, mind you, not those dry pseudo-cinnamon rolls from the supermarket."

"You got it, Victoria. I promise," said Thomas with a smile, waving goodbye from the pavement outside.

It was almost midnight and Thomas was still sitting on the aft deck in his plastic chair, his newly acquired CD cover in one hand and half a glass of gin in the other. He'd had to dispense with tonic and music. He forgot the former, and the lack of the latter was due to a defect in the electrical cable that he'd been unable to fix. During said attempt he had, however, managed to short-circuit the boat owners' communal electrical fuse box supply on Christianshavn quay. At least two irate fellow boat owners had already paid him a visit to complain about the lack of electricity. Preben would give him hell tomorrow, but right now, that was the least of his concerns. If he couldn't get his CD player working again, he would have to go back to The Sea Otter and Johnson, whose stunt the other day

Thomas had still not forgotten. He sipped his gin. *What the hell was Johnson thinking?* Why should he, Thomas, help Johnson's cleaning lady find her daughter? He didn't know the woman from Adam—he didn't even know that Johnson had a cleaning lady! And Johnson even had the gall to play on his conscience. It was ridiculous and utterly unfair, Thomas thought, shaking his head.

In the six years that he had spent working as an investigator at Station City, he had seen more than his share of human tragedy. And it took more than some runaway teenager to rattle his chain. But all at once the electricity kicked in, the lights came back on in his cabin and the CD player began to play. Music flowed up to the deck to meet him. Thomas leaned back in his chair and peered over to the fuse box on dry land. He couldn't see anyone up there, but he raised his glass in a toast of gratitude nonetheless. He took another huge gulp of gin. The alcohol doused his feverish brain, and he began to feel a pleasant intoxication rising. Johnson had really irked him. He ought to have put a fist in the man's face for mentioning Eva.

Eva had been an extraordinary human being. She had the consistent habit of putting everyone else's interests above her own. There wasn't a defence attorney in the country more dedicated than she was. He couldn't count the number of times she used to work late into the night to prepare for a case. There had been times when he was even jealous of her work, but most of all, he'd been proud of her. Even though he had never told her so. Instead, he used to joke that no sooner had he caught the criminals than she got them released again. ". . . and that's why we make such a good team," she'd replied cheerfully. He had not just loved her; he was *in love* with her, and he remained in love with her for the entire nine years that they were together. His relationship with Eva had been the most important part of his life. He could barely remember the time of his life *before* he met her.

But he clearly remembered the first conversation they had. It always made him smile when he thought about it:

"What's your dog's name?" she asked.

"Møffe," he replied.

"That's a pig's name, not a dog's."

"Hmm. Maybe that's the reason he acts the way he does?"

She smiled.

She was standing on the quay, looking down at him, and her smile had revealed those dimples of hers for the first time. She was wearing her blue summer dress, the skirt of which fluttered in the breeze . . . He promptly invited her to join him on board. She had hesitated, but he insisted and at last he was able to convince her to have a drink with him, and they had sat out on the aft deck late into the night. Stupidly, he let her leave without getting her phone number or an address. He didn't even know her surname. In the days that immediately followed, he tried in vain to find her. He asked around everywhere in Christianshavn. Eduardo, Victoria, and most of all Johnson, of course, had teased him relentlessly about his marvellous talents as an investigator. Hahaha. When at last he had stopped looking for her and given up all hope of ever seeing her again, there she was, standing on the quay as before.

The very first thing he did when he saw her was ask for her phone number. And she gave it to him. Then she joined him on board. They drank white wine and kissed till the sun came up. He could still hear her laughter ringing in his mind, and this time he heard it right behind him.

Thomas swivelled slowly in his plastic chair.

Eva was wearing her blue summer dress. But her face looked a little older. Her shoulder-length hair was caught up in the silver clip that he had bought from a hawker on Strandgade. He stood up and looked at her, penetratingly, as if he would nail her to the ground with his gaze. Eva gave him a warm smile.

"I know it's just because I'm drunk, and I'm out of my mind, and you might disappear at any moment, but dear God it is good to see you, Eva!"

He wasn't sure if he'd actually uttered the words out loud, but she smiled again, as if she had heard him. Thomas took two steps up to the railing, afraid to get too close lest she disappear the moment he reached out to her. "You have no idea how much I have missed you," he said.

"Yes, I know," Eva said sweetly. "But you look terrible. Are you okay, Thomas?"

"No, I'm not. I miss you like hell, Eva. There is so much I regret. So much I wish I had done for you."

"There's nothing to regret."

"Yes, there is, Eva. I wasn't there for you. I don't understand why you put up with all my shit."

"No, you were wonderful to me, Thomas. The best man by my side that I could have hoped for."

"No, I was not. I never even asked you to marry me, even though I knew how much it meant to you."

"It doesn't matter." Eva shrugged. "Don't give it another thought."

"It *does* matter. I was selfish. A big, fat, egotistic arse."

"Rubbish. You were just a little slow on the uptake," she said with a smile, and he couldn't help smiling in return.

"That's true," he said. "There's just so much we didn't get to do together."

Her face showed pure concern. "You don't deserve this, everything you are doing to yourself."

Thomas looked away, only for a moment though, afraid that she would disappear. "I can't bear being without you."

"The Thomas I knew would never talk such nonsense, and he never gave up; he was a fighter and absolutely dedicated to his job. Most of all, you are a man with a keen sense of right and wrong."

"Times have changed."

"*No*, they haven't. There is no reason to be selfish. And you know it."

He sighed in resignation. "It's just that . . . I can't see the point of going on . . . nothing makes sense."

"You deserve so much more than this."

Thomas shook his head, feeling the tears prick his eyes. "I was too late. I didn't get there in time to save you. If only I had come home earlier, you would not have bled to death."

"You cannot keep blaming yourself."

"I can't help it."

"It was an accumulation of unfortunate circumstances. That's all there is to it."

"Yeah, goddamn unfortunate," he said bitterly, choking on his tears. "Some psychopath breaks into our home to steal a stupid watch and a computer that cost you your life. I can't even find him, Eva. I can't even find the one who . . . killed you. Do you have any idea how unbearable that is?"

"Yes, I know you, Thomas," she said quietly. "I understand."

Thomas wiped his cheeks and sniffed loudly like a child. "You didn't happen to see who did it, I suppose? I could really use some kind of sign."

Eva smiled. "Nope, sorry, sweetheart. I can't help you there." Her gaze wandered over the deck, and she pointed to the cabin. "Is that . . . ?"

"Hall and Oates, yes."

"'Every Time You Go Away'?" Her dimples appeared. "The first time we heard that together was over at Johnson's place. You called it . . ."

". . . the best song ever written."

She laughed. "You played it six or seven times or more, just so we could keep dancing. Johnson almost blew a fuse."

"That much hasn't changed." Thomas smiled.

She looked at him sheepishly. "Aren't you going to ask me to dance, sailor?"

"You promise you won't disappear?"

"I wouldn't dream of it," she said, and jumped on board.

Thomas took a step closer and put his arms around her. He could feel the warmth of her body, feel her breath against his neck. They swayed to the music, and he inhaled the familiar smell of vanilla in her hair.

"We will always have this moment together," Eva whispered. "But you have to move on, Thomas."

He hushed her.

"You have to let me go. Sooner or later. You have to take charge of your life again."

"I don't know how."

"Find a way. You owe that to both of us."

"I know," he mumbled.

Eva kissed him gently on the mouth and then pushed herself free of his arms. "Take care of yourself, my darling."

Thomas wanted to say something—anything that would hold her back. He searched desperately for the right words. In vain. Then he watched her jump back onto the quay. She brushed her hands off on her skirt and smiled down at him. Waved goodbye. And then she was gone.

The lights cut out and the music died.

Thomas was alone on the aft deck.

18

Mälarhöjden, December 1979

Erik stood next to his father at the workbench, carefully following Bertil's craft on an Arctic owl that was a work in progress. Arctic owls are quite rare in Sweden, and this one must have been looking for a mate when a hunter in Åkersberga came across the owl and killed it. Bertil spanned out the left wing carefully, trying to find the best angle to attach it to the body of the bird. "Does this angle look natural to you?" he asked his son.

Erik narrowed his eyes. "I think it should be slightly lower," he said. He reached out and pressed the wing down a little. "Round about here. Then it looks like it's just gliding on the wind."

"You're right," said Bertil. "This makes him look rather graceful," said Bertil.

"And in this position the inner down feathers are displayed in flight."

Bertil nodded. "Yes, indeed. You learn fast, Erik."

"Bertil!"

Lena's voice rang out from the kitchen above. When she didn't get an answer, she came to the top of the cellar stairs and yelled his name again. "Bertil!"

Bertil sighed and laid down the wing carefully. "What is it?"

"Hurry up!" Lena's voice demanded, without her providing any further explanation.

Erik followed his father up the stairs. When they came up to the kitchen, they found Lena standing by the window, cigarette in hand, looking out into the road.

"What's going on?" asked Bertil, wiping his fingers on his leather apron.

Lena turned her head and blew a ring of smoke into the air. "What is that car doing in our garden?" she said, jabbing her cigarette at the offending vehicle outside.

A large van was parked half on their drive, half in the road. One set of wheels had ploughed tracks through the snow that covered their front lawn. The van was in a despicable state of disrepair, and the words *Monson's Trädfällning* with a telephone number underneath were painted on the driver's side door. Large patches of rust were visible through the green paint on the side panel, and it was idling and coughing from its exhaust so aggressively that Lena's glass figurines on the window sill clattered against one other.

"Who the hell *is* that, Bertil?"

"I honestly have no idea," he replied.

As if on cue, the passenger door opened, depositing a little cascade of empty beer cans onto the snow-covered lawn. Moments later, two hunters in almost identical thermal coats stepped out onto their drive with cackles of jolly laughter. The first guy stretched his limbs, ran a hand through his long hair and looked up at the front door.

"Hey, isn't that Johan?" asked Erik behind his parents.

"Good heavens, you're right," Bertil said in surprise.

"Johan?" said Lena, blowing a jet of smoke out the corner of her mouth.

The hunters greeted Erik and Bertil with a cheer on the front steps, all three of them filthy drunk. Erik recognised both the men standing just behind Johan; it was Söbring and Olofsson, his father's hunting mates. He knew that one guy's family had worked in the steel industry for generations, and that the other guy was a banker, just like his father, but he couldn't remember which was which. All three men were unshaven and had dark rings under their eyes. Erik guessed that they had been drinking for several days on end.

"You guys look in great shape," Bertil said with a smile.

"Yeah, aren't we a pretty sight?" Söbring said. He put his arm around Bertil and planted a wet kiss on his cheek. Then he ruffled Erik's hair. A stench of stale sweat and alcohol burnt a trail into Erik's nostrils.

"Have you been on a hunt?" asked Erik, superfluously.

Söbring tried to focus his bleary eyes on Erik. "Damn right we have, son," he said with a forceful grunt. The alcohol fumes almost knocked Erik off his feet. Bertil disentangled himself from Söbring's embrace, leaving Söbring swaying on his feet for a moment.

"That's some vehicle you guys have got yourselves there." Bertil glanced at the van, and the large tyre tracks that encroached his garden. "Did you steal it?"

"Steal it?!" guffawed Johan. "Good God, no. The van belongs to my good friend Monson—Monson!" he yelled.

A thin man wearing a hunter's cap and a padded vest stepped out of the vehicle. He smiled, revealing the absence of teeth in his upper jaw.

"Monson is my good schoolmate from my days at Kungsholmen High," Johan explained.

Söbring and Olofsson laughed.

Johan joined in the merriment. "Monson was voted the 'most promising' pupil in the class. Ain't that right, Monson?"

Monson made no reply, simply let the other men have their laugh. Apparently, this wasn't the first time he had been reminded of the fact.

"Where have you guys been?" asked Bertil.

"Hunting," the three visitors said simultaneously.

"Yes, I can see that, but for how many days?"

"Three," they said in unison.

"Well, it must have been a poor hunt, considering the shape you're all in," Bertil remarked drily.

Johan rested an arm on Bertil's shoulder. "Don't get cheeky, Bertil, my boy. Or I shall have to ask Prefect Monson to punish you." Bertil reluctantly allowed himself to be drawn around to the back of the van. Erik followed on their heels. He didn't like the way that Johan treated his father. He became even more arrogant than usual when he was drunk, it seemed.

At the back of the van, Johan let go of Bertil and began untying the rear hatch. When at last it came undone, the ramp fell down heavily and revealed the contents of their load.

"Good heavens," said Bertil.

With a satisfied grin on his face, Johan stepped back and allowed Erik to come closer.

"Check this out, son. Have you ever seen a larger specimen?"

On the ramp before them lay a massive elk bull. Long and intricate antlers like the branches of a small tree crowned its huge head.

"Isn't it magnificent?"

"Yes," said Erik. "Impressive."

Johan turned to Bertil. "We tracked him for the better part of the weekend. This morning the brute came within range. I shot him at a three-hundred-metre distance," he added with a large burp, "despite the most brutal hangover in hunter history."

"How many shots did it take to bring him down?"

Johan smiled. "Just the one, Bertil. Straight to the heart. You should have been there."

Bertil nodded. "It must have been a great moment." He shifted his gaze from the elk to Johan. "So, what now? Where are you boys headed?"

"Home. I haven't slept since Thursday. You know how these drunkards are," said Johan.

The drunkards laughed.

"Actually, I meant: What are you going to do with the elk?"

"We have brought it to you."

"Thanks, but no thanks. Thoughtful, but we have plenty of meat in the freezer."

Johan laid an arm on Bertil's shoulder again. "You misunderstand me, Bertil. I want you to stuff him for me."

Bertil let out a high-pitched sound that wasn't quite a laugh. "That must be the booze talking."

"Not at all," replied Johan. "This brute will have pride of place in my hallway entrance."

Erik looked at his father in excitement. This could be their largest project yet—a masterpiece! But his happiness was quashed almost immediately.

"That may well be, Johan, but I'm not the one who is going to conserve him for you," Bertil replied in a cool tone.

All present looked at Bertil with disappointment painted on their faces.

"Bloody hell, Bertil," said Johan, "we were counting on you."

"I'm sorry to hear that, Johan. But it's impossible. I mean, how would we even get it down into the cellar?"

"Can't you just do it outdoors?" asked Söbring. "We could help you to carry it out back."

"No, the cold would hamper the process," Erik chipped in, taking a step up onto the tailgate of the van. He picked his way around the animal, inspecting it carefully. "We would need at least five kilograms of alum. And the same quantity of salt to prep its hide."

"Holy shit," Johan said with a snort of laughter. "Perhaps I should hire your son instead if you don't have the balls to do the job, Bertil?"

"Get down from there, Erik," Bertil snapped. Then he turned to Johan. "I'm sorry, old boy, but I'm not interested."

The men looked up as Lena appeared in the doorway, wearing white trainers and a grey mink coat slung over her shoulders. Her lithe, naked legs drew appreciative glances as she sauntered towards them. "Nobody but you, Johan, could make such a commotion on a Sunday morning," Lena said, giving him a big smile. Her lips were coated with a fresh layer of deep-red lipstick. One of her front teeth bore a little red smudge on the tip.

"Terribly sorry," Johan said with a fat grin on his face.

Söbring and Olofsson greeted Lena, and she replied with a polite nod for each of them as she walked past to the back of the van.

It was obvious that Bertil didn't want Lena there. "You should go inside. You'll freeze to death out here, my dear," he said.

"Oh my God, it's HUGE. Did you shoot it, Johan?"

Johan took a step towards her. "Right through the heart," he said, as soberly as possible.

"Was it dangerous?" Lena asked, her eyes wide.

Johan nodded. "A male elk is no joke. If you don't bring him down with the first shot, he can become just as aggressive as a grizzly."

"A grizzly?" Lena said with a vacant expression on her face.

"A large bear," Bertil explained.

"I see," said Lena, arching an eyebrow. "A daring thing to do, I'm sure," she added, looking at Johan.

Johan shrugged, nonchalant. "I guess that's just part of my nature."

"All right, then, I'll mount the elk head for you," said Bertil irritably.

Johan removed his gaze from Lena and looked at Bertil. "Seriously? You'll do it?"

"Unless you'd like us to mount his arse on a pedestal instead," said Bertil.

The drunkards guffawed and Bertil winked at Erik. "Isn't that right, my boy? We could stuff his rear end, couldn't we?"

Erik smiled, and his cheeks turned red in embarrassment.

"Don't be vulgar, Bertil," said Lena, without anyone taking any notice of her.

"But it will cost you," said Bertil.

Johan nodded. "Of course, old boy. Not a problem. How much?"

"Fifty thousand," said Bertil.

Söbring and Olofsson shot glances at him. "Jesus. You could buy a brand-spanking-new Volvo for that price," Söbring barked.

"Then buy yourself one, Söbring. A Volvo would suit you perfectly," Bertil answered, without bothering to turn his head in Söbring's direction. "It's up to you, Johan. As far as I'm concerned, you can transport the elk into the city. I can give you the contact details of three or four professional taxidermists. They could do a fine job for you for half that amount. But if you want to park the elk here for work, I have named my price."

"But we can talk about the price, surely," said Johan, treading carefully now.

Bertil shook his head. "This is not a trading post," he said, turning on his heel.

"Okay, okay," said Johan. "If that's your price."

Söbring and Olofsson shook their heads. Lena smiled and lit herself a cigarette.

"Do you have a chainsaw with you, Monson?" Johan said.

Monson looked at him as if he'd asked a ridiculous question. "What do you think?"

No more than five minutes later, Johan stood on the ramp with a roaring chainsaw in his hands. Söbring and Olofsson sat on the animal's back to brace its body, while Johan began to cut through its neck. Flesh and bone fragments flew up, splattering Johan's clothing and face with blood.

Lena stared at the macabre scene in fascination for a moment. Then she took a step back, mindful of her precious mink coat.

Not long after, Johan let the severed elk head slump down into the snow.

Bertil and Erik stared at it, spellbound. "This is going to be fantastic," said Erik.

Bertil nodded. "Let's drag him around to the back and see if we can get it through the cellar door entrance."

19

A few days later the huge, skinned head of the elk was strung up in the hoist and tackle just below the cellar ceiling. Erik and Bertil had sawed off the tree-like antlers and the upper part of the cranium was cranked open. Like threaded rope, its tendons rang along its exposed cheeks, and the animal's black eyes stared, embedded in bloody flesh. Despite the cool temperature in the cellar, the carcass was starting to rot and gave off a nauseating stench. But neither the macabre sight nor the stink bothered Erik. Armed with a vernier calliper, he was measuring the head with minute precision, recording the figures in a little black moleskin notebook.

At the workbench, Bertil stood next to the enormous elk mould that they had bought for the purpose. As soon as Erik had completed the measurements, Bertil adjusted the mould accordingly to ensure that it had the perfect fit for the hide, which was soaking in the large zinc bath in the corner.

The preparatory measurements of the animal hide had become one of Erik's favourite stages in the conservation process. The past months working alongside his father in the cellar had taught him that the more meticulous you were in the preparatory phase, the better the final result. And he was already better at it than his father, both with respect to precise measurement of the subject and tanning the hide to preserve its shine.

Bertil put a little cardboard box on the workbench in front of them. It contained four pairs of glass eyes whose tinted gloss was almost identical, apart from the size of the pupils and the form of the eyeballs. The subtle variations gave each trophy its own unique expression.

Bertil turned his head and yelled in the direction of the stairway. "Johan!"

He received no reply, so he turned to his son. "Erik, could you go and fetch Johan so we can ask him what kind of eyes he would like?"

"I'm just in the middle of something," mumbled Erik.

"Now," said Bertil, "before your mother talks a hole in the man's ear."

Erik sighed and put down his measuring device, reluctantly turned away from his work and dashed up the stairs.

The kitchen was deserted. He looked around for Johan and his mother, but one of his mother's slender cigarettes, still glowing in the ashtray, and two empty coffee cups on the table were the only signs of them. Wondering where they could have gone, Erik walked through the kitchen and down the corridor to the entrance hall. The door to the living room was ajar, so he headed that way. He could hear muffled voices inside, so he pushed the door open quietly.

In the furthest living room, he saw his mother and Johan. Lena was bent forwards over the dining room table, holding onto the curved edges with both hands. Her dress had ridden up her thighs, revealing her full buttocks. A pair of pale-blue cotton panties dangled from her left ankle. Behind her stood Johan, thrusting into her. "You're a whore," he grunted, "nothing but a fucking whore."

"Yes," Lena said. "Yes . . . I am."

Erik stumbled back down the corridor and down the cellar stairs. His father was standing next to the cadaver, measuring the eye sockets. He turned round when Erik approached. "Where is Johan?"

"I couldn't find him."

Bertil sighed irritably, pushed past Erik and called from the foot of the stairs. "Johan, we need you down here! Right now!"

Not long after, they heard Johan's footsteps in the kitchen above and moments later, he appeared at the top of the stairs. "I was in the bath," he explained, out of breath and red in the face. He came down the stairs and smiled at Bertil.

"At least you didn't drown in it," said Bertil.

"No danger of that," Johan replied, slapping Bertil on the shoulder jovially, but then he caught sight of the elk hide, which looked like a crumpled old raincoat in the bath. "Yuck, that looks disgusting!"

"We need to concentrate on the eyes first," said Bertil. "Which expression do you want your trophy to have?" he asked, handing Johan the little box.

Johan glanced inside. "What do I know? You choose for me."

"Then I would suggest these," said Bertil, selecting a set.

"Sure, why not," said Johan. "Hopefully, he will look more presentable once you guys are done."

"Don't you worry about that. We'll fix him up nicely," Bertil replied in a cool tone. "He'll be worth the trouble and every krona."

Erik stood a little way off, watching his father and Johan in silence. His mother's characteristic footsteps sounded on the kitchen floor above. His brain could not comprehend what he had just seen upstairs. All he knew for sure was that nothing would ever be the same again, and the cellar was no longer a safe haven for him. More than anything else, Erik just wanted to run far away.

If only he knew where to go.

20

Christianshavn, 2013

The door to The Sea Otter opened and Thomas stepped inside. It was bitterly cold outside, and he rubbed his arms, trying to warm up his body. Johnson looked up from his morning newspaper, which he was reading behind the bar.

"It's early—even for you, Ravn," he said. "We don't open for another hour," he added, reaching out for his coffee cup. He took a sip demonstrably, put it down and picked up the unfiltered Cecil that was smoking in the ashtray in front of him. "Besides, you still owe money for the drinks you had yesterday."

Thomas took a seat on his barstool. "I'm not here for a drink, Johnson," he said, sliding a 50-kroner note across the bar.

After ransacking *Bianca*, he'd managed to increase his capital by 675 kroner. He was in a better position to settle his debts now. "I think that ought to cover it."

Johnson took the 50-kroner note and stuffed it into the breast pocket of his check shirt. "We still don't open for another hour."

Thomas shrugged. "So tell me the story again. About your cleaning lady's missing daughter."

Johnson eyed him critically. "Why are you suddenly interested in her?"

"You asked me for help, right?"

Johnson stubbed out his cigarette in the ashtray, keeping a wary eye on Thomas. "Yes, I suppose I did."

"All right, then. So tell me what happened."

"Well, as I said, Nadja's daughter has been missing for more than two years now."

"Yes, I remember as much. But what would you like me to do about it?"

"I'd like you to check if the police have any information about her."

"Check what? If she hasn't already been reported missing, there is not much I can do, unless . . ."

"Unless what?"

"Unless she is reported dead or injured. Was she staying in the country illegally?"

Johnson shook his head. "I don't think so, but I'm not sure about the exact circumstances of her disappearance. Perhaps it would be best if you spoke to Nadja directly?"

"Okay, so where can I find her?"

"At home, I guess."

"And where is home?"

"A few streets away from here."

Thomas got up from his stool. "Okay, so let's pay her a visit."

"But . . . I can't leave the bar!" Johnson said, obviously horrified by the suggestion. "We open in less than an hour."

"Exactly. We'll be back by then. Come on, Johnson!"

"But . . . but Nadja doesn't know that we're coming."

"You can give her a call on the way."

Johnson shook his head. Then he folded his newspaper, grabbed his keys from the hook behind the counter and gulped down the dregs of his coffee. "You're acting very strange this morning, Ravn. Are you sick or just sober?"

Nadja's flat was located in the cellar of a redbrick residential block on Burmeistersgade. Inside, it was just as damp as *Bianca*'s cabin on the canal, but the ceiling was even lower. However, unlike his boat, Nadja's living room was painfully neat and tidy.

Johnson's cleaning lady invited her guests to take a seat on one of the white plastic chairs around the kitchen table and offered them some coffee and homemade cookies. Nadja was a thin lady with grey hair and dark rings under her puffy eyes. Once she had poured them each a cup of coffee, she took a seat at the head of the table. She eyed Thomas suspiciously, as if she was having a hard time believing that this scruffy man with a beard and unruly hair was really a police officer.

"So, what is your daughter's name?" asked Thomas politely, putting down his coffee cup.

"Masja," said Nadja.

"And how old is she?"

"She turns twenty-three next month—on the fourteenth," Nadja said. She spoke Danish with a strong accent, and Thomas had to concentrate to understand what she was saying.

"And when did you last see her, Nadja?" Thomas asked.

"Two and a half years ago," she said, her eyes brimming with tears.

"And you have no idea where she could have gone?"

"No. I have looked for her everywhere. She just disappeared."

"You have tried to reach her on her phone, of course?"

"The number is dead. Her phone doesn't work anymore."

"Did she live here with you?"

"At first, yes. Then she moved in with a girlfriend from work. Then she moved in with another friend. A man. I didn't like him," Nadja said, wrinkling her nose.

"And where does this man live?"

"I don't know, only saw him twice. When Masja came to fetch some of her things here."

"What's his name?"

"Ivan . . . Igor . . . something like that. I'm not sure."

"What does he look like?"

"Ugly man, a Russian. He always wore sunglasses. Like for cycling. He drove a big car with trees inside."

"Trees?"

"Yes, the stinky ones that you hang from the mirror."

"Ah . . . 'Wunder-Baum,'" said Johnson. "Do you mean those little Wunder-Baum?"

Nadja nodded and looked down. "I met him on the street about a year ago. Asked him if he knew where Masja was, but he just ignored me. I ran after him and kept asking, but he said he didn't know any Masja . . . that I was crazy, *pamišęs*."

"What did Masja do for work?" asked Thomas.

"This and that. I wanted her to study—she has a good head on her shoulders—but Masja wanted to earn money . . . Who can blame her for that?"

"So what did she do for a living?"

"At first, she cleaned houses for other people—like I do—but she hated it. Then she got a job at a clinic."

"What kind of clinic?"

"A beauty salon. Did people's nails, make-up, that kind of thing."

"Where is this clinic?"

Nadja shook her head. "I don't know. She never told me anything."

"What about her friends?"

Nadja shook her head again. "Masja didn't invite anyone around here. She was ashamed of this," she said, pointing around the spartan living room. "She was ashamed of me."

"And what do you think happened to her?"

"I fear the worst," Nadja said, the tears welling up in her eyes again.

"Is it possible that she met a new boyfriend—somebody who you don't know? Or perhaps she has gone back to Latvia—"

"Lithuania," Johnson interrupted, correcting him.

Thomas shrugged apologetically. "Someplace else, other than Copenhagen," he said. "That could be one reasonable explanation, perhaps?"

Nadja shook her head firmly. "Masja always kept in touch. In the end, she seldom came to visit me, but she still came. She has a room here. She . . . she also paid my rent. She was . . . she *is* a good daughter," Nadja said, letting the tears flow now.

Johnson leaned forward and rested a hand on her shoulder. "We'll find out what has happened to her. It's probably not as bad as you think, Nadja."

"Could I take a look in her room?" Thomas asked.

From the looks of it, the little room facing the courtyard had clearly been decorated just after Nadja arrived in the country and had not been touched since. On the walls hung faded idol posters of Britney Spears and Jon from *Popstars*. On a pink bedcover a row of teddy bears was propped against the headboard. Her daughter's desk was littered with make-up, and in the far corner there was a framed photograph of Nadja holding a little girl's hand in front of the Little Mermaid statue on Langelinie Pier.

Thomas picked up the picture. "Is this you and your daughter?"

"Yes," said Nadja. "That's my little princess."

Thomas carefully returned the frame to its place on the desk.

A selection of expensive Louis Vuitton handbags, three or four fake pearl necklaces and a worn grey rabbit-fur coat with one arm torn and limp like a broken arm. Thomas continued to the clothes cupboard and opened it. The shelves bulged with clothing. High-heeled shoes and boots cluttered the bottom. "Do all of these belong to Masja?"

"Yes," answered Nadja. "Masja loves clothes. Clothing and shoes. She was always wearing a new pair when she came to visit me."

"And all this?"

"Old clothes. Masja loves new things. She always has."

"Do you have a more recent picture of Masja?"

Nadja nodded and retreated from the room. A moment later, she returned with an envelope containing photographs of her daughter. She took out four or five that showed Masja posing next to Christianshavn canal. If the photographer had zoomed out a little to the left, he would have captured *Bianca* in the background.

"One of her girlfriends took these. The girls wanted to send them to film companies and fashion photographers. Masja wanted to be a model, or an actress maybe."

"She's very pretty. I'm sure she could be either," Thomas replied, and gave Nadja a friendly smile. "Can I keep one of these?"

"Of course," said Nadja.

They left Masja's room and made for the front door, where Thomas extended Nadja his hand. "I will see what I can do, Nadja. I will talk to the police and find out if anyone has seen her."

"The police?" said Nadja, all at once very anxious. "I don't want any trouble with the police."

"There will be no trouble whatsoever," Thomas assured Nadja in parting.

Thomas and Johnson took the route along the canal back to The Sea Otter. The wind had picked up and Thomas was shivering in his thin jacket.

"So what do you think has happened to Masja?" asked Johnson.

"I have no idea."

"None whatsoever?" Johnson looked at him with a frown.

"Well, she made a lot of money for someone who earned a living doing other people's nails."

"What do you mean?"

"I mean that she would have to be earning a *lot* of money to be able to afford luxury clothing *and* her mother's rent every month. Those designer handbags alone cost at least five thousand kroner each. I know because I bought one of those for Eva when she turned thirty. I thought the salesgirl was pulling my leg when she told me the price, but by then it was too late to say no."

"Do you think Masja stole the bags?"

"Maybe. But it's not easy to lift one in those boutiques. There are guards at the door, and they secure their items carefully. They know perfectly well how valuable they are."

"Perhaps she got them from the guy . . . Mr. Wunder-Bbaum."

"Yes, maybe."

"You don't seem convinced. What are you thinking?"

"That she wouldn't be the first girl in history who would give a man a massage for the right price."

"You think she was a prostitute?!" Johnson burst out.

Thomas shrugged. "It wouldn't surprise me if she were."

"Okay. So what now?"

"Well, it looks like I'll have to go into City and run a search on her name in the system," Thomas said. He started to develop a twitch in his right eye. "It will be strange to go back after . . . after such a long time."

A few minutes later, they arrived in front of The Sea Otter.

Johnson gave Thomas a look of concern. "Would you like to come inside? First round is on the house."

"Thanks, but no thanks, Johnson. I'll let you know if I find anything." With that, he turned on his heel and headed back to the canal.

"Ravn," Johnson called after him. "It's decent of you to help."

Thomas paused and cast a look over his shoulder. He nodded briefly in reply to Johnson. Then he made his way to *Bianca*.

21

Mälarhöjden, January 1980

Erik opened his eyes. Only the pale moon outside cast some light through his bedroom window. There was a draught coming from the hallway. The old filigree woman with her ducklings in the wood-carved wind-chime above his head spun around once. Erik pushed himself up onto his elbows and cast a glance at the clock on his bedside table. It showed just before two thirty in the morning. Then he heard voices coming from the far end of the corridor; it sounded as if they were arguing. Someone was crying, but he couldn't make out who it was. Deciding to investigate, Erik whipped aside his duvet and hopped out of bed. His striped pyjamas slipped off his bottom in the process, but he pulled them up and sneaked to the door.

The corridor light was still on, and he could hear his mother complaining, but he couldn't understand what she was saying. So his parents were still up, Erik thought, tiptoeing to his parents' bedroom at the end of the corridor. Their door was ajar, and he hesitated for a moment before creeping over to it. He took a quick peep inside.

His mother was in bed. She was wearing a pink nightdress and rested her back against the headboard as she manically filed her nails. His father was pacing up and down before the bed, wearing a pair of striped pyjamas almost identical to his own. Erik noticed that his father's eyes were bloodshot. So *he* was the one who had been crying. This scared Erik, much more than if it had been his mother crying.

"I just don't understand . . . I cannot understand it, Lena."

"You don't *want* to understand it, Bertil. We have been through this so many times."

"Then explain it to me one more time," Bertil spat out.

"If I stay in Mälarhöjden much longer, I will *die*. Do you understand what I'm saying now, Bertil? If I stay here, there will be no more life in my body than those bloody animals of yours in the cellar," Lena spat at him as she moved on to the next nail, which was given the same vicious filing treatment as the first.

"Fine, so let's sell this house and move into the city. I'm open to that," Bertil said, taking a seat on the edge of the bed.

Lena jerked her legs away so that she did not come into contact with Bertil.

Bertil tried again. "We can make a fresh start," he said. "And if we lived in Stockholm, it would save me driving into work every morning. We could go out and eat at restaurants more often, go to the theatre, the movies . . . do all the things which you say we never do."

"You really don't understand, do you?" Lena said with a sigh.

"Yes, I do," Bertil replied in desperation. "I understand that it isn't much fun for you, being in this house all day, so we'll move into the city, just like you've always wanted to."

"Bertil, stop. Not *us*. I said *I* am moving. It is not just the lack of life out here in Mälarhöjden. It is also *you* I want to get away from. We have simply . . . drifted apart."

"How can you be so cold?" said Bertil, casting his eyes to the floor, "after all these years, after everything we have been through together."

"I am not cold, Bertil, I am realistic. I am making a decision that will make us *all* happier in the long run."

"What about Erik? You can't just desert your son."

"Don't you dare play that card, Bertil. Erik can come and visit me. We will make a suitable arrangement."

Erik could not hear another word. His knees buckled and he slid onto the floor. He shrank away from the door. He covered his ears with his hands, but it was not enough to keep out his parents' voices.

"I won't let you go," said Bertil.

"That is not your decision to make, Bertil."

"I'll kill myself if you go, Lena, I swear to you. I'll go down to the cellar and hang myself from the tackle in the ceiling."

Erik removed his hands from his ears and peeked around the corner of the bedroom door again. He saw that his father had got up from the bed. And he was crying again.

"I'm begging you, Lena."

"Stop it, Bertil." Lena leaned forward and slapped one of Bertil's legs, the one that was closest to her. "You're just making everything so much harder than it needs to be. We have had . . . a good time together, as long as it lasted . . . but now we all have to move on," she said. She put down her nail file and helped herself to a cigarette from the pack on the bedside table.

Bertil got up and stood at the foot of their bed, as if turned to stone, staring at the carpet on the floor. Lena exhaled a cloud of cigarette smoke that curled like grey mist around his body. *Not Papa's finest moment,* thought Erik. It was not a pose worthy of a pedestal. The image burnt into his memory.

But suddenly and without warning, he saw his father jump onto the bed and straddle his mother. Then he put his hands around her throat and squeezed down hard. The cigarette slid out of her hand and fell onto the carpet beside the bed. She thrashed about with both arms, trying to free herself from the iron grip around her neck, kicking her legs in an attempt to get him off her. Erik froze. Fascinated and horrified, he stared at his father. He wanted to yell at him to stop, that he was hurting her, but Erik could not speak. He wanted to help his mother, but his legs would not move. Paralysed with fear, Erik watched the cigarette burn deeper and deeper into the plush carpet as a gurgling sound escaped from his mother's throat. A thought came to his mind: *Perhaps this was for the best. She was going to leave us anyway . . .*

A howl came from his father and his hand flew to his face. Blood seeped through his fingers where Erik's mother's nails had flensed his cheek. Coughing and gasping for breath, his mother hammered her fists against his father's chest. At last, his father slid off the bed and landed on the cigarette on the carpet. He did not appear to feel it though. His father remained where he fell, sobbing like a child.

"You fucking psychopath!" his mother screamed in a hoarse voice, lashing out and hitting him over the head. His father made no attempt to defend himself. He let her beat him about the ears. Finally, his mother fell back onto the pillows. Then she raised a hand to her throat. She wore a necklace of his father's deep red finger marks.

"I'm sorry, Lena . . . I don't know what got into me. Forgive me."

"You are sick . . . sick in your head."

"I'm so sorry, Lena, so sorry," his father said, reaching out for her.

"Stay away from me," his mother croaked, slapping the hand away.

Bertil withdrew his arm and stared vacantly at the floor. "All right. If that's really what you want, I will let you go, Lena. We can look for an apartment for you. We will make sure that you recover in the city and get some rest. Then we can see how you feel after six months—or a year or whenever it would suit you to come back. I will wait for you. I will gladly wait for you."

"Stop!" his mother yelled. "Just stop talking, Bertil. I don't want anything from you."

"But Lena, you cannot simply move out. It's terribly expensive to live in Stockholm. How will you survive? Get a job?" his father said sarcastically.

"I can take care of myself, Bertil."

His father looked at his bloody hand. "Well, that would be the first time . . . unless . . . have you found someone else?!"

His mother coughed again and reached out for another cigarette.

"Who is he?! Answer me, Lena!"

His mother lit her cigarette and levelled her eyes at his father. Her mascara had smudged like black garlands under her eyes. The dark-red fingerprints on her throat gave her a grotesque appearance. "Does it matter who he is, Bertil?"

"Answer me!"

"Johan," she said, leaning back against the pillows. "Are you satisfied now?" she said, blowing a cloud of smoke up to the ceiling.

His father made no reply, but he struggled to his feet instead. Without looking back, he went into the ensuite bathroom and locked the door behind him.

Erik watched his mother from the doorway. She was smoking in the bed, staring at a remote spot on the ceiling. She had never been more inaccessible to him. Erik felt a violent urge to throw himself into her lap and bury his face into the soft material of her nightdress. Instead, he turned on his heel and made for the stairs.

Erik put on the light in the cellar. The mould for the elk head was fastened to the workbench. He and his father had stitched the hide onto its face and only a few minor adjustments were required before the trophy was done. It was almost as if the enormous animal had been restored to life, staring sombrely over the room with its amber eyes. Erik observed the elk. It had been their greatest project thus far, and his father had called it Erik's "apprentice piece." But now he felt as if the dumb animal's half-open mouth was regarding him with a mocking smile. His eyes fell on the scalpel that lay on the table. He gripped the shaft tightly in his hand and jabbed it into the elk's face, perforating the hide and penetrating deep into its head. Erik pulled out the scalpel and stabbed it again. And again. He could not stop. He lunged at it, faster and faster till he ran out of breath and at last the blade broke off in the animal hide.

Beads of sweat dripped from his brow. Erik tried to wiggle the blade loose, but it was wedged in too deep. Armed with the shaft, he attacked the right eye. It was glued in place with epoxy glue that would not budge easily, but with a single-minded perseverance, he managed to get in under it and pry the eye out of its socket. It clattered onto the floor.

At last, Erik threw down the shaft and stared at his handiwork. The animal looked hideous, as if it had been pelleted with automatic gunfire. Then he caught sight of his father's toolbox. The large syringe that his father had warned him about protruded from the top. He considered using it on the elk, but he wasn't sure how. Besides, all his energy was spent, so he simply slipped the syringe into his pocket and crept back to his bed upstairs.

22

Copenhagen, 2013

It was morning at Station City and the rush hour had set in. Arrestees of the night before were being hauled out of their cells in the cellar and led out to patrol cars that would transport them to the law courts for preliminary hearings. Thomas passed two uniformed officers who had their hands full trying to bustle two handymen in dirty overalls and boots out the front door. The handymen were unruly and quite drunk, and even though they were handcuffed behind their backs, they managed to put up a serious resistance to being hauled out of the station.

"Need a hand?" Thomas asked the officers in passing.

The first officer looked at him suspiciously.

By way of explanation, Thomas produced his badge from his jacket pocket. The officer looked at it, then he shook his head. "That's all right," he said, a little out of breath as he heaved on the arm of his charge. The officer yelled at the prisoner and threatened to kick his arse, which appeared to be enough to persuade him to proceed to the exit.

Thomas returned his badge to his pocket. Then he continued down the long corridor towards the Crime Ops Division. He'd cleaned himself up as best he could in the sink on *Bianca* and was now wearing a relatively clean hoodie and a pair of dark-blue jeans. He'd had every intention of having a shave, but unfortunately, he couldn't find a disposable razor and the electric one was useless because he still hadn't fixed the short-circuit to the communal fuse box, and judging from the look that the guard in reception gave him upon his arrival, he surmised that his attempts to make himself presentable had only been partially successful. Never mind, at least the guy at reception had let him into the fold.

"Ravnsholdt?" A voice stopped him in his tracks. He turned around slowly to greet the man coming towards him from the opposite end of the corridor.

Police Chief Inspector Klaus Brask was a chubby man in his midforties. He sported a moustache that had more substance than the wispy fluff on his scalp. Brask was sweating and his sleeves were rolled up to his elbows. A stack of files was clenched under one arm. "I thought you were still on leave," Brask said.

"I am," Thomas replied.

"How are you?" Brask asked, looking him up and down.

"I'm all right."

"Marvellous," Brask replied, without conviction. "Are you still seeing the folks at Bispebjerg?"

Thomas smiled inwardly. "Bispebjerg" was Brask's oblique term for the psychiatric ward he had been referred to at Bispebjerg Hospital, "referred to" being the operative phrase, as he was yet to take them up on their offer of counselling while he was "on leave." "Yes, of course . . . every Tuesday," said Thomas. "It's been very useful."

"Marvellous," Brask said again. "Ultimately, they're the ones who have to evaluate when we can have you back," he added with his eyes cast somewhere near the tips of his shoes. "*If* you can come back," he corrected himself. "Did you remember to deliver your badge to reception before you left?"

"Naturally," Thomas said with a genuine smile.

Brask did not return it. Instead, he leaned in and lowered his voice confidentially. "Incidentally, the public prosecutor has decided not to press charges against you."

"I wasn't aware of the fact that I had been charged at all."

"That's what I just said: They've decided to drop the case against you." Brask used a tone and a look that implied Thomas was a complete idiot.

"I'm not sure I understand," Thomas said. "Why were charges raised against me in the first place?"

"You really don't remember?"

"No, I really don't."

Brask shifted the load of files to his other arm and let out a deep sigh. "It's hardly police protocol to interview a suspect with the barrel of your service pistol buried in his mouth, is it?" he said.

Thomas stared at him in surprise. "I . . . I don't recall that incident."

"Uh-huh. Then it appears that the folks at Bispebjerg still have work to do."

Thomas nodded. "What about Eva's case? Anything new?"

Brask averted his eyes. "You know how it is."

"Nothing new whatsoever?"

"I'm not going to lie to you," Brask replied reluctantly. "Unless a witness turns up or we find some of the goods that were stolen, there's not much more we can do." Brask clapped Thomas on the shoulder. "I hope you feel better soon, Ravnsholdt. I mean it."

"Thank you," said Thomas. He almost added "same to you" but managed to bite his tongue in time. Then he turned on his heel and continued to his old department. As he came to the door of the Crime Ops Division, he vaguely recalled the incident involving his service pistol. It was just before he was sent on leave. He and Mikkel had pulled over two Polish men in a van on the Køge Bugt Motorway. Upon closer inspection, it turned out the van was loaded with contraband—everything from lawnmowers to children's bikes, clothing, computers, and luxury jewellery. Thomas had proceeded to ransack the van. Like a maniac, he threw everything out onto the motorway. He was desperate to find something. He remembered that quite clearly now. It was the same day that Eva's case had run aground. He had searched for anything from their flat among the stolen goods. But of course he found nothing. He remembered threatening one of the Poles—although he remembered nothing about using his pistol on the guy in the process. He *did*, however, recall that he had tried to get the Pole to confess to the break-in at his flat, confess that he had murdered Eva. It was pure madness. He knew it then, and he knew it now. For their own part, the Poles hadn't been anywhere near Christianshavn on the night in question. But someone else had—someone who had got away scot-free. The mere thought cut his heart to shreds.

Thomas pushed open the door into the Crime Ops Division. Everything looked the same as he remembered, the shabby office furniture, peeling wallpaper, and a computer set-up that dated back to the turn of the century. It was amazing that their success quotient on busting crime in the city was relatively high, in spite of it all. A group of investigators in civvies was huddled in a briefing by a whiteboard against the far wall. He noticed quite a few new faces, cleanly shaven young men. Thomas was not happy to be back. The office was a painful reminder of late shifts and countless reports to write before you could go home. Before *he* could go home. To Eva.

He caught sight of Mikkel, who was gnawing on the lip of his plastic cup—as usual—all the way around, millimetre by millimetre. *The fucking rodent*, he thought affectionately. Five minutes later, the briefing was over, and the officers returned to their seats. Mikkel tossed his cup in the nearest waste basket, and when he looked up again, he caught Thomas's eye.

Mikkel's face broke into a broad grin, showing the gap between his front teeth. "Hey, Serpico, have you gone undercover, or what?" Mikkel quipped in his broad Jutlandic accent, revealing his roots in Aalborg.

"What do you mean?" Thomas grinned back.

"You look like one of those guys peddling hash in Christiania, mate. God, it's good to see you," he said, giving Thomas a brief hug before sitting down at his computer. He immediately tapped in his password and looked at his screen. "This is one helluva time to pay us a visit—we've got all guns blazing."

"What's going on?"

"A raid. Got a tip on one of the boys from Blågårds Plads. Apparently, they'll be shovelling a large load of snow today—at least two kilograms—and we're going to nab them," Mikkel said, flashing another one of his charming grins. Thomas could practically see the adrenaline pumping in his friend's veins. He recognised that rush, and he knew how easy it was to become addicted to it.

"Good luck," Thomas said. He meant it.

"When can we welcome you back?" asked Mikkel as he flipped through the papers on his desk. "I miss you, buddy."

"I need a little while yet."

"Of course," mumbled Mikkel, turning his attention to the computer screen. "We'll grab a cup of coffee one day, right?"

"You bet. Mikkel, I need you to do me a favour."

"Yeeaah?" Mikkel said distractedly.

"It involves a missing person . . . and, as matters stand, with me being on leave and all, I can't get into the system."

Mikkel shifted his gaze from his computer and looked at him sympathetically. "I sincerely hope this has nothing to do with Eva's case. If so, it's an absolute no-go. Especially after that stunt you pulled on Køge Motorway. Brask will be all over you like a rash in a minute."

"No, not at all, it's something else entirely."

"Okay, spit it out," said Mikkel.

Thomas briefly explained Masja's disappearance and the promise that he had made to her mother. Then he gave Mikkel the piece of paper listing Masja's personal details.

"This remains between the two of us," Mikkel replied, quickly logging into the central Criminal Register of the Copenhagen Police. He entered the details, and after what felt like the better part of eternity, Masja's picture appeared on the screen, in connection with an arrest.

"We do have something on the young lady," Mikkel said, swivelling the screen towards Thomas. "She was arrested in 2009: civil disorder and minor theft involving an elderly German tourist was reported outside Hotel Sankt Petri," he added, scanning the report. "But Fritz subsequently withdrew the charge."

"Is there any indication as to what she was doing at the hotel?"

"No, but I guess you can figure that out, right?" Mikkel smiled.

"You got anything else on her?"

Mikkel shook his head.

"Is it possible that she was deported from Denmark?"

Mikkel shook his head again. "If she had been, it would be listed here. And these days it takes a lot before the girls are evicted. We have our hands full. Perhaps she's working the streets out there," he added, pointing at Skelbækgade just outside his window. "It's mostly African girls we see these days, but perhaps she was moved about, to another country. They often move their girls around."

"Who does?"

"The underground, the Eastern European gangs slash Baltic Mafia. Did she have a pimp?"

"No idea. She had a boyfriend, a Russian, apparently."

Mikkel shrugged. "I'm afraid there's no happy end to this story."

In that moment, Dennis Melby came past and clapped Mikkel on the shoulder. "Shall we get going?"

Thomas glanced at Melby. He never could stand that prick.

"Two seconds," said Mikkel.

"Are you guys watching porn in office hours?" Melby chuckled. He nodded at the picture of Masja on the screen. "Is that your new dame, Ravn?" He snorted with laughter again, realising too late that he had stepped over a line.

"Don't be a moron, Dennis," said Mikkel, logging out of his system.

Melby shrugged. "It was just a joke, man. I didn't mean no harm. Sorry, Ravn."

Thomas didn't answer and merely glared at him. Melby had always been trouble. That time that anabolic steroids were found in the locker rooms, everyone knew it was him, but the charges were dropped. He sucked up to Brask and got away with it. And now he had apparently moved up in the ranks and become Mikkel's partner. *One more word*, thought Thomas. *Say just* one *more word . . .*

"He didn't mean it, Thomas." Mikkel pulled him away from Melby and nudged him towards the door. "We'll have that coffee real soon, okay? I'm sorry I couldn't be of any more help."

Mikkel shook his hand and hurried back to Melby.

Thomas surveyed the Crime Ops Division before him for a moment. All at once he felt completely out of place. He was having a hard time comprehending that this place had been his life for six years. Now all of a sudden he wasn't so sure that he wanted to come back.

23

December 2010

Christmas, 2010. *Mumija*, I remember that you used to send Christmas cards to everyone—the family, neighbours, your friends, former colleagues. The post made a mint on you. You loved to send your cards, so now I am sending one to you. In my thoughts. I will write that everything is going well. That we are happy, my husband and I and our two children. In our house. We earn millions. We are happy, have I already mentioned that? And we miss you, my husband and me. We send you a thousand kisses. A million.

What I don't write, and what you will never know, is that I actually miss serving customers in the Key Club. I know it sounds crazy! But this only goes to show how desperate things have become. Most of all I miss the warmth inside the club. I miss the music and the rush, which could sweep my mind away. I miss that little bit of security that, in spite of everything, we still had at the club. Now that Slavros literally sends us out in the cold to walk the streets, the other girls and I are in danger 24/7!

It is the coldest winter of the decade, minus twenty degrees in a miniskirt without any underwear. If the bulls don't kill me first, the cold will finish the job. It's only warm in their cars. We give them extra time so we can be warm, to avoid the icy wind. It was Slavros's idea: If the bulls don't come to us, we must go to them. It's a desperate move on his part, which shows us how deep in the shit he really is.

On average, I have a single bull every other night, which is still more than most other girls. I figured it out myself: It would take five years to work off my debt to Slavros. But new expenses keep cropping up all the time. But I would do anything to avoid this. The bulls on the streets are seedy, even more so than the ones that came to Key Club. They keep trying to push down the price. They try to cheat us. Persuade us to do it without a condom.

Lulu ran away after the third night we had to work out here on the streets. She wanted to go home to Łódź. Slip out of her debt. But Slavros wouldn't have it. Had men waiting for her in Warsaw Airport. They put Lulu on the next plane back. And doubled her debt. It is almost impossible for her to walk after what Slavros did to her. He punished her without leaving a single mark on her body. Lulu would not say what he did, but she pisses blood all the time. No one has mentioned running away since. We might as well be handcuffed to the nearest streetlamp. We are prisoners on the open streets.

Masja scanned the icy road. In the reflected headlights of the cars, the lanes looked like the dance floor in a cheap nightclub. The snow crunched under her stilettos as she made her way along the pavement. Her feet were frozen blue and completely numb. She tried in vain to stay warm in the thin satin jacket she was wearing. At the end of the street lay the railway yard where they went to service the bulls. Fucked them in their cars or up against the tool sheds while the trains rushed past nearby. The power lines crackled like fireworks above them. She hadn't had a bull in over an hour; the cold kept them indoors. Only the coppers slid past on patrol, but they were too lazy to get out of their cars. She had a measly two grams on her, shit-quality powder that barely contained the goods. It wasn't much for a night's work, but it was enough to get arrested by the pigs, and she dare not think of the consequences if that happened. Slavros would follow her, wait until she came out of detention. He would follow her to the ends of the earth to collect his debt—with interest upon interest. As matters stood, she still had to claw 2,500 kroner home before her debt was paid.

She had reached the No Parking sign that marked the boundary to Iza's territory, so she turned on her heel. She wouldn't dream of crossing this line, even if Iza had gone off with a client. She scanned the deserted parking lot, then began walking back to the dark office buildings at the other end of the street. She needed a bull right now, or she would freeze to death.

A few cars slowed down as they came past. She smiled at the dark windows, but no one stopped. After she had walked for a while, she lit a cigarette and cast a glance at the classic black Mercedes that was parked on the other side of the road. It had been there most of the night. A man was seated behind the wheel. It was too dark inside the car to see his features, but she knew that he had been watching her and the other girls—which was not unusual in this neighbourhood. As a rule, these guys were only after a freebie; they jerked off in the car and drove off when they were done. But it was unusual for anyone to hang around for so many hours. Masja reckoned that either he was a psycho, or it was his first time. If the latter, then he needed a little push just as much as she needed a client.

Making up her mind, she tossed her cigarette and sauntered over to the Mercedes. When the man behind the wheel caught sight of her, he started in fright. Well, at least at first she thought that she had scared him, that he was about to drive away, but then he leaned over and rolled down the passenger-side window instead. Masja bent down and looked into the dark car. She couldn't see the man properly because he was wearing a dark pair of glasses and a cap that was pulled down low.

"Hello, sweetheart," she said in her professional voice. "Is there something I can do for you?"

"What's your name?" he said in a gentle voice.

"You can call me whatever you like."

"I would like to know your real name."

"Karina," she said. "Do you like it?"

He didn't reply. Instead, he rubbed his chin, as if he was considering her question. "How old are you, Karina?"

"Eighteen," she said, forming her mouth into a pout. "It's a good age, don't you think?"

"Do you take drugs? Do you shoot up?"

"Not that it's any of your business, but no, I don't. So, what can I do for you?" she added, getting impatient now. "Do you like it kinky?"

"Have you seen the sun dance?"

"What do you mean, sweetheart?" she asked, arching her eyebrows.

"I mean: Have you seen the moon and the stars dance before your eyes?"

"You're turning me on, sweetheart," she said tonelessly. "It sounds like you're going to give me a wild ride. Why don't we sort out the boring money business first so we can have some fun together?"

The man removed his hand from his face and rested it on the dashboard. "I don't think you're ready, not yet."

"I was born ready. I'll give you a good price."

"No, you're not there yet. One day I will come for you. One day I will show you my cellar."

"What the hell are you talking about?" Masja snapped, withdrawing from the open window immediately.

"One day we will see if you have the potential . . . or if you're just a fallen angel . . . but I think you are the right one, so I have added you to the list of possible candidates," he added. Without another word, he leaned over and pressed the button to raise the window, which began to roll up.

"You psychopath!" Masja yelled at him.

The man waved from his dark seat as the black Mercedes set in motion. She swung her handbag and brought it down hard onto the roof. "You fucking swine!" she yelled after the car as it disappeared down the road.

Masja's body was shaking when she crossed the road again. The man's voice, the way he savoured every word, told her that he was extremely dangerous. Experience had taught her that he was the kind of bull that wanted to act out his darkest desires—fantasies of violence and abuse. She promised herself to be more careful in future, no matter how desperate her situation became. There had been so many stories of girls who had disappeared without a trace, and she had even heard rumours about some Eastern European girls who had been found dead and mutilated at a scrapyard. She needed a line of angel dust so bad—and she needed it *now*!

Masja stood in the parking lot, spying down the deserted road. Not seeing anyone suspicious, she took her little stash of coke out of her pocket and sniffed it directly from the bag. The rush set in almost immediately, but she knew that it wouldn't last long and tried to enjoy every single second.

"Karina?" a frail voice said behind her.

Ignoring the voice, Masja rubbed the remaining powder against her gums.

"Karina?"

"Yes, what is it?" Masja said irritably. She tossed the bag and cast a look over her shoulder. "What is it now, Tabitha?" she added, wiping her nose with the back of her hand.

Tabitha was shaking with cold in a pink latex minidress—which she had bought with the money that Masja had loaned her and never got back. "I said what do you want, Tabitha?"

"Do you have any more?" Tabitha said, pointing at the crumpled bag on the pavement.

"More? What the hell are you talking about?! Of course not. Get your own!" Masja snapped, and began walking up the road.

"Okay," said Tabitha, following in Masja's footsteps dejectedly.

Masja stopped to light another cigarette and realised that Tabitha was right behind her. She rolled her eyes. "Why are you following me, Tabitha? Your territory is over there," she said, pointing to the office buildings.

"There aren't any customers anyway. Just wanna talk."

"I'm not here to talk," Masja said. "Push off, will you?"

"Okay," said Tabitha, standing her ground.

Masja sighed. "Do you need a smoke?"

"Okay."

Masja gave Tabitha the cigarette she was smoking and lit a new one for herself. Tabitha sucked on the cigarette without inhaling. And it didn't look as if she had any intention of leaving.

"See you later, Tabitha."

"Karina?"

"What?"

Tabitha was staring at her feet. "I have a problem."

"We all have problems. That's life."

"I don't know what to do."

Masja looked up at the red car that came past. Deep bass tones were blaring from the car radio. The two boys sitting in the front seats made rude gestures at them. Masja gave them the finger in reply.

"What do your problems have to do with me?" Masja said.

"I don't know who else to ask."

Masja turned to look at Tabitha. "Okay, so what is your problem, puppy-dog?"

Tabitha threw down the cigarette and crossed her arms over her chest. "I . . . I'm pregnant."

Masja shook her head in disbelief. "No . . . you can't be serious!"

"Yes, I am."

"How far along are you?" Masja said, uncrossing Tabitha's arms to look at her tummy. She couldn't see any signs, but Tabitha had always been an overweight girl, and her belly didn't look any larger than usual.

"Four months. I think. I don't know what to do."

"Slavros is going to be furious."

Tabitha started to cry.

Masja frowned. "Stop that nonsense. If you keep bawling like that, I'm not going to help you."

"Okay," said Tabitha, but she didn't stop crying. "I don't know what to do."

"You have to talk to Slavros."

"I won't dare tell him."

"You don't have a choice. You have to."

Tabitha dried her eyes and looked at Masja. "Can't you talk to him for me? Get him to help me?"

"I most certainly will not! If I do, he'll think I knew about it all along. Don't involve me in this, Tabitha."

"But he likes you. He will listen to you. He hates me. Please get him to help me. I'm begging you, please." Tabitha took a few crumpled notes out of her bra and extended them to Masja. "I have three hundred fifty krona. The money is yours if you'll help me."

"Don't be silly," said Masja, slapping Tabitha's hand away. "And would you please stop bawling already? You look like a drowned rat," she added in a softer tone.

"Okay."

"Four months?" muttered Masja, shaking her head again.

"Maybe more."

"Slavros is going to be so mad. No, not just mad. Fire-spitting fucking furious."

24

Mälarhöjden, January 1980

Three suitcases were waiting by the main door in the entrance, filled with his mother's clothing, just the absolute essentials. In the next few days, a van would be sent for the rest of her things. After the episode in their bedroom, Erik's parents had taken him aside in turn and given him the bad news: They were getting a divorce.

It had taken his father an exceptionally long time to explain because he kept stuttering and choking on his tears. In the end, it was all Erik could do to assure his father that everything would be okay.

His mother had no such difficulties. She had called him into the kitchen and—most extraordinarily—went to the fridge and served ice cream, which he'd had a very hard time forcing down his throat, but he managed it in the end. Unlike his father, his mother's explanation was simple: She informed him that she was moving to Gamla Stan in Stockholm with "Uncle Johan."

Erik did not like the sudden familiarity with Johan Edel. The word *uncle* sounded wrong the first time she said it. And the mere fact of her repeating it did not help.

As Erik slowly picked his way down the cellar stairs, the solution that he and his father used to clean the hides before tanning filled his nostrils with an acrid smell. His father was busy with the raccoons that they had left in the freezer for much too long.

Erik pulled the collar of his jumper up over his nose and mouth and walked over to his father, who was squatting beside the zinc tub. Several hides were floating in the solution inside it. On the ground beside the tub, the skinned animals looked like newborn babies. His father was manically scouring one of the skins with a steel brush. He was wearing a thick pair of latex gloves, and his nose and mouth were covered by a big black respirator that distorted his panting breath into a metallic whine.

"You're brushing them much too hard," Erik said.

"Mind your own business," Bertil said, scrubbing away regardless.

"Mama is about to leave."

"And?"

Erik lowered the jumper from his face. "Can't you talk to her? Please, Papa. Get her to change her mind."

Bertil stopped his scouring and looked at his son with tears in his eyes. "I *have* talked to her, Erik. No, I have *begged* and *pleaded* with her, but it's no use. We . . . we are no longer good enough."

Erik looked away.

"She's in love—in love with *Jo-han*." Bertil spat out the syllables of his name.

"Can't you try again anyway?"

"No. It's over," Bertil said, resuming his work. "Do you have any idea what a fool your mother has made out of me? Any idea just how much everyone is laughing at me?"

"But . . . I thought . . . you said that you don't care if they laugh."

"A man's honour is all he has—don't you get that?!" Bertil shouted, flinging the brush into the tub so hard that a spray of cleansing solution soaked his arms and face.

Erik started and stared at his father in fright. Then he spun on his heel and ran for the stairs.

"Erik! Erik, please don't go, I'm sorry!"

When he pushed open the door to the bathroom, he could hear that she was in the shower. Through the foggy glass wall that separated the shower from the rest of the bathroom, Erik caught a glimpse of the contours of his mother's naked body. He stepped into the bathroom and went towards her. Lena had her eyes closed, washing the shampoo out of her hair. Erik noticed the caesarean scar like a knotted rope across her bow. It was an ugly stitching, a job badly done. Fascinated, he stared at her pubic hair, which formed a little tuft that dribbled the gathered beads of water. There was a bruise the size of a thumbprint on her inner thigh, and Erik wondered how it got there.

"Erik!" shrieked his mother when she opened her eyes and saw him standing there. "What are you doing in here?" she asked, quickly turning away.

Erik goggled at her but made no reply.

"You know very well that I don't want you in the bathroom when I'm having a shower."

"I know. I'm sorry," he said, casting his eyes to the floor. "It's just that . . . you're leaving soon."

Lena took half a step out of the shower and ruffled his hair with her wet hand. It didn't feel particularly good, but Erik let her do it anyway. "Everything will turn out all right," she said. "I promise you that. You mustn't be sad."

"How can it turn out all right if you're leaving us?"

"Don't do that, Erik," Lena said, reaching out and gently lifting his chin. She looked deep into his eyes. "I'm not leaving you. As soon as Uncle Johan and I have settled in properly, you can come and visit us."

"But in that case, you would still be leaving us."

"You need to be a big boy about this, Erik." Lena's voice broke. "This is . . . this is hard for all of us. Do you understand?"

The doorbell rang downstairs. "Already!" Lena said, stepping back under the shower of water. "Go downstairs, Erik. Tell Uncle Johan that he can take the three suitcases in the entrance out to the car."

Erik felt a constant pain at the back of his eyes. The tears pressed hard to come to the fore. "Don't go, Mama."

"Not now, Erik," Lena replied. "Hurry up, will you? Go downstairs and let me finish up now."

He could see that she was holding back her tears.

"Can't you stay? Please, Mama?"

"Erik, we need to talk about this another time," Lena said, turning her back.

Erik could not move.

Soon, it would all be over. Soon, she would reach out for the tap and turn off the water. Soon, she would take the towel off the hook and dry herself. She would go into the bedroom and get dressed. Underwear, stockings, bra, and the short blue dress that was laid out on the bed. Little steps, which would bring her further and further away from him, till she would walk out the door and never come back. Never, as in . . . *never.* And that visit she had promised was a lie. She only said it to get him out the way. She would move into the city and forget about him. It was just like Papa said: They weren't good enough anymore. *It's all over,* Erik thought. *It's not fair.*

Erik stuck his hand into his pocket and brought out the large syringe from his father's toolbox. He removed the little cap from the needle and stepped closer to his mother. As she reached out for the tap to turn off the water, he jabbed the needle into her side and pushed the plunger home. She screamed in pain and turned towards him. Erik looked at her in horror. The needle was jammed in her flesh and was bobbing up and down in time to her movements.

"What . . . what have you done, Erik?"

Erik stumbled back a few paces till his back was pressed against the wall. He leaned against the cold surface. "I . . . I'm sorry, Mama."

The first cramps set in after a few more seconds. Lena tried to steady herself against the glass wall. Her free hand felt for the needle, and she ripped it out of her side, but her body had already started to shake uncontrollably, and she dropped it. Then her legs gave way beneath her, and she crashed to the tiled floor. She tried to get up again, but her hands slid over the wet surface. Now her entire body began to convulse, and her legs smashed against the glass wall, which shattered around her. Froth appeared at the corners of her mouth, mixing with the blood that she coughed up in an inarticulate gurgle in her throat. Erik watched her death throes under the running water. It seemed like an eternity till his mother finally lay still, her tongue sticking out of her mouth, her eyes staring vacantly at him.

The doorbell rang.

* * *

Like a sleepwalker, Erik descended the stairs slowly and glided into the entrance hall, past the three suitcases and on to the main front door. He opened it. Outside, stood "Uncle" Johan.

"*Hej*, Erik, good to see you, lad," he said cheerfully.

"Uncle Johan," he said tonelessly.

Johan's gaze wavered, but he stuck out his hand.

Erik did not take it. His arms hung loosely by his side.

Johan withdrew his hand. "You can just call me 'Johan,'" he said. "The 'uncle' part was your mother's idea, but I don't think either of us likes it very much, am I right?" he added with an awkward smile.

"No."

Johan looked over Erik's shoulder. "Are those Lena's . . . I mean . . . are those your mother's suitcases?"

Erik made no reply.

"Are they?"

"I don't know."

"I see." Johan looked at him with concern. "Are you okay?"

Erik nodded.

"Well . . . is she ready?"

"Yes."

"Could you go and get her for me?" asked Johan, shifting from one foot to the other on the step.

"She's upstairs."

Leaving the door open, Erik turned on his heel and walked across the entrance hall, continued into the kitchen and headed for the cellar door. From the top of the stairs, he could hear his father tinkering away. The smell of animal hides and turpentine rose up to meet him at the top of the stairs. When he reached the bottom, he found his father sanding the wooden frames they used to suspend the hides during the drying and tanning process. His father's black respirator was discarded on the workbench. Erik picked up the mask and pulled it over his head. He yanked on the straps at the back so that the respirator sat tight over his mouth and nose. For a moment, he stood listening to his breath distorting through the filter. It almost sounded like Papa's, and there was something comforting about the sound, just like there was something comforting about the acrid smells in the cellar.

Erik bent down and crawled in under his father's workbench. He sat there in the relative darkness with his back resting against the wall, listening to his own breathing, listening to his father pottering about above, till the sounds were drowned out by Johan's screams from the first floor upstairs.

25

Copenhagen, 2013

It was early in the evening and business at The Sea Otter was slow. Patsy Cline was crooning "Crazy" from the jukebox. Thomas took his seat at the counter and ordered a round. Johnson regarded Thomas evenly as he popped the cap off his beer and put it in front of him. "Did you find anything?"

Thomas shook his head, waiting for Johnson to pour his shot. When it was filled to the rim, he downed his shot and chased it with the Hof as usual. "Naturally, this is confidential," he said, extracting the photocopied pages from Masja's police case file from inside his jacket and sliding them across the bar counter. Johnson snatched them up and fished his reading glasses out of his breast pocket. His lips moved in sync with the words he read. Once he had made his way through the report, he looked up at Thomas. "This doesn't say jack shit."

"It indicates that she's probably walking the streets somewhere," said Thomas.

"Yes, thank you. But *where*? And how am I supposed to tell her mother *that*?!" Johnson waved the pages in Thomas's face.

Thomas took a slurp from his beer. "Gently."

"Gently?"

"Yes. Break it to her gently. Don't you think her mother already suspects what Masja has been doing for a living?"

"I don't know," Johnson said, laying the pages on the counter between them. "Can't you do the rounds?"

"The rounds? What do you mean?"

"Ask some questions in the underground."

Thomas put down his beer and leaned on the counter. "No," he said. "I most certainly can*not*."

"But you're the one who is familiar with the underground, Ravn."

"That's exactly why I cannot do it, Johnson. Do you really believe that a trip up and down Skelbækgade is going to do the trick?"

"It would be a good place to start."

"No. Listen to what I am saying: I promised you that I would ask the guys at Station City if they had anything on Masja, and I did. That's the end of it. This case is closed," he added, crossing his arms over his chest.

Johnson refilled his shot glass with Jim Beam. "That report isn't going to bring Nadja's daughter back."

"You could ask around yourself. You take a look around, if you think it would help."

"But you're the one who knows the underground."

"Johnson, I swear to God, if you say *the underground* one more time, I'm leaving."

Johnson bit his lip, took out his dishcloth and wiped down the counter instead. "I'm just saying. You're the one who knows how to handle this kind of thing. You're a police officer, for Pete's sake."

"I'm on leave."

"You have the know-how, Ravn."

Johnson's gaze rested on Thomas, and he was reminded of Møffe—the drooping jowls, those big sad eyes that stare at you, unblinkingly and quietly insistent till you crack. "Johnson, the girl could be anywhere in the world by now," said Thomas, retrieving the pages from the counter and returning them to his inside jacket pocket. "She might have left the country for all we know," he said, sipping his Jim Beam thoughtfully. "The only people who might know something are the girls at The Nest."

"The Nest sounds like an excellent plan," Johnson said quickly. "So . . .what is The Nest, exactly?"

Thomas scratched his forehead. "An organisation that helps the girls who work the streets. There's a shelter over on Gasværksvej. I know the woman who runs it. Or at least, I used to. From the old days."

"Perfect!" said Johnson. "So ask her!"

"I'm not sure she'll remember me."

Johnson snorted. "You're not the type of guy who folks forget in a hurry."

Johnson was about to return the Jim Beam bottle to its spot above the bar, but Thomas held onto it. "I think I deserve another shot."

"Of course," said Johnson. "I just wasn't sure you'd drink while you were on duty."

It was raining cats and dogs on Gasværksvej. The kind of downpour that sends people running for cover. Thomas stepped onto the wet asphalt, strode across the road and immediately heard the screech of brakes followed by a prolonged honk. He cast a sidelong glance at the vehicle's driver, who showed him the middle finger through the windscreen. Thomas glared at him and continued over the far lane towards the glowing sign that hung over the entrance to The Nest.

The moment he entered the reception area, a stout woman in a pink jumpsuit blocked his way. "I know it's pissing down rain outside, comrade, but you've taken a wrong turn," the woman said in a voice like a blowtorch.

"Is Rosa here?" asked Thomas, whipping back his soaking-wet hood.

The woman narrowed her eyes at him. "You're a cop, aren't you?"

"I have an appointment with Rosa. She's expecting me."

"You're possibly undercover, but I can always spot a copper. *Always*."

"That's a great skill to have. Can you get Rosa for me now, please?"

The woman led the way through the living room, where a few women sat drinking coffee. They continued to a small kitchen that was set up in the rear.

"This copper here says he has an appointment with you," the blowtorch said.

The woman stirring a pot on the stove looked up. Rosa was in her late thirties, suntanned and dressed in a peach-coloured summer dress. Her blonde hair was pulled back by a broad cloth band that matched her dress.

"Vesterbro's answer to Grace Kelly," quipped Thomas with a smile.

"*Thomas?!*" Rosa said, staring at him briefly. She left the soup to simmer and came forward to give him a big hug. "I was very surprised when you called."

"My calls usually have that effect on people."

Thomas knew Rosa from the days when he first started out at Station City. At that time, Rosa was a newly appointed social worker on a project based in the red-light district in and around Istedgade, Copenhagen Central Station and Halmtorvet. Thomas's unit often instigated raids against the hookers, which meant that he and Rosa had clashed on a regular basis. There was bad blood between them till the night the Danish football team won the European Cup, and Thomas bumped into her—Rosa just about as blind drunk as he was—in Fælled Park behind the stadium. Against all odds, the two of them ended up at her place. He could still remember the night they spent together. It was just that one time, but they got on much better after that.

"It's been a long time . . . Are you still working for Station City?" Rosa asked.

"Yup, you could say so."

"I barely recognised you . . . you've grown a beard and you have a more . . . relaxed attitude," Rosa said, glancing at his scruffy attire.

"We all get older."

"Got yourself a wife? Children?"

Thomas looked away. "Neither."

"Still the lone wolf, huh?"

"Something like that. What about you?"

Rosa shook her head. "I have all this to take care of," she said, casting her arms wide. "It's more than enough to keep me busy. Time flies."

"Yes, it does."

"So, have you moved up in the ranks? You the one calling the shots now?"

"On the contrary. I'm on leave."

Rosa frowned. "It's nothing serious, I hope?"

"Nah, I just needed a break. Nothing more than that," Thomas said. He knew it sounded like a crock of shit, and Rosa was the kind of woman who could see right through it. Luckily, she didn't press the issue.

"Listen," Thomas said, unzipping his jacket, "the reason I called is that I need some information about a girl." He pulled out the picture of Masja, but before he could show it to her, she laid a hand on his arm.

"You know I can't talk about the girls who come here, Thomas."

"But I'm really just trying to help her," he said quickly.

"Help?" Rosa said, leaning back against the kitchen counter. Her brows formed two perfect arches over her eyes. "The police definition of that word has not always agreed with ours."

"As I said: I'm on leave," Thomas replied. Then he gave Rosa a brief explanation of Masja's disappearance and his own search in the Criminal Register, which indicated that she was a prostitute.

"So, you're not investigating any charges against her?"

"I am here because her mother misses her. That's all there is to it."

Rosa took the photograph from him and looked at the picture of Masja posing by the canal.

"Have you seen her before?" Thomas asked.

Rosa shook her head. "The picture doesn't ring any bells. Did she work in this neighbourhood?"

"I don't know. I think she concentrated on the hotels."

"Hmm. I don't work with the escort girls much. They generally keep to themselves, until the drugs take over and they end up on the streets."

"Are we eating soon?" a voice behind Thomas said. One of the women from the living room came into the kitchen. She reeked of cheap perfume. "I am ssso . . . hungry, Rosssa," she said with a lisp through her false teeth. Her face was gaunt and haggard from sustained drug abuse.

"I'll be done in five minutes," said Rosa. "Jackie, have you seen this girl?" she added, holding up the picture of Masja to the woman with the lisp.

Jackie leaned forward and narrowed her eyes. "No, does ssshe sssay that ssshe knows me? What's her name?"

"Masja," Thomas replied. "She's missing. Disappeared about two years ago."

"Masja? It's a common name. Sssounds like one of the Baltic girls."

"She comes from Lithuania."

"It doesn't matter what country they come from—Latvia, Lithuania or Long-way-away-stan—they all undercut the fucking prices on the street . . . Isn't that right, Rosssa?"

Rosa smiled sweetly. "Have you seen her about, Jackie?"

"Nope," Jackie said, shaking her head. "When can we eat?"

"Five minutes, I said. You're impatient today," Rosa remarked good-naturedly and returned the photograph to Thomas. He returned it to his inside pocket.

"Thanks for the help. It was lovely to see you, Rosa."

"Likewise, Thomas. Maybe we should have a glass of wine sometime?"

"Sure."

"No need to wait until our boys win the European Cup again," she added with a smile.

"I'll call you," he said, knowing full well that it was never going to happen. He was about to leave when the thought struck him: "Masja had a boyfriend, probably her pimp, a Russian called Ivan or Igor. Does that sound familiar?"

Rosa shook her head. "It's mostly Nigerians and Romanians on the streets at the moment, but why don't you try asking at the Russian Club?"

"The Russian Club?"

"It's near the main station, on Colbjørnsensgade. The kind of dive where only bandits and convicts hang out."

"Thanks, Rosa."

26

It was still pissing down rain when Thomas left The Nest, and there wasn't a taxi to be seen within a mile's radius. Flipping his hood over his head, he started walking down Istedgade in the direction of Colbjørnsensgade and the Russian Club. It was worth a shot, even if it was a long one. Thomas had never heard of the place. Melby probably would know it because the Baltic Mafia had always been his turf—at least until his new partnership with Mikkel—but he wasn't inclined to ask that prick for help.

Thomas turned down Colbjørnsensgade. When he was halfway down the block, he came to a building with opaque windows that appeared to be closed for business, but the door was ajar, and the sound of a running television commentary spilled onto the pavement. He spied through the crack of the door and caught a glimpse of three elderly men seated at a table, watching a football match on the screen above. All three had a Slavic appearance and he was pretty sure that this was the place that Rosa had mentioned. Thomas briefly considered going inside, but if any of the customers actually knew Igor, they probably wouldn't admit as much to a bum who had just walked in off the street—least of all a bum who turned out be a cop.

As Thomas continued down Colbjørnsensgade, he came across a black BMW with shiny hubcaps and a spoiler mounted on the rear hatch. There was nothing unusual about the car—it looked like every other pimped-up BMW in the red-light district—apart from a single exception: a green Wunder-Baum was dangling from the rear-view mirror. It could have been a coincidence, but his gut told him that the car could belong to Igor.

Thomas was soaked to the bone, but habit borne of hundreds of stakeouts rather than refuge from the rain made him duck into a quad a little further down the road. Despite the habit, or perhaps because of it, he struggled to settle down and blend into the darkness. The situation reminded him too much of his last stakeout with Mikkel. Following up on a tip, the two of them were posted across the road of an apartment block in Vesterbro belonging to a Bandidos gang lord who they knew was expecting a delivery of hash. The drop never happened, but the stakeout prevented Thomas from being home that night. Prevented him from finding Eva in time to stop the bleeding from the blow to her head. Prevented him from stopping the blood soaking into the oak floorboards in the living room.

Unable to stand still, Thomas fled out of the quad and darted over to the twenty-four-hour kiosk diagonally across the road. He had only intended to buy a couple of beers, but then he noticed the bottles of spirits lined up on a shelf just behind the broad shoulders of the Pakistani shopkeeper. He ordered a quart-sized bottle of Tullamore Dew and three Elephant Beers, basic provisions for a sleepless night on *Bianca*. The shopkeeper put his beverages in a plastic bag and asked for 175 kroner. While Thomas was rummaging in his pockets for some cash, a young couple came into the kiosk. He watched them out of the corner of his eye as he paid for his items. The girl had a pink faux-fur coat slung over her shoulders, and the man was wearing a black leather jacket and a pair of sunglasses on the back of his neck. Oakleys. The man ordered a pack of twenty Prince Reds, all the while bickering with the girl in Russian. His sentences were punctuated with loud sniffs, which Thomas guessed was a nasty case of the cocaine cold. Thomas picked up his plastic bag, exited the kiosk but remained standing just outside the door. A moment later, the Russian couple came out and headed in the direction of the black BMW. The man pointed his keys and the car responded with a beep and blinking indicators.

"Igor!" yelled Thomas.

The man cast a glance over his shoulder, obviously trying to place Thomas, but his face showed no signs of recognition.

Thomas walked resolutely towards him, his Tullamore bottle clattering against the Elephants in his bag with every step. "You *are* Igor, aren't you?"

"Mind your fucking business," the man answered, yanking open the driver's seat door of the BMW.

"Hang on a minute . . . I'd just like to ask you something."

"What do you want, man? Are you drunk or what?"

"I want to talk to you about Masja."

The mention of her name made the man freeze for a moment. "I don't know any Masja. Who are you?"

"Why would you say that? Masja was your girlfriend, after all."

The man's gaze wavered. "Who the hell are you?!"

"Do you know where I can find her?"

"I have no idea who you are talking about."

Thomas narrowed his eyes. "Come off it, Igor. I know when someone is lying to me."

Without warning, Igor stepped forward and shoved Thomas in the chest. Thomas was sent flying over backwards and came down hard on the asphalt, shattering his provisions against the pavement.

"What's going on, Igor?" squealed the girl in the faux-fur coat.

"Get in!" Igor shouted at the girl over the roof. "Now!"

The girl complained under her breath but did as she was told.

Igor looked down at Thomas. "Stay the hell away from me, do you understand, fuckwit? If you don't, I'll break you in half," Igor said. Then he turned on his heel and got into his car. Moments later, the BMW roared to life and sped away down the road. Thomas struggled to his feet and brushed the dirt off his hands. His palms were scraped and bloody, but he was only vaguely aware of the pain. Something else filled his mind now.

It had been buried for a long time, but it was back: his hunting instinct. No matter what the cost, he was going to track down that piece-of-shit Igor.

And he had to find out what happened to this girl called Masja.

27

December 2010

Slavros was seated behind the enormous mahogany desk in his office. The beautiful antique filled the better part of the room. It was a stark contrast to the cheap black leather furniture and pin-ups of naked women that hung on the walls. The lighting was dim, and the deep bass beat throbbed like a jungle drum from the club somewhere above. With the help of his sidekick, Mikhail, Slavros was wrapping Christmas presents, and his tight leather jacket squeaked whenever he moved his arms or reached for more Sellotape. "Not so much tape, you moron!" he snapped. "Else they won't be able to get the darn presents open!"

Mikhail nodded apologetically and removed some sticky-tape from the gift in front of him.

Slavros glanced at Masja, who was sitting on the edge of her chair on the opposite side of the desk.

"I always decline when the salesperson offers to wrap my gifts. I find this more personal. Don't you agree?" Slavros said, lifting the package in front of him.

Masja nodded and swallowed the spit that had gathered in her mouth.

"Not that my kids know the difference." He laughed. "They're more interested in what's *inside* the package. But the personal touch is important to *me*. I think it's important to make an effort."

Masja nodded again.

Slavros swore under his breath as he struggled to free his fingers from a wayward bit of sticky-tape. Giving up, he crumpled it into ball and extracted a fresh strip from the dispenser. At last, he sealed the ends of his package and inspected the result with satisfaction. "So, when are you going to open your trap and tell me why you've come to see me, Masja?" he said, reaching for a fresh roll of wrapping paper.

"I . . . something has happened—something that shouldn't have happened."

"I realise that. Are you going to tell me what it is?" he said, picking up the scissors to cut himself a sheet of wrapping paper.

"Someone has had an accident."

"An overdose?"

"No, no, it's nothing like that." Masja took a deep breath. "An accident . . . as in . . . fallen pregnant."

Slavros put down the scissors and looked at her belly.

"How far along are you?"

"No, no, it's not me. It's . . . Tabitha."

"The Nigerian girl?"

"Yes."

He shook his head. "The Nigerian girl is so bloody stupid."

"Fucking stupid," said Mikhail in agreement. "I told you that you shouldn't take a chance with her."

Slavros sent him a look and Mikhail fell silent. "So how far along is she?"

"Much too far, four months, maybe more," said Masja. "I only found out about it yesterday," she added quickly.

"Is that so!" Slavros said, leaning back in his chair. "Only yesterday?"

"Yes."

Slavros gave Mikhail a sidelong glance. "Next time we need new girls, remind me to avoid the fat ones."

Mikhail nodded. "No fat ones, no Black ones. Noted."

"How did you find out about this?"

"She came to me and asked if I would talk to you."

"It is never a good idea to get involved in other people's business."

"No, obviously not," said Masja. "I didn't want to get involved either. Usually, I mind my own . . . and stick to our . . . agreement. I just thought that you would want to know. That you might be able to help her," she added, trying to keep her knees still, but they had started to clap against each other.

Slavros cocked his head and smiled at her. "Of course I will help her. We help each other here. I'm glad that you came to me. Where is she now?"

"In her room," Masja said.

Slavros nodded at Mikhail. He immediately put down the wrapping paper and slipped out the door. Slavros pulled a roll of notes out of his pocket and gave her two. "Here," he said.

"That's not why I came."

"That's not what it's for. Merry Christmas, Masja."

Masja got to her feet and grasped the notes between her forefinger and thumb, but Slavros didn't let them go.

"Do you also have a gift for me?"

He let go of the notes and unzipped his trousers.

"Of course," she said. Masja squeezed her way around the desk and straddled his lap. Then she started to moan mechanically as she moved her body up and down.

Christmas Eve, 2010. Merry Christmas, *Mumija*. I am thinking about you. Thinking about our Christmas Eves together. You always tried to be home early from work. You always tried to arrange some nice things for us. Sweets and biscuits. Once, you even brought a tree home with you. I remember that it didn't have many branches left. But it was *our* tree. *Our* Christmas. I'm so ashamed that I wasn't grateful. That I never bought you a gift. That I never thanked you for the gifts that you gave me. I thought it wasn't good enough. Not expensive enough. Can you ever forgive me?

. . . I thought that Slavros would send Tabitha to a hospital. That it might be her way out of this—with or without the baby. I thought he would write off her debt. As long as she kept her mouth shut. I thought it would be best for everyone. But I don't know jack shit. All I know is that Slavros will never give up on anything. That he's the devil.

Tabitha is in her room now, pumped full of drugs and poison

and all kinds of crap to kill the baby. To "induce contractions," Lulu said. She said that it will take about six hours to kill the little one, and all the tissue in Tabitha's womb. It would be "expelled," she said. A stillborn child, one helluva way to come into the world. Lulu says that it's murder, that Tabitha's baby is a human being. Albeit a tiny one. No one in the club knows how big it is. Some say five centimetres, others say twenty. But everyone says it looks exactly like a little child—with arms, legs, fingers, and toes and eyes and everything. The thought makes me sick at heart. I feel like screaming. At least my Valium pills help to control the urge.

Christmas Day. Tabitha is bleeding. Bleeding, bleeding, bleeding. I didn't see it, the birth—if that's what you could call it. But the baby is gone. Lulu carried the bloody sheets, bloody toilet paper and bloody clothing down the stairs to the container behind the club. I doubt that there is any blood left inside Tabitha. Everyone is worried about Tabitha, or at least say that they are. Maybe they are just afraid because they could just as well have been the ones who lay there bleeding to death.

Slavros and that psychopath doctor are with Tabitha right now. His name is Poul. Apparently, he was the closest thing to a doctor that Slavros could get hold of. Poul used to be a porter or a carer or something in a hospital, till he was fired for stealing medication from his employers. I've had him as a client just once. He gets off on whips and pain. I'll bet he's having a field day with Tabitha, the poor girl.

26 December. The holidays are golden. I've never made so much money on a single day, not even in the club—the bulls are back! Back home, their families are exchanging gifts, so they take the gap to drive down the street and score a girl for a thrill. We're kept busy.

Tabitha has stopped bleeding. She sleeps all the time. It's impossible for her to walk. She doesn't talk about what happened. Lulu says that Poul has removed most of it inside her. *Scraped* her out, she said. The word makes me feel sick. Lulu says that Tabitha will probably never be able to get pregnant again. Tabitha says nothing, just stares up at the ceiling, popping those yellow pills that Poul has given her.

The other girls always called her lazy. A "lazy bitch," they say. I know that it is only a question of time before Slavros kicks her out of bed. Tabitha's debt has grown. Big time. All the trouble she has caused costs money, and Slavros is keeping tabs on every single sheet she has ruined with blood. My own balance sheet is looking good though. This week, at least. I still have a long way to go—seven or eight months, I reckon—but I can see the light at the end of the tunnel. The day will come when I have settled my debt to Slavros. And then I'll come home to you, *Mumija*. I will visit. Maybe next summer . . . maybe.

28

Mälarhöjden, January 1980

From the dark corner under the workbench, Erik could hear his father's footsteps rush down the stairs. He closed his eyes, pulled his legs up underneath him and held his breath, trying to block out the world around him. But then he felt his father's hands, rubber gloves clawing at his jumper and dragging him out from underneath the workbench.

Bertil yanked the respirator up over his son's head and flung it across the room. "What have you done? What the hell have you done?!" he screamed, beating his son about the head, completely beside himself.

The pain felt almost like a relief. "S-s-s-sorry," Erik stammered, slipping to the floor.

At last, Bertil stopped lashing out at him and sank onto the floor next to his son. Staring up at the ceiling, Bertil choked back the sobs in his throat. He brought his hand up to his chin and tried to wipe away the snot from his face. Then his arm reached out and found Erik, pulling his son close.

"I didn't mean it, Papa. I didn't want her to die."

"What on earth were you thinking?"

"I don't know . . . I . . . I just didn't want her to leave us."

"Good God, Erik . . . you killed her . . . How could you?!"

Erik started to cry. "It just happened . . . I . . ."

"That's not true. You must have been thinking about it for a long time because . . . why the syringe?"

"You said it was dangerous."

"But *why*? It doesn't make sense, Erik."

"I don't know, Papa . . . I saw the two of you in the bedroom . . . I saw you on top of her with your hands around her throat . . . I . . . I just wanted to stop her, just like you wanted to stop her leaving, don't you understand?"

The tears ran unchecked down Bertil's cheeks. "Yes, I suppose I do, in a way," he said. Then he sat up and brushed back his thin hair. "But I doubt that other people will understand."

Erik looked up at his father. "What's going to happen to me, Papa?"

Bertil shook his head. "I'm so sorry for everything we have put you through, Erik. It's my fault."

"No, Papa."

"Yes, it is. But we need to fix this."

"Shall we call the police?"

Bertil nodded. "I'm afraid we don't have any other choice."

Erik started to cry again. "Okay, Papa. I understand. What will they do with me?"

"I don't know, Erik. None of this is fair," he said. His thick leather apron creaked as he got to his feet and helped Erik up next to him.

"I'm scared, Papa," said Erik. His body was shaking.

"So am I," said Bertil, putting an arm around Erik's shoulders. Then they made for the stairs together.

When Erik and Bertil came into the master bedroom, they heard Johan's moaning above the sound of running water. Erik tried to hide behind his father when they reached the doorway of the ensuite bathroom. Johan was in the shower, holding Lena's lifeless body in his arms. Blood was coming out of every orifice in her body, and he was trying to resuscitate her with mouth-to-mouth.

"It's too late for that, Johan," said Bertil.

Johan looked up at him. "We . . . we have to do something."

"Her organs are no longer functioning. Death occurs within seconds of the injection," said Bertil.

"But . . . but have you called for help . . . an ambulance?"

"She's dead, Johan. There's nothing we can do to save her."

As if Bertil's words had extinguished what little hope he might have had, Johan let go of Lena's body and slumped against the tiled wall behind him. Then he began to sob uncontrollably. "Why . . . why . . . why?"

"It's a tragedy," mumbled Bertil.

Erik squeezed his father's hand, dimly aware of the cold rubber surface of his father's glove.

Johan was staring vacantly ahead of him. "We have to call the police. How the hell could this happen?" he said to no one in particular.

Bertil let go of Erik's hand and walked towards the shower. "That's what we need to figure out," he said.

"What the hell is there to figure out? Lena was murdered . . . by him," Johan said, pointing at Erik, who immediately bowed his head.

Bertil did not reply. Instead, he drummed his fingers against his lips, all the while inspecting the bathroom thoughtfully. "You came to fetch Lena."

"Yes, you know that I did."

"You were going to take her away from her family."

"That doesn't give that boy the right to kill her!" Johan yelled directly at Erik.

"Hmm . . . no," muttered Bertil. "But Lena had changed her mind. She no longer wanted anything to do with you. She loved her family—loved her son—too much to go through with it."

"What are you talking about?" Johan said, sitting up against the wall. "Have you completely lost your mind?"

"Not at all, Johan. *You* were the one who lost your mind. You fell into a jealous rage. You could not tolerate her rejection, which you interpreted as an unforgivable betrayal. So you broke into our house while Lena was in the shower. Erik and I were down in the cellar."

Johan stood up. He tried to push past Bertil, but felt the older man grab hold of his arm.

"Let go of me," Johan snapped. "If you're not going to call the police, I will."

"And what are you going to tell them, Johan? It will be your word against mine . . . *ours*," he corrected himself, looking at Erik. "Your fingerprints are all over the bathroom, and *you* are the one with a motive."

"You're out of your mind."

"No, not at all. I am protecting my son."

"Not at my expense," hissed Johan. "That boy killed his mother with a syringe from *your* workshop downstairs. How do you intend to explain that to the police?"

"You know, you're right," said Bertil. "That might be the decisive point that could tip the scales in your favour."

Johan yanked his arm free. "You're both fucking crazy," he said, looking at Bertil and Erik in turn.

Bertil nodded. "Possibly, but at least Erik and I are alive."

Before Johan could react, Bertil extracted the scalpel he had in his left glove and slashed a fine arch across Johan's throat, a nice clean cut that severed the carotid artery, and the blood gushed out of the open wound. Johan brought his hands up to his throat. He had an expression of surprise on his face, and he tried to say something, but only blood came out of his mouth.

Bertil frowned thoughtfully again. "I think that he must have stolen the syringe the last time he visited us in the cellar. Erik and I have been looking for it ever since."

Johan sank to his knees. His entire chest was covered in blood now.

"Naturally, all of this is pure speculation," Bertil continued. "But I think that the police will agree that my explanation is plausible. Especially when I tell them that Lena was afraid of you, Johan. That she had taken the scalpel from the cellar to defend herself, so afraid of you that she took it with her into the bathroom. This is the only logical explanation for this tragedy."

Johan toppled over onto the floor.

Bertil dropped the scalpel beside Lena in the shower. For a moment, he stared down at her, then he turned to Erik. "Do you think it looks better if she's still holding the scalpel in her hand, Erik?"

As if he had turned to stone, Erik could neither speak nor move a muscle.

"Erik?"

At last, Erik took a tentative step forward and looked down. "Y-yes," he said. "That would appear more authentic."

Bertil bent down, picked up the scalpel and put it in Lena's hand. Stepping over her corpse, he picked up the syringe between his thumb and forefinger and placed it carefully in Johan's palm. He closed Johan's hand over the syringe, then threw it in the far corner of the bathroom.

"Does everything look right to you now, Erik?"

Erik had withdrawn to the doorway, and he surveyed the tableau thoughtfully. A thick pall of mist had settled over the corpses. Lena's legs stuck out of the shower, and behind the cracked glass wall, he glimpsed the outline of her naked body. Johan lay on the floor with a surprised expression on his face. The tendons in his neck were exposed, almost like the elk's.

"We need to call the police now."

"Yes, Father."

"It's important that you don't break down, Erik. We have to stick to the story I have just told."

"Yes, Father."

"It was best that it ended this way, Erik," Bertil said firmly. "Any other conclusion would have left a terrible mess that would have hit us very hard. Let's remember your mother for all the good things that she brought us. Let us honour her memory."

"Yes, Father."

"As for Johan: The world is a better place without him. Believe me, no one is going to miss him."

"No, Father. No one will miss him."

"I love you, Erik. You know that."

"I love you, too, Papa."

Erik looked around the bathroom one last time. *This* scene was worthy of a pedestal. He imagined that it would sit very nicely between the hovering buzzard and the squirrel eating a hazelnut. "Here he comes, here he comes . . . here he comes . . ." The theme song of *Hopalong Cassidy* sounded somewhere in the recesses of his mind.

Erik turned to his father. "Do you think we will be able to repair the elk?"

29

Copenhagen, 2013

The stairway was ice cold and reeked of urine. Thomas was standing in the dark on the third-floor landing, in front of Igor's door. Igor's flat was in the old industrial quarter near the abandoned soya bean factory in Islands Brygge. Initially intended as an exclusive residential location on the harbour front, the complex rapidly became a ghetto in the wake of the financial crisis. No one could feel safe in this area after dark.

The rope of Thomas's police badge chafed around his neck. Standing on the landing in the dark, it almost felt like the old days, and he could feel the adrenaline rushing through his veins. He had asked Mikkel to do a search on Igor's number plate so he could track down his address. Mikkel had warned him not to do anything stupid; it would only give Brask an excuse to throw him out of the police corps for good. But the only thing that mattered to Thomas right now was getting into Igor's flat so that he could search for anything that might give him a lead on what had happened to Masja.

Thomas cautiously bent down and levered the hatch of the letterbox. The entrance to the flat was dark and all was quiet inside. He straightened up and took his set of picklocks out of his jacket pocket, selected the appropriate size and stuck it into the cylinder. Mikkel's search in the Criminal Register had revealed that Igor had a suspended sentence for theft. Unfortunately, the charge had not been enough to expel him from the country, but if Igor as much as pissed in public, he would end up behind bars for a few years, as well as receive a one-way ticket to Minsk—or wherever the hell the dickhead came from.

Thomas swore under his breath. His hands were shaking so much that he couldn't pick the damn lock. At last, he gave up and took a step back from the door. One hard kick with his right leg shattered the door-frame. *Mission accomplished.* He stood still and listened to the silence in the stairwell for a moment, then he entered the flat.

Apparently, Igor had fired his cleaning lady. The entire living room was littered with half-empty beer bottles, as if after a wild party. On the coffee table, among empty bottles, a shiny silver platter glowed in the dark. Beside it, there was a fine layer of white dust.

Thomas walked through the living room and headed for what appeared to be the bedroom. The bed was unmade, and clothing was strewn on the floor. The room stank of sweat and beer. Thomas stepped over a used condom and took a few paces to the built-in cupboard against the far wall. The first two doors revealed a jumble of men's clothing only. This was not the only indication that Igor lived alone. When Thomas opened the last cupboard door, an assortment of junk spilled out onto his head and the floor. Thomas bent down and started to sort through the contents: old receipts, porno mags, football shoes, and a guitar with broken strings, among all sorts of other shit. He upended cardboard boxes onto the carpet. When he had been through the contents of those, he noticed a crumpled photograph right at the back of the shelf: Igor sitting on the hood of the BMW with a girl. Thomas recognised Masja immediately and put the photograph in his pocket.

Now he had found what he was looking for, but the investigation did not stop there. He wanted something else on Igor—something more that would pin him down. The cocaine dust on the table and the constant sniffing indicated to Thomas that there might be drugs in the apartment. From experience, he knew that there were three common places where most pushers liked to stash their stuff: under the bed, in the fridge and in the tank behind the toilet.

He bent down and looked under the bed. He couldn't see anything suspicious, so he ran his hand along the planks of the bedframe. After a few moments, his fingers found a small plastic bag wedged under the mattress. He pulled it out and saw that it contained a white powder, cocaine or some kind of amphetamine, he reckoned. So Igor seemed relatively predictable.

His search was interrupted by a burst of Russian expletives coming from the entrance. Thomas stuffed the little plastic bag into his pocket and retraced his steps into the living room. Igor was standing in the doorway, his face red with rage. His eyes opened wide when he caught sight of Thomas. ". . . you?" Igor said in disbelief. "What the hell?!" he said, balling his fists and taking a step towards Thomas.

Thomas calmly took out his police badge and presented himself. "Yes, me, Igor. Thomas Ravnsholdt, Copenhagen Police, Crime Ops."

Igor stopped in his tracks and looked at the badge, which clearly threw him off balance.

"You've had a break-in," said Thomas.

"I've had a what?"

"A break-in," Thomas repeated clearly. "As in: Somebody has broken down your door and entered your home."

"What are you doing in here?"

"I was in the neighbourhood when it happened. Luckily, nothing has been stolen. They didn't even take the drugs that I found under your mattress," Thomas said, taking out the little bag and waving it in front of Igor's face.

"That . . . that's not . . . mine."

"Oh, of course not," said Thomas with a lopsided smile. "But I'm pretty sure that Forensics will have a field day when they tear your place apart."

"Fucking hell," said Igor, swallowing hard.

"Yes, that's exactly where you are right now. Take a seat on the sofa. You and I are going to have a little chat—right now!"

Igor did as he was told and sat down.

"With everything you have laid up against you already, you're going to jail for a long time, Igor. And afterwards, I will have the honour of personally putting you on a plane home."

"Who talked?"

Thomas stared down at him. "Is *that* your biggest worry right now?"

Igor shrugged. "Who?"

"Masja. Masja talked."

Igor's jaw dropped. "Masja?!" He gawked at Thomas. "I . . . I don't know anybody by that name."

Thomas took the crumpled photograph out of his pocket and threw it on the table in front of Igor.

Igor glanced down. Then he hunched over and buried his hands in his hair. "Masja squealed on me?"

"What do you think?"

Igor stared ahead without blinking. "I can't blame her. I'm ashamed of what I did to her. When you see her again, please tell her I'm sorry, will you?"

Thomas sat down on the arm of the black leather chair next to the table.

"I have no idea where she is. That's why I came to look for you here."

"But . . ."

"Listen to me, Igor, right now I'm your new best friend," Thomas said, jiggling the bag of white powder, "but it's essential to our friendship that you tell me where she is."

"I really do not know."

"When was the last time you saw her?"

"It was at least two years ago, I swear."

"And where did you see her?"

Igor bowed his head. "Over on Amager someplace."

"Can you be more specific?"

"On Yderlandsvej, at an abandoned auto workshop."

"Interesting. And what were the two of you doing there?"

Igor fished a pack of cigarettes out of his breast pocket.

"What was she doing there, Igor?"

"She was helping me out of a deep fucking hole."

"What kind of hole?"

"The kind you cannot get out of on your own," Igor said, lighting a cigarette. He inhaled deeply and blew out a large cloud of smoke. "A gambling debt. Big time."

Thomas nodded. "And Masja had to take care of clients out there?"

"She did a bit more than that."

"What do you mean?"

Igor looked up. "You gotta understand how deep in the shit I was, man," he said desperately.

"Tell me what happened."

Igor shook his head and stared at the floor again. "I made a deal. Passed the debt on to Masja."

Thomas stood up. "Let me get this straight. You *sold* your girlfriend to settle your own debt?"

"Yes . . . no . . . it wasn't like that. I . . . I got her a job. Yeah, a job, that's how it was."

"You don't really believe that story yourself, do you?"

Igor didn't reply.

Thomas could see that it was eating the guy up inside.

"I need names, Igor."

"I cannot do that. You know how it is."

"Yes, I know *exactly* how it is: Either you tell me who you made a deal with out on Amager that day, or I'm going to hand you over to the system—for possession, dealing, sex trafficking, the whole fucking rigmarole. Afterwards, I'm going to pay a visit to your club on Colbjørnsensgade and tell everyone that you're holed up in Station City, spilling your guts. After that, we won't have to bother with finding flight connections to Minsk. I'm pretty sure your friends will get hold of you before we get a chance to book the ticket."

"They were Eastern Europeans. I didn't know them," said Igor.

"I need names—now!"

"It was such a long time ago . . ."

"Right now!"

"Milan. One of the guys was called Milan."

"Like the football club?"

"Yeah, whatever. And the other guy's name was Lucian."

"So Masja is with these guys now?"

"No."

"Then where the hell is she?!"

"Lucian sent her to another guy that she would work for."

"Name."

Igor took a frantic puff on his cigarette. "His name is Slavros. Vladimir Slavros. Gangster. Big-time pimp. Mega organised."

"And where can I get hold of this Slavros guy?"

Igor leaned forward and stubbed out his cigarette in the ashtray. "I have no idea. You don't find Slavros; he finds you. Most people only see him coming when it's already too late."

"I'm pissing in my pants," said Thomas, deadpan.

"You'd have good reason to if you were dumb enough to start poking around in his business."

Thomas shook his head, grabbed the coke, and made for the door.

"What about my stuff?" asked Igor, pointing at the plastic bag in Thomas's hand. "I could really use a line right now."

"The coke? I'm going to flush it down the toilet."

"What the fuck?! It's worth twenty thousand!"

"You're testing my patience, Igor," said Thomas. On the way to the door, he sidestepped into the bathroom and flushed the coke down the toilet.

Thomas had no idea who Milan, Lucian, or Slavros were, but they sounded like the kind of bad guys that Melby or Mikkel would know. It looked like he would have to beg Mikkel for one more favour.

30

December 2010

It was long after midnight and the streets of the upper-crust villa quarter in Mälarhöjden was deserted. The dim glow of TV screens in the living rooms of several houses revealed that the neighbours were having a late night. On Lake Mälar, spread out at the edge of the lawns of the homes on the bank, you could catch a glimpse of the red lanterns of the occasional container ship that slid past soundlessly. In front of the villa at the end of the street, a 1972 Mercedes-Benz SEL was parked in the driveway, gleaming black and chrome under the streetlamp, in the same mint condition it was the day it left the dealer's in Sollentuna thirty-eight years ago.

The man behind the wheel put on a pair of dark glasses and pulled his flat cap down low. He extracted a pair of black calf-leather driving gloves from the inside pocket of his lambskin coat and laboriously put them on. When he turned the key in the ignition, the 6.5 litre V8 engine responded like a distant thunderclap. The man leaned forward and retrieved a small metal box from the glove compartment. Inside was an ampoule of morphine and an old-fashioned syringe made of metal. The man removed the cap from the needle and perforated the lid of the ampoule. He drew the morphine solution into the chamber and held it up to the light, carefully pushing on the plunger till a few drops appeared at the tip of the needle. Satisfied, he returned the cap to the needle and laid it in the console between the front seats. He was ready. Everything had been planned down to the last detail. Now all he needed was one of the candidates on his list.

Twenty minutes later, the black Mercedes was cruising through Stockholm city centre. The deserted office buildings of the Norrmalm business district towered on either side of the road. The yellow light from the Mercedes' raised headlights spilled onto the iced-over pavements and revealed the girls standing along the walls, shivering in their scant clothing. They stared at the car, as if they were deer blinded by the headlights. The sight lifted the driver's spirits and he started to hum cheerfully as he drummed his gloved fingers on the wheel. When he was about halfway down the length of Mäster Samuelsgatan, he pulled over to the kerb. A thin blonde in stilettos stepped out of the shadows and came over to the car. The man rolled down the passenger side window and the girl leaned down to looked into the car.

"You again," she said, somewhat disappointed. She blew a bubble with her chewing gum till it burst. "Are you still just gawking, or are you ready to take the plunge?"

"Would you be so kind as to show me your breasts?" the man said.

"Kind?" the girl mocked. "You're a weird one, all right," she said, taking a step back. Then she zipped down her satin jacket and flashed her naked boobs. "I hope you're not a 'chubby chaser,' sweetheart, because if so, you've come to the wrong place." She lifted her sagging breasts in her hands and pinched her nipples between her forefingers and thumbs till they went hard.

"On the contrary. I like thin girls," said the man. "I reckon that your body fat percentage must be around five or six—which is excellent," he said cheerfully, opening the passenger door for her.

The girl zipped up her jacket and got into the car.

As they set off down the road, she rummaged in her bag for a condom. "It costs five hundred, and I don't do anal or any kinky shit. Just so you know . . ."

"That's fine by me. Have you been ill long?"

"What do you mean?"

"You've lost a lot of weight since I last saw you."

"What can I say? Life's a bitch," she said in a monotone, staring out the window. "We can go down to the railway yard," she said, pointing down a side road, but the man kept driving, and she turned towards him. "Or . . . perhaps you have a different place in mind?"

"Paradise," the man said. "We're going to paradise." In one swift movement, he retrieved the syringe from the console, jabbed the needle into her thigh and pushed the plunger home. The girl had no time to react, and the morphine took effect immediately. She collapsed in her seat and the man returned the syringe to the console.

"Sweet dreams, darling," he said, stroking her hair gently.

The girl slowly woke up from her sleep and squinted into the sharp fluorescent light. She tried to get up but discovered that thick leather straps were holding her down. She was naked and strapped to a pallet that was raised at a 45-degree angle to the wall, giving her an unhindered view of the low-ceilinged room that stretched before her.

The walls were lined with a series of narrow metal shelves that held a variety of bottles and glass jars filled with liquids and row upon row of crates and cardboard boxes. The girl studied the jars on the top shelf. The first contained a frog floating in formaldehyde. The next was a similar jar containing some kind of snake. To her horror she realised that all the jars on the top shelf contained a variety of preserved toads and reptiles. She craned her neck to get a better view of the animals on the lower shelves: pheasants, crows, squirrels, foxes, a puppy, and a grotesque animal that appeared to be half owl, half hare.

At the other end of the room, a man in a white lab coat was standing at a workbench with his back to her. A series of glass jars containing strange liquids stood on the workbench before him. The man extracted the liquids with a glass pipette and mixed them in a test tube with an elegant rotation of his wrist.

The girl strained against the leather straps. "What the hell are you doing?" she said.

The man turned towards her, and she gawked at the sight. He was wearing a dark pair of goggles and a large black respirator that covered his nose and mouth. Holding the test tube at arm's length, he made his way towards her between the metal shelves.

The girl writhed and struggled to free herself. A sharp pain in her lower body made her look down. A fat needle was planted in her left groin, and a slim line of rubber tubing connected it to a strange apparatus that stood on the top surface of a trolley beside her.

"Help!" she yelled, but there was no one to hear her call.

The man was next to her now and rested a hand on her shoulder. "Please keep still," he said in a hollow voice from inside the respirator. "You will only hurt yourself if you move."

"Let me go, I'm begging you," the girl said. "I promise, I won't tell anyone about this."

"There, there," said the man, clapping her on the head. He turned to the trolley and bent down. On the trolley, rubber tubing ran from the apparatus on top to a row of three jars on the shelf underneath. Very carefully, the man poured the contents of the test tube in his hand into the third jar. The translucent liquid in the jar immediately took on a bright yellow hue.

"Please . . . please let me go," the girl sobbed.

The man raised his index finger to hush her. "Would you kindly refrain from saying anything right now?" he said, turning back to the apparatus. "You will disturb the process."

The man punched a series of numbers into a keypad. The apparatus began to hum as the liquids were drawn out of the glass jars below and pumped along the clear rubber tubing.

"Let me go!" screamed the girl. "Let me go, you psychopath!"

"This is not appropriate behaviour," said the man calmly.

The girl swore at him, calling him all sorts of names, and at last it appeared as if the man had heard enough, for he punched the first of three green buttons on the keypad, and a clear liquid entered the rubber tube and inched towards the needle in her groin. The effect was immediate: The girl grunted and stopped yelling instantly. Her gaze clouded over, and she licked her lips, as if after a luscious meal.

"What . . . what have you given me?" she said.

"Morphine solution, one hundred fifty milligrams."

"Please don't hurt me," she wailed. "I'll be good to you, treat you real nice, better than anyone has ever treated you before, I promise."

The man nodded. "I'm glad you've decided to cooperate. It makes everything so much easier. And I'm sure it will aid the process."

"The processh," she slurred.

The man entered a new combination of figures into the keypad and pressed the second green button. "I'm terribly sorry, but this might cause you some discomfort."

"I've had my share of discomfort," the girl said, staring at him with hazy eyes. "What are you giving me now?"

"A mixture of formalin, hydrochloric acid, and zinc."

"W-what?"

The liquid pumped through the rubber tubing, and when it entered the girl's bloodstream, her body went into spasms, and she screamed in pain. The leather straps cut into her flesh as her body strained against them. Froth protruded from the corners of the girl's mouth, and she stared with bloodshot eyes at the man.

"Easy now, it's all part of the process," the man said, observing her response clinically. "It will all be over soon." The man studied his watch.

Now indecipherable words came from the girl's mouth. Then her body convulsed again and her back arched away from the pallet. The leather straps around her wrists and ankles squeaked but held fast.

After precisely forty-three seconds, the girl's body went limp.

The man pressed the third green button on the keypad and took up his post next to the corpse. Her tongue stuck out, partially severed at the root, and he gently pushed it back into her mouth and lowered her lids to cover her staring eyes. When the bright yellow liquid infused her blood, the glow came back to her face, and her skin tone changed. Her cheeks regained some colour, as if awoken from the dead.

"At last," the man said, clearly moved, as he stroked her hair fondly, regarding his handiwork.

But all at once the glow started to drain from the girl's face, and it took on a sallow discolouration, which became increasingly pronounced. The man removed his hand from her hair and hurried back to the apparatus.

He checked the figures on the display. "No, no, no, this is not right . . . it's not fair!" he wailed, close to tears. He glanced at the girl. Her skin already looked parched.

Crestfallen, the man walked over to the hoist and tackle in the ceiling and guided it over to the pallet. He untied the straps that had held the girl's arms and legs to the pallet and secured the tackle around her chest instead. Then he hauled on a chain that hoisted her body into the air, about one and a half metres off the ground. Putting his back into it, he ferried the girl to the other end of the cellar, up and over the rim of the zinc tub.

He whipped a well-worn leather apron from the hook on the wall beside him and fastened it around his waist. From a small wooden toolbox on the workbench, he selected his favourite Havalon scalpel. It had a deer beautifully etched into the shaft. With utmost care, he replaced its twenty-six-millimetre blade with a fresh one. A deep sigh escaped from his lips as he regarded the corpse dangling from the ceiling. *The experiment has failed*, he thought dismally. So much work lay ahead. *Never mind.* Bending over the head, he traced a fine incision along the left-hand side and slowly began to cleave the skin from the girl's face.

A week later, the man was back in his cellar. A piece of polystyrene foam that had the shape of a human left arm was mounted onto his lathe, and he was systematically polishing the surface with a 140-millimetre-grade piece of sandpaper. He stopped to take measurements of the anterior shoulder joint with his vernier calliper. Cross-checked the measurements with the figures in a little notebook that was always within reach on the workbench surface beside him. Sanded another millimetre off the shoulder. Leaned back and inspected his work. Satisfied at last, he dismounted the polystyrene arm from the lathe. Turning on his heel, he walked over to the far wall, where he had propped his life-sized mould, which was a patchwork of foam pieces screwed together. It looked very much like a dressmaker's mannequin except that the face was a lot more detailed, and you could almost recognise the dead girl's face below the hard foam surface.

Twenty minutes later, he had successfully mounted the arm onto the mould, and he returned his attention to the zinc tub. The tanned sheaths of skin rested in the solution inside. He would have liked to skin the girl whole, but it was a finnicky process, and he had been loath to cut the hide in six smaller parts. In truth, it would not have made any difference one way or the other because, in order to hide the stitching, he had to lime-wash her from head to toe anyway. He bent down and selected the back-sheath part from the tub. Carried it dripping-wet back to the mannequin.

Taking his time, he carefully draped the sheath of tanned skin over the back and shoulders of the mannequin mould, as if it were a loose-fitting coat. Once the skin had dried, it would shrink and fit snugly over the form. He inspected his work in progress: Ultimately, the girl would be more beautiful, more majestic than she had been during her lifetime. But she would be far from perfect. She was a stop-gap solution, an amateur's attempt to hide his own imperfection. And he knew it. He was suitably ashamed. But one day, the process would succeed. He would create his masterpiece. And fortunately, there was more than one candidate on his list. Stockholm had no shortage of supply. The country was full of run-away Eastern European girls.

He resolved to do a better job next time.

31

New Year's Eve 2010

The night sky was illuminated by fireworks that exploded over an entire city celebrating New Year's Eve. Cascades of gold, silver, blue, green, and red lights rained down over the rooftops, which were almost hidden in smoke. Cannon shots resounded over the Norrmalm district, making prostitutes and clients alike jump in fright every time there was an explosion in the skies above. A gentle stream of cars cruised past the girls. Local boys having the party of their lives yelled insults at the girls, instigating each other, occasionally mooning the prostitutes through rolled-down windows as they drove by. The girls responded with a volley of insults and rude gestures of their own.

A red Audi pulled up to the kerb and Masja opened the door and got out of the passenger seat. "Happy New Year!" the man behind the wheel called after her.

"Same to you, sweetheart," she said, and smacked the door behind her. She walked over to Iza, who was standing on the pavement with two other girls.

"Did you get anything out of him?" Iza asked.

"Four hundred," said Masja. "The moron wanted to do it without a condom, of course. 'Because it's New Year's,' he said. What kind of a bullshit argument is that?!"

"So, did you do it?"

"Do I look like an idiot to you?" said Masja, taking a little plastic bag out of her pocket.

"Did you score that stuff from him?"

"Yes, indeedy," Masja said.

"What is it?" asked Lulu from behind them.

Masja shook her head. "Lulu, if it looks like coke . . ."

". . . then it probably *is* coke," said Iza. "Are you sharing?"

Masja relented. It was New Year's Eve, after all. The girls cut the coke between them on Lulu's make-up mirror and snorted the entire four grams through a rolled-up 50-krona note.

Iza took a half-empty bottle of Smirnoff out of her shoulder bag and passed the vodka round. "It was brave of you to go to Slavros, Karina. Respect. Even if it was for that girl's sake. I've seen him beat the shit out of people for sticking their noses in other people's business."

"Fuck Slavros," said Masja, taking another big gulp of vodka.

The other girls winced and giggled behind their hands, as if Slavros could hear them all the way from Key Club.

"Where is Tabitha anyway?" asked Masja, glancing up and down the street.

"Down by the railway yard with a client," said Lulu.

"Hopefully not with the Mercedes wacko?"

"Who?"

"That guy who cruises around in a black Mercedes—the freak I warned you girls to stay the hell away from!" Masja yelled.

"They're all freaks," said Iza, taking the bottle of vodka from her.

"No, this guy is different. This one is . . ." Masja's gaze wavered, her throat was dry, and she could already feel the rush subsiding. "This freak is a devil."

"Relax," said Lulu. "Tabitha was picked up by a yellow van. She struggled to get inside, poor thing. It must hurt like hell after Poul scraped her insides out."

"Arrgh, Lulu, please don't say that word again. It hurts all the way up."

A can of beer landed on the pavement right in front of them, spraying foam at their feet. "Happy New Year, you whores!" a pimply-faced lad yelled from a passing car. His mate stepped on the accelerator and the car sped down the road. Iza chucked the empty vodka bottle after them, but the bottle missed and smashed on the kerb. Despite the ruckus, no one took any notice. Not even Slavros's three goons who sat at a café across the street, staring through the glass panes with vacant expressions on their faces. Nothing to do but smoke cigarettes as they waited for yet another night to pass.

"Hey, I have one more we can drink," said Lulu, drawing a quart bottle of Tullamore Dew out of the inside pocket of her jacket.

Over Lulu's shoulder they heard the screech of tyres as another car swung around the corner. Masja and the other girls looked up and saw a large yellow van career towards them.

"Are the cops after him or what . . . ?" Iza said to no one in particular.

When the van reached the kerb, the driver slammed on the brakes. There were bloody handprints on the passenger side door, Masja noticed. The driver, a chubby little man wearing velvet trousers that were much too short, had already jumped out of his seat and rushed to the passenger side door, his fly gaping wide open. "It's bad," he said frantically. "It's really fucking bad!" He ran one hand through his mop of hair. Masja and the other girls shrunk away from him as he yanked open the passenger door.

Tabitha was slumped over on the passenger seat. The chubby man hauled her out of the seat and pulled her onto the kerb, leaving a bloody trail behind. "You need to take care of your friend!" yelled the man, dumping her roughly onto the pavement. Blood trailed down Tabitha's inner thighs and gathered in a dark pool under her body. The girls stared at Tabitha in horror.

"What . . . what have you done?" asked Masja.

"Nothing! . . . We didn't even get to . . . before this . . . this started to happen," the chubby man said, already hurrying back to the driver's side.

"You have to take her to a hospital," Masja yelled after him.

"No way, I can't get involved!" he said.

"But you have to help her, you arsehole!"

"Hey! I brought her back here, didn't I?! I could just as well have left her behind!" the chubby man snapped. The driver's door slammed shut and moments later, the van sped away and disappeared from sight.

"Is . . . is she dead?" said Lulu with her hand to her mouth.

"If she looks dead . . . she probably is dead," mumbled Iza, taking another swig of Tullamore Dew.

Masja sat on her haunches next to Tabitha and rested a hand on her shoulder. "Tabitha! Tabitha!" she said, shaking her gently.

Tabitha made no response.

A crowd of curious onlookers had started to gather, and moments later, Slavros's goons arrived. Mikhail ordered everyone to clear out immediately. Masja felt his hand on her shoulder. "Come on, we have to leave," he said.

"But . . . but we can't just leave her here."

"We're leaving, Karina. Right now!" Mikhail said, dragging Masja to her feet.

2011. New Year's Day. The first day of a year that is just as rotten as the one before it. No one is talking. No one knows what has happened to Tabitha. No one *wants* to know. I dreamt about her. She looked like an angel, a Black Santa Lucia bride. She smiled at me, and she looked so happy, humming something to herself as she hovered above me. Then she smiled and said: "O-kay." "Okay, okay, everything is going to be okay," she sang to me while the clouds floated by. But I know that nothing is "okay." I know that 2011 is cursed. I'm so scared. I'm so fucking scared of everything that is going to happen. Everything that is waiting for me just around the corner . . .

32

Christianshavn, 2013

Late in the afternoon, a blue Golf pulled up on the quay beside *Bianca*. Sitting on the rear deck, Thomas saw Mikkel and Dennis Melby get out of the car. He was not inclined to have them on board, so he got out of his deck chair and clambered up onto the quay to meet them. Mikkel greeted him with a high five. Melby gave him a measured nod over the hood of the car.

"What can you tell me?" asked Thomas.

"Not much," said Mikkel.

"Was Igor bullshitting me?"

Mikkel shook his head. "No, there's no reason to believe that he was lying. Word on the street is that Kaminsky often hosts poker games for the bigwigs, and it's quite possible that Igor could have been invited to sit at their table."

"Why hasn't Station City locked down the joint already?"

"Because they're very good at making the money disappear before we arrive," said Melby. "Is that your boat?" he added, pointing at *Bianca*.

"Yes," said Thomas.

Melby snorted. "She could use a lick of paint."

Thomas ignored Melby and focused on Mikkel. "Do you think that Kaminsky knows about the dirty deal with Masja? Can we put some pressure on him?"

Mikkel shrugged. "The Russians are not the talkative sort. As a rule, when we call them in for a chat, the iron curtain comes down."

"What about the other guy, Milan?"

Mikkel shook his head. "We did a search on him and came up empty."

"Lucian?"

"Zero."

"And Slavros?"

"Slavros is a bad boy," Melby cut in. "Russian veteran from the war in Chechnya. According to our information, he was involved in some nasty shit over there. Now he's running his business all over Europe. Interpol has been watching him for quite some time—without any luck. He's a smart guy, careful not to get caught."

"What kind of business?" Thomas asked.

"The three biggies: weapons, drugs, and sex trafficking," said Mikkel. "Till now, they haven't been able to pin anything on him. His organisation is efficient, highly skilled and strictly disciplined."

"Do we at least know where he is?"

"He has family in Sweden and owns a few strip clubs in Stockholm, so he's possibly up there. But he's adept at keeping his business on the move."

"Do the Swedes have anything on him?"

"Last year there was an episode involving a couple of Eastern European hookers in Stockholm. One of the girls died under suspicious circumstances at Stockholm Central. Slavros was implicated in the death, but an official investigation was never made."

"I don't care about Slavros. I'm looking for information on Masja's whereabouts."

"There have been other cases in Sweden involving dead prostitutes. Stockholm is not a safe place to be for a girl like her."

"Copenhagen is not much better."

Mikkel shrugged. "All things considered, I don't think there's much chance of finding her. She's just a statistic by now."

"What statistic?"

"The one that tells us that every month more than five thousand hopeful Eastern European girls come over the border, looking for work in the European Union. Most of them go home again—when they're worn out—but some of them simply disappear from the face of the earth. No one ever finds them again."

"That's a lot of pussy coming over the border every month," said Melby with a snort of laughter. "And some of them are actually really pretty."

Melby's mobile phone rang, and he turned his back to take the call.

Thomas met Mikkel's gaze. "You should have come alone."

"I know. But Melby is the one who works the Baltic Mafia. It's his territory, Thomas," said Mikkel apologetically. "When are you coming back to Ops?"

"I'm not sure that I am."

"Why not?"

"It doesn't make sense to me anymore."

"And *this* does . . . ? This . . . freelance investigation of yours?"

Thomas turned to gaze over the canal. "No, not really. And that's why it ends here."

Mikkel looked at him with genuine concern. "You look like shit, my friend."

"Yeah, I know."

"What do you think Eva would say if she saw you like this?"

"Don't, Mikkel. I really don't need that right now."

Mikkel dropped his gaze to the ground. Kicked at some pebbles with the toe of his boot. "I'm sorry, Thomas. We miss you. Don't you understand?"

Melby waved from the car. "Mikkel, we've gotta go!" he yelled, getting into the car.

Mikkel made to leave, but Thomas put a hand on his arm.

"What about Igor?"

"What about him?"

"That piece of shit is not going to get off so easy."

"What do you want me to do?"

"I flushed at least thirty grams of coke down his toilet. My guess is he'll be making a trip to his pusher real soon."

Mikkel nodded. "Then I guess I ought to pay him a visit in the next couple of days."

"Thanks," said Thomas. "Look under his mattress."

"See you round, Ravn," said Mikkel. He turned on his heel and jogged back to the car.

Half an hour later, Thomas was on his way to The Sea Otter to tell Johnson what he had learned from Mikkel.

Johnson listened in silence, looking more and more depressed by the minute.

"Whatever happens to that piece-of-shit Igor, he will be getting off too easy," said Johnson, taking a sip from his coffee cup. "He ought to be strung up by his balls."

"I agree," said Thomas. "There's no justice in this world."

"We ought to pay the bastard a visit. Spell it out to him that he's not going to get away with it."

Thomas took a sip of his beer and regarded Johnson evenly. "Well, Igor will have a problem when Mikkel and the entire Forensics Unit from Crime Ops show up at his door. If they find something, he'll be kicked out of the country for good."

"I still think he's getting off easy," Johnson said, shaking his head in disgust. He patted down his breast pocket for his Cecils, lit one and exhaled a huge cloud of smoke. "But does this mean that Masja is in Sweden?"

"Who knows?" said Thomas. "But it's a reasonable possibility. In any event, I think it's highly unlikely that she's still in Denmark. Not after such a long time."

Johnson scratched the stubble on his chin thoughtfully. "I don't know what to say to Nadja. Won't you come with me?"

Thomas stared at him in surprise. "*Me?* Why in the world would I do that?!"

"Well . . . aren't you . . . trained for things like this?"

"Things like what?"

Johnson drew on his cigarette, hard. "Delivering bad news," he said.

Thomas shook his head. "That's not something you can train for—like a football match."

"No. But you know what I mean. You're a cop; surely you've had to do this kind of thing before?"

"Yes, exactly. And that's why I know that it never gets any easier. It's not a routine. Ever. As I said before: There's no justice in this world."

"Yes, I know. But *I'm* the one who has to tell that to the girl's mother."

Thomas put his beer bottle down on the counter and let out a deep sigh. "I could go on about this all day, Johnson: THERE—IS—NO—JUSTICE—IN—THIS—WORLD. On the other hand, you don't have to give Nadja *all* the details."

"What do you mean?"

"You could tell her something . . . positive."

"Which would be?"

"That Masja went out in the world to make her fortune," Thomas said, taking another sip of beer. "That has a kernel of truth to it."

"Are you out of your mind?!" Johnson looked at him furiously and viciously stubbed his cigarette out in the ashtray. "That would be lying straight to Nadja's face."

"I'm just trying to make it a little easier for you," said Thomas.

"Never mind. It's about being honest, Ravn," Johnson said, tapping another Cecil out of his pack. "Anything less just doesn't work."

"Fair enough. As long as you keep me out of it," Thomas said, and downed the rest of his beer.

33

Stockholm, January 2011

Malmskillnadsgatan has been raided. There's not a single girl on the street. Instead of bulls the place is crawling with cops. I didn't even know what our street was called until they mentioned it on TV. It looks like every other street I know. There's nothing special about it. The news is choked with stories about us. Reports about all the girls who have been arrested and deported. They say it's illegal to buy sex in this country. Hahaha! It's a joke, a sick joke, when you think about how many bulls come to us. Last night there was a politician on the news—a minister of some kind—who stood right on the spot where Tabitha was dumped, feeding the reporters a whole lot of bullshit about prohibitions, more cops on the streets, and a lot of other stuff that I didn't understand. What about laws to help *us*?!! It doesn't change the fact that Tabitha almost got her ticket out of this world. She's in a coma in hospital. I guess that means that Slavros will have to write off her debt, but you can't be sure about that. Poor Tabitha, she was not particularly bright to begin with, but still, she doesn't deserve to wake up as a vegetable.

Masja had taken a seat in a booth with Lulu and Iza, as far away from the stage as possible. She blew smoke rings up to the ceiling listlessly, as one of the new girls danced under the blue strobe lights in Key Club. The new girl strutted about, parading her naked silicone boobs. She gyrated athletically around the pole and ended her performance with splits on the floor, all of which was a complete waste of time and energy because there were no bulls to be had.

"Will they ever come back?" said Masja, looking out over the empty booths.

"Who? The bulls?" said Iza. "When this blows over, they'll be back. Their dicks will make that decision for them. And they'll be horny as hell. But right now, they're more scared than horny."

"The bulls are so fucking pathetic." Lulu laughed.

"But you miss it anyway," replied Iza.

"Their money, Iza. I only miss their money."

"That's what I meant, you bloody idiot!" Iza snapped. She snatched her bag and got up from the table in a huff.

"Hmm. Looks like somebody misses her cola," muttered Masja, watching Iza storm off. In the bar, Slavros was yelling at one of the bartenders. Masja couldn't hear what the argument was about, but Slavros kept slapping the back of the guy's neck as he screamed into his face. Now that he wasn't making any money, Slavros was more irritable—more evil—than ever before, and she made a point of staying the hell away from him.

Masja stubbed out her cigarette in the ashtray and immediately lit another. She reckoned that business must be close to zero now that Slavros could neither make them walk the streets, nor get the bulls to come to the club. She understood his frustration. Worst-case scenario, he would end up in prison, and if this situation went on for much longer, he might have to cut his losses, perhaps even be forced to write off their debts and let them all go home—just so he wouldn't be nabbed by the cops. Masja smiled to herself. Perhaps it wasn't so bad that this had happened after all—except for poor Tabitha, of course . . .

The door to the rear entrance burst open and Mikhail rushed into the club. "The cops!" he yelled, gasping for breath. "The cops are coming!"

The music died immediately, and the bright ceiling lights came on. Panic spread through the room as strippers toppled off the stage, trying to cover themselves with the tops they'd discarded only moments before. Masja, Lulu, and Iza followed on the heels of the strippers while Slavros and his men shooed them up the stairs. Fortunately, due to the current situation, everything had been prepared for a potential raid and their scant belongings were already packed and ready so that they could vacate the premises without delay.

The moment Masja got in her room, she kicked off her stilettoes and pulled on a pair of trainers. Then she grabbed her black Nike sports bag that stood on her table and dashed out the door. Downstairs, there was one helluva commotion in the club: glass shattering in the bar, furniture overturned, the cops yelling at the people to get down on the floor, but Masja did not look back. She headed up the stairs, following the train of girls making a run for the door to the loft.

"Go, go, go!" shouted Mikhail, waving them through the door, as everyone fumbled their way through the dark. Iza tripped in front of Masja, and she reached out and grabbed her just before she hit the ground. "Th-th-thank you!" said Iza, looking at Masja with both terror and surprise.

The moment they reached the other end of the corridor, Mikhail yanked open the door that led to the fire escape of the neighbouring building. A white-haired old man in a stained vest stuck his head out his door, and his eyes opened wide at the sight of so many women plunging down the stairs. He slammed his door shut again. Everyone knew it was only a matter of seconds before this guy called the police.

Masja and the other girls burst out onto the dark courtyard behind the building. The cold hit them full in the face like a fist. Police sirens rang out from the road. "*Go, go, go!*" the men shouted again as they piled into the back of two vans waiting for them.

Police cars with blinking blue lights swung onto the pavement in front of Key Club, followed by the first news team to arrive on the scene. Slavros himself appeared in the doorway in handcuffs. Flashlights hailed over him as the press clamoured to take his picture.

A few minutes later, the two vans slid past the massive police barricade in front of Key Club. Masja lay pressed to the floor in the back of one of them. A uniformed guard stepped out and impatiently waved them past. The driver nodded, inched past the crowd and disappeared down the road.

It was ice cold in the empty room. A naked bulb in the ceiling cast a pale glow over the girls huddled together on the living room floor. Loud voices penetrated the walls of the flat next door. From below, the bass rhythm of a stereo on full blast. Mikhail and his sidekick started dealing out blankets. Masja grabbed one gratefully and wrapped it around her shoulders, even though it stank of cat piss.

"No noise, no light, see you tomorrow," said Mikhail. Without another word, he turned, flicked off the light and left with the other man at his heels.

Masja stared into the darkness, listening to the men's footsteps fading down the stairwell. Once she had warmed up a little, she got up and went to the doorway to switch on the bulb. Some of the girls complained, repeating Mikhail's orders to keep the lights off.

"Shut your mouths!" said Iza.

Masja went over to the window and lit another cigarette. They were on the fifth floor, and she had an unhindered view over Rinkeby, where there were rows of residential blocks like cement silos in an industrial landscape.

"We ought to get the hell out of here," said Lulu behind her.

"And go where, Lulu?" said Iza. "Slavros won't let anyone go until they've settled their debt."

"He might not have a choice," replied Masja.

"What do you mean?"

"Wait and see," Masja said. She stubbed out her cigarette on the window sill and returned to her seat on the floor. She closed her eyes and tried to block out everything around her, just like she did when she was with a bull. It worked sufficiently well for her to doze off for a while.

The next morning two men arrived with Mikhail. Slavros's right-hand man looked as if he had aged ten years overnight. He clapped his hands loudly, which echoed through the empty room and woke up the girls, who were scattered over the floor. "We are faced with a rotten situation," he said in English with a strong Russian accent. "The cops have closed Key Club and arrested Slavros. They have raised several bullshit charges against him. Our operation is in chaos." He brought the back of his hand to his mouth and bit into it. "Right now, the pigs are looking for you girls all over Stockholm."

The girls looked up at him in fear. Some of them started to wail and complain bitterly.

"Listen to me!" Mikhail said, letting his eyes wander over the heads in the room. "If anyone asks—no matter who they are—you have never met Slavros. You have never heard of the man. You are simply tourists, on your way home. Are we all clear on that?!"

Iza leaned a little closer to Masja and lowered her voice. "You know, I think you might be right. We are on the move."

Masja replied with a little smile.

Mikhail went on: "If any of you breathes a word about Slavros, I will beat the shit out of you myself. Understood?!"

A murmur ran through the room and the girls nodded in agreement.

"So when do we get out of this hole?" asked Iza.

Mikhail glared at her. "We will bring you some food and coffee. Then we will try and find some mattresses for you."

Iza looked at him suspiciously. "Are you suggesting that we bring clients up here?"

"No, of course not. Before the week is out, all of you will be working at tanning salons in the city."

"Tanning salons?" Masja gaped at him.

Mikhail nodded. "Mr. Arkan has a chain of twenty-five tanning salons, all of which have suitable locations for your work at the back. The cops are clueless, but the clients know perfectly well what is on offer in Stockholm. Getting a tan has never been more popular among the Svenssons," he said, laughing at his own joke.

"Who the hell is Mr. Arkan?" asked Masja.

"He's your new boss, Karina. Everything has been arranged. There is no need for concern. You will be making good money."

"But what about our debts?"

"Debts? What the hell are you talking about?" Mikhail snapped.

"Does this Arkan guy know how much each of us still owes Slavros?"

Mikhail shook his head. "You misunderstand me. Everyone will start from scratch. Your debt is fixed at ten thousand euros—across the board," he said with a shrug.

Masja jumped to her feet and the blanket slid to the floor. "I don't owe Slavros ten thousand euros! I don't owe him nearly that much!"

"You do now. Sit down!"

"Fuck you, Mikhail! I have an agreement with Slavros. I keep a record. I owe him four thousand. Not a cent more."

Mikhail glared at her. "Slavros has not mentioned a word of this to me. As far as I am concerned, everyone pays the same. We are all in the same boat. Why should you get special treatment?"

"Because I have been keeping score. And because I have earned more money for Slavros than anyone else in this room," she seethed. "Understood?!"

A twitch appeared at the corner of Mikhail's right eye. He strode over to her, put his hand on her throat and pushed her up against the wall, bashing her head against it.

"I'm getting tired of your complaints, Karina. Do you understand, or do I need to make myself crystal clear?" He took a knife out of his pocket and placed the tip under her right eye. "Tell me again. How much did you say you owe Slavros?"

"As much as . . . as you say I do," said Masja.

"Good answer. Am I going to hear any more complaints from you?"

Masja swallowed the spit in her mouth. "Not at all."

He removed the knife and loosened the grip around her throat. "You're not so dumb after all."

Masja brought a hand to her throat and gasped for breath.

"Sit down," he said, pointing to her blanket on the floor.

Masja did as she was told.

Mikhail looked around the room as he folded his knife and returned it to his pocket. Everyone in the room was looking at him with fear in their eyes, and it was obvious that he was enjoying the situation. "Remember. None of you has ever heard of Slavros," he said.

The girls nodded in unison.

Mikhail smiled coldly. "Don't worry. Before the week is out, it will be business as usual. None of you have anything to worry about."

34

Christianshavn, 2013

It was early in the morning and the sun was rising over Christianshavn canal. Thomas was standing on *Bianca*'s flybridge, inspecting the teak wood at his feet. He had treated the deck with a strong saline solution that would get rid of the layer of moss that had covered the planks like a plush green carpet. Satisfied with his work so far, he picked up a brush and began scrubbing.

"You're up and about early, Ravn," yelled Eduardo from his own cockpit. He was wearing nothing but a pair of jogging bottoms, and he scratched his beer belly and yawned. "Cleaning your deck, eh?"

"It's high time that I did," said Thomas.

"At seven in the morning?"

"I'm sorry if I woke you. I couldn't sleep last night. I've been up since five."

"*No problema*. Your deck is looking better already," Eduardo said. "I'm sure you can fix her up real nice."

Thomas nodded. "Yeah, the right owner will get her up and running."

"Sounds as if you're thinking of selling?"

"I think I ought to give her up." Thomas stopped scrubbing to inspect his progress. "And I'm thinking of moving back into my flat."

"Cool. But that doesn't necessarily mean that you have to sell your boat."

"I don't think I can manage the upkeep anymore. It's a pity to let *Bianca* go to rack and ruin like this. She deserves better."

"But you love *Bianca*."

"Yes, I do," said Thomas. He picked up his bucket and poured some water over the deck.

"And you're one of us. You belong here, on the canal."

Thomas made no reply and started scrubbing again instead.

Eduardo rubbed his eyes. "I can give you a hand with the repairs. You know that, Ravn."

"Thank you, Eduardo. But I think *Bianca* needs a bit more work than our combined efforts can muster. Nothing works properly anymore."

"Is it really that bad?" Eduardo stood on his toes and peered at *Bianca*'s flybridge critically.

"The aft deck is rotten to the core. The gear box is broken. And you know what state the electrical wiring is in," Thomas said, jabbing his thumb in the direction of the fuse box up on the quay. "The patient is barely breathing, doctor," he added drily.

"I still think it's a pity," said Eduardo, rubbing his belly and yawning again. "Just say the word if there's anything I can do to help."

"Spread the word, Eduardo. You can tell people that I will sell her for a good price."

Eduardo nodded and disappeared into his cabin.

Thomas emptied the bucket of water over the deck. Steam rose up towards him as he swept the water over the sides. Even though his dream of a grand escapade had never materialised, he was struck by the thought that so many good memories involved *Bianca*. In the middle of the city, his boat had been a haven for him and Eva, their own little slice of paradise where there was always an ample supply of chilled white wine and grilled sausages on the aft deck.

When Thomas was done with the flybridge, he started cleaning the wooden railings. Despite the cool wind, he was sweating so much he had to take off his jacket. Just after midday, he had been all the way around. He found the tub of linseed oil in the cabin and pried open the lid with a screwdriver. The smell of the oil infused with sea air filled his nostrils. He felt the sun on his cheeks and closed his eyes to enjoy the moment, feeling as if the physical exercise had done him a world of good. If the dry weather lasted, he would be able to finish oiling the railing before it got dark, he reckoned.

"Thomas Ravns . . . holdt," a frail voice said up on the quay. Thomas looked up and saw an elderly lady shivering in the wind. It took him a few moments to recognise Masja's mother, Nadja. "Johnson told me that I would find you here. With your boat."

"Okay," Thomas said with a smile. "Would you like to come aboard?"

Nadja glanced anxiously at the deck, which lay 1.5 metres below her. "No, thanks," she said, shaking her head. "I don't want to intrude. I just wanted to say thank you for taking the time to look for my daughter."

"I'm sorry that I was unable to give you much information," he said, smiling again.

Nadja stood on the quay without saying another word. After a few minutes of silence, Thomas felt obliged to ask whether she had anything else on her mind.

"Yes," Nadja said quickly, but fell silent again for a while, clearly hesitant to continue. "I . . . er . . . I want to get in touch with my daughter."

"Yes, of course," said Thomas. "I understand, but . . ."

"Johnson told me that she lives in Sweden now . . . Where in Sweden, exactly?"

The question surprised Thomas, and he took a moment to scratch the back of his neck. "Er . . . I'm not sure, exactly. Stockholm, I think."

"Do you have an address for her?"

"No. Wait. What exactly did Johnson tell you?"

"Well, he said that Masja is in Sweden. That she went to find her fortune. That she works for a very important man. And that she is doing well. Do you know this man?"

Thomas swallowed hard. "No, I'm afraid I don't," he said, inwardly damning Johnson to hell for his bullshit sermon about the importance of telling the truth and nothing but the truth . . .

"So . . . you don't have an address for her in Sweden?"

"No, I'm afraid I don't."

"But . . . Johnson said . . ." Nadja fell silent and looked at him with an utterly forlorn expression on her face. "Something has happened to

Masja," she began again. "Something that Johnson is not telling me. Am I right?"

"No, I don't think so." Thomas went over to the railing and looked up at her. "Things are just a little more complicated."

"Is Masja in danger?"

"To be honest, I really don't know."

"But you know this man that she is working for. I can see it in your eyes. They can't lie."

"I don't know this man. But yes, I have heard of him. His name is Slavros. He's a criminal, but this doesn't necessarily have anything to do with Masja."

"Johnson said that she was a babysitter. That she was looking after this man's house and children."

"Sometimes Johnson has a very big mouth," Thomas muttered irritably, but managed to bite his tongue before saying anything else he would regret. "I wish I had been able to give you more useful information about Masja. Perhaps it's best to wait till she comes back of her own accord."

Nadja started to cry. "She's not coming back. Not now. Not this time."

All Thomas could do was wring his hands and look at this poor woman helplessly.

Nadja dried her tears. "Could you go there?"

"Where?"

"To Stockholm. To look for Masja."

"No, I can't do that," said Thomas, trying to smile. Without success.

"I will pay for your trip, Mr. Ravn. I'll pay you. It's not a problem. I have savings."

"It's not about money. I don't have time."

"I'll pay you for your time."

"Look, I don't even know where she is. It's not even certain that she's in Stockholm at all."

"But you could look for her. Like you did here. So I would know. If she's lost somewhere, you can find her. I'm sure of it."

Thomas could see that Nadja was becoming more desperate by the minute. He'd be damned if *he* was going to be the one who had to tell this woman that her daughter had been sold to some or other pimp and might not even be alive anymore. If Johnson thought that he could palm this off on him, he'd better think again. On the other hand, Thomas didn't want to let Nadja down. And she deserved to know the truth. He reached for his jacket, which was hooked on the back of the cabin door.

"You'll help me?" asked Nadja, a glimmer of hope appearing in her eyes.

"I think you and I should go and have a little chat with Johnson," said Thomas.

35

The Sea Otter's first guests of the day had already found their places by the window, chatting over a beer or two. Thomas flung open the door and Nadja followed at his heels. Johnson was at his post behind the bar, reading his newspaper as usual, but when he looked up and saw the two of them approaching, he bit the inside of his lip nervously.

Thomas pulled a barstool out for Nadja and offered her a seat, but she shook her head and simply stood instead, clutching her handbag with both hands. "Would you like something to drink?" he said, taking a stool without further ado.

"No, thank you for asking," Nadja said, clearly uncomfortable.

Thomas shrugged and ordered a Hof. Johnson popped the cap and put the bottle in front of him on the counter. Thomas curled his fingers around the beer, but kept his eyes trained on Johnson. Nobody said a word or made a move. At last, Thomas lifted the beer to his lips and took a sip.

"What . . . what is this about?" said Johnson, looking at Thomas and Nadja in turn.

Nadja looked down quickly and fixed her eyes on the tips of her shoes.

"Nadja tells me that you have explained the whole situation concerning Masja's disappearance," said Thomas, resting his beer on the counter.

"Yes . . . as best as possible," replied Johnson. He grabbed a dishcloth and started polishing the nearest beer glass vigorously.

"She tells me that you have explained that Masja is in Sweden, possibly made it all the way to Stockholm."

"Yes, that is what you told me, Ravn." Johnson turned to face Nadja. "At least she got away from that Igor guy."

Nadja made no reply.

"And what kind of work did you say Masja was doing, Johnson?"

Johnson stared at him, blinking furiously. "But . . . but you know that perfectly well, Ravn."

"Remind me."

"Masja is . . ." Johnson glanced at Nadja, who was watching him with her sorrowful eyes. "Masja is . . . something to do with babysitting, right? Wasn't that it, Ravn?"

"No, not as far as I know."

Johnson put the beer glass down and immediately grabbed the next. "I'm pretty sure that you said—"

"No!" snapped Thomas, taking a deep breath. "The truth exists, Johnson, and it's worth sticking to, right?"

Johnson didn't reply. He didn't even look in Thomas's direction.

"The truth is that no one really knows for certain what has happened to Masja," Thomas said evenly, controlling his temper. "No one knows where she is and what she is doing right now." He placed a hand on Nadja's arm.

"But . . ." said Nadja.

"And that's why I cannot help you anymore," Thomas said. "That's why it ends here."

"Yes . . . of course," mumbled Nadja, looking at her hands, which were still clutching her handbag.

"Ravn has done what he can," Johnson cut in quickly. "We just have to hope that Masja shows up soon. Cross our fingers that she's okay . . . wherever she might be," he added, nodding at Thomas and trying to smile. Thomas did not return the gesture.

"It's just that . . . I can't just give up on her. She's my daughter," said Nadja, clearly on the verge of tears. "That's why I asked you to go to Sweden and look for her. As a last resort."

"I'm really sorry, Nadja," said Thomas, bringing his beer to his lips and taking a big sip.

Johnson looked at Thomas thoughtfully and put the polished glass aside. "You know, maybe it's not such a bad idea."

"What is?" said Thomas

"To see if she's up there or not," Johnson said, smiling at Nadja. "It's actually a very good idea, Nadja."

"No, it is not," said Thomas, putting his beer down.

"Why not?" asked Johnson.

"For starters, because I don't have time."

"But you're on leave, right?" said Johnson.

Thomas ignored the question. "Based on the information that we have, it's in fact an *extremely* bad idea. I'm sorry, Nadja, but there is very little chance of us finding her up there."

Nadja nodded and looked at the floor.

"But there is *a* chance that you'll find her," Johnson persisted.

Thomas gave him a sharp look. "I'm not going anywhere."

Johnson put down the dishcloth. "Bloody hell, Ravn, Stockholm is just a short flight away. And you know the kind of neighbourhoods where you need to start looking," he added in a lowered voice.

"Don't start with the 'hood' crap again."

"Perhaps you could talk to the local police up there. You coppers talk to each other, right?"

"Listen to me: I am *not* going anywhere."

"Hell, it's quicker to fly to Stockholm than take a train to Jutland."

"Fine, but I am going to neither Jutland nor Sweden. I'm not going anywhere."

Johnson leaned back and regarded Thomas stubbornly. "Ravn, we're talking about a missing girl here."

"Well, you can go and look for her yourself."

Johnson shook his head. "No, I can't. Not like you can. You know what to do, Ravn." Johnson turned to Nadja. "Ravn knows what to do." He returned his gaze to Thomas. "Just look what you were able to find out when you started digging over here . . . It was a brilliant piece of work . . . I was imp—"

"Just stop!" Thomas yelled. The other guests in the pub turned around and looked at him briefly, then carried on chatting among themselves.

Thomas faced Nadja. "I'm sorry that I have to tell you this, but . . . Masja has got herself into a terrible situation—something connected to what she was doing in Denmark . . . I don't think she ever told you the truth about how she earned a living. But something tells me that in your heart of hearts, you already know. All those handbags, dresses and shoes she bought aren't cheap. You can't earn that kind of money doing other people's nails—"

"Bloody hell, Ravn," Johnson cut in.

"It's . . . yes, I had a suspicion," Nadja said quietly.

"Her relationship with Igor didn't make her situation any easier," Thomas went on. "If you really fear for your daughter's life, I recommend that you go to the police and file a missing person's report. Get them to look for her, even though she disappeared such a long time ago. Perhaps the Danish police can contact the Swedish authorities, or Europol."

"Okay," said Nadja. Her voice was barely audible.

"But . . . but that won't make a difference," Johnson sputtered. "Not one jot of difference." He fumbled for his Cecils and managed to light himself a cigarette. "Not one jot of difference," he repeated, puffing smoke like a dragon. "And you know it, Ravn. How high do you think the cops will prioritise Masja's case?"

"I don't know."

"Like hell you don't," said Johnson. "All they'll do is kick Nadja out of the country. They don't give a shit about a missing girl from Eastern Europe." He glanced at Nadja apologetically. "I'm sorry to say so, Nadja, but that's the truth."

Thomas dug a 50-kroner note out of his pocket and put it on the counter.

Johnson crossed his arms over his chest. "Ravn, you are the only one who can make a difference here."

"Do you want money for your beer or not?"

"Forget it. Just go."

Thomas shrugged and put the note back in his pocket.

Nadja gave him a weak smile. "I'm sorry that I bothered you with this, Mr. Ravn. This is not your problem. I'm so sorry. I'm grateful for what you have done already. I hope that you understand."

Thomas nodded and glanced at the door.

"Let's pray that Masja comes home soon," she said, choking on her tears. "She's a smart girl. She can take care of herself. I'm sure of it. Sorry that I got you involved in this."

"There's no need to apologise for that."

"It's just that . . ." Nadja smiled self-consciously. "Ever since she disappeared, I go into her room every morning to look for her. I look at her little table with the mirror where she used to sit and get ready for her day. She loved it when I came in and brushed her hair. Masja has long, thick hair like a princess."

"Oh," mumbled Thomas, rubbing the hair on his cheek furiously.

"That's what I used to call her: my little princess."

"Okay, I give up."

Nadja looked up at Thomas in surprise.

Thomas looked at Johnson. "You'll pay for the flight?"

"Of course."

"And a decent hotel."

"Put it on my bill."

"And whatever other expenses might come up."

Johnson raised his hand. "Within reasonable bounds."

Thomas turned to Nadja. "Okay. I'll go up and take a look. I cannot do any more. And after that, I'm out. Understood?"

"Thank you. Thank you, thank you, thank you," said Nadja, putting her thin arms around Thomas.

Thomas was embarrassed by the sudden intimacy and awkwardly tried to untangle himself from her embrace, but Nadja was surprisingly strong. She gave him a huge hug. "Thank you, Thomas. You're an . . . an angel."

"Far from it," he mumbled.

36

Stockholm, February 2011

Hawaii sun—as if you were already there" promised the faded sign that hung on the wall above the entrance. The thin yellow curtains that were drawn in the windows appeared luminous in the blue glow that escaped from the tanning pods.

In the cramped reception area, ten men were waiting in their seats. Most of them seemed restless, casting impatient glances at the very tanned blonde behind the counter. Chewing gum, she counted the clients with the tip of her ballpoint pen raised in the air. The receptionist blew a bubble and pressed the button on the intercom with her handy pen. "I'm gonna have to start sending clients through to you girls. It's mega stressful out here."

Static sounded on the other end before a voice replied: "We're on lunch, Blondie. Get that through your thick skull, or I'll rip your hair out."

An elderly man came up to the counter. "How long do we have to wait?"

The receptionist waved her pen in the air. "I believe the girls are on lunch."

"Is it okay if we get some sun while we wait?" said the man, jerking his thumb at the glowing pods behind him.

"Sure, whatever."

* * *

Masja and Iza were in their dressing gowns, sitting at the table in the kitchenette out back. The air was thick with cigarette smoke. There was a monotone creak of bedsprings coming from the room next door. Masja deliberately failed to return the intercom receiver to its cradle so that they wouldn't be disturbed. Then she poured generous shots of vodka into the three mugs that stood on the little table squeezed against the wall. "I reckon Lulu will have time for a drink when she's done."

Iza lit herself another cigarette and regarded Masja with glassy eyes. She seemed even more high than usual. Masja wondered where Iza kept her stash. It would be worth knowing—if she ever ran dry herself. Or if Iza kicked the bucket. It would be a shame to let the drugs go to waste.

"I almost believed you when you told that swine Mikhail about your arrangement with Slavros," said Iza, pointing at Masja with the glowing end of her cigarette.

"What do you mean? Slavros and I have a deal."

Iza snorted with laughter and smoke puffed out of her nose and mouth at once. "A *deal* with Slavros?! *Please* don't tell me that you are stupid enough to believe anything that Slavros says."

Masja took a sip from her mug. "Of course not. I made that up on the spur of the moment, hoping that Mikhail would fall for it," she said, and looked away.

Iza laughed again. "I'm not an idiot, girl. I know that you actually believed Slavros."

"And what if I did?" Masja snapped. "If you're so fucking smart, why haven't you left already?"

"And go where? To the moon? Slavros will find you no matter where you go."

"But if you don't have a deal with him, what do you have to lose?"

"My fucking life," Iza said, glaring at her. Next door, the monotone creak picked up its pace, and Masja rubbed her temples with a tired sigh.

"Haven't you saved any money at all?" asked Iza.

"Nah," said Masja. "What about you?"

"Well, I have an expensive habit," Iza said with a loud sniff.

"We ought to take the chance," said Masja.

"What do you mean?"

"Who's going to stop us? Blondie out there?" Masja said, jerking her head in the direction of the door to reception.

Iza shook her head and stubbed out her cigarette in the ashtray. She lit another immediately. "You shouldn't say shit like that if you don't mean it."

"I do mean it. We ought to split. Right now."

"You're forgetting about Slavros."

"Slavros is in the can. And Arkan—that old prick—wouldn't dare come after us. What's he going to do? Set his poodle after us?"

"I can't stand that fucking dog. It keeps licking its own arse," Iza said.

"Arkan has too much to lose. The last thing he needs is to attract the cops' attention to his tanning salon business. And we ought to take advantage of the fact that all the pimps have gone into hiding after the raid on Key Club."

Iza narrowed her eyes. "You shouldn't sit there shooting off your mouth unless you're serious about this. You know I could earn a couple of thousand by repeating what you just told me to Mikhail or Arkan."

"You're not a snitch either."

"Says who? Perhaps you're being naïve again, Karina."

"I didn't know you were scared, Iza."

"Who says I'm scared? I'm not scared of anything."

"No?" Masja smiled at her. "The other day I found out where Blondie keeps the money," she said, changing the subject.

"The daily turnover?"

"Maybe even a bit more than that. You know how terrified Arkan is of coming here, because of the cops. My guess is that the pot holds at least a week's worth of turnover. You don't have to be a genius to figure out how much money that is."

Iza frowned, as if she was trying to do the math in her fuzzy head. Masja helped her out: "Fifty thousand. Perhaps even a little more, if we snatch it tomorrow."

"Where would you go?" asked Iza with her cigarette dangling in the corner of her mouth.

"Home. To Denmark. To my mother. Start over."

"You're dreaming, you are."

"It can happen. What about you? What would you do?"

"I don't know. Go home to friends—those who are still alive. But why don't you just steal the money on your own?"

"Because I'm scared."

Iza took a final drag on her cigarette, then killed it in the ashtray. A loud cry sounded from the room next door. Iza downed the rest of her vodka in one gulp without moving a muscle in her face. "What's your name?"

Masja looked at her in surprise. "You know my name . . . Karina."

"Not your working name, your *real* name. What is it?"

Masja swallowed hard. "Masja. My name is Masja."

It felt very strange—terrifying—to say her name out loud. Right there, in the kitchenette.

"Miiisha," said Iza, trying it out on her tongue. "It's pretty. My name is Petra. Fucking ugly, huh?"

Masja shook her head. "Not at all. It actually suits you."

Petra extended her hand across the table. "It's nice to meet you, Masja."

Masja laughed and took her hand. "It's nice to meet *you*, Petra."

Petra took her hand and held it tight. "You realise there's no going back now, right?"

"No way back," Masja agreed.

Lulu suddenly appeared naked in the doorway with her bull, a painter's apprentice, apparently, wearing a white overall. He greeted the ladies and quickly scooted through the door to reception.

Masja handed Lulu her mug of vodka.

Lulu accepted the mug and looked at Masja and Petra with a stony expression on her face. Then she downed the contents of the mug in a single swallow. "Are you two not going to work at all today?" she asked.

Neither Petra nor Masja replied.

37

Christianshavn, 2013

Thomas packed Møffe's bowl, his food, and his new best friend—a chewed trainer that he had found outside The Sea Otter—into a plastic bag. Thomas had just been up to his flat to take a bath and pack his kit for the trip to Sweden. It felt strange being up there, as if he were on the run, and it gave him a guilty conscience.

Møffe whined and looked up at him with his big, sad eyes.

"Oh, come off it, Møffe, don't give me that look. It's only for a couple of days. I'll be back before you get a chance to miss me."

Møffe licked his chops and shook his head, flinging drool in all directions.

"Eduardo is going to take real good care of you, Møffe. You'll have a great time on his boat. Just do me a favour: Don't shit on his deck, okay?"

Thomas put on his jacket and patted his breast pocket to check that he had the postcard for Masja that Nadja had given him. On the front was a photograph of two kittens playing with a ball of yarn. Nadja had asked him to give the card to Masja—if he found her. The text on the back was written in Lithuanian, and he had no idea what it said, but he guessed it was a quiet prayer for Masja to come home. Letting out a deep sigh, Thomas bent down and clipped on Møffe's leash. Then he grabbed his kitbag and the plastic bag with Møffe's things, headed for the bridge, and hauled Møffe over to the stern. "Eduardo!" he yelled down into the cockpit of his friend's ketch.

Moments later, Eduardo emerged from the cabin door in a pair of jogging bottoms.

"It's two o'clock in the afternoon," said Thomas. "Why aren't you dressed? Are you ill or something?"

Eduardo shook his head. "I have company," he said, jerking a thumb over his shoulder to the cabin.

Thomas shook his head. Then he lifted Møffe over the railing and handed him down to Eduardo, followed by the plastic bag containing Møffe's things. "It's decent of you to take care of him while I'm away," said Thomas.

"*No problema.* It's the least I could do now that Johnson has palmed this case off on you."

"You know Johnson."

"That brickhead should have gone up there himself."

A smile played at the corners of Thomas's mouth. "That probably wouldn't have got us anywhere."

"Are you armed?" asked Eduardo, looking at him with concern.

"What do you mean?"

"Your service pistol. Do you have it with you?"

Thomas raised an eyebrow and picked up his bag. "Do you honestly think I'm going to board a plane with a gun in my bag?"

Eduardo shrugged. "You're going to a dangerous country, *amigo.* A man can't be too careful."

"I'm going to Sweden, Eduardo. The home of Volvo. I feel pretty safe, thank you. Besides, I handed over my service pistol when I left Crime Ops."

Thomas nodded in farewell.

"Just a moment, Ravn," Eduardo said and disappeared into his cabin. A few minutes passed, long enough for Thomas to become impatient, but finally Eduardo returned with a thick paper folder in his hand. He handed it up to Thomas.

"What on earth is this?"

"Research. I thought you might find it useful."

"Research on what?"

"I printed out a few articles on prostitution in Sweden."

"Eduardo, that's very thoughtful of you, but I'm just going up to take a look." He passed the folder back over the railing, but Eduardo raised his hands in protest.

"Just read it, okay. Then you'll understand my concern."

"Eduardo?" a woman's voice called from inside the cabin. "Are you coming?"

"It's the Wild West up here, *señor.* Bandits and guys who are much worse," said Eduardo.

Thomas stuffed the folder into his bag.

"They have a serial killer on the loose up there," Eduardo added.

"Okay, I'll watch my back. Thanks."

Eduardo nodded and waved. Moments later, he disappeared into his cabin and closed the door behind him.

Thomas walked down Dronningensgade and headed for Christianshavn Square. There was still plenty of time to get to the airport, so he crossed the road and ducked into Lagkagehuset bakery on the corner. A few moments later, he emerged with a bag of *kanelsnegle* and headed down Sankt Annæ Gade to Victoria's second-hand bookstore. The bronze bell clanged a little as he pushed open the door, but he was greeted by the familiar smell of freshly ground coffee as he stepped inside the store.

"Sweden?" said Victoria, clearly aghast, her mouth full of cinnamon, sugar, butter, and pastry.

They had taken a seat at her desk behind the counter, and Victoria had cleared some space between the stacks of books for their coffee cups and the bag of *kanelsnegle* from Lagkagehuset. She was already on her second "cinnamon snail" and showed no signs of stopping before the bag was empty. Considering her appetite for pastry, it was amazing that she was petite, thought Thomas.

"Why would you want to go to Sweden? It's so crowded with elks and neo-Nazis," Victoria said.

"Eduardo has already warned me."

"Then you ought to have listened. Did you know that Sweden has the second-highest frequency of interbreeding in Europe after Bulgaria?"

"No, Victoria, I did not."

"I don't understand," Victoria ranted on. "For years you've spoken about taking a long trip to all the exotic destinations in this world, but the first place you go when you get a chance is Sweden?"

"I guess that's just how things turned out."

"I didn't even know your boat could sail."

"Actually, she can't. My plane leaves in two hours." Thomas half-turned in his seat and looked at the shelf containing travel guides.

"You don't happen to have a map of Stockholm, do you?"

"Stockholm?" Victoria stared at him open-mouthed. "Are you seriously telling me that you're going to *Stockholm*?"

"That's what it says on my ticket, yes. Arlanda Airport."

"Sweden is one thing, Thomas, but Stockholm? Not even the Swedes can stand the Stockholmers!"

"Do you think you could find a map for me?" said Thomas in a tired voice.

"God help you," Victoria replied, "but now at least you've been warned," she said, getting to her feet. One of her braces had come loose and she tightened it over her shoulder as she walked towards the bookshelf containing travel guides. She ran her index finger methodically along the spines. When she had found what she was looking for, she tipped the book off the shelf and tossed it over to Thomas, who caught it in the air.

Thomas looked at the worn copy of *Turen går til Stockholm* in his hand. "This guide was published in 2002," he noted. "It's more than ten years old, Victoria."

"Didn't you say that all you needed was a map of Stockholm?" she said. "That guide has a large map of the region, as well as detailed maps of the various districts in the city. You can't go wrong with that one."

"What do I owe you?"

Victoria joined him at the table and took another pastry out of the bag. "Consider it a gift," she said. "Just remember that the Swedish word *korv* means *sausage*, then there's no danger of you going to bed with an empty stomach. But stay the hell away from their *kanelbullarne*. They sell them on every corner, but they don't come anywhere near the taste of these babies," she added, taking a huge bite of the next *kanelsnegle*.

"Gotcha," Thomas said, slipping the guide on top of Eduardo's folder in his kitbag.

"When do you get back?"

"Very soon, hopefully."

"Stockholm," Victoria repeated, giving him the evil eye. "God help you."

Thomas reached for his mug of coffee. "By the way, I don't think I've ever thanked you."

Victoria paused mid-chew. "Thanked me? For what?"

"For not treating me like a leper or something after Eva's death. Everyone else either avoided me or kept telling me how sorry they were for me, but not you. You kept on being the same cantankerous pain in my arse that you've always been. It's liberating and I really appreciate it."

Victoria chewed for a few seconds, swallowed, then gave him a fat grin. "No need to thank me for that. It's only 'cause I really liked Eva, even if I was never particularly crazy about you."

Thomas raised his mug in a toast to her. "The feeling is absolutely mutual, Victoria," he said, then he downed the dregs of his coffee.

38

February 2011

Sitting at McDonald's at Stockholm Central, waiting for Petra, who has gone to the toilets. We arrived a lousy two minutes too late to catch the train to Copenhagen. Now we're waiting for the Swedish "high-speed" train, which isn't particularly speedy—it takes five hours to get to Copenhagen! But God knows I'm so excited! I can hardly believe it. My brain cannot get around the fact that we are actually sitting here, at the station. There is so much I want to tell you, *Mumija*, and so much that I don't ever want you to know. So many things I regret that I did to you. So many things that I would like to change. I promise that everything will be okay again. I wish I still had your number. I wish I could still remember it, but your number is gone, just like so many other things that used to live in my head. I hope you still live in the old flat on Burmeistersgade. Would you believe that I'm actually looking forward to seeing that little flat again? But we can move to a different place. You and me. I have money now. Me and my friend, Petra, we did it! You should have seen us, *Mumija*, when we split from Arkan's tanning salon. Blondie lay bleeding on the floor, the clients were gobsmacked. We were just like those two girls in that film that we saw together, the one where they flee from the cops and then drive over a cliff at the end. You know the one that I mean . . .

. . . We planned our little coup to the last detail. Never breathed a word of it to anyone else. Not even Lulu knew about it. Which is best for her, so she doesn't get into trouble with anyone. She's been smacked around more than enough in her lifetime. Anyway, at ten in the morning we were driven from the flat to "Hawaii," as always. We packed both Petra's clothing and mine into one sports bag (mine) so that no one would get suspicious. We even had a story ready, if Mikhail or one of the drivers asked about the bag: that we were going to wash our clothes at the salon. But no one asked, no one cared, or maybe they're just thick as snot—I choose to believe the latter! We knew that Arkan would waltz in with his poodle around midday to fetch the weekly turnover and stow away our money in his silly file. Petra and I took care of the walk-in clients in the morning, and when Lulu was busy with her fifth, Petra and I struck. The blonde receptionist (whose name is actually Tea) glared at us in confusion when we came into reception fully clothed. She asked us where we thought we were going, said that there were bulls waiting . . . and we just told her to shut up and went over to the last tanning pod. Arkan (or maybe it was Tea) had put an "out of order" note on the lid, but I knew that the only reason that pod wasn't working was because all the pipes in the upper section had been removed to create a hiding place for the stash. When we opened the back panel, we were shocked to the core. Inside, there were no less than *ten* envelopes of cash!! It was the turnover of not only "Hawaii" but also a few of the other tanning salons nearby. I wanted to leave immediately, but Petra started counting the money . . . She'd counted the cash in six of the envelopes before Blondie pitched up with a bread knife—there was more than 100,000 Swedish krona in there!! Blondie flipped out and tried to take the money from Petra. Tea said that we would be dead meat when Arkan found out about us, so Petra simply head-butted her. Holy shit! I've never seen a *woman* do that before! But Petra clearly knew what she was doing, because Blondie ended up on the floor with a broken nose, bleeding all over the place.

There was no reason to stick around, so Petra and I split. The bulls just stared at us. None of them dared lift a finger, even though

> Blondie was yelling for help. 141,000 Swedish krona!!! We counted the rest of the money in the taxi on the way to Stockholm Central. We now have 140,000 left because we gave the taxi driver with the turban and the funny accent 1,000 for his great driving and keeping his mouth shut . . . He was a really cool dude.

Masja looked up from her notebook and gazed over the tables where seemingly zillions of travellers were hunkered down with their shopping bags, belongings and suitcases as they wolfed down their lunch. For her own part, she'd polished off two portions of fries and a king-sized strawberry milkshake. She looked at her watch and wondered what was taking Petra so long. The toilets at the restaurant weren't working, so she'd said that she would go find one in the station somewhere.

Masja tucked her notebook back into her sports bag and cast another nervous glance at the door of McDonald's. Petra had been gone for just over half an hour now. She would have loved to just stay put at the restaurant. Here she could blend with the other guests, rather than roam around in the Arrivals Hall and risk being recognised. It was not just Mikhail and Arkan who she was afraid of. If some overeager copper wanted to see their travel documents, they might be detained—and *definitely* lose all their money. Masja looked in her bag again. The two fat envelopes were still there. Petra was holding the remaining eight, which meant that she was running around Stockholm Central with more than 100,000 krona in her pocket. The latter thought made Masja jump to her feet and head for the door, despite all her misgivings.

Masja walked through the cathedral-like Arrivals Hall, where hundreds of travellers were milling about. Looking up, she was surprised to spot the sign for the toilets straight ahead of her. She was about to head that way when she noticed two uniformed police officers coming towards her. One of them was holding a walkie-talkie to his mouth, the other was scanning the crowds. Her heart pounding in her chest, Masja turned her back and made as if she was searching for something in her pocket. As they came past, the officer's walkie-talkie sputtered, scaring Masja half to death. The policemen kept walking and headed for McDonald's.

"Hey, baby!" an ecstatic voice said just behind her.

Masja spun on her heel and stared into Petra's beaming face. Without warning, Petra kissed her deeply. Masja took a step back. "What the hell are you doing?!" she said. Then she noticed the size of Petra's enlarged pupils, the languorous smile on her lips. "Are you *high* right now?!"

Petra grinned innocently at her.

"But this morning you said you didn't have anything on you!"

"I didn't," Petra said with a laugh.

Masja lowered her voice. "Goddammit, Petra, did you buy some?"

Petra shrugged. "Well, I had to go to the toilet. And then I bumped into Silas."

"Who the hell is Silas?"

"You know Silas. The guy with the cleft palate and a tiiiny dick," Petra said, demonstrating the lack of size with a commensurately tiny space between her forefinger and thumb.

Masja shook her head. "Don't know the guy. What did you tell him? Did you say anything about where we were going?"

Petra put her hands on her hips. "Damn straight I did," she said with a snort. "I told him we just screwed over that dickhead Arkan for a hundred forty thousand—and that we're splitting to Denmark!"

Masja closed her eyes and shook her head in disbelief. "What was Silas doing in the women's toilets?"

Petra glanced at the floor. "Er . . . well, I might have just popped over to Klaraberg Bridge. I wasn't gone for more than five minutes, I swear."

"Have you lost your mind, Petra?!"

"Relax, will you? Only Silas was there. All the other dealers aren't up yet. Not at this hour. Stop being so paranoid. Come on, let's go to the toilets and take a quick hit."

"No, thanks."

"What do you mean no?"

"I don't want to get high. Not when I'm going home."

Petra burst out laughing. "The train won't be here for another two hours. And didn't you say it takes five hours to get to Copenhagen?"

Masja nodded.

"Besides, Silas's coke isn't that good. You'll be straight by the time you get home to your mother."

"No, I mean it, Petra. I don't want to do that anymore."

Petra raised her eyebrows. "Okay, okay, if you say so. But don't start whining when you get the shakes halfway to Copenhagen," she said, leaning in and kissing Masja on the mouth again. "Goddamn, you look hot today, sister."

"And you're bat-shit crazy," Masja said, looking over her shoulder. "The cops have just gone up to McDonald's. Why don't we go over to the other end of the hall and see if we can find a quiet spot to sit and wait for our train?"

Petra smiled, hooked her arm into Masja's and they set off through the station hall together.

Petra wanted to go into every shop they passed, and Masja let herself be dragged along. It was so much fun, and half an hour later, they had two plastic bags filled with magazines, pastries, sweets, a leg of ham, two scarves, two Build-A-Bear teddies—called Princess Green, for Masja, and Biker-bear, for Petra—and a sixpack of Pripps Blå beer.

At last, they managed to find a free table in the seating area of a cafeteria close to Platform 10. Petra sat down with all their gifts and paraphernalia while Masja went up to the counter to get them each a latte. On her way back to the table with their coffees, Masja caught sight of three skinhead men who towered over everyone else around them, sniffing out their prey like wolves on a hunt. Mikhail was leading them. Masja dropped the coffees in fright, splattering milk all over Petra's legs.

"Ouch! What the fuck?!"

"We have to leave! Now! It's Mikhail . . . they're here."

Petra got up and started gathering their bags.

"Leave it! We have to go right now!"

"But Princess Green and . . ."

Masja grabbed Petra's arm in desperation to get out of there and literally dragged her friend through the crowd, keeping one eye on the three men approaching.

"What are we going to do?" asked Petra, squeezing past a stocky man who almost dropped his tray.

Masja craned her neck, peering over the heads of the masses. She spotted the escalators and stairs leading down to the tracks behind the café. "Come on, this way!" she said.

As they made a dash for the stairs, Masja heard a commotion behind them. Casting a glance over her shoulder, she saw Mikhail and his fellow goons elbowing their way directly towards them.

"They've seen us!"

Masja tried to force her way through the stream of passengers coming up the stairs, but it was almost impossible to get through, and Petra was too high to keep up with her. She grabbed Petra's hand and pulled her back the way they came.

"Where are we going now?" Petra gasped.

Masja didn't take the time to reply, making a beeline for the escalators that led to the Underground trains. She scoured the screens, looking for the next available departure.

"There they are!" Mikhail's voice shouted from above.

Masja and Petra looked up. Mikhail was standing by the balustrade on the landing just above, glaring down at them.

"Come on!" said Masja, hauling Petra along behind her.

Mikhail clambered up onto the railings and let himself drop the two metres to their level. His pals hesitated for a moment, but then followed suit.

Masja and Petra dashed down the narrow stairway to the Underground platform. "Come on, Petra, we're almost there!"

"I'm c-coming . . . as fast . . . as I can," Petra gasped. Moments later, they were standing on the platform, which was relatively deserted. A rumble came from the tunnel as the next regional train approached.

"Where's that fucking train already?!" Petra yelled.

Masja looked around desperately. There was nowhere to flee.

Then Mikhail and his men arrived on the platform. Mikhail shook his head ominously when he caught sight of them.

"What . . . what do we do now?" said Petra as they backed away from the men.

"I don't know," said Masja.

"I can't go back, Masja, I can't . . ."

"HELLLLP!" Masja shouted as loud as she could, and her voice rang out in the tunnel.

A few of the other passengers looked up. She called for help again, but no one made a move to help them. Mikhail was heading straight for them, banging his fists together. "Last stop, you whores!"

At last, the train came out of the tunnel. Petra turned to Masja and smiled.

"See you around, Masja," Petra said, giving her a quick kiss on the mouth.

Petra turned to face Mikhail, who had stopped only two feet away from them, and took one of the envelopes out of her jacket pocket. "If you want your money, you'll have to come and get it!" she screamed, tossing the money at him.

Mikhail tried to grab the money in the air, and the next second, Petra jumped.

Her body hit the windscreen of the oncoming train with an almighty crash and was flung onto the tracks ahead. There was an ear-piercing screech of brakes, and the train eventually came to a halt among a fluttering cloud of banknotes, which Petra had strapped around her middle.

Mikhail grabbed Masja, who stood as if rooted to the platform. *Petra.*

"Let me go!" Masja screamed, beating violently against Mikhail's chest as he hauled her away from the edge and dragged her up the stairs.

No one came to their aide.

On the stairs, Mikhail pulled out his pocket knife and stuck the point just below Masja's ribcage.

"If he were not expecting you, I would take care of you right now," Mikhail hissed in her ear.

"Tell Arkan he can lick his poodle's arse."

"Who said anything about Arkan?" Mikhail said. "You're not that lucky, Karina. The cops have just released Slavros. He's expecting you."

Masja stared at Mikhail in terror.

39

Sweden, 2013

The Boeing 737 and its eighty-three passengers, which primarily consisted of Scandinavian businessmen and -women, took off in a thick fog that hung over the Øresund. Thomas turned to the window and just managed to catch a glimpse of the Øresund Bridge before it disappeared below the clouds. When the flight attendant came down the aisle a few minutes later, Thomas promptly ordered a double vodka with plenty of ice. The guy sitting next to him, an elderly gentleman in a double-breasted suit, glanced in his direction. "Business or pleasure?" he said in English with a thick Swedish accent.

"Excuse me?"

"*Aaarbejde eller feeerie?*" the Swede said again, going for Danish this time, and deliberately drawing out those pesky Danish vowels that the language was infamous for.

"Neither nor," Thomas replied, and deliberately turned to look out the window. The Swede got the message and left him in peace.

Once he had his drink in hand, Thomas retrieved from the seat pocket in front of him Eduardo's folder as well as his newly acquired map of Stockholm from Victoria's bookstore. Some of the newspaper articles had been written by Eduardo himself, Thomas noted, but there were so many of them that it seemed as if Eduardo had included everything on prostitution in Sweden that his news rag had published in recent history. He read that sex trafficking in Sweden had escalated—despite various

Swedish resolutions, initiatives and regulations enacted in an attempt to stem the flow of girls over the borders. Thomas leafed through the pile and recognised the name of the Swedish Chief Commissioner, who was quoted in connection with a coordinated raid against a chain of tanning salons. Apparently, the salons had been operating as illegal "massage clinics" all over Stockholm. The Commissioner had the rather unfortunate name of Karl Luger. For his own part, Thomas had met Karl at an international conference at Scotland Yard. As far he could remember, Karl was a fine fellow. His wife was heavily pregnant at the time. She went into labour while the conference was underway, and Karl kept nipping out to call and check how she was doing, but by the time the conference was over, she still hadn't given birth to their child.

Thomas knew that Eduardo only wanted to help. It had been decent of him to print out all this material, but it was just too much to bloody read. All he really needed was an indication of where in Stockholm, more or less, he should start his search for Masja.

Thomas flipped through the articles randomly and finally found one about a raid against prostitutes on the streets. According to the article, the part of the sex trade that operated above ground was practised in the district around Stockholm Central and the large boulevards in the Normalm business district, mostly along Malmskillnadsgatan and Mäster Samuelsgatan. A few strip clubs just north of the city centre were also mentioned. He marked the various locations in his own Stockholm map. He was about to return the folder to the seat pocket when the final article with a pixelated portrait of a man caught his eye. The man in the photograph had a meticulously trimmed goatee and slicked-back black hair. His eyes were narrow, and the sardonic smile on his face gave him the air of the prototypical psychopath. Involuntarily, Thomas was reminded of the killings orchestrated by Charles Manson. He read the caption underneath: "Vladimir Slavros, a Russian businessman, connected to a prostitute's death at Stockholm Central . . ."

Thomas skimmed the contents of the article, a report on a Stockholm Central incident involving an unidentified woman in her thirties, presumably a prostitute, who was run over and killed by an oncoming train. The pictures from the security cameras on the relevant platform identified three of Slavros's men, including a man named Mikhail Ivanov, but charges were never brought against them. This must be the case that Mikkel had mentioned, Thomas thought, downing his vodka. The world was full of arseholes like Slavros. Which, fortunately, was not his problem. His own task was straightforward: He had given himself a maximum of three days to find Masja. If he found her, he would simply hand her the postcard from her mother and go home. He would not make any explanations, nor would he try to convince her to come home. If she had some deal going on with Slavros, it was none of his business. The sooner he got himself back to Christianshavn, the better.

Thomas raised his empty glass and signalled to the flight attendant that he would very much like another.

40

Stockholm, February 2011

Masja felt the fist like a hammer in her solar plexus. The wind was knocked out of her, and she gasped for breath as the next blow landed, then the next and the next. Every successive blow made it harder and harder for her to breathe, as if slowly suffocating her. At last, she fell to the floor. The other girls' silhouettes seemed to dance before her eyes. She managed to draw some air into her lungs and tasted blood on her tongue. Her left eye was swollen closed. In his black leather jacket, Slavros towered over her, both hands clenched into fists. His knuckles were stained with blood. Her blood. She crawled away from him till she reached the far wall and slumped against it.

Slavros turned towards Mikhail, who was standing next to the two other men who had chased them through the station. "How long have I been out, Mikhail?"

"A day?" Mikhail said, his shoulders twitching nervously.

"Wrong! Four and a half hours!" Slavros said, flicking his forearm against Mikhail's chest so hard that the big man stumbled backwards.

"It . . . it's good to have you back," Mikhail mumbled feebly.

"You should also know that the pigs interrogated me for over a week, without respite and without sleep because they put me in a cell between two paedos who kept me awake all night with their filthy talk. Do you have any idea how that makes me feel? Do you, Mikhail?!"

"Mad?" Mikhail said, staring at the floor.

"Oh, much more than that, I can assure you. And what do I find in my organisation when I get out? Chaos. A bunch of amateurs who let three lousy whores steal money from my good friend Mr. Arkan."

Slavros turned towards the only person in the room who was sitting down.

Arkan looked about sixty years old. He had acne scars on his cheeks and his thin top lip disappeared under a badly dyed soot-black moustache. A rust-red poodle was coiled in the folds of his lambskin coat in his lap. "That is very disssapointing," Arkan lisped, shifting in his plastic chair, which creaked in protest under his weight.

"I am deeply sorry for the inconvenience, Mr. Arkan," said Slavros. "I thought my girls could be trusted. And if you cannot trust a person's word, what can they possibly have left to offer you?"

"We had a deal," Masja said in a choked voice.

Slavros turned to face her. "What did you say?"

"We had . . . a deal . . . not the one who broke it," she stammered, still trying to catch her breath.

Slavros took a step towards her and Masja curled into a ball, shielding her head with her hands. "Exactly—we *had* a deal!" he yelled. "So why the hell did you steal from me?! Why couldn't you show me some respect and wait until I got out? After everything I have done for you, for all of you," he said, pointing at Lulu, who was standing among the other girls. Lulu's nose was bloody, and she had red fingerprint marks on her throat.

"Lulu had nothing to do with it," Masja said. "It was me and Petra . . . Iza . . . who took the money. And only because Mikhail suddenly said that we owed you ten thousand euros each, regardless."

"So instead, you thought you could steal two hundred thousand Swedish krona from me."

"It was a hundred forty thousand," Masja said, looking demonstrably at Arkan, who lowered his eyes to the poodle in his lap.

"It was at leassst two hundred," said Arkan. "At leasst. And now the money is scattered in the Underground tunnel."

Slavros glanced at Arkan suspiciously but made no reply.

"I don't care if it was just a five-krona coin that was missing from the till. I promised Mr. Arkan reliable girls who he could trust. Who can I trust now?" He looked around the room.

"It was only Iza and me. The others had nothing to do with it," Masja insisted.

Slavros looked at the poodle. The dog was turned over on its back with its paws in the air, while Arkan lovingly scratched its belly. "Is that a Gucci collar?" he asked.

"Nothing is too good for Pelle," said Arkan.

"*I* wear Gucci," said Slavros. He loosened his belt buckle, and with the flick of his wrist, he freed the Gucci belt from his trousers. "Lulu," he said.

Lulu looked up with fear in her eyes.

"Lulu had nothing to do with it," Masja said again.

"Lulu, show me that you can heel," Slavros said.

Lulu took a step forward.

"No," said Slavros. "On all fours. Show me that you can obey orders, just like Pelle here."

Lulu did as she was ordered. She got down on all fours and crawled up to Slavros's feet. His knuckles had turned white around the belt. "Did you know that you can only hit a dog so much, Arkan?" he went on. "At some point, the animal's brain simply gives up the ghost. It no longer obeys you, no matter how long or hard you keep beating the shit out of it. And yet, the power of fear alone can make a dog walk through fire for you."

"P-p-please," stammered Lulu. "I didn't know anything."

Slavros put his index finger to his lips and hushed her. Then he bent down and fastened his belt around her throat. "See, now you have a stunning collar that is just like Pelle's. Can you bark like a dog, Lulu? Can you say 'woof' for me?"

"Woof," Lulu said quietly.

"One more time. There's a good doggie, Lulu."

"Woof, woof."

"Give me your paw."

Lulu raised her right hand as if it were a paw, and one of the other girls sniggered.

A broad grin spread over Slavros's face. "See, this one *can* obey orders."

"Possibly," Arkan replied drily. "But I'm still out of pocket."

"Yes, I realise that," said Slavros. "The problem is that I cannot keep Lulu or any of the other girls on a leash all the time. Which is why proper training is so important. Do you know Pavlov?"

"The guy who owns Club Lux?" Arkan said.

"No. Ivan Petrovich Pavlov, the Soviet neurologist who won a Nobel Prize for his work."

"Never heard of him."

"Dr. Pavlov did behavioural experiments with his dog, which made him famous. Every time he fed it, Pavlov rang a bell. Soon, the dog knew that whenever the bell rang, he would get something to eat. Soon, whenever Pavlov's bell rang, it began to salivate. It was an automatic response. That means that Pavlov effectively changed the dog's behaviour, you see? Unfortunately, the effect was only temporary, and as a result, Pavlov had to repeat the conditioning of his dog regularly."

"What's your point?" asked Arkan.

"My point is that you can neither beat nor brainwash a dog to be one hundred percent obedient. The dog is and remains just a dog, which will always follow its instincts in the end. Submit to its own greed. Which means that you have to show it—remind it constantly, by way of example—what will happen if it does not obey. It ought to be something relatively dramatic, something that will make an impression on its mind and solidify the memory, something that will resound for a longer period than Pavlov's bell."

Slavros ended his explanation with a smile. Without looking down, he leaned back and pulled on the belt with both hands, tightening the pressure around Lulu's throat.

Lulu clawed at the belt and tried to free herself. But it was impossible.

Now, Slavros braced one boot on Lulu's shoulder and heaved on the belt even more.

"Stop!" yelled Masja, struggling to her feet.

Slavros turned his head towards her. "Do you want to take her place, Masja? Do you?!" he snapped, pulling the belt noose even tighter around Lulu's neck.

Masja fell silent and slumped back against the wall.

Lulu's head thrashed from side to side. Then a crunching sound came from her cervical spine, and she was still. A dark river of urine spread down the inner thighs of her jeans and left a puddle on the floor. All her energy spent, Lulu began to sink to the floor as she slowly choked to death. At last, Slavros let go of the belt and Lulu crashed onto the ground.

Arkan swallowed hard and hugged his precious Pelle to his chest.

Behind Arkan, the other girls started to cry.

Slavros stepped over Lulu's corpse and walked over to Masja. Bending down, he took hold of her chin and forced her head upwards so that she had to look him directly in the eye. "Remember this: Iza and Lulu were the lucky ones. You, on the other hand, will pay dearly for your disobedience," he said. "I pulled you up out of one kind of hell in that grease pit, and now I will send you to another. But this time, you will know what hell really is. I will make sure that every psychopath in this town knows your name. They will know your name and they will know your body inside out. But do not flatter yourself into thinking that this is just a punishment for your disobedience. It's not just about you; this is good business. Because the perverse people I know in this world also happen to have money. And they pay generously to have their darkest desires fulfilled."

"You can go to hell."

"No, sweetheart, not me. That's where *you* are going."

Slavros straightened up and looked round the room. "Ring, ring, ring," he said, flicking his wrist as if ringing an imaginary bell. "Back to work, girls. Mr. Arkan is still out of pocket, and you need to fix that."

41

Stockholm, 2013

Thomas opened the minibar and snatched the four little bottles that were neatly lined in a row on the shelf inside the door. Without bothering to read the label, he unscrewed the lid of the first one, gripped it between his front teeth and threw back his head. *Gin*, he registered, screwing off the lid of the second. Skirting the bed with its stained and crumpled cover, Thomas took up vigil by the window.

Darkness had fallen outside and there was light in the living rooms in the residential block opposite the hotel. His eye lingered on an elderly couple who were holding hands, their eyes glued to a large television screen. Thomas threw open the window, letting in a gush of icy air that tore at the curtains. The noise from Västmannagatan four storeys down flooded into his microscopic room. It was Saturday night, and the excited voices of a flock of teenagers heading into town rose up to meet him.

Thomas had chosen the Colonial Hotel, a two-star establishment that did not live up to its grandiose name. But the location was perfect, central and within walking distance of Malmskillnadsgatan, where the hookers reportedly walked the streets. It was here that he would start his search for Masja, or at least someone who knew her.

His phone vibrated insistently beside him on the bed. A glance at the display confirmed that it was Johnson calling, his fifth call in as many hours. The first came when Thomas was on the Arlanda Express, the shuttle that brought him in from the airport. Thomas had taken the call reluctantly, and Johnson immediately asked how the investigation was coming along, if he had found any trace of Masja. Thomas had explained that he was yet to arrive at his hotel in Stockholm.

Ignoring the phone, Thomas rummaged in his bag for a jumper and pulled it over his head. Ten minutes later, he was heading down the stairs to the lobby. He patted his breast pocket, making sure he had remembered to bring the photo of Masja and the postcard from her mother.

Thomas had intentionally left the Stockholm city guide in his room, memorising the map and the places he wanted to visit instead. He was loath to look like a tourist who had lost his way. There was no reason to stand out like an easy prey. He wasn't familiar with Stockholm streets, but he knew that if he were in a similar situation on Skelbækgade in Copenhagen, it would be a matter of minutes before someone like that exposed himself to all sorts of trouble.

He turned down Tunnelgatan, which he knew would lead him onto Malmskillnadsgatan. The wind bit into his skin and he cursed himself for not wearing a thicker coat. There was a good chance that his walk about town could turn into a long and bitterly cold night. He flipped up his hood as he went past the pub on the corner. KGB Bar, the sign over the door said. The bar was full, there was a lively crowd at a long counter and it looked like a cosy place. People laughing. People who were having a good time. If it hadn't been for this investigation, he would have gone inside and taken a seat at the empty stool he spotted through the bar's panoramic window. Even a bar in Sweden would have single malt, he told himself. He made a mental note of the address and hoped that the place would still be open on his return to the hotel later.

Malmskillnadsgatan lay directly in front of him. Ugly and uninspired, the office buildings were deserted. A constant stream of buses and cars trundled through the night. Thomas walked along the broad pavement of Malmskillnadsgatan. Music boomed from one of the cars passing by. Before long, Thomas came across the first hookers walking the streets. Their provocative clothing and glossy boots glittered in the headlights of the passing cars, sending an unambiguous message of their availability. Every time a car pulled over to the kerb, the girls came out of the shadows and propositioned the drivers. Malmskillnadsgatan could easily have been Skelbækgade. Indeed, it could easily have been any red-light district in any city across the globe. Which saddened him to the pit of his stomach.

He came to three girls who had taken cover in the bay entrance of a large office complex. They puffed on their cigarettes and hopped on the spot to ward off the cold, but they spotted him at once. "Hey, b-baby," one of them called to him through chattering teeth.

Without slowing his pace, Thomas glanced at the girls, dark complexions all three, possibly from Latin America, eighteen or nineteen, no more than twenty years old. He wondered what had brought them all the way up here. Why would they come this far from home to this shitty job on the other side of the globe? Whatever they might be running from, Thomas had a hard time imagining that it could be much worse than banging Swedes on the street at a temperature of minus ten degrees. He continued down the road, passing one group of girls after another. All of them were relatively young, and all of them were foreigners. It looked as if street girls from every nationality on earth were represented.

The traffic at the kerb kept up a lively pace. Taxis and private cars constantly pulled up, either picking up or returning girls from the shadows. Thomas wondered where they actually performed their services. As far as he could remember from his map, there was a large park not too far away. There was also a railway yard just behind Stockholm Central. After about an hour, Thomas had combed most of the Norrmalm business district. Most of the girls took up posts along the main arteries of the district. Because they were pitifully young, he had an impression that the transvestites and elder hookers, those who had been in the game for a longer period of time, had been forced out to the side roads. Unfortunately, he hadn't seen anyone who looked even remotely like Masja. So he decided to head back to Malmskillnadsgatan to see if there had been a change in the guard.

No sooner had Thomas returned than the first girl came on to him. They had noticed him, of course, just like they noticed all the other men who habitually trawled the streets. The girl who approached him must have been about twenty years old. But her features were hard, giving her the appearance of a much older woman. She had a pale complexion and dyed blonde hair. "Hello, loov, looking for some fooon?" she said in English with a thick Slavic accent. She was also wearing a short rabbit-fur coat, and Thomas was reminded of the one he had seen in Masja's bedroom at her mother's place on Burmeistersgade, but otherwise there was no resemblance. "*Hej*, I'm looking for a particular girl," he replied.

The girl said that he had come to the right place, and immediately asked what particular things he had in mind. Thomas shook his head, unzipped his jacket and took out the photograph of Masja. "I'm looking for this girl. Her name is Masja. Do you know her?"

The Slavic girl took no more than a glance at the photo and shook her head. Then she propositioned him again. This time, she licked her lips. "Make you reeeal happy," she said.

Thomas asked her to take another look at the photo, just to be sure. The Slavic girl shook her head firmly.

"Okay, thanks," Thomas said. He returned the picture to his pocket and continued down the street. The Slavic girl yelled something inaudible after him.

He tried talking to some of the other girls further down the street. To no avail. He had the feeling that the girls didn't actually know each other. And all they seemed to care about was getting the cars to stop along their particular stretch of pavement—and keeping the competition the hell away from their turf.

Thomas worked his way through the district, and every time a girl came up to him, he showed her the photo, but nobody recognised Masja. The third time he came along Malmskillnadsgatan, the Slavic girl in the rabbit-fur coat yelled a string of words in Russian—nothing flattering, he was sure—and spat in his direction. Suddenly, two guys in padded coats and winter boots came out of the shadows and confronted Thomas. Both men had crew cuts and resembled the Yugo gangsters on Skelbækgade back home.

"Hey, man," the first called after him. "What do you think you're doing?"

"So you're hassling our girls, are you?" the second asked, before Thomas could reply to his pal.

Thomas shook his head. "Not at all. I'm just looking."

They blocked his way. The first smacked into Thomas's shoulder with his own, keeping his hands in his pockets. "You can't just look. You buy, or you piss off. Understood?"

Thomas nodded.

"I'm not sure that you do," said the second, taking his hands out of his pockets. Both fists were clenched.

They scanned the street quickly.

"*Davaj*," the first said. Without another word, they brushed past Thomas roughly and disappeared.

Moments later, a squad car cruised past. Inside, two uniformed cops gave Thomas the once-over before continuing down the road. The squad car drove past the hookers and their clients without stopping. Unlike in Denmark, it was in fact illegal to *buy* sex in Sweden—it had been illegal to do so for more than ten years, Thomas knew that perfectly well—but there was no sign of police intervention on the streets, he noticed.

This was an impossible task, Thomas realised. He had more chance of winning the lottery than finding Masja in Stockholm. The thought of the KGB Bar and the empty stool by the counter became more and more appealing as he walked down the road in the freezing cold. Even so, he turned and headed in the opposite direction, where he knew he would find a few strip clubs where he could continue his search.

42

Thomas stopped in front of the boutique on Drottninggatan. Two rubber sex dolls dressed in erotic underwear were on display in the window, and he was momentarily confused. He checked the street number. There was no correlation between the boutique in front of him and the address he had noted for a strip club called Heart Beat, so he went inside to ask for directions.

The little shop was crammed with all kinds of sex toys. Behind lock and key, a glass cabinet of dildoes in every shape and size was displayed along the entire length of the back wall. The corner right at the back appeared to be reserved for leather, whips, chains, and handcuffs. On either side of the counter stood two large scented candles that oozed a sickly sweet smell into the air. Thomas went up to the shop assistant, a woman with piercings in both lips, her ears and her nose. She was reading a biker magazine behind the counter. A pair of Gothic warrior tattoos on her powerful arms seemed to bare their teeth at him as he approached.

"I'm looking for a strip club called Heart Be—"

"Downstairs in the cellar," the woman said, cutting him off. Without looking up from her magazine, she jerked her head in the direction of the stairs in the corner to her left. "Entrance is six hundred."

Thomas glanced at the stairwell. He took the photo of Masja out of his pocket and placed it on the counter in front of the shop assistant. "Perhaps you could tell me if this girl is down there?"

"Take a look for yourself," she said. "Entrance is still six hundred krona."

"I just want to see if the girl is there."

The big woman lifted her gaze from her magazine. "As I said: Entrance is six hundred to get in."

Thomas found the money in his wallet and slapped the bills onto the counter.

"Watch your head when you go down the stairs," the shop assistant said, sliding the bills into her inside jacket pocket. "The ceiling is rather low."

"Thank you."

Thomas ducked as he went down the narrow spiral staircase to the cellar. The blinking red strobe lights in the ceiling were as insistent as the pumping techno music from the loudspeakers mounted in the bar against the far wall. A thin girl wearing nothing but a G-string was gyrating around a pole in the middle of the stage. Three men were lounging in the leather sofas arranged in a semicircle in front of it. An Asian-looking girl wearing a tight corset was tending the bar, her arms raised over her head, clapping in time to the music, presumably in an attempt to whip up some enthusiasm.

Thomas went up to the bar.

The bartender smiled at him. "Hey, honey," she said, batting her false eyelashes at him.

Thomas said "Hi" and asked for a beer. The girl plopped a can of Pripps Blå on the counter and fluttered her eyelashes again. "Happy times, right?" she said in English.

Thomas leaned on the counter. "How many girls are working tonight?" he asked.

The girl pointed at the stage and then at herself. "Would you like a lap dance?" she said with a smile.

Thomas shook his head and took out the picture of Masja. "Do you know this girl?"

The bartender picked up the photo. She looked at it briefly, shook her head and gave it back to him.

"Sure you've never seen her?"

"Sorry," she said with a shrug.

When the dance performance was over, the two girls swapped places. The new bartender also appeared to be of Asian descent. She smiled just as broadly as her sister-in-arms and began clapping her hands over her head as soon as the music started to blare again, and the former bartender began to dance. Thomas showed the second girl the picture of Masja, but she claimed not to recognise her either. In the hopes of gleaning some information from her, Thomas bought the bartender a drink. He was partially successful. She told him she and the girl on the dance floor had come to Sweden about three months ago. Before that, they had worked in the Netherlands and Germany.

"Berlin, Leipzig, and *Hamburger*." She smiled. Then she asked if he wanted a private lap dance. Thomas politely declined, and the girl abandoned him in favour of the three men on the sofa.

Ten minutes later, Thomas was making his way back down Drottninggatan. The next stop on his list was a place called "Kitty Club, which lay on a corner a few streets away. His telephone rang, and when he fished it out of his jacket pocket, the display revealed that it was Johnson. *Again.* He took the call.

"Anything new?" Johnson's voice rasped in Thomas's ear.

"No."

There was a grunt on the other end of the line. "Are you sure you're looking in the right places, Ravn? This is important, you know."

"I'm trawling the freezing fucking streets of Stockholm to look for her."

Thomas heard shouting in the background. "I . . . I have to run."

"I promise I'll call as soon as I know."

The other end of the line went dead.

Thomas turned the corner by the 7-Eleven store and headed up the steep alley where Kitty Club was located on the map. The smell of fried foods filled his nostrils as he paused in front of Shawarma Grill next to the club. Thomas bought himself a falafel and leaned against the wall on the opposite side of the street, keeping a watchful eye on the club as he ate his dinner.

The club's façade was a sorry sight. The name appeared in large silver letters on a sign above the entrance, and one of the Ts in KITTY dangled askew from its nail. The sign was old and painted over, but he could still make out the letters underneath. He looked more closely: K—E—Y Club. The name rang a bell from Eduardo's file of articles. This was the place that used to belong to Slavros.

Thomas tossed the rest of his falafel in a rubbish bin and headed for the entrance.

Kitty Club was not in any way more exclusive than Heart Beat, but it was much bigger and there were many more clients inside. Most of the guests were middle-aged men, or groups of boys barely out of their teens. The clients and the girls, typically dressed in tight miniskirts, were seated in a series of oval booths placed in front of the stage, where two girls were engaged in an erotic show accompanied by the title song from *Titanic*.

Before he could take another step, a dark-skinned girl in a cobalt-blue satin dress came over to him. "We have an empty table available," she said with a smile, pointing to one of the sofas.

"Okay," said Thomas.

"There is a cover charge, of course, but it includes a bottle of bubbly," the cobalt girl said, hooking her arm into his, clearly intent on ushering the way.

"And how much does it cost to sit there?" said Thomas, standing his ground.

"Usually, a table costs thirty-five hundred, but you can have it for twenty-seven hundred, honey."

"Thanks," said Thomas, disentangling himself. "But I'd rather take a seat at the bar."

Only half the stools by the bar were occupied. Thomas took a seat and had a look around.

The *Titanic* performance came to an end. A blonde in a red latex corset started to strip to Joe Cocker's "You Can Leave Your Hat On." Bouncers were stationed at the door and on either side of the stage, all of them muscular, body-builder types with crew cuts and Slavic features. Thomas figured the bouncers were either Balkans or Russians, which indicated that Vladimir Slavros might still be the owner of the club, despite the change of name. None of the ten to fifteen girls, who he watched working the crowd, resembled Masja. They were even younger than she was, he noticed, again feeling sick to his stomach.

"Hey, handsome, you look just like Daniel Craig," said a blonde who had sidled up to him from the crowd. "A rugged version, that is," she added with a smile.

"Who?"

"You know, 007. The guy who plays James Bond. You know him, right?"

"But isn't he blond?"

The girl shrugged. "I'm sooo thirsty."

"Would you like one of these?" Thomas said, pointing at his glass of *lättöl*, Swedish piss beer.

The blonde shook her head, and before Thomas could respond, a waitress appeared and plonked a champagne glass in front of them. Thomas was well aware that he'd be paying a small fortune for it, regardless of what it contained. He and the blonde chinked glasses.

"So, you're from Denmark?" she said. "What's your name?"

"Thomas."

"Cheers, Thomas from Denmark. My name is Lizza—with two z's. Are you on holiday, or up here for work?"

Thomas let his eyes wander over Lizza's shoulder. "I'm looking for a girl—someone who ran away from home."

"Then you've come to the right place," Lizza said with a snort of laughter. "That's the only kind of girl we've got. We're all running away from some place or another. But we're still sweet," she added with a pout.

"How long have you been here?"

"In Sweden? Much too long.

"And how long have you been working in this club?"

"Why do you ask? You're not a cop, are you?" she said, arching her thin painted brows.

Thomas shook his head. "No, no, I'm not a cop. I'm just trying to find out what happened to this girl. I'm helping her mother find her."

"A real gentleman." She smiled. "What's the girl's name?"

"Masja," Thomas said. He took out the photograph and showed it to Lizza.

"So you've met her?" Thomas asked, putting down his beer glass.

Lizza nodded her head. "Yeah, there's something about her that looks familiar."

"When? Where?"

Lizza leaned closer and slipped the photo back into his pocket. "Why don't we go upstairs together, where it's a little more private," she whispered in his ear. "Then we can talk about her . . . Masja." Lizza leaned back and looked him in the eye. "But there has to be something in it for me."

"Do you know where Masja is?"

"I have the bridal suite upstairs," Lizza said. "Why don't you come up with me?" Without waiting for his reply, she turned and started walking away.

Thomas watched her head for the stairs in the far corner. She had a word with one of the Balkan bouncers guarding the doorway, nodded in Thomas's direction, and disappeared up the stairs.

Thomas wasn't sure if Lizza was telling the truth. But he knew for a fact that if he left now, without getting clarity on this point, it would gnaw at him for the remainder of his trip. He downed the rest of his piss beer in a single gulp.

Five minutes later, he was standing on the narrow landing on the first floor of Kitty Club. He knocked on the door of room number 3. At top of the stairs, he had paid 2,500 krona to the bouncer in a cheap tux guarding the corridor. "You have twenty minutes," the bouncer informed him. "Behave yourself," he added, giving Thomas a hard stare.

Lizza opened the door to room number 3 and invited Thomas inside. She had discarded her dress and was standing before him in a black G-string and matching brassiere that barely covered her large silicone breasts. He looked around the tiny room in the near darkness. A bed, a cupboard and a make-up table in the corner were all that the bridal suite had to offer.

"Why don't you lie down so I can give you a little massage for starters?" Lizza said.

Thomas removed her hand from his zipper. "I'd rather you told me about Masja. Where can I find her?"

Lizza took his hand. "Come and lie down with me. Forget about Masja. I can be your little Mas-ja."

Thomas freed himself and took a step away from her. "I mean it. If you know where she is, I would really appreciate your help. Naturally, I will pay you for it."

"Show me that photo again," Lizza said, putting out her hand.

Thomas showed her the picture and she snapped it up. "She's very pretty. Innocent-looking. Is this a recent picture of her?" asked Lizza.

"It was taken a few years ago. She disappeared in 2010."

"In 2010?" Lizza rolled her eyes. "Then I'm honestly not sure I know her."

He was about to take back the photo, but Lizza kept it out of his reach. "Wait here," she said, taking a thin silk kimono off the hook on the wall. She wrapped it around herself and disappeared out the door.

Thomas looked around the pathetic room, grimacing at the sight of the large damp stains on the walls. If this was the "bridal suite," he dared not think what the rest of the rooms in the club looked like. A sports bag stood on the little dressing table. Lizza's precious few belongings, he guessed. It wouldn't surprise him if she worked and lived in this little room.

A few minutes later, Lizza returned. "I talked to a few of the other girls. One of them remembered her," she said, returning the photo. "But she left a long time ago."

"Left? Where did she go?"

"Home."

"Back to Saint Petersburg?" he asked, testing her.

Lizza nodded and hung the kimono back on its nail. "Yes, exactly," she said. "Shall we?" she asked, pointing to the bed.

"Who owns this place?"

"No idea."

"Slavros? Vladimir Slavros?"

"I don't know anyone by that name. You ask too many questions. Come and lie down."

Thomas returned the photo to his pocket. He took out a 500-krona bill and gave it to her. There was no reason to stick around. Apparently, Lizza was lying to him. No one here knew Masja.

"Thanks for your help, Lizza. Look after yourself," he said, and made for the door.

"Thomas from Denmark?"

He cast a look over his shoulder.

"Tell her mother that she's okay."

43

Thomas woke up to the vibrating sound of his phone somewhere close by. The sharp morning light was shining through the window and made it impossible for him to open his eyes completely. He fumbled for the source of the sound so he could kill the bloody thing. When his fingers made contact with the vibrating object, he pressed buttons manically till the noise stopped. He let it slip out of his hand in relief. Goddamn, his head hurt. And his throat was cork-dry. He realised dimly that he was still fully clothed.

"Ravn . . . Ravn . . ."

He heard his name from somewhere in the distance.

"Ravn! Pick up the bloody phone already!"

Thomas opened his eyes. *Fuck*. In his fumbling, he'd involuntarily accepted Johnson's call.

"Yes?" Thomas said in a hoarse whisper. "What do you want?"

"Are you drunk?"

"Not anymore. Why?"

"It's after twelve, and you sound like someone who hasn't even got out of bed yet."

"I'm awake and dressed," he said. The effort prompted a coughing fit that seemed to shake the walls of his tiny room.

"What have you found out?"

Thomas sat up in the bed, which made the room spin and he felt the nausea rise. "There's not much to be found up here."

"Perhaps you'd get better results if you weren't blind drunk half the time," Johnson said in a peeved voice.

"I haven't been drinking . . . only a little. I spent most of the night combing the streets of Stockholm in minus ten degrees. But she's not bloody here, Johnson."

"Nadja has been around to see me today. She says she believes in you. She told me to tell you that she's keeping her fingers crossed and hopes that you'll come home with good news soon."

Thomas scratched his aching head. "Well, I can't perform miracles, can I?"

"You can't let her down, Ravn. This is her daughter we're talking about."

"For fuck's sake, Johnson. It wasn't *my* brilliant idea to fly to Sweden to look for Masja."

"Just make sure that you—"

"I've gotta run." Thomas threw down the telephone and lurched over to the bathroom. He just managed to reach the toilet bowl before he doubled over.

A few minutes later, Thomas was sitting on the bathroom floor, leaning against the glass wall of the shower. In his hand he held a plastic cup of water that he was trying to get down. Of course bloody Johnson would have to wake him just at the point when his hangover was at its worst. If only he could've slept for *one* more hour, he could've avoided this little chat with the toilet bowl. He tried to recall what had happened the night before.

After meeting Lizza at Kitty Club, he had visited a few more strip clubs, each dive more heart-rending than the next. And in every club he imagined finding Masja. She had stood in front of him and said: "Hello, how are you? Special price for my special friend . . ." The truth was that he saw Masja in every girl he had met in those clubs, no matter where she came from, or what colour her skin was. They were all like her. Running from something or other. Sold to someone or other. Bought by a third party and sold again. Without a glimmer of hope for the future. But all the girls seemed younger than Masja. And he couldn't help but wonder how long it would take before they were worn out. A year? Six months?

Three? How long could they last in such an environment? As the night wore on, his investigation started to feel like a waste of time. In the end, he gave up and sought refuge in the KGB Bar. He found that empty stool at the counter and drank single malt and Heineken and made friends in "the hood" in Stockholm—not that he would recognise these people if he ever bumped into them again. But it was entertaining and a relief to get away from the strip clubs. At the KGB Bar, he could drink and sing along with everyone else—*Swedish troubadour songs by Evert-fucking-Taube, so help me God*—all in the name of jovial inter-Scandinavian one-upmanship. They told jokes in Swedish and in Danish—the Swedes made fun of the Danes; the Danes made fun of the Swedes—and he met a woman called Monica, who looked like the brunette from Abba. She flirted with him, said he was *snygg*, but he couldn't remember if he kissed her or just wanted to.

Eva's face swam to the surface, came into focus, and his heart dropped.

Thomas got up from the bathroom floor, stepped into the shower, and let the warm water soothe him.

The morning buffet at the Colonial Hotel was long since over, so Thomas kept his head down and made for Kungsgatan in the Norrmalm district, where he found a little café with a seat by the window.

Thomas ordered black coffee and two croissants. A young waitress with a bouncy ponytail and rings on every finger told him that they only had *kanelbullar* left. Recalling Victoria's advice, he said he would settle for a black coffee. He sat back and helped himself to the *Express* lying on the empty table next to him.

In the mid-section of the newspaper, he found a report about an ongoing murder investigation. An unknown perpetrator had killed six prostitutes, who were preserved, limewashed and ultimately propped like white statues in a local scrapyard. The perpetrators motives were still unknown, but a number of psychologists interviewed in connection with the case believed that the perp had either a religious or sexual motive for the murders.

When the waitress returned with his coffee, he put the newspaper down and let his gaze wander to the window, watching the traffic and streams of people hurrying past on the pavement. Thomas tried to convince himself that he had done what he could. That it would be a waste of time *and* money to continue. He had already spent at least 6,000 krona on the strip clubs alone. He doubted that Johnson would fork out that kind of money—and Thomas wouldn't dream of asking Nadja to reimburse him. He considered changing his flight and going back home immediately, even though he knew he would get an earful from Johnson for giving up so easily. God knows he would never hear the end of it at The Sea Otter.

Thomas downed the remainder of his coffee. He desperately needed another. He took the postcard with the kittens on the front out of his pocket. He figured that he could simply tell Nadja a white lie and leave the postcard here on the table. That could work. That would be the easiest way out. But it went against his code to lie to a nice old lady who had lost her daughter. "Tell her mother that she's okay," Lizza had told him.

"Goddammit," Thomas muttered under his breath.

"Excuse me?" the waitress with the ponytail said.

Thomas looked up, startled to see her standing there. "Could I have another coffee, please? And I'll have one of those cinnamon bun things of yours."

The waitress nodded, spun on her heel, and bobbed over to the counter immediately.

As soon as she was gone, Thomas fished his mobile phone out of his pocket and scanned his contacts. At last, he found the one he was looking for and placed the call.

"*Rikspolisen*," the duty sergeant said on the other end of the line.

44

Karl Luger extended his hand and smiled at Thomas, revealing deep dimples in his chubby cheeks. It appeared that Karl had gained quite a lot of weight since they'd met. At least fifteen or twenty kilos, Thomas guessed.

"Good to see you, Ravn," Karl Luger said. "I was rather surprised to get your call. How long has it been? Four, maybe five years?"

Karl loosened the marine-blue tie around his neck that looked as if it were about to choke him.

"Closer to six, I think," said Thomas. "Not since the seminar at Scotland Yard. I see you still have the teddy bear." He smiled, pointing at the Bobby teddy bear that was leaned up against a picture frame on Luger's desk. The bears had been a souvenir for all the foreign delegates upon completion of the seminar.

Karl glanced at the bear. "Yup. Pretty pathetic, huh?"

"Not at all. I still have mine back home," Thomas lied. "Is that your wife and daughter?" he asked, pointing at the picture frame.

"Yes. That's Susan with our Louisa. She starts school next year."

"Right. I remember that Susan was about to give birth when we met in London."

Karl grinned. "What about you? Children?"

Thomas shook his head.

"But you were married to . . ." He clicked his fingers, trying to remember the name.

"Eva," Thomas said, helping him out.

"Eva! Yes, the defence lawyer. I remember. You joked that you caught the criminals, and she . . ."

"She set them all free, yes." Thomas nodded and tried to smile.

"Are you two still together?"

"Yes, of course, we're very well, thank you," Thomas said, averting his eyes. The Criminal Division of *Rikspolisen* was very different from Station City back home, he noticed. The office was open plan and well-lit with an air of painstaking order to the desks and computers lined up in a row. Every investigator sat in front of his own monitor in a shirt and tie. He felt as if he'd walked into the local branch of a bank, not a crime unit.

Karl offered him a cup of coffee, which they drew from the vending machine in the corridor. While they waited for their coffees, Karl told Thomas about his promotion: He had been appointed Chief Commissioner of the Swedish IT-Investigative Unit. "Here in the IT Unit, we still investigate the same crowd of people," he said. "The criminals in this country haven't stopped breaking the law; they've just moved their operation to the internet, regardless of its nature: prostitution, sex trafficking, drug dealing, or theft. Even the biker gangs have iPads now," he added with a chuckle as he picked up their coffees. "But at least I no longer have to run around on the streets at night. You know how exhausting that can be."

Thomas nodded in agreement and followed Karl back to his office.

Karl put their paper cups down on his desk and invited Thomas to take a seat. "How are things on your end?"

"Same as usual. No promotion for me. I still run around on the streets at night," Thomas said with a smile.

"You Danes take a more casual approach, I see," Karl said, picking up his cup and jabbing it at Thomas. "You look like a rock star with that beard of yours. That would never be allowed in here." He chuckled again and took a sip of his coffee.

"No, probably not. I noticed that you Swedes have a more streamlined approach," Thomas replied, scratching his beard and smiling in return. "Although, if you ask my boss, he'll tell you I'm hardly up for Station City's Police Detective of the Year Award."

"That surprises me. As I recall, you were one of the sharpest delegates at the Scotland Yard seminar."

Karl extracted a Kleenex from a metal holder, folded it neatly in half and smoothed it down on his desk. "So tell me more about this case you mentioned on the telephone," he said, resting his coffee down on his Kleenex coaster.

"Yes, of course. As I said, I'm looking for a Lithuanian girl who disappeared in 2010. She was a prostitute, and the evidence suggests that she was sold in Copenhagen and trafficked to Sweden via a middle man."

"Like so many other girls, I'm afraid. In recent years, there's been a veritable flood of prostitutes from all over the world."

"But I thought it was illegal to buy sex in Sweden. Doesn't the prohibition help at all?"

Karl leaned back and stretched in his chair. "Ah, that *jävla* prohibition," Karl swore, "it's the work of the Devil. Before the prohibition was enacted, we had good connections with the girls and their *hallickarna*, their pimps. But now they've all gone underground, and we no longer have an ear to the wire. This means that the girls are more vulnerable than ever. They are raped, beaten up, subjected to all kinds of abuse. On top of it all, we've got a psychopath on the loose who has murdered six girls. The perpetrator finds his victims among the prostitutes working on the streets and preserves them like stuffed animals!" Karl shook his head in horror.

"Do you mean the guy who dumps the girls on the rubbish heaps?"

"The scrapyard, yes. You're familiar with the case"

"I read about it in the *Express* this morning. Nasty business."

"So, how can I help you?" asked Karl.

"I was wondering whether you had any information about the girl I'm looking for in your system."

"Is this an official request for assistance?" Karl asked in a serious tone.

"No, I'm afraid not," said Thomas. "I'm doing this as a favour to the girl's mother. That's all."

"Do you have any idea how many girls disappear each year?"

"A hell of a lot, I've been told. Even so, I'd really appreciate your help on this."

Karl smoothed down his tie, which draped over his paunch like a dead snake. "But if this isn't an official police investigation . . ."

Thomas leaned forward in his seat. "Karl, all I am asking is that you punch her data into your system. See if her name pops up, if you have anything on her, anything at all that might give me a clue as to where she might be, or what has happened to her."

"Naturally, I sympathise with your investigation," said Karl. "But I still need either an existing case file or an official request from Station City before I can run a search on your girl in *Rikspolisen*'s system. I've fired colleagues for lesser contraventions of the rules. The Swedish system cannot be used for private purposes, you know that, no matter how noble your intentions might be," he added firmly.

"Okay, I understand," said Thomas.

Karl glanced at his watch, signalling that their brief meeting was already coming to a close.

"The man she was sold to is named Slavros. Does the name ring a bell?"

"Vladimir Slavros?"

Thomas nodded.

"Has this been confirmed?"

"I have a witness who has implicated Slavros's involvement."

"Do you have a witness statement or a confession to this effect?"

"No, neither, and I doubt very much that I ever will. The Baltic and Russian Mafia operating in Denmark are not known for snitching on each other."

"Yes, it's much the same in Sweden." Karl regarded Thomas thoughtfully as he tapped his fingertips together just in front of his mouth. "Do you think the girl would testify against Slavros—*if* you found her, that is?"

"That possibility always exists."

"For, if that were the case . . . *Rikspolisen* would very much like to talk to her."

"Well, for starters, you could fire up your PC," Thomas replied with a smile, nodding at the monitor in front of Karl.

Karl let out a heavy sigh and pulled his keyboard over. "All right, what do you have on this girl?"

Thomas quickly gave him the data he had on Masja, and Karl tapped the information into his system. A moment later, the result appeared on the screen: "No matches found."

"Well, that would have been too easy," Karl remarked.

"What do you mean?"

"Ever since I started working here, we've been trying to nail Slavros."

"That's a long time."

"Myself, Dahl, and Lindgren," Karl said, swivelling in his chair and pointing to the two deputy investigators who were sitting at their desks opposite him. "We've spent thousands of working hours on the man."

The two deputies looked up and nodded briefly in Thomas's direction. "So, why haven't you guys caught him yet?" Thomas asked.

The three investigators smiled among themselves and looked at Thomas as if he'd asked a stupid question.

"Slavros is clever enough to never get directly involved," Lindgren replied. He was about the same age as Karl, with large fleshy lips and a side parting that cut a straight line through his slicked-back dark hair. "There is always a straw man between Slavros and any illegal activities," he explained.

"And in the few times that we've managed to raise charges directly against Slavros," Karl added, "no one was prepared to testify against him."

"We came close to catching him only once," said Lindgren.

"When was that?" asked Thomas.

"It was a couple of years ago, when we instigated a large-scale raid against Key Club, which is one of his strip clubs."

"The establishment that is now called Kitty Club, right?"

"Yes. It's changed names several times, but it's still owned by Slavros."

"So what happened?"

"He managed to evacuate the girls just before we entered the building, so we couldn't pin anything on him, and the case fell apart."

"But there are still girls working there," Thomas said incredulously.

"We know that, of course, but times have changed," Lindgren replied. "Now even the royal family goes to strip clubs," he said drily, raising his pinkie finger in a mocking gesture.

"And Slavros? Do we know where he is?"

"Everywhere and nowhere. Slavros knows how to stay under our radar," said Karl.

"But he's still under investigation?"

"Officially, yes. But at the moment, other cases have a higher priority," said Karl. "No one is prepared to take real action for the well-being of a handful of foreign girls on the streets. The politicians know they can't win votes with that kind of thing at the moment. Creeps like Slavros take advantage of that."

"I read about an incident at the railway station a couple of years ago," said Thomas. "One of the cases that I believe *you* were investigating, Karl. You arrested some of Slavros's men. What happened to them?"

"The . . . railway station? Do you mean Stockholm Central?" Karl asked.

"Yes. Apparently, a prostitute was hit by an oncoming train in the Underground."

Dahl looked up from his computer and smiled. "Yes, the girl with the money. Our boys spent two days hunting for thousand-krona bills between the tunnel tracks. They found more than 100 of them down there."

"But did you raise any charges against his men?"

"No. It was suicide," said Dahl. "But we knew that the money belonged to Slavros because security cameras caught three of his men chasing the suicide victim and another girl through the station just before the incident occurred."

"Who was the other girl?"

"We have no idea. Only the three men were interviewed. But it's highly likely that she was also a prostitute. We had no contact with her."

"But Slavros was definitely involved?"

"To one extent or another, yes," replied Karl. "As far as I can remember, it was some guy called Aron."

"Arkan," said Dahl. "The owner of the tanning salons."

"Exactly . . . Arkan was his name," said Karl. "One of Slavros's business pals. Arkan owned a chain of tanning salons that were a cover for his brothels. The dead girl and the money came from there."

"Arkan supervised a large chunk of the prostitution trade at that time," added Lindgren.

"Would Arkan have known about the deal with Masja?" Thomas asked.

"He might have," said Karl, "but whether he would talk is another matter altogether."

"Arkan is silent as the grave," said Lindgren.

"Where can I find him?"

"In a prison near Södertälje called Hall. He'll be there for the next five years." Karl glanced at his watch again. "I'm afraid I'm going to have to wrap this up, Ravn."

"Of course, I won't keep you any longer." Thomas got to his feet and said goodbye to the two deputies.

Karl walked Thomas to the door. "It was good to see you, Ravn. I'm sorry that I couldn't be more helpful. If you find her, and if she has anything at all to share about Slavros, you'll let me know, right?"

Thomas nodded. "What will it take for me to have a word with Arkan?"

"A ride in a taxi. Hall is only half an hour's drive from Stockholm."

"Could you give the guys over at Hall a ring and get me on Arkan's visitors list?"

Karl smiled. "Sure. Arkan doesn't pose any kind of risk in our books. As Lindgren said, it's rather a question of whether he'll talk to you or not."

45

It was just after nine the next morning when Thomas got into a taxi and headed for Södertälje along the E4 motorway. The old Volvo negotiated morning rush-hour traffic with Lisa Nilsson crooning "Let Me In Your Heart" on the radio. They drove at a snail's pace along the motorway with a languorous view of IKEA on one side and Lake Mälar on the other. *Could it get any more Swedish than this?* Thomas thought.

"Heading out to see one of your bros?" The taxi driver, a man sporting long red sideburns and a leather cap that was much too small for his head, gave Thomas a bleary-eyed glance in the rear-view mirror. Thomas muttered something in reply that signified either *yes* or *no* but most of all that he had a hangover and was not in the mood to talk.

The night before he had taken another pass at the strip clubs—without becoming any wiser as to Masja's whereabouts. He had ended his search at the KGB Bar, which was not nearly as lively as the first night, but there was enough Jim Beam and piss beer to go around.

"I know several blokes doing time in Hall," the driver went on in Swedish. "Not a fun place to be. The guards ride you hard in there, if you know what I mean," he added, glancing in the rear-view again. He had a snus pouch like a black slug pasted against his upper gums that revealed itself whenever he spoke. "Soon, you won't be able to take a shit in the woods without getting arrested. So what did he do, your bro?"

"What?!"

"Your bro, your friend, your pal. What's he in for? Drugs? Theft? Beating up his ol' lady?" The driver laughed at his own joke.

"He's not my friend."

"No? What then? Does he owe you money?" The driver laughed again but stopped when he saw Thomas's stony expression reflected in the rear-view. "You've come a long way," he said, changing tack. "Do you live in Denmark?"

"Yes."

"Copenhagen?"

"Yes."

"Are the cops over there also pigs?"

Thomas sighed heavily. "More than you know," he said, leaning forward to show the driver his badge. "Tell you what. Why don't we just let Lisa Nilsson sing in peace for the rest of the way, okay?"

The taxi driver starting coughing so much he nearly swallowed his slug. "Sh-sh-sure thing."

Thomas leaned back in his seat and looked out the window. Here and there, bare trees rose up between large boulders. He caught a glimpse of Lake Mälar. A heavily loaded container ship sailed over the grey surface of the water. They'd once made plans to sail *Bianca* up the eastern coast of Sweden together, just the two of them. Eva suggested that they take the route to Gothenburg, then make their way further north to Krabbefjärden. From here, they could take the Södertälje canal and sail over Lake Mälar, directly into the heart of Stockholm at Wasahamnen. They would sit on the aft deck, eating lobster and drinking champagne as the sun went down over Gamla Stan . . .

Thomas shivered in his seat. He could not get home fast enough so he could sell the goddamn boat.

His mobile phone vibrated in his pocket. On the display he could see that it was Eduardo returning his call. "What have you got for me, Eduardo?" he said into the receiver.

In the early hours of the morning, Thomas had called Eduardo and asked him to find out what had been reported in the news about Arkan, any information that might help to loosen his tongue. Half asleep, Eduardo had promised to take a look when he got to the office.

"Arkan came to Sweden from Turkey with his parents in 1968," Eduardo replied. "He was fourteen years old at the time. His family was part of the guest worker boom in Western Europe."

Thomas could hear a great deal of noise in the background, and he had to concentrate hard to hear what Eduardo was saying.

"Arkan was the eldest of four brothers. His father worked as a baker and the family lived in Rinkeby, Stockholm's answer to the Vollsmose district for low-income households on the fringe of Copenhagen."

"Do you have anything on his criminal record?"

"Very little. Can't you get that information from the local Swedish police?"

"The local police guard their archives as if it were a matter of national security."

Eduardo laughed into the phone. "In Arkan's case, it probably is."

"What do you mean?"

"Arkan had his heyday in the 1980s and 1990s. He used to arrange so-called hunting trips for prominent high-level VIPs. The trips were basically a cover for wild parties complete with prostitutes and large quantities of drugs. They took place in discreet locations deep in the Swedish countryside."

"How prominent?"

"All the way up to the top, including senior management in large-scale industry. There were even rumours that members of the royal family were involved. For his part, Arkan got off with a fine and a slap on the wrist, even though he could have been charged with several years' imprisonment—which speaks volumes about the kind of connections he used to have. He was the Swedish jetsetter's darling. But after that, they distanced themselves from him. In 2002, *Expressen* wrote a feature about his fall from grace to nothing but a friendless bum on the dole."

"How did Arkan come into contact with Slavros?"

"I have no idea. The only case on record that connects them is the tanning salon brothels, which sounds like a similar operation to the hunting trips, albeit for the everyday Swede rather than the rich and famous . . . Do you think that Masja might have worked at one of these places?"

"This is what I need to find out. Is that all you have for me?"

"Yep, that's it."

"What about Møffe? How is he?"

There was a sigh on the other end of the line. "I think he misses you. He's chewed his way through the better half of my wardrobe."

"Well, he's always appreciated quality."

"*Realmente?* Do you have any idea what a bad stomach your dog has?"

"*Sensitive*. His stomach is sensitive."

"Be that as it may, you're not the only one who has a close relationship with his dog."

"What do you mean?"

"Arkan was Chairman of the NSPF for several years in a row."

"Sounds like some kind of neo-Nazi organisation."

"Hardly. It's the Swedish Poodle Foundation."

"I see. Thanks, Eduardo."

"*No problema*. When will you be back?"

"I'm planning to be on the plane tomorrow night, unless something comes up."

Thomas said his goodbyes to Eduardo and popped the telephone back in his pocket.

Twenty minutes later, his Volvo taxi exited the Nynäsvägen artery and swung onto Halldalan, which led to the old Hall prison behind its massive walls.

The metal table was nailed to the floor, Thomas observed idly, as he waited for Arkan to be brought down from his cell. A pair of fluorescent neon tubes above his head enhanced the anything-but-cosy atmosphere in Hall's visitors' room, which had less charm than most police interrogation rooms that he had frequented. It was almost as if the ghost of the educational institution that was originally located in the building in the previous century still haunted the premises, despite extensive renovations to transform the buildings into a modern correctional facility. A clatter of keys announced the prisoner's arrival, and moments later, Arkan entered the room. The guard nodded to Thomas in greeting and locked the door behind him as he left. Thomas stood up and extended his hand. Arkan came forward and shook it with a grip like unleavened dough.

Arkan smiled and smoothed down the thin moustache on his upper lip. Thomas noticed that he had clumps of black mascara in the dyed bristles on his lip. The prisoner was dressed in a pair of meticulously ironed grey trousers, a pink shirt, and a polka-dot silk scarf at his throat. Arkan's attire was dapper but seemed much too large for him, as if he'd lost a great deal of weight.

"I'm curious, Mr. Thomas Ravnsholdt, how do we know each other? From the old days?"

"No," said Thomas. "We've never met," he said truthfully. He opened the paper bag from the bakery, took out the four *kanelbullar* he had brought with him, and placed them on top of the bag.

"*Kanelbullar*? Don't mind if I do," said Arkan, helping himself. "You with the Christian Brothers' Association? We can talk about God and Jesus if you like, not that either one of them ever show their faces around here," Arkan remarked drily, using the tip of an index finger to brush some crumbs and cinnamon sugar out of his moustache.

Thomas smiled. "I'm neither a Christian Brother, nor particularly religious. I'm here because I need your help."

"Is that so? With what, I wonder?"

"I'm looking for a girl."

Arkan chuckled. "I've known an incredible number of girls, more girls than most. Have you fallen in love?" he said, winking at Thomas.

"No, it's nothing like that."

"If you ask me, you should stay the hell away from women. They can't be trusted. The Devil's spawn is what they are. I've helped hundreds of them. Gave them work, a roof over their heads. Without a single word of thanks in return."

"At your tanning salons, for example?"

Arkan smiled. "Ah, you were a client, perhaps? Did you partake of their services? The salons were a 'nice set-up,' as the Americans would say."

"Yes. A savvy arrangement, a bit like your hunting parties in the old days," Thomas remarked.

Arkan slapped his thigh enthusiastically. "Ooh, yes! Those were the days, ooh-la-la." He chortled. "No one can beat my hunting parties—what a ball we had!"

"I heard that *everyone* was there."

"Yup, *all* the VIPs."

"Even the King." Thomas winked at him.

Arkan smiled. "I cannot comment . . . nor confirm the size of His Majesty's penis." He grunted.

Thomas smiled as if on cue and discreetly took the photo of Masja out of his pocket. "You're a witty man, Arkan, I'll give you that. But, getting back to the purpose of my visit . . ." He put the photo of Masja down in front of Arkan. "I need to find *this* girl."

Arkan glanced down at the photo. His eyes wavered briefly before he looked away. "Never laid eyes on her."

"Are you sure?" Thomas tapped the surface of the photo lightly, drawing Arkan's attention back to it.

"Positive," Arkan said in a quivering voice.

Thomas looked him directly in the eye. "Her name is Masja. Her mother misses her."

Arkan's lips drew into a thin line. "That girl is lucky to have someone who misses her. I'm all alone here. Completely forgotten by the world. You are the first visitor I've had," he said bitterly.

"A few years ago, Masja was sold to a man name Slavros. A man who I know you've done business with."

"Are you a cop? Are you?!" Arkan said, pushing back from the table.

Thomas ignored the question. "There's no reason to protect the man who got you locked up in here. *You're* the one who took the rap for both of you back then, am I right?"

Arkan folded his arms across his chest in silence.

"Why hasn't he been around to say thank you?"

"Is this another one of *Rikspolisen*'s ridiculous attempts to get me to squeal on Slavros?" Arkan said, getting to his feet. "Do they really think that some Danish copper could break me?"

"Sit down, Arkan, I'm not finished."

"But *I* am. I want to go back to my cell now."

"Sit down!"

Arkan looked at him in surprise for a moment, then slid back into his chair.

"Thank you," Thomas said calmly. "I'm just trying to help the girl's mother find her. I don't give a shit what business you might have had with Slavros. That's not why I'm here. But I have to find the girl."

"But you're a police detective, right?"

"I'm on leave. Indefinitely. Without any plans to return. Some might say I'm currently unemployed. Hell, I may well end up on the dole," he added with a sympathetic smile.

"Why does the girl mean anything to you? Did you fuck her?"

"I've never met her."

"Are you fucking her mother?"

"I barely know her mother. An old friend of mine introduced her to me, and she told me about her problem."

"An ex-cop with a bleeding heart." Arkan snorted. "And I thought *I* was pathetic."

Thomas leaned back in his chair and regarded Arkan evenly. "Come on, Arkan, help me out here. The sooner I find the girl, the sooner I can go home to Denmark."

"Home to your family? Your wife and kids?"

"No. As you said, one cannot trust women. The truth is: I have to get home to my dog. He misses me."

Arkan raised his eyebrows. "What kind of dog do you have?"

"A poodle," Thomas said. "I don't know what it's called in Swedish."

"A poodle," Arkan said softly. "How old is your dog?"

"Two years old. His name is Møffe."

"So he's really just a puppy."

"Well, he certainly behaves like one."

"I had a poodle once. I've had many, actually, but Pelle, my last one, was something special."

Thomas smiled. "Where is Pelle now?"

"They killed him. Put him down when I was sent to prison," Arkan said sadly, his eyes staring into thin air. "And they say there's no death penalty in Sweden."

"Poor Pelle," said Thomas. He picked up the photo of Masja and returned it to his pocket. "If you really don't know the girl, then there's nothing to be done here. I'm sorry for wasting your time. It was nice to meet you, Arkan."

Arkan was startled out of his reverie. "There's no reason to keep Møffe waiting."

"What do you mean?"

"The girl. I remember her now. I think she was called something else, but I'm sure I've seen her."

"Okay. When? Where?"

"It's irrelevant, considering the fact that she's dead."

"Dead? Are you sure about that?"

Arkan nodded. "Listen, for various reasons, I cannot explain the circumstances, and if this should ever come out, I would deny any knowledge of this conversation, understood?"

"Of course. I just need a few details that I can take back home to her mother."

"The girl worked at one of my tanning salons. But I never met her personally," he said, averting his eyes. "She stole some of the profits. It was a great deal of money and Slavros was the one who was . . . responsible for her, so it was his obligation to punish her, as a lesson to the other girls."

"So he killed her?"

Arkan hesitated. "No, not her. He did something that was much worse."

"What is worse than death?"

"Arizona. Slavros took her to Arizona."

"Slavros took her to the United States?"

"Good Lord, no. He took her to Arizona Market. It's just north of Rinkeby and Hjulsta. Even the police stay the hell away from there. The Market is named after its Yugoslavian model."

"I'm afraid you'll have to explain that to me."

"During the civil war in the Balkans, there was an area where the borders between the countries converged, a neutral zone that was no larger than two or three football fields where a lively black market flourished among the combatants. Here you could trade everything from caviar, alcohol, weapons, drugs, and women to spare parts and canned goods. Everything was for sale—provided you had sufficient dollars. When the war ended, NATO forces razed the place to the ground. But the network remained. Serbians, Croats, Roma, Russians and Turks," Arkan said, pointing at himself. "We still work together, and since, other nations have joined in. Now every large European city has its own Arizona Market—London, Paris, Berlin, and Stockholm, for example. Contraband leaves the country from there. People are smuggled in and sold in auctions. A large proportion of weapons, goods and narcotics change hands. Rumour has it that some of the largest robberies in Scandinavia are planned from the Market."

"And what is Masja doing there?"

"Arizona Market is hell on earth, but even in hell the damned need a little entertainment. Slavros owns a brothel out there. Not a nice place—downright horrifying, to call it like it is. Slavros's place is a whorehouse for every kind of psychopath."

"And Masja works there?"

"*Worked.* Past tense. It happened years ago. There's no way she's still alive. Nobody lasts more than a couple of months in Arizona Market. She's gone, believe me. Loooong gone."

46

Arizona Market

Withdrawal symptoms made it difficult for Masja to hold the pen, and she had to grip onto it with all her strength, chiselling the words onto the soft paper notepad. Wearing a dirty nightdress, she was curled up on a narrow bunk under the only source of light, a naked bulb in the ceiling, in her claustrophobic room. The only other furnishing was a stinking basin in the corner that she and her clients used as a toilet. Screams and a constant tumult could be heard through the paper-thin walls of the rooms on either side. Masja had become accustomed to the noise, but to help her concentrate she clasped her free hand over one ear and hoped that the ruckus would be over soon.

2011, I think. I have no idea of the date, what season it is outside. I have lost all sense of time. Time is irrelevant here. We don't count the hours, but the number of ills we suffer between each period of sleep, which never lasts long. Sleep is always interrupted. I have not written since Slavros brought me here. Life before this place seems like a strange dream. Like a story that someone once told me. I cannot remember colours because it is so dark. I try to remember what music sounds like. All I hear are screams. It's hard to remember words. All I hear are groans. And men panting, in every mother tongue. I have stopped talking myself. At first, I spoke to the other girls through the walls. Not anymore. What is the point? What should we talk about? What should we dream about? What can comfort us? There is no hope. The scars on my wrists tell my story. I tried to run away. They stopped me. Tied me up. They check on me when I don't have clients. Check on their investment . . .

Mumija, you would no longer recognise me. I barely recognise myself. The heroin they give us sucks in my cheeks. My teeth are falling out. I am haggard. I am a shell. An empty sack. Only the heroin numbs the pain. I have so many clients. We are busy. We work like slaves. I think the cops have cleared the bulls off the streets of Stockholm and driven them out here to us instead.

Masja heard the rattling of a chain at her door. A key was inserted in the lock. She closed her notebook and hid it under her mattress. She wondered how many clients she would have that day. The door opened and a scruffy guy in baggy trousers and a hoodie appeared in the doorway. It was Kemal, one of the youngsters who ran errands for Slavros. He cast her a sandwich wrapped in clingfilm. "Eat," he said.

Masja picked up the sandwich. They always got the same thing to eat: cookies, sweets, Twix, sandwiches. Kemal probably stole from the kiosk at the railway station and kept the money that Slavros gave him to buy food for himself.

Kemal dug in his pocket and pulled out a crumpled ball of foil and tossed it at her. "Here, junkie."

Masja tried to catch it in the air, but it fell on the filthy floor, and she scrambled after it.

Kemal laughed. "You're hungry, huh?"

"I could really use one more, Kemal."

He shook his head lazily. "You know how it is."

Masja stuck out her hand to show him how much she was shaking. "You gave me shit last time. You have to give me another so the clients don't complain."

Kemal turned his head and checked the corridor. "What's in it for me?"

Ten minutes later, Kemal locked the door behind him. Masja got up from her bunk and put on her nightdress again. She laid the two nuggets of foil on the floor next to the sandwich and briefly listened to see if she could hear footsteps in the corridor outside. When she was satisfied that the coast was clear, she pulled the bunk away from the wall. With both hands she pried open a panel in the wall. A hollow the size of a matchbox revealed itself. She removed the ten nuggets that she had hidden inside. Little by little, she had saved what she needed. Now she had enough.

By sheer strength of will, she had collected a large dose. Her body had screamed for drugs. She had almost lost her mind. But the hardest part was letting them do whatever they wanted with her, as the withdrawal symptoms wracked her body. Twelve pieces would be enough for her exit.

Masja lit her candle and boiled the heroin. With precision and practised ease, she drew the drug into her syringe, wrapped the rubber tubing round her arm, found a vein she could shoot up, and finally pressed the plunger home.

The rush set in immediately and blew the room away. Masja felt warmth flooding through her veins. She was dimly aware of faltering light that danced before her eyelids, as if she were being carried away towards the light, which became increasingly sharp. She saw a frost-white sun filter through naked trees that were planted next to the road as she calmly floated by. She was seated in the passenger seat of an enormous car, leaning back with her feet up against the windscreen, her head resting on the driver's shoulder. A Wunder-Baum dangled from the rear-view mirror. Watching it sway made her dizzy. She tried to lift her head and look at the driver, but it was much too heavy. It was impossible to move a muscle, so she simply watched the landscape sailing by . . . trees and the sun so low in the sky, slowly disappearing below the horizon, leaving absolute darkness behind . . .

Masja opened her eyes, and her dream ended abruptly, as if the enormous car had crashed into one of the trees on the roadside. She gasped for breath, her body ached as if she'd been skinned alive, and Slavros was standing over her, his eyes like a wild animal's. He had an adrenaline injection in his hand. "Welcome back," he snarled. "It took a while to bring you around."

Masja backed as far away from him as she could, cowering in the corner of her bunk. Behind him stood Kemal and two other men. Blood was streaming from Kemal's nose. Probably Slavros's work. Clearly, he had been busy: broke a nose, procured an adrenaline shot, then resuscitated a junkie.

Slavros wiped the sweat from his brow. "Did you really think you could slip away so easily?!" he said, flinging the injection across the room. "You leave this world when I say so. Not a second before!"

He looked at her for a moment and grimaced. "Jesus, you look like hell. And you stink."

Masja looked down at her soiled mattress and filthy nightdress.

Slavros was in a quiet rage. "You used to be beautiful. There was something special about you. Like an angel. But you're no longer a good investment. It costs more money to keep you here than the cash you bring in. Do you realise that?" he said through gritted teeth.

"So just let me die."

"All in good time," he said, scratching his goatee. "I'm impressed that you have lasted for so long. You're an interesting experiment."

He bent over and gathered her syringe, lighter, candle stump, and scraps of silver foil and returned them to her little pouch. "It appears that I don't need to waste dope on you. Considering the fact that you survived just fine without it . . ."

"Slavros, I'm begging you . . ." She grabbed onto his arm.

He snatched it away and hushed her. "It's too late to pray to Slavros, or God, or anyone else. Do you understand? No one can hear you. You no longer exist."

47

Stockholm, 2013

Thomas walked through reception and took the stairs up to the second floor, which was the hub of *Rikspolisen*'s Criminal Division: the IT-Investigative Unit. He was soaked to the bone after getting caught in a downpour on his way over from the Metro station. Heading home for the day, police officers filed down the stairs, and Thomas found himself jostling his way up against the stream. Occasionally, an officer gave him a suspicious look, as if wondering what business this drenched and shabby man with the long beard could have in the heart of Sweden's national security facility.

By the time Thomas entered the double doors of the IT Unit, he was out of breath. Only a few investigators were still in the office. Karl Luger was one of them. He was standing with his coat on, next to his desk, obviously ready to leave, as he dumped brown case files into his briefcase for the evening's home office session.

"I'm glad I caught you," said Thomas.

Karl looked up in surprise. "Ravn? How on earth did you get past reception?"

Thomas cleared his throat. "I showed my badge and said I had a meeting with you."

"A meeting?"

"Well, it's more like a debriefing to keep you in the loop. I thought you might like an update after my meeting with Arkan."

"You could have just called," Karl said tonelessly as he snapped his briefcase shut.

"Do you still have the CCTV footage from the day that prostitute was killed at Stockholm Central?"

"No, I doubt that very much. Why?"

"Because I'm almost certain that the other girl on the platform was Masja."

"Did Arkan say so?" Deputy Investigator Lindgren asked from his desk behind them.

"Between the lines," said Thomas, glancing at Lindgren before fixing his gaze on Karl. "Who could have access to those tapes?"

"Listen," Karl said, taking his black leather gloves out of his coat pocket. "We watched the footage at Security at Stockholm Central. I'm pretty sure that those tapes have been wiped out ages ago."

"Didn't you take the tapes into custody as material evidence?"

"No," said Karl, looking at his computer. "No charges were raised after all. And even if Masja does appear on those tapes, it doesn't really prove anything, does it?"

"It would prove that she was alive at that time. That she was here, in Stockholm. And that she might have information about Slavros."

"Circumstances which took place more than two years ago," said Karl.

"Even so," Thomas insisted. He was having trouble understanding where Karl's apparent reluctance was coming from. "Arkan also mentioned where Masja could have disappeared to."

"And where might that be?" asked Karl.

"A place called Arizona Market. It's a place where—"

"Thank you," Karl said, raising his hand. "I know the place. But even if Arkan is telling the truth, several years have passed since then."

"He *is* telling the truth. He described the Market to me in detail. And Masja's life is in danger. He tells me that the girls don't last very long out there."

"I'm not aware that there is or was a brothel at Arizona," said Karl. He glanced over at Lindgren, who looked up from his screen and shook his head. "Not that I know of either," he said. "But Arizona is a hellhole."

"So what are we waiting for? Why don't we go there and check it out?" Thomas said, pointing at the door as if he meant *right now*, which prompted a smile from Karl.

"We only go out there if absolutely necessary and, as a rule, under severe political pressure."

"This could prove to be important for all parties concerned," Thomas pointed out.

Karl ignored him. "We never go into Arizona without a Special Ops team for back-up. That is to say, approximately a hundred and fifty men in full combat gear, armed with tear gas, batons and dogs. And afterwards, we have the particular displeasure of mobilising forces in Rinkeby and Hjulsta—and all the other neighbourhoods—where containers are set on fire by protesting local gangs who believe that their interests are threatened by our actions. Last time we raided Arizona, it took our team an entire week—which is roughly six thousand man-hours—before we regained some semblance of order in the community."

"Actually, what I have in mind is more of a quiet Recon Op, just you and me—sans tie and briefcase," he said, pointing to both items on Karl's person as he spoke.

A snigger escaped from Lindgren, and from the corner of his eye, Thomas could see that the deputy was shaking his head.

"Ravn, my days in the field are over," said Karl.

"Geez, you sound like a burnt-out ol' man," Thomas said with a smile.

"No, a realistic one. In fact, we catch more bad guys on our laptops than we do running around on the streets. Isn't that right, Lindgren?"

"It's like playing video games, sir." Lindgren laughed. "And *we're* the ones with the highest score."

"I don't give a shit about the bad guys. I just want to find Masja."

Thomas took his guidebook out of his pocket and unfolded the map of Stockholm. "Could you at least show me where I can find this place?"

Karl frowned and looked at him sceptically. "Do you really want to go out there on your own?"

"Damn right, I do."

"Have fun," Lindgren quipped sarcastically.

Karl squinted at the map, which Thomas held up in front of his face. "It . . . it's not on this map," he replied reluctantly. "It's further out of town. You have to go beyond Rinkeby and Hjulsta, past the scrapyard. I think the T-Rail can take you most of the way. But I strongly advise that you do *not* go out there."

Thomas closed the guidebook and put it back into his pocket. "The scrapyard? The same location where the murdered girls were found?"

"Yes. Why?"

"Is there a connection between Arizona and these cases?"

"Not that I know of," said Karl. "Ravn, I need to go now. I'm already late. It's my turn to take Louisa to her dance class."

"Could there be a connection?"

"No. There is nothing connecting the murders to Arizona. For God's sake, these cases have been investigated more than the assassination of Prime Minister Olof Palme."

"Whose murderer you still haven't found," Thomas reminded him.

"Okay, bad example. But, as I said, there is no reason to believe that the murderer has any connection to Arizona."

"What about the victims? Do you have a profile on them?"

Karl glanced at his watch. "Caucasian girls between the ages of eighteen and twenty-two. Neither their DNA nor their fingerprints have given us any indication of a connection. We've had intense collaboration with Europol, without any success in identifying them."

Lindgren scraped back his chair and got to his feet. "I'm leaving now. See you tomorrow, Karl," he said, and pushed his chair back under the table.

Karl nodded in Lindgren's direction impatiently.

"Do you have any idea why the murderer paints the corpses white?" Ravn asked.

"He doesn't paint them; he chalks them. And no, we don't," said Lindgren, pulling on his long winter coat. "And it's not really a corpse, as such."

"What do you mean?"

Lindgren was silent and glanced at Karl, as if he'd already said too much.

"The perpetrator stuffs his victims, tans their skins and preserves the corpses," said Karl. "He appears to choose his victims among prostitutes, girls who nobody will miss anyway."

"The kind of girls you'll find in Arizona, according to Arkan," said Ravn.

"As I said: We have never found any prostitutes in our raids out there. So perhaps Arkan has told you a wild story."

"Perhaps, but I doubt it. He seemed truthful on this point. Could Masja be one of the victims?"

"No . . . or rather, she could be, in principle, because the murders occurred during the period that she was involved in the sex trade in the Stockholm area."

"Do you have pictures of the victims?"

"That's classified information," replied Lindgren.

"Classified? Are you kidding me? Those pictures were published in the press." Thomas smiled at Karl. "Give me a break, Karl. Won't you just let me take a peek at the case files? Please."

"Ravn, for the tenth time, I'm going to be late for my daughter."

"At least you have a daughter to be late for!" Thomas snapped. His voice was so loud it rang out in the large office. Both Karl and Lindgren started in surprise.

"I'm sorry," said Thomas. "I just want to find the girl and bring her home to her mother and . . . and deliver Slavros to you on a silver platter. Instigate a little inter-Scandinavian police collaboration," he added with a conciliatory smile.

Neither Karl nor Lindgren returned the gesture.

"After your last visit, I called Station City and spoke to a Chief Inspector by the name of Brask—your boss, I believe. He told me that you were on leave."

Thomas scratched the back of his head. "Did he mention why?"

"Personal reasons, he said. Stress. Perhaps it's time you went home, Ravn, instead of looking for some girl. I'm sure your family misses you just as much as mine misses me."

Thomas bit the inside of his cheek. "Please. If you could just show me the pictures of the victims, then I'll be out of your hair."

Karl shook his head and let out a deep sigh as he put his briefcase down on his desk. Then he opened the file cabinet behind Lindgren's desk and leafed through the files till he found the report from the Forensic Institute. One after another, he slapped the photographs of the dead girls onto the desk, as if a deck of cards in a macabre game of solitaire. "You can exclude the first two victims, because they were killed back in 2009."

Thomas studied two of the limewashed victims. Their agonised expressions made them look surprisingly similar, as if they were twins. The marble-white skin blotted out any semblance of life that might otherwise have remained.

"They look like statues," said Thomas.

"The press called them 'white angels,'" said Lindgren.

"One possible theory is that the perpetrator is motivated by extreme misogyny and therefore desecrates the women's bodies in this manner before dumping them on the scrapyard," said Karl.

"How does he kill them?"

"We have a theory that he poisons them intravenously by injection into the groin," said Lindgren, pointing out the needle marks on close-ups of the victims. "Forensic experts found traces of hydrogen peroxide, formalin, glycerine, zinc, and hydrochloric acid in their bodily tissue. A highly toxic cocktail."

"That sounds quite intricate. Any idea why?"

"Some of the ingredients Lindgren mentioned are habitually used to embalm a corpse," Karl said.

Thomas picked up one of the photos in order to study it more closely.

"But didn't you say that he stuffs the bodies, and only uses the tanned skins?"

"Yes, but . . ."

"In that case the preservation technique hardly seems necessary."

"No, it's not. We have no explanation or plausible motive for the way he chooses to kill his victims. Other than the assumption that he is severely mentally disturbed."

"Any suspects?"

Karl shook his head. "None, unfortunately. I think I must have interviewed every single living taxidermist in Sweden."

"As well as a string of pathologists, without getting any closer to our perpetrator," Lindgren added.

"What about Slavros? Could he suffer from this kind of psychosis?"

"As I said: We haven't found any connection between Arizona Market and the victims. Nor, for that matter, any connection to Slavros."

Karl looked at the pictures. "Is Masja among the victims?"

Thomas shook his head. "No, fortunately not."

"I really have to go now," said Karl, gathering up the photographs again.

"Thank you very much for your help," said Thomas.

Karl nodded. "Get home safely to Copenhagen, Ravn."

It sounded like an order rather than a farewell.

48

Arizona Market

Masja opened her eyes. The room was completely dark. She had no idea how long she had been sleeping. It could have been minutes, a quarter of an hour or more. Time was non-existent.

She could sense someone else in the room. Her body tensed and she retreated into the corner. Usually, she could hear the bulls coming. It was almost as if she could sense their approach long before they reached the stairs to the cellar, and she was prepared by the time they opened her door, all feelings locked away before they touched her.

Masja fumbled for the light switch, but when she pressed it, nothing happened.

"It doesn't seem to work. I tried it a moment ago," a man's voice said in the dark.

He sat down on the bunk, and she automatically shrank away from him. "I don't mind though. I like the dark."

"Okay. We can leave the light off," she said. Withdrawal symptoms made her body shake uncontrollably. She felt as if she was freezing and sweating all at once. She couldn't wait to get it over with so the bull would leave. "Don't you want to take your clothes off?" Masja asked.

"I think I'd just like to sit here for a while, if that's all right with you," he said.

"Do whatever you-you want," she said through chattering teeth.

"Are you okay?"

"Yep."

"I could get you a glass of water?"

"No, thank you. I don't think water will help."

"I have a couple of pills. And you can have a sip from my hip flask if you like."

"Hip flask?" It was a strange word that Masja had never heard before. She strained her eyes in the dark, but the man was merely a shadow near the wall. "I could use something to give me a kick," she said.

The man took out the pills and gave them to her. She caught a whiff of his citrus aftershave, which surprised her. Usually, the bulls reeked of alcohol and tobacco, vomit, and sex. She swallowed the pills and took a gulp from the little leather-bound flask that he had given her. *Brandy.*

"I'm sorry. I think I might have drunk it all by mistake," she said, returning the empty flask. "It was good, thank you."

"That's all right."

Masja started to cough violently, and he clapped her gently on the back. "You sound unwell."

"I can't remember ever feeling healthy."

The man took a deep breath and exhaled. "I'm not surprised with the damp in here. You're breathing fungi directly into your lungs."

"I think bad air is the least of my problems," she said with a sniffle.

"Do you protect yourself? Forgive me if talking about this makes you uncomfortable."

"It's okay. And yes, I take care of myself as best I can."

He gently reached out for her arm.

At first, she thought he wanted to hold her hand, but then she felt his thumb on her wrist.

"What are you doing?"

"I'm trying to take your pulse, but it's very weak. If you turn your back to me, I can listen to your lungs."

"Are you a doctor?"

"No."

He put his hands on her shoulders carefully and turned her back to face him. "Breathe in deeply for me," he said, resting his ear against her spine. She started to cough again.

"I wouldn't be surprised if you have pneumonia, perhaps even tuberculosis. Do you cough blood?"

"All the time."

He felt along her arms, her hollow chest and thin legs. His touch was clinical, not groping like the bulls did. "What is your body fat percentage?"

"My what?"

"Your body fat percentage. My guess is less than ten. What do you get to eat in here?"

"I don't know. A sandwich now and again. Some sweets or a chocolate bar. I don't really eat that much. Tell me, have you been here before?"

"It's important that you get enough liquids. Drink lots of water. So you don't dry out."

"You make me sound like a plant." She snorted a laugh. The pills and the brandy were making her feel light-headed. Masja leaned forward to get a closer look at him, but she couldn't see his expressions in the dark. "Hey, you, I asked if you've been here before?" she said, gently slapping him on the chest.

"No. When did you start cutting back on the drugs?"

"Cutting back?" She snorted with laughter again. "Cold turkey is more like it."

"Okay. So when did you stop taking them?"

"I haven't touched anything for several days, I think. Where did we meet, then? I'm sure we've met somewhere before. Was it at Key Club?"

"I've never been to that dive. So you've only been clean a couple of days?" he asked, sounding disappointed. "Then we'll have to give it more time."

"Time? What do you mean?"

"For the withdrawal symptoms to subside. Till your body stops shaking uncontrollably."

"Yes, that will take a while yet. Why do you ask?"

"Because it disturbs the process," he said, and stood up.

"What do you mean? What process? Tell me where we've met before. I recognise your voice."

"Impressive, after such a long time. I almost take that as a compliment."

Masja tried the light switch again, even checked to see if the bulb was loose, but she could not get the light to work. "Tell me where we met. Right now."

"It was last Christmas. On Malmskillnadsgatan. It was freezing cold."

"It was always cold on Malm."

"I'd been looking for a girl like you. For a long time. And then suddenly there you were, shining among all the others. I couldn't take my eyes off you. I must have parked there for hours, just watching you. I have never been so reckless before. So stupid. At last, you came over to me. I think you had been standing in the cold for so long that you'd decided to take the chance. You came over to my car. I opened the passenger window, and you stuck your head through. We spoke. Very briefly."

"What kind of car do you have?" she asked, her voice trembling.

"I could see that you weren't ready yet. You were too plump. And much too stubborn. Do you remember I said I would be back . . . that I thought you had the potential? That you were not one of the fallen angels."

"What kind of car do you have?! Answer me!"

"Mercedes SEL."

"Black?"

"Yes, 1972 model. It's a true classic. You remember now?"

Masja moved as far away from the man as she could. Crawled into the far corner and balled her fists. "Don't you dare touch me. If something happens to me, Slavros will kill you."

"Are you sure about that?"

"He never lets anyone touch his . . . investment. You're a dead man."

"Has it not occurred to you that Slavros might be the one who has summoned me from the dark?"

Masja couldn't speak. Couldn't even breathe.

"We'll see each other again soon. Once the withdrawal symptoms are over. Remember to drink lots of water so your skin is taut. Hydration makes your skin more supple. That is very important. It is essential to the process."

The man turned and made for the door. Unlocked it.

Masja stared at him in terror. The bulls did not have keys, only Slavros and his men did. Which meant that he was telling the truth. *Slavros wanted to get rid of her.*

The man stepped out into the corridor. In the dim light she caught a glimpse of his dark hair and smart grey suit. Then he locked the door behind him.

49

Stockholm, 2013

It was 11:30 p.m., and Thomas was sitting in the last car in the T-Rail to Hjulsta. Apart from three Somali youngsters in hip-hop clothing and colourful caps worn back to front, he had the entire place to himself. One of the boys was writing something on the wall with a black pen, while his pals lounged in their seats, smoking their cigarettes as they listened to booming music with intermittent bouts of static on their headphones. Once in a while, the immigrant boys would stare him down, as if marking their territory. This was *their* train, *their* kingdom. For his own part, this was actually the first time since he'd landed in Stockholm that Thomas felt at home. As if it were here, in the last car of the T-Bana that stank of piss as the train hurtled through the night at 110 kilometres per hour, that Stockholm had finally bid him welcome. Thomas smiled to himself. It felt like the good old days when he and Mikkel used to patrol the streets in civvies, unshaven, hoodies flipped up, hunting the bad guys . . . They didn't just *own* the street; they *were* the street. Maybe his mind was simply conjuring up a false sense of security for his trip to Arizona Market, but it sure felt good.

The brakes screeched and the train slowed down as it pulled into Rinkeby Station. The Somali boys got up and swaggered over to the door. The one who had been writing on the walls raised the pen and aimed it at Thomas in a threatening gesture. Then the door opened, and the boy uttered a litany of abuse in his direction before jumping off the train. Thomas didn't flinch.

He remained on the train through Tensta and got off at the final station at Hjulsta. The station was located right in the middle of a residential complex, and the area in front of the station building was humming with people. He walked past a shopping arcade where a grocery store and grill stand were still open for business, despite the lateness of the hour. According to Karl's directions, he had to walk down Tenstavägen and follow the almost one-kilometre-long walking bridge, which crossed over private gardens to the industrial area on the other side.

Twenty-five minutes later, Thomas was standing at the foot of a high wire fence around a Schenker industrial railway terminal. The wind had picked up and he was freezing cold. Something told him that he might have taken a wrong turn somewhere, and he chided himself for not asking Karl for more precise directions to Arizona. But he decided to continue walking down the dark road instead of turning back. He came past two metre-high gates that marked the entrance into the scrapyard. Large projector lights lit up the mounds of twisted metal that towered up to the night sky. Thomas reckoned that this must be where the murdered girls were found. He paused for a moment and studied the layout of the scrapyard. Two vicious-looking guard dogs came charging up to the fence, barking madly and frothing at the mouth. They jumped up against the fence and Thomas involuntarily took a few steps back. It could not have been easy to get the corpses inside, least of all six times in a row. This suggested to Thomas that the perpetrator must have some local knowledge of the area—perhaps he even frequented the area on a daily basis. If this had been *his* case, he wouldn't have wasted time questioning the taxidermists. He would have looked for a perpetrator who was familiar with the location. A man who felt secure on the grounds. Someone who enjoyed finding his victims in the slums, stuffing them in a garage nearby, and then dumping them on a rubbish heap. But this was not his case.

Thomas reached the end of the road, which was a dead end, apart from a narrow gravel path that led to a nearby forest. He caught a glimpse of pine trees swaying in the wind. A rumbling noise made him turn around, and he saw a large truck with its headlights turned off come round the corner. It was driving at such speed that the trailer at the back almost tipped over. Thomas stared after the cloud of dust in its wake before the truck was swallowed by the night.

Thomas smiled to himself. He had found the way to Arizona.

About 200 metres into the dark forest, Thomas could see the glow of a bonfire. He approached carefully. A group of men, apparently of Slavic descent, were standing around the fire in front of two low-slung barracks. One of them took an empty crate from a stack nearby and threw it on the fire. The wood burst into flame, sending sparks into the sky. A bottle of vodka was being passed around, and the men were stamping their feet and rubbing their arms as if trying to ward off the freezing cold. Thomas cast a look over his shoulder. A row of pickup trucks were parked along the outer walls of a narrow alley to his right. He headed that way, nodding at the men by the bonfire as he went, but no one took any notice of him.

He came past two pit bulls that were chained to the tailgate of the first truck. The smaller of the two dogs was bleeding badly from its ear and looked as if it had been in a fight. The pit bulls growled at him, and Thomas deliberately crossed to the other side of the alley.

Thomas arrived in front of an open gate, in fact the massive doors of a ship container vessel, which had been bolted into the brick walls surrounding the complex. Just inside the grounds he came to a crumbling warehouse of some sort. The window panes were broken and on the side wall was a red sign with the letters *Johanneson's Bygg AB* in black paint. He continued down the alley, bypassing the adjacent grounds. From the dilapidated state of the premises on either side, he surmised that the buildings belonged to enterprises that had long since gone bankrupt.

There was a bend up ahead where the alley narrowed. The high walls on either side formed a bottleneck, and it appeared as if straight ahead was the only way into Arizona Market. Perhaps this was why someone had felt inspired to spray paint the words *sniper alley* on the wall, Thomas observed.

Loud techno music was coming from a building further down the alley on his right. Directly to his left another group of men was crowded around four or five parked trucks. A lively trade of alcohol and cigarettes was going on from the ramps of the respective vehicles. Most of the traders appeared to be Russian or dealers from the Middle East.

Thomas heard the loud whine of a blowtorch coming from an auto workshop just up ahead. He glanced through the open gate. A long line of luxury cars were parked in a makeshift garage: Mercedes, BMWs, and a single Maserati. Sparks from the blowtorch were flying as the men worked, and Thomas guessed that the cars were probably stolen and that their chassis numbers were being changed before the vehicles were delivered to their new owners in Eastern Europe.

As Thomas continued past the workshop, he caught sight of the big truck that came rumbling past him earlier. Large cardboard boxes with Samsung and Sony logos on the side were being unloaded from the trailer and reloaded into the holds of two waiting trucks whose engines were running. Stockholmers with the right connections could wake up to great deals on a brand-new flatscreen the next morning.

Approximately halfway down the alley, he arrived at a clearing in front of two low-slung barracks adjacent to each other. The loud techno music he had heard was coming from the open door of the front barrack. Thomas sauntered over and went inside. No more than ten men were sitting on benches that stretched from one side of the room to the other. Topless women with large breasts were serving them jugs of beer. The tables between them were overflowing with rifles and handguns, amidst a clutter of vodka bottles, beer jugs, cartons of cigarettes, and hard cash.

Thomas slipped out the door and walked over to the adjacent barrack. The second building had a similar layout to the first, apart from the fact that the benches were replaced with rows of white plastic chairs that faced a makeshift stage, where two anorexic-looking girls in shabby corsets embraced one another in a pathetic dance. The girls rocked from side to side and appeared to be oblivious to the boos from the audience.

Thomas made his way to the bar at the far end of the room and ordered a beer. The bartender was a dark-skinned young guy with a green hoodie obscuring his face. He filled a jug from the beer tap and plonked it on the counter in front of him.

"I'd also like a glass with that, thanks," said Thomas.

The bartender took a sticky glass off the shelf closest to him and put it down next to the jug. "Two hundred," he said.

Thomas paid for his jug. Despite the green hoodie, he could see that the guy had recently been in a fight. His nose was swollen and sat slightly skew on his face. "Quiet night," said Thomas, pouring himself a glass.

Hoodie took a step back and leaned against the wall without further reply.

"Any other girls coming on tonight, apart from those two?" Thomas said, pointing at the girls on the stage.

Hoodie shrugged in reply.

The beer was flat and tasted like piss, but Thomas managed to drink half his jug before the girls finally stripped out of their respective corsets and wrapped up their performance. When they stumbled off the stage, some of the men in the audience threw beer after them, and the girls took cover behind the bar as fast as they could. Shortly afterwards, a plump middle-aged woman took to the stage. Plastered out of her mind, the woman teetered from one end of the stage to the other in a solo performance, not unlike a circus bear on a bike, and the audience jeered again.

Thomas hung around at the bar, waiting to see if other girls would take over, but when the woman had, with great difficulty, managed to strip out of her clothing, the anorexic girls from before took to the stage again. He abandoned the rest of his beer and went to the second barrack, where the techno music was still blaring relentlessly from the loudspeakers. More people had arrived, and the benches were almost full now. As one of the topless waitresses came past, he ordered a jug of beer and asked offhand if Masja was working tonight.

"No idea," the waitress said, giving him a vacant look.

"You don't know Masja, or you don't know if she's here?"

The waitress stared at him through a mask of heavy make-up that made her look like a zombie. "Who the hell are you?!"

"Just a friend," Thomas said, slipping her three 100-krona bills.

The waitress stuffed the bills into her G-string. "What you see is what you get," she said, pointing around the room. "But if you give me two hundred more, we can figure something out," she added with an arched eyebrow.

"Where?" he said, hoping to find out if there was someplace else the girls took their clients, a place where Masja might be.

The waitress shrugged. "You got a car, right?" she said and sashayed back to the bar. Thomas did not wait for her to return with his beer.

Outside again, he saw nothing that remotely resembled a brothel. But Masja had to be around here somewhere. Then again, it was such a long time ago, and he had to agree with Arkan: No one could survive out here for that long.

He caught sight of Hoodie having a smoke in a corner, texting on his phone. Thomas decided to approach him. He had no other option but to take a risk with this guy. "I'm looking for a girl," he said.

Without looking up from his phone, Hoodie pointed to the stage.

"A particular girl," Thomas said.

Hoodie tapped the ash off the end of his cigarette. "Uh-huh."

"There's money in it for you."

"Uh-huh."

"A lot of money."

"Uh-huh."

"Five thousand."

Hoodie looked up. "Five thousand?"

Thomas nodded. "What's your name?"

"Kemal."

"Okay, Kemal. I'm looking for a pretty girl called Masja."

Kemal laughed, his teeth a flash of white in the dim room. "Then you've come to the wrong place, man. There are no pretty girls here and no one called Masja. We only get the ones from the bottom of the heap—all the junkies. But for that price you can have any girl you want—hell, you can get those two at once for that same price," he said, nodding in the direction of the stage. "And you can do whatever you want with them."

"No, thanks. Five thousand, if you can find Masja for me." Thomas took out the photograph.

Kemal lit up the photograph with his display and took a look at it: "Wow, she sure was beautiful once."

"What do you mean? Do you recognise her?"

Kemal nodded. "But she's not so beautiful anymore."

"That's irrelevant. Where is she?"

"Where's my five thousand?"

"You'll get the money when you bring Masja to me."

"If you give me two thousand up front, I'll see what I can do."

Thomas hesitated.

"She'll do whatever you ask, man. We train them well. You won't be disappointed." Kemal's pearly whites shone in the dark again. Thomas was much, much more inclined to knock out the guy's teeth and stuff them down his throat, but he stuck his hand in his pocket and pulled out two 1,000-krona bills.

"Wait here," said Kemal. With another white flash he snatched the bills from Thomas and disappeared around the back of the second barrack.

Thomas's heart was hammering in his chest. He looked around the parking lot in front of him. More men had arrived. He cursed himself for not thinking this through properly. He patted down his pocket to make sure that he still had the postcard from Masja's mother. He'd just give her the card. Then his mission would be over, he told himself. But he knew damn well there was no way he was going to leave her behind, especially after he'd seen this hellhole. This could only end badly. *Really fucking badly*. He briefly considered calling Karl Luger. Getting him to send the entire fucking Stockholm cavalry. It would be worth their while if Masja's testimony could bury the gangster, this guy . . . Vladimir Slav—

The door behind him opened and Thomas spun on his heel.

Kemal had returned with three other guys. Thomas recognised the one with the ponytail and the devil goatee: It was Vladimir Slavros in person.

50

Thomas watched the men take up positions around him, blocking all means of escape. He concentrated on his breathing and clenched his fists in his pockets. Slavros regarded him with a cool expression on his face as he fingered his black goatee. He cocked his neck, cracking his cervical joints like an old boxer getting ready for a fight.

"I heard you're interested in one of my girls," he said.

"Yes," said Thomas. "That's quite a show you're putting on in there," he said, nodding in the direction of the barrack behind Slavros. "So I think a little good company would not go astray."

"Are you Danish?"

Thomas nodded. "Originally, yes."

"Do you live nearby?"

"Södermalm," Thomas said, trying to smile.

"Kemal says you're looking for a particular girl?"

"Masja, yes, I couldn't see her in there. Is she here tonight?"

Slavros took a step towards him. "Where do you know her from?"

"From Key Club, Kitty Club, of course. Great place."

"So why are you here?"

Thomas swallowed the spit that had gathered in his mouth. "Someone or other told me that she'd come out here, but perhaps that's bullshit?"

"Someone or other?"

"Yes, I don't remember exactly who it was," said Thomas with a nonchalant shrug. "Is she here?"

"And what if she is?"

"Then I'd really like to see her. I've already paid the lad."

"Kemal said you offered him five thousand. That's a lot of money for a hooker."

Thomas nodded. "Yeah, but she's something special."

"Well, then I'd better give you what you came for," said Slavros. Without warning he planted a well-placed blow to his liver. Thomas doubled over. He was having a hard time staying on his feet, and the next blow, which hit him on the chin, sent him flying backwards.

Slavros bent over him and grabbed onto his collar. "I can spot a liar a mile away," he hissed. "If there is one thing I cannot stand, it's a liar. And you are one of the biggest fucking liars I have ever met." He hauled Thomas back onto his feet only to headbutt him down.

Thomas brought a hand to his brow and felt the blood seep through his fingers.

"Search him, Mikhail," said Slavros, smoothing down his own meticulous black leather jacket.

Thomas felt one of the men searching his pockets. The man found his wallet, mobile phone, keys, the postcard from Masja's mother, and finally, his police badge.

Mikhail turned the badge in his fingers, as if he couldn't believe his eyes. Then he looked up at Slavros. "This guy's a fucking cop."

Slavros ripped the badge out of Mikhail's hand and stared at it. "Is this real? Is it?!" he yelled, taking another swing at Thomas.

"Yes," he said. "Of course it's real."

"I told you I could spot a liar when I saw one. So much for coming from Södermalm . . . Where are you from?"

"Copenhagen. I work for Station City, Crime Ops Division."

"And what is the Copenhagen Police doing on my doorstep?"

Thomas slowly picked himself up from the ground. The blow to his liver still hurt like hell, his vision was blurred and he felt as if he might throw up any minute. "We're working with *Rikspolisen*," he replied as convincingly as he could.

"You look very much as if you're on your own out here, pal," Slavros said with a smile, looking around.

"We both know that if we needed it to be more than one, we would be here with an entire Special Ops team."

"So you're just the scout?"

"Scout and back-up. Right now, I'm the whole team. But one call from me can change that in an instant."

"Is that so?" Slavros fingered his diabolical goatee again. "So, what do you want with the girl?"

"We have raised serious charges against her in Denmark," Thomas lied. "It's my job to bring her back home."

"And the Swedish police are helping you with this?"

"Of course."

Slavros's fist hit him in the face and sent him to the ground with a taste of blood in his mouth. Then a boot landed in his stomach, knocking the air out of him.

"How stupid do you think I am?! Don't you realise who I am?" he raged, kicking Thomas again. "Do you seriously think I don't know *exactly* what is going on in my operation? Where every cop is at any given moment. Which one of my whores they are fucking and when. Which raid will be sanctioned and when. I know *everything.* Which is why I also know that you are full of shit, and that you don't have any back-up. You should have stayed in pathetic little Denmark instead of wasting my time," he spat, giving Thomas one more kick in the ribs.

Slavros stepped back to catch his breath and pat down his hair. "I cannot understand why you would lie to me—twice in a row for that matter. Do you really think that wouldn't have any consequences for you? Are you really that stupid? So arrogant, so fucking *Danish* that you think you can get away with it?"

Thomas spat out the blood that had gathered in his mouth and looked up at Slavros. "Think whatever you want, but I would advise you to let me go."

Slavros shook his head incredulously. "Fetch the dogs."

"Fucking hell, Slavros, this guy is a cop," Mikhail replied.

"So what? Are you afraid of that Mickey Mouse badge he carries around with him? Fetch the dogs, I said—now!"

Mikhail immediately did as he was told.

Thomas tried to get up, but Slavros put a foot on his chest and held him down. "Not so fast. Why don't you tell me the truth so we can avoid the bloody mess, not to mention listening to you scream when my dogs start tearing you apart?"

"If you don't let me go, the entire Stockholm police force is going to come out here."

"What makes you so sure of that?" Slavros shook his head again.

Mikhail returned with two pit bull terriers that were straining on their chains. Both dogs were frothing at the mouth, and their yellow eyes looked rabid in their black faces. Slavros took over the dogs and gave them a few inches on their chains till their fangs were snapping right in front of Thomas's face.

Thomas shrank away from the pit bulls, but Slavros's men blocked his path.

"These boys can peel the skin off a man's face in less than twenty seconds. They're quicker and more effective than piranha, in fact," he said, giving another inch on the leashes.

Thomas felt the jaws of one of the dogs clamp over his shin and pull him backwards. The other one went for his head with teeth bared, and Thomas shielded his face with his arm. The dog bit into his hand, but Slavros yanked on the chain, and it reluctantly let go.

"Last chance, you Danish pig, what do you want with the girl?"

Thomas gripped his hand, which was bleeding badly. "I just want to get her home. Home to her mother."

"Very noble of you. But it's a lie, just like everything else you've said. Why does she have to go back to Denmark? What kind of charges do you guys have against her?"

"There are no charges."

"You're full of shit. I know everything about Denmark. You pigs have been after Kaminsky for years. Does this have anything to do with him? Anything to do with me?"

"No. I promised to deliver a message to Masja, that's all. Give her that postcard if I found her."

He pointed to the card that Mikhail had thrown on the ground. Slavros bent down and picked it up. He saw the two kittens on the front and turned it round. Read the text on the back and crumpled it up in his fist and threw it down. "Very touching, but none of this changes the fact that you're a pig. Don't try to deny that you are pursuing a case against me."

"I'm on leave. And no, I'm not denying it. I'm sure that charges have been raised against you here in Sweden, in Denmark, and the rest of Europe. And I'm sure there are many a police corps out there who would like to see you behind bars, but none of that has anything to do with me. All I want is to see the girl so I can give her the message. Then I'll be gone."

"You're on leave? Why?"

"Stress. It doesn't matter why."

"You don't look like the stressed type. Why are you on leave?"

"None of your business," Thomas said, and looked away. The dogs growled at him.

"Do you want to keep your face or not?"

Thomas looked at the pit bulls, then at Slavros. He spat blood. This time, mostly with disdain. "Do you really want to know?"

"More than anything else."

"Okay, because some loser broke into my home and killed my wife while I was on duty. That's why."

"Did you catch him?"

"No, the fucker is still running around scot-free. Satisfied?"

Slavros looked down at him, rubbing his goatee as he tightened his grip on the dogs' chains. Then he laughed in Thomas's face. "That is the most pathetic story I have ever heard. But at least now you're telling the truth. God must be really pissed at you," he said, cackling to himself as he handed the dogs' chains over to Mikhail, who hauled them away.

"Can I see Masja now?" Thomas asked, slowly getting to his feet.

"No."

"Why not?"

"Because I say so. And because she's not here anymore."

"Do you know where she is?"

Slavros shook his head. "No, the girls don't stay here very long."

"You have no idea where she could be?"

"Your guess is as good as mine. Forget her. For your own good. Now piss off while you still can. And don't come back, Danish-Pig."

"You heard Slavros," a voice behind Thomas said. A hard shove in the spine helped him on his way and Thomas stumbled back to the road.

51

Masja heard footsteps outside her door and pulled the blanket up under her nose. The blanket was her only protection, and she was completely at his mercy. The man who had chosen her to be his next prey. But when the door opened, it was Slavros, who came in with Mikhail and Kemal.

A little while ago, she had heard Slavros's dogs barking wildly, and she had wondered who they had attacked this time. Probably another drunkard who had pissed off Slavros and was now torn to pieces for his trouble.

Slavros grimaced and held his nose. "Fucking hell, doesn't anyone ever clean this place? It stinks worse than a latrine in here."

Kemal shrugged. "The clients don't care."

Slavros came over to the bunk and looked down at Masja.

"She looks more dead than alive," said Mikhail, standing just behind Slavros. "But she's still breathing. And she's becoming a problem. She knows too much. I can get rid of her for you. The dogs are still hungry. And whatever is left of her can be buried in the woods."

"And cheat the Hyena out of his meal? When are you going to use your head, Mikhail?"

"I'm sick of that psycho. We ought to get rid of him as well."

"Seriously?" Slavros shook his head. "One look at my dogs reminds me: Never bite the hand that feeds you," he said, and cracked his neck.

"Or, when it comes to the Hyena: the one who protects you. When did he say he would be back?"

"When she no longer has withdrawal symptoms," Kemal replied. "He said something about it 'disrupting the princess,' but I don't know what he means by that."

"The *process*, you idiot, 'disrupting the process.' The man is an artist," said Slavros. He kicked the bunk bed so hard that Masja jolted. "Do you still have symptoms, you whore? Do you?!"

Masja made no reply, just stared at him with a blank expression.

"She looks fine to me. Call him. Tell him she's ready. I want her out of my face," said Slavros.

Once they had gone, Masja pulled her notebook out from under the mattress and sharpened the stump of her pencil against the brick wall. The lead crumbled between her fingers. There was not much left, but it didn't matter. She didn't have that much more to write, and no time left to do it. The Hyena would come for her now, like he did for the other girls. At least they would find her body. She knew that much. It would come in the news, and maybe her fate would be published in the papers. Perhaps it would bring her mother some peace to know what had happened to her.

If you still remember me, *Mumija*, forgive me.

52

Stockholm, 2013

Soft bossa nova music came from the loudspeakers in the ceiling of the men's toilets at Stockholm Central. It was one thirty in the morning, and Thomas was standing in front of the basin furthest from the door, trying to clean the bite wounds on his hand. After he had managed to hail a taxi on the main road, the driver offered to drive him to the local A&E. Thomas had politely declined and asked if he would take him to the nearest 24-hour chemist instead, and they found one on Klarabergsgatan. Thomas had bought three rolls of gauze, bandages, plasters, and a bottle of iodine to disinfect his wounds. He had used most of the iodine on the leg wound, which ran down the length of his left shin. After bandaging his leg, he tended to his mutilated hand.

After he had cleaned and bandaged the hand, he looked at himself in the mirror. It was not a pretty sight. The split eyebrow had left a trail of blood down his cheek and congealed clumps of dried blood in the shaggy beard on his chin. He touched the swollen bridge of his nose. It hurt like hell, but luckily nothing was broken. He clawed paper towels out of the dispenser on the wall next to him and began washing his face. When he had done a half-decent job of unclogging his beard, he tried to patch his eyebrow with plasters. But the wound had split again, and he couldn't get the damn things to stick. He gave up on patching the wound effectively and grabbed what was left of the paper towels to dab his eye on the move. It would definitely leave a scar—a souvenir from Stockholm to remind him that arseholes like Slavros always win.

Thomas took the direct route from Stockholm Central down Olof Palmes Gata to the KGB Bar. As he approached, he could hear the music coming from the bar and the cheerful voices of the guests who were standing outside for a smoke. He went up to the door and pushed his way through the crowd. A broad-shouldered bloke in a black coat barred his way. "*Beklagar*," he said—we're closed.

"Really? Doesn't look like it to me," said Thomas, looking round at the other guests.

"Perhaps you should just go home. It looks like you've already had a rough night."

"I just want to have a beer. I could really use a beer," Thomas said truthfully.

"I'm sorry, but you'll have to drink someplace else. This is a respectable establishment," the bouncer insisted, giving Thomas a stern look.

"Is that so?"

"Yes," the bouncer said, squaring his shoulders.

Not in the mood for a fight, Thomas brushed past the bouncer and made his way back through the queue.

Two streets further down, he found an Irish pub on Kungsgatan. The Irish were more accommodating, and he didn't have any problems getting through the door. The place was half-dead though, and he took an empty stool at the long mahogany bar. He ordered Guinness and Jameson, downed the shot and ordered another, which he downed with equal speed.

"Tough night?" asked the strawberry-blonde bartender.

Thomas nodded. "More than you know."

The kind bartender responded by pouring him another and telling him it was on the house. This was probably the best thing that had happened to him since he'd arrived in Sweden, he thought with genuine gratitude. After half an hour and a few more shots, he could no longer feel the pain in his battered body. The place had livened up a bit, and Irish folk songs were blaring from the loudspeakers. He picked up his phone from the counter and made his way to the toilets, which were at the far end of the bar. He went into the last cubicle, locked the door behind him and took a seat, not bothering to put the lid down. The silence was deafening. Taking a deep breath, he placed the call. It took a long time for someone to pick up.

"Johnson," the voice finally said on the other end. There was music in the background and a woman screeching with laughter. Clearly the party at The Sea Otter was still in full swing. In a tired voice, Thomas greeted his friend.

"Ravn? Are you okay?"

"Yeah, yup, just a little tired."

"It's really late to call. I was just about to close up shop. Any news?"

"No, it's . . ."

"Did you find her? I've had Nadja on the phone all day."

"What did she say?"

"She asked about your search, of course. Any trace of Masja?"

Thomas bowed his head. He had no idea how to say it. His head throbbed.

"Are you still there, Ravn?"

"Yes, I'm still here."

"So, any news?"

"News?" he said, trying to win time. He leaned back against the tank.

"You don't sound like yourself. Are you sure you're okay?"

"Yes, yes. I . . . I found Masja."

"You found her?! Jesus, that's good news!"

"Yes, it's . . ."

"Is she okay?"

"Yes, under the circumstances."

"What do you mean? Where did you find her?"

Thomas rubbed his eyebrow. The wound had opened again, and he was bleeding on his cheek. With one hand he managed to rip off a handful of toilet paper and dab the wound. "At a club. Swanky place. The bouncer wouldn't let a guy like you in. Rich clientele, businessmen in suits, you know the type."

"I see," said Johnson, sounding disappointed. "So she's still a prostitute?"

"Yes, but she says she's only doing it part-time. And that she's finally paid off her debt. She's working for herself now, studying on the side . . . cosmetics and skin care, I think."

"Well, at least that's something."

"It's her choice, after all, but she looks well . . . healthy."

"Did you give her the postcard?"

Thomas spread his legs and threw the bloody toilet paper into the bowl. "Yes, of course. She was really touched. I could see that it meant a lot to her. She seemed very grateful. Please tell Nadja that."

"Did you get her address and telephone number?"

"No."

"Bloody hell, Ravn, Nadja would like to speak to her."

"I had the impression that Masja didn't want to be contacted, not right now. There was no reason to put any pressure on her. But she's well. Please tell Nadja that."

"Okay. I guess that's the main thing, for now. Perhaps with time . . ."

"I have to run."

"Make sure you come home safely. I almost miss hearing that song you always play on the jukebox."

"Talk soon."

"Ravn?"

"Yes?"

"I'm proud of you."

"Please don't be."

"I damn well am. There aren't many of your kind left. You're a mensch, you know that?"

Thomas knew that in Johnson's world, this was the biggest compliment there was to be had. "If you say so," he said, utterly exhausted.

"Maybe this case can be the beginning of something good, something better. Perhaps the tide is finally turning for you."

Thomas ended the call.

He went back to the bar and picked up where he'd left off. And when the Irish bar closed, he took out his Visa card, paid for the rest of the Jameson and stuck it under his coat on the way out.

53

It was three o'clock in the morning, and Thomas had given up trying to find his way back to his hotel. At the intersection of Drottninggatan and Mäster Samuelsgatan, he stopped walking and supported himself against the front window of a boutique. It felt as though he was walking in circles. The dark office buildings and the endless shopping arcades made one street in the middle of the city look identical to the next. The bottle of Jameson, which was now empty, had not helped the accuracy of his internal compass either. His legs gave way, and he slid down the window and ended up sprawled on the sidewalk. The ice-cold wind had picked up, and even though the alcohol had numbed his senses, he could still feel the frost bite into his face.

He crawled into a doorway, which offered some shelter, and curled into the foetal position. He reckoned that the temperature on the street must be below minus ten degrees. It was in weather like this that the homeless, drunks, and drug addicts froze to death. In his early days on the force, he'd seen a few such cases. He dimly recalled that the people who had frozen to death had looked surprisingly peaceful, except for that homeless man they found in the Sydhavn Quarter. But that was mostly because his dog had begun to snack on him, and the man was missing the lower half of his face as a result.

Thomas closed his eyes and dozed fitfully in the doorway. Despite the lateness of the hour, there were still people on the streets. Girls in scant clothing and high heels strutted back and forth as their clients came and went. Business had never been livelier. There were dozens of Masjas right in front of him, but he couldn't help a single one of them. He closed his eyes again, feeling the alcohol and cold slowly numb him to sleep. It *was* peaceful. He sank into a wonderful calm that he hadn't experienced since . . . he did not know when.

He must have passed out, he had no idea for how long, but after a while a shining figure came up to him. She was dressed in a golden robe, and her hair was silver. The figure laid a hand on his shoulder, and he could feel her warmth. She was tugging his shoulder gently, as if she wanted to draw him into the sharp light behind her. He tried to get up and follow her, but his legs could not support his weight. More glimmering figures appeared and stood before him. They looked like angels, and he smiled at them in a drunken stupor.

"*Snälla vän*, you can't stay here," said the angel with the silver hair.

Thomas blinked in fright at the three women standing in front of him. They were wearing identical golden-yellow padded winter coats.

"You'll freeze to death," the silver-haired women said with a smile.

"Why don't you come with us and get a nice warm cup of soup?" She pointed over her shoulder to the little van that was parked at the kerb with its rear doors thrown open. Inside, Thomas glimpsed what looked like a field kitchen arranged on the tailboard. From a huge metal pot, one of the women was serving steaming cups of soup to a group of prostitutes that had gathered around.

"Who are you?" Thomas asked in confusion, staring at the middle-aged women in gold.

"We are the *Nattuglorna* Sisters. Volunteers who help to make our city more safe."

"Shouldn't you be taking care of yourselves out here?"

The women chuckled among themselves. "Mother Tove has been on the streets for twenty years," one of the sisters said, nodding in the direction of the silver-haired woman. "She's a legend. A genuine hero."

"Eighteen years, to be precise. And I'm no hero," said Tove, giving Thomas a critical but concerned once-over. "Why don't we get you to a hospital, my friend? You're looking pretty beat up."

Thomas shook his head and struggled to his feet. "That's all right, thank you, I'll manage. But if you could point me in the direction of my hotel, I'd be very grateful. The Colonial Hotel?"

"Not until you've had some soup, and I've had a chance to take a look at that eye of yours," said Tove, gently but firmly guiding him over to the van, where there was more light.

"Won't you please pour this good man a cup of soup?" Tove said to the young African woman in the back of the van. The woman stared at Thomas suspiciously. "I only serve the girls. Why should I serve this guy?"

"Because we help all of God's street children in Stockholm," said Tove as she took a pack of plasters out of her pocket.

"It is because of jerks like him that we are here in the first place," said the woman. She did as Tove asked but added testily: "He's not getting any bread though. We don't have enough."

"I'm sure a cup of soup will be more than enough for the gentleman," Tove replied, and smiled at Thomas as she handed him the cup.

"Thank you," said Thomas.

Tove asked him to look up into the street light as she carefully applied a plaster to the cut over his eyebrow.

"I'm sure I don't have to remind a grown man like yourself that there are precious few matters worth getting in a fight over?" Tove remarked drily.

"No, you don't. Nor was it my intention to pick a fight," Thomas replied.

He took a sip of the hot soup. "So you know most of the girls on the street?"

"Many of them, yes."

"I'm looking for one who disappeared a few years ago. Perhaps you might recognise her?" He unzipped his coat and took out the photograph of Masja.

Tove studied the picture carefully. "No, I don't think I've seen her, but I can't be sure. Unfortunately, we see more and more girls on the streets. It must be about a thousand girls a year. There is a huge turnover."

"Where did you get that picture?!" snapped the African woman, and she snatched the photograph from Tove.

"Tabitha, honey," said Tove. "Take it easy, will you? And give back the photograph, please."

"Not before he tells me where he got it."

"From . . . from her mother," said Thomas, taken aback by the woman's outburst.

"You're lying!" she said, her eyes wild and furious.

"Do you know Masja?"

"I know who you are!" she screamed, ignoring his question. "You're the guy she warned us about. The guy with the black Mercedes. The madman who stuffs the girls and paints them white. You're the serial killer!" She pointed at Thomas with an outstretched arm.

The three prostitutes who were standing around the van quickly stepped away from him.

"Call the police! It's him, the murderer!" yelled Tabitha.

With a flick of her wrist, one of the girls pulled a jackknife out of the pocket of her satin coat. The blade flashed under the street lights.

"Easy now," said Tove, resting a hand on Tabitha's shoulder. "Sara, put that knife away. You know how I feel about weapons."

The girl called Sara folded the knife away.

"I've come over here from Denmark to find her," said Thomas. He took his police badge out of his pocket and showed it to Tabitha. "I'm just doing her mother a favour. If you know where she is, we'd be very grateful for your help."

Tabitha returned the photograph and crossed her arms over her chest.

"Tabitha, do you know this girl?" Tove asked.

Tabitha nodded. "She saved my life once. She was like a big sister to me," she added. Tears sprang to her eyes.

"When was the last time you saw her?"

"It was years ago. Before I landed in hospital."

"Do you have any idea where she could be now?"

She shook her head. "Back then, we all worked for Slavros, that bastard. He would know."

"I've already had a word with that guy," said Thomas, pointing at his battered face.

"Slavros did that to you?! When?"

Thomas briefly told them about his trip to Arizona Market.

"Arizona is hell on earth," said Tabitha. The terror in her eyes suggested she feared this place more than anything or anyone else.

"Slavros said that Masja had already left."

Tabitha shook her head doubtfully. "Girls don't come out of there alive. It's more likely that she's dead."

"Well, I could find no trace of her there."

"I'm sorry that we couldn't be more helpful," said Tove. "But we have to move on to the next stop on our route now. Good luck."

Thomas nodded and threw his empty cup in the waste basket.

Tove gave him directions to the Colonial Hotel, which was just a few streets away. Then she turned her attention to her sisters, who were packing up the field kitchen and ready to move on.

"I'm sorry I yelled at you," said Tabitha. "You don't look like the kind of guy who stuffs other people like animals."

"That's all right," said Thomas.

"Perhaps Masja is better off dead. At least she won't have to work in Slavros's underground brothel anymore."

"Underground . . . brothel . . . what do you mean?"

Tabitha stared at Thomas. "The place that Slavros has at Arizona. Deep under the ground."

54

Thomas entered the café on Hantverkargatan, which was just two streets away from *Rikspolisen*'s headquarters. The long rectangular room was full of people who sat on rows of benches, eating their warm lunches. A sour smell of fried food and cooked sauce emanated from the open kitchen that was situated at the far end of the room. The café had about as much class as a harbour-side shack peddling grilled sausages. Thomas scanned the crowd, which primarily consisted of white-collar employees who worked for *Rikspolisen* or the nearby local government office building. He caught sight of Karl Luger on one of the benches near the window, having lunch with Dahl and Lindgren. Thomas limped over to their corner table and greeted them. Karl looked up in surprise.

"They told me over at your office that I could find you here," said Thomas.

Thomas took a seat in front of Karl. Both Lindgren and Dahl gave him a curious look. Twelve hours after his run-in with Slavros, Thomas's face was still swollen, and the injuries around his eye were blue-black.

"Take a fall?" Lindgren quipped. The other two men at his elbows smiled.

"Something like that," said Thomas. "The kerbs at Arizona are a bit higher than the ones I've had to negotiate in Stockholm."

"You went out there alone, despite my warning?!" Karl looked horrified.

"There was no other way."

"Did you find the girl?" Karl asked, attacking the tough piece of grey, indefinable meat that lay in front of him.

"No, but I did gather some mighty interesting information," said Thomas.

"*Mighty* interesting? Is that so?"

Thomas nodded. "Yes, I met this woman last night who told me that—"

"Listen up, Ravn," said Karl, interrupting him. He deliberately put down his fork and the hefty steak knife and regarded Thomas patiently as he loosened the navy tie around his neck. "My day starts at six a.m., when Louisa wakes up. And for all the joy that she brings me, I still have to bathe her, dress her, make her lunch, help her pack her school bag and make her breakfast before I take her to school. Afterwards, I have the pleasure of driving Susan to work at Karolinska Hospital, only to turn the car around and drive back through the city in rush-hour traffic, while taking the first meetings of the day over the phone. And when I finally get to the office, my working day starts with a vengeance. Ten hours, sometimes more. Meeting after meeting, investigations, interrogations, interviews, briefings follow debriefings, you know how it is. When my working day is over, I again have the pleasure of driving back to Karolinska to fetch Susan, if she hasn't already taken the Metro home, because I'm too late. Then I pick up Louisa from dance class, scouts, or gym, depending on what her busy little calendar dictates for any given day. If it's my turn, I also have to organise the shopping, make dinner, eat dinner—the latter is usually done in front of my computer—and then I watch the news on TV with Susan, if only to say that we have a life together, and then we go to bed. The next day, it starts all over again. Can you see where I'm going with this, Ravn?"

"Nope, not really, sorry."

"There is only *one* precious moment of my day that I have to myself, thirty minutes to be precise. Thirty minutes when I can be myself, think what I want—if I want to think at all. Thirty minutes in which I can keep the whole world at arm's-length. Do you know which thirty minutes I mean?"

"Er . . . when you're sitting here?"

"Exactly, Ravn. Right here," Karl said, pointing to his spot on the bench. "Here, I can switch off compleeeetely," he said, and glanced at his watch. "And I have seven minutes left. So, my question to you: Is this important?"

Thomas shrugged and leaned back in his chair. "I know you're a busy man, Karl. And I'm sorry that life in the suburbs is not treating you as well as you might deserve, but the fact is that I've received a solid tip on Masja's whereabouts."

"So why don't you just go there yourself?" said Lindgren with his mouth full of fried food.

Thomas ignored him and kept his eyes trained on Karl. "Last night, after my visit to Arizona, I got a tip from a woman who works for . . . the 'night owls,' I think they call themselves."

"Ah, the granny brigade," said Karl ironically. "The ladies who dish out hot cups of coffee?"

"Soup. One of the women recognised Masja from her days on the streets, and *she* told me that Slavros runs a brothel at Arizona."

"So why didn't you find it last night?"

"Because it's *under the ground*," he said, pointing to the floor under their feet. "It's *under* the strip club he has out there. Apparently, all the worn-out prostitutes are shipped out there."

"So why didn't your contact report this ages ago?"

"How should I know? Perhaps she doesn't have the greatest faith in you guys?"

"How do you know that she is telling the truth?"

"I don't think she has anything to gain by lying about this."

"Maybe she has a grudge against Slavros or the police or *you*."

Dahl and Lindgren laughed at Karl's remark.

"Or against men in general," Lindgren added for good measure. "A lot of whores feel that way."

"Speaking from experience, are you?" Thomas snapped at Lindgren and returned his attention to Karl. "Seriously, I think it would take one quick raid to confirm if she's telling the truth or not. And it would give us cause to shut the goddamned place down for good."

"Seriously?" he replied with the same irony as before. "If you were in my shoes, if *I* were the one who had come to you in Denmark with this story, how would you respond? Wouldn't you want to see some semblance of evidence for the wild allegations that you're making right now?" Karl did not bother to wait for a reply. Instead, he threw his paper serviette onto the table and pushed himself to his feet. "My break is over. I have to get back to work. I have about two hundred serious crime cases on my desk that require my immediate attention."

"So you're not going to send a team to Arizona because it's too difficult?"

"I believe I have already explained what kind of resources that would require—resources which we can use much more effectively elsewhere."

"But you could bring in Slavros. Doesn't that mean anything to you?"

Karl sighed heavily. "So what if it was true that Slavros runs a brothel out there? There are illegal brothels all over the city. It makes no difference to me if they are in Hjulsta, on Södermalm or in Gamla Stan, whether they are above or under the ground; they are *all* illegal. In time, we will hopefully shut them all down. Once we have cleaned up the centre of town, we can expand our parameters a little further out. It's all a question of priorities, Ravn. This is the reason why one can never, *ever* get personally involved in a case."

Thomas dropped his gaze.

"I don't recommend the Jäger steak," said Karl, pointing at the tough meat on his plate in parting. "Have a nice day."

"Have a good trip back to Copenhagen," Lindgren added, clapping Thomas on the shoulder on his way out.

Thomas remained in his seat and watched Karl leave the café with the two deputies at his heels. Once they were out the door, he turned towards the empty plates. He didn't have any appetite and the food in front of him only increased his nausea. But next to Karl's plate lay the gleaming steak knife. He leaned over and picked it up. He wiped off the brown sauce with a paper serviette and popped it into his pocket.

Thomas gazed out the window. It had started snowing heavily.

Nope, there was no other way. He would have to go back to Arizona.

55

Arizona Market

Evening fell while a blanket of white snow covered the rooftops of Arizona Market. From his perch on an old crane that was abandoned in front of AK Byggnadsfirman, Thomas had an unhindered view of the entire area. He had decided to avoid the gravel road that led directly into Arizona and make his way through the woods on foot to see if he could find a rear entrance instead. All the premises were surrounded by a high wall, but he eventually found a place where the bricks had crumbled sufficiently for him to break his way in. Slavros's club lay on the far end of the entire complex, and he was yet to figure out how he was going to scale the neighbouring buildings without being spotted. He considered waiting until he could slip through Sniper Alley under the cover of darkness, but the chances of being seen were relatively good. He studied the white mosaic of roofs below. It was impossible to discern whether they would provide passage all the way to the other end, but he reckoned he had a fighting chance that the buildings could bring him within reach of Slavros's two barracks.

He crept along the crane towards the tipping point at the end, and the rickety construction protested under his weight. When he had reached the hoist, he grabbed the rusty wire dangling from it and looked down. He figured that the large hook at the end could function reasonably well as a springboard onto the garage building that lay about six metres down below. He began to ease his way down the wire, but a wound on his hand split open, making it hard to hold on to the wire properly. Soon he was descending too fast, he realised, and the friction burnt like hell, so he let go and dropped the last few metres. He landed on his target with a loud crash, which immediately alerted a few dogs that started barking wildly in the distance. He rolled onto his back and lay dead still, staring up at the black sky, and the snow, which gently wafted down onto his face as he took a moment to catch his breath.

At last, the dogs shut up. He crouched on his knees and peered out over the grounds. Luckily, it appeared that his fall hadn't attracted any other unwelcome attention, so he continued over the tin roof of the garage and headed towards the wall of the next property. He picked his way over the roll of barbed wire on the neighbouring wall and dropped half a metre onto the flat roof below it.

Keeping his eye on Sniper Alley, which ran alongside it, he scurried over the roof. A small group of men were sharing a case of canned beers in the headlights of a car. Thomas passed close by their heads, and his boots displaced a shower of powdery snow over the eaves, but none of them noticed. Before long, he ran out of roof but continued along some scaffolding that brought him to the next lot, which appeared to be an old auto repair workshop. He counted five men in the workshop, splitting apart a Bentley Continental. They were battling to hoist the engine out of the hub, and Thomas reckoned that the spare parts of the Bentley were destined for the black market.

He hopped down onto the closest carport and inwardly cursing the cracked Plexiglas that squeaked under his boots. He jumped onto the neighbouring carport and peered through a gap between the two structures. Snow filtered through the cracks onto the black BMWs that were parked underneath. One of the men splitting the Bentley looked up and gave his pal next to him a jab in the ribs.

"What?" the pal said.

"Did you hear something?"

"Nothing apart from you farting about. Do you think you could pull your finger out and help me now?" The pal returned his attention to the shiny V8 engine that was dangling just above the hub of the Bentley. The man turned back to the hoist and yanked on the chain, which rattled its way up to the ceiling. Thomas took the gap to scramble over onto the next carport.

On all fours, he crept over the next carport, painfully aware of the men who were directly underneath him now. He could see their heads through a hole in the Plexiglas. They had their eyes fixed on the hoist, and they would discover him if he tried to hop over onto the next roof, so he decided to change tack and crawled to the opposite edge, which flanked a stack of scrapped vehicles. The cars had been compressed into sheets of mangled metal, stacked in four layers, and Thomas clambered over them. From up here, he had a good view of the parking lot in front of the barracks.

The techno music was still blaring from the first, and through the open door he could see that the benches were packed. Red light glowed along the façade of the second barrack, where he had seen the strippers doing their ridiculous dance routine the night before. He was relatively sure that he would find the brothel underneath this building.

Thomas climbed down the final stack of scrapped cars. Flipping his hood up over his head, he made his way across the parking lot. He spied through a window of the second barrack. The place was almost empty. He cursed under his breath. It would've been much easier to blend in if there'd been a crowd. He opened the door and stepped into the dim red light. The room reeked of sweat and beer. Apart from the constant hum of a generator behind the bar on the far side, all was quiet.

Thomas took the steak knife out of his pocket and slipped it up his sleeve. He crossed the room, walked past the bar and went into the back room, which was filled with crates of beer and other alcoholic beverages. The rear entrance was open, and a man was standing just outside, talking on his mobile phone. He made a quick survey of the room, and beside the diesel generator he spotted a hatch in the floor. He managed to slip past the back door unseen, made it over to the hatch and took the steep wooden stairway that led underground.

In some kind of cellar underground, he walked through a narrow tunnel that had a single defective fluorescent pipe that provided intermittent light along his way. The rank stench of stale sweat, urine, and human faeces filled his nostrils and his stomach heaved. There was another long corridor before him. There was a solid wall to his left and doors leading off to his right. Moaning and grunting sounds came from behind the first door.

Suddenly, footsteps sounded on the wooden stairs behind him. Glancing over his shoulder, Thomas saw a pair of clunky boots come into view. He took two steps forward and laid his ear against the second door. Taking his chances, he slipped inside and closed the door behind him.

It took a moment for his eyes to adjust to the darkness. On a narrow bunk in the corner lay an emaciated girl in a filthy nightdress. Her skin was pale, her hair dishevelled and wild as a thorn bush. As if a robot, the moment he took a step towards her bunk, the girl lifted her dress and exposed her crotch. He noticed the deep cuts running along her inner thighs. She was not looking at him but stared off into space. And she was humming something to herself. Thomas took another step and covered her up again. The girl stopped humming, slowly turned her head and looked at him in surprise.

"I need your help, so we can all get away from here," he said. "I'm looking for a girl about your age. Her name is Masja. Do you know which room she's in?"

The girl smiled vacantly, averted her gaze and stared up at the ceiling again. After a moment, she exposed her crotch again and resumed her humming.

Thomas left the girl in peace and stepped back to the door, put his ear against it and listened. Once he was satisfied that there were no footsteps outside, he carefully opened the door and peeked out. The corridor was empty. He realised that he would have to search every room for Masja, whether there were clients in the rooms or not. He made for the next door, but before he could listen for sound, the door opened in his face, and he found himself looking at Kemal's pearly whites. They stared at each other in surprise, then Thomas reacted, drew the steak knife and backed Kemal into the room behind him. Inside, he put the knife to Kemal's throat and pinned him against the wall.

"Where is she?" Thomas hissed.

"You . . . won't . . . get out of here . . . alive," Kemal managed.

"That makes two of us," Thomas said, tightening his grip on the knife till it drew blood from the skin on Kemal's throat.

"The r-room at the end of the corridor. She's in the last room on the corner, for f-fuck's sake," Kemal choked.

Little more than skin and bone, a young woman got up from the bunk next to them. She was completely bald, and her left eye was swollen, as if she'd suffered a hefty blow to the head. "*Puta!*" she screamed in Spanish and started to lash out at Kemal, clawing at his face. In the scuffle, Thomas dropped the knife. He bent down to pick it up and Kemal rammed a knee into his stomach and dashed out of the room. Thomas gasped for breath and set after him. By the time he got back into the corridor, Kemal was already at the foot of the wooden stairs. In a split-second decision, Thomas spun round and sprinted down the corridor in the opposite direction. When he reached the last door before the corner, he yanked it open and stepped into the dark room. "Masja?!" he said.

There was no answer.

Thomas stepped closer to the bunk bed, which contained nothing other than a rolled-up blanket. The next moment the bald Spanish girl appeared in the doorway behind him.

"Do you know where Masja is? Where is the girl who lives here?!" he yelled at her.

"Masja is gone. She's the lucky one."

"Gone? What do you mean? Gone where?"

"Taken, *señor*. By the Hyena. He takes away the weak ones."

"Do you know where he's taken her?"

"Of course I know. *Con los ángeles blancos, señor.* To the white angels, mister. She's dead now. Resting in peace."

"When? When did she leave?!"

"Yesterday. Or the day before. Maybe it was last week, last year. Time disappears . . . just like we do. Time becomes an angel," the girl said, waving her arms as if they were wings. Then she turned on her heel and disappeared from the doorway. From the stair end of the corridor, Thomas could hear the sound of loud voices and barking dogs approaching. His hand flew to his pocket, but then he remembered that the knife lay on the floor in the Spanish girl's room. He looked around quickly, searching for anything he could use to defend himself, but there was nothing. Desperate, he tipped over the mattress, and something fell to the floor.

Thomas bent down and picked it up. It was a notebook. He opened it at random and read:

> **29 November 2010. DAY 33.** More than 400 to go. I am Masja. I am twenty-two years old, and I have come to hell. This is my diary. It is *mine*. Do you understand? It is written for no one else. Just for me . . . To survive. So I can bear to be alive. To remind myself that I am still alive . . .

Thomas stuffed the notebook under his jacket and dashed out the door. Kemal and Slavros were headed in his direction. The two pit bulls straining at their chains led the way. Two half-dressed clients came out of their rooms and stared. The dogs snarled when they caught sight of Thomas. Slavros let go of the chains and the animals charged. Out of options, Thomas turned and ran in the opposite direction, turned a corner and came up against a blind alley with the dogs at his heels. He saw a ladder leaned up against the end wall, and he scaled the first few rungs. The first dog snapped at his pant legs, but Thomas managed to kick himself free. He could hear the techno music above him, just beyond the closed hatch in the ceiling. He put his back against the hatch and leaned his weight into it, just as Slavros appeared around the corner.

"It's over, Danish-Pig," Slavros said.

At last, the hatch gave and Thomas scrambled up the last few rungs of the ladder and smacked the hatch down. He immediately shifted two cases of Ballantine's over it. The topless waitress behind the bar gave him a bleary-eyed stare.

"What the fuck you doing?" she slurred.

"There's a psychopath down there," Thomas said to the waitress. "Make sure he doesn't come up. I'm going to look for Slavros," he added. He took two 100-krona bills out of his pocket and gave them to her.

"There's nothing but psychopaths in here, mister," the waitress said, stuffing the bills into her underwear.

Thomas was already striding across the room, and he didn't look back. But when he got to the door, a large hand on his chest made him stop in his tracks. "We told you not to show your face here again," Mikhail said. He was blind drunk and unsteady on his feet.

Thomas took hold of Mikhail's collar and head-butted him. His aim was a little off. The contact between Mikhail's thick head and his own hurt like hell and momentarily disoriented him, but luckily it was hard enough to bring the big Russian to the ground. And he stayed down.

Thomas ran out the door and legged it across the parking lot. He spotted a few rubbish containers lined against the far wall, clambered up over them and scaled the wall. Behind him, Slavros came out of the barracks with two of his goons and the pit bulls. The dogs sniffed the air while the men peered around in the darkness, looking for any sign of him.

Thomas jumped and landed on the snow-covered undergrowth almost three metres down. He rolled when he hit the ground and immediately set off into the dark woods. Patting his abdomen as he ran, he made sure he still had Masja's notebook clamped between his belt and the sweaty skin on his stomach.

56

Stockholm, 2013

Sitting at McDonald's at Stockholm Central, waiting for Petra, who has gone to the toilets. We arrived a lousy two minutes too late to catch the train to Copenhagen . . . There is so much I want to tell you, *Mumija* . . . I have money now . . . You should have seen us, *Mumija*, when we split from Arkan's tanning salon . . . We were just like those two girls in that film that we saw together, the one where they flee from the cops and drive over a cliff at the end. You know the one that I mean . . .

"*Thelma & Louise*," Thomas muttered to himself. He was sitting at the table right at the back of a little café in Stockholm Central's Arrivals Hall, diagonally across from the McDonald's where Masja had written these words. He jumped ahead a few more pages and read about Mikhail chasing them through the station . . . and her friend Petra, who had jumped in front of an oncoming train in the Underground . . . the terrible night when Slavros strangled Lulu—a blatant murder that Karl Luger and *Rikspolisen* could certainly hold him accountable for.

Thomas looked up. The digital station clock above the café showed 22:39.

He had been reading Masja's diary from the moment he boarded the T-Rail at Rinkeby Station. He was reading and intermittently calling Karl Luger, who had not yet returned his calls. With the testimony in the diary and everything he had seen at Arizona, they had more than enough evidence to make a strong case against Slavros, testimony that not even Karl could ignore or refuse to investigate. But all this evidence was cold comfort in light of the fact that he had been too late to save Masja.

"We're closed for the night," said the hefty waiter. He had a nose ring that made him look like a bull. Without asking first, he cleared away Thomas's coffee cup and proceeded to wipe his table with a dirty cloth. Thomas closed Masja's diary and got to his feet.

He called Karl again as he walked through the Arrivals Hall. The answerphone came on immediately, but this time he ended the call without leaving a message. He looked up and stared at the huge dome in the ceiling. He was struck by the similarity between this dome and the one in the Church of Our Saviour in Christianshavn. He recognised the same Gothic style, even though he was no expert on architecture. Eva's coffin had stood in the aisle, right in front of the altar. Mother-of-pearl white, almost hidden under a sea of flowers and wreaths. The immediate family, comprised of her parents and two elder brothers, had shared the front pew in the church with him. The rest of Christianshavn sat in the rows behind them or stood out in the rain—hundreds of complete strangers who had heard about the murder in the news had pitched up to show their sympathy. To him, the entire ceremony seemed like a farce, as if the coffin were empty, as if Eva were far away—at work or at home or doing the shopping at SuperBrugsen on Christianshavn Square. He had felt removed and distant throughout the entire proceedings, his frustration mounting by the second as he watched all these people who were obviously grieving the loss of his Eva. He had wanted to scream at them, tell them they could go straight to hell with their invasive sorrow, not just because he didn't know who the hell they were but because *he* could feel absolutely nothing but an inexpressible and all-consuming emptiness that seemed to be eating him alive—and he only realised this now, as he stared up at the dome of the Arrivals Hall of Stockholm Central Station.

Thomas's hands began to shake uncontrollably. The notebook slipped out of his hand and landed on the floor with a dull thud. He bent down quickly to pick it up, feeling the panic rise in his chest, the cold sweat break out on his spine. Suddenly, he felt as if he could not breathe, and he leaned against a bench next to him to steady himself. The hall spun before his eyes, and in spite of himself, he slid to the floor. He opened his coat, his hands clawing at the zip of his hoodie, trying to breathe. He was determined to hold back the tears, but they came out anyway. In bouts, spraying snot everywhere, he started to cry and, ultimately, sob uncontrollably. Thomas was mortified by the display, but all he could do was let the tears flow.

After a few minutes, it was all over. The sobbing stopped and he calmed down a little. His eyes and throat burned. He took a deep breath, stuck his hand in his pocket and pulled out his phone. After searching the net he found the Swedish Name Register and tapped in Karl Luger. There was only *one* result for that name in the entire district of Stockholm. Thomas punched in the private number that stood just below an address in Mälarhöjden.

"Susan Luger," said a frail voice on the other end of the line.

Thomas introduced himself as Karl's Danish colleague and apologised for calling at such a late hour. "Is Karl home?"

"I'm afraid he isn't," said Susan. "Is this about the speech?"

"The speech? I'm sorry, I don't quite understand."

"The Police Inspector's annual war cry for the troops. Afterwards they always hold a dinner at the Academy—for a 'nightcap,' as they like to say."

"Exactly, the dinner," said Thomas. "I was not quite sure where it was being held."

"The Police Academy on Myntgatan 5—Karl's second home," Susan replied cheerfully. "It's on Brantingtorget, on the old town island, Gamla Stan. Just follow all the uniforms."

"Right, thanks for your help."

"You're welcome. You're quite late for the party, aren't you?"

"The story of my life," Thomas said.

He heard the frail voice chuckle on the other end of the line.

"Thanks again for your help, Susan."

57

Thomas leaned on the bench and pushed himself to his feet. Despite the lateness of the hour, the Arrivals Hall was still buzzing with activity, and he followed the stream of passengers to the main exit of Stockholm Central. It was snowing heavily, and people were vying for taxis outside. At last, he managed to flag one down, gave the driver the address to the Academy and gratefully sat his frozen arse on the back seat. Once the taxi had made it through Norrmalm and was on its way over the Vasa Bridge to Gamla Stan, Thomas extracted Masja's diary from his inside jacket pocket. He stared at the faded cover where she had written her name in a handwriting that looked like a child's. It was almost unbearable to read Masja's diary, and it hurt to keep turning the pages, but he felt obliged to keep reading, not only to discover if the notebook contained any more evidence against Slavros, but also to find some indication of what had happened to her.

Thomas read about the Hyena's visit, about how he had examined her body and told her that she would be ready soon. The horror of Masja's situation made it difficult for him to think rationally, but he forced himself to make a sober assessment of the facts described. At first, he had suspected Slavros of being the perpetrator, but regardless of how evil he was, the diary appeared to absolve him of these murders. If the Hyena had collected Masja from Arizona days ago, as the Spanish girl in the cellar had said, then in all probability her limewashed corpse would soon be found planted in the scrapyard near Hjulsta. He had persuaded Karl to increase surveillance, perhaps even extend the parameters of their search to other scrapyards in the greater Stockholm area. In the meantime, they could try to track down the car that Masja had mentioned. This shouldn't be too difficult, because the list of black Mercedes from the 1970s registered in Sweden would be limited, he reckoned—less than a hundred, perhaps as little as twenty.

"We need to take a detour," said the driver when they reached Gamla Stan.

"Excuse me?" said Thomas distractedly.

"Roadworks. They've closed Myntgatan to two-way traffic," said the driver, pointing to the barricade and blinking lights up ahead.

"All right, but please get us there as soon as you can," replied Thomas.

He returned his attention to the notebook in his lap, skimming over the pages, and it was heart-wrenching: her fight to survive in the cellar; how she had braved her withdrawal symptoms to save enough coke to take an overdose; how Slavros had brought her back to life only to deliver Masja to the Hyena:

If you still remember me, *Mumija*, forgive me.

Thomas bit the inside of his trembling lip.

His hatred for Slavros mounted with every word he read, and on the last page, Masja described the Hyena as someone higher up in the hierarchy, as if he were protecting the fucker. Thomas had no idea what to make of this, but perhaps it meant that someone other than Slavros was pulling the strings. He grabbed his phone and called Karl again. The Chief Commissioner of *Rikspolisen* must know more than he was telling him about Slavros's organisation.

"How long till we get there?" Thomas asked the taxi driver impatiently.

"Two minutes."

Karl's answerphone came on automatically and Thomas ended the call. "I don't have two minutes," he snapped in frustration.

The driver mumbled something that sounded like a curse. Moments later, the taxi turned onto Myntgatan. A little further ahead Thomas could see a group of policemen in gala-uniform, having a smoke and a chat under the arch of the entrance to a large yellow-brick building.

The driver pulled over to the kerb. "So, looks like we made it after all," he said in a sour voice.

Thomas handed him two banknotes.

While the driver organised his change, Thomas noticed the text on the back of the notebook. He held it up to the light. The handwriting was smudged, as if it were written with charcoal or dirt.

"Here you go," said the driver, handing Thomas his change.

"That's all right," said Thomas, still trying to decipher the writing:

> This is my last entry. I know who the Hyena is. Not that it helps me in the least. Mikhail came by last night. He was drunk. Luckily, too drunk to touch me. He taunted me. Said I was going to die. Told me that there was no way out. That my body would soon be found on the junk heap. He told me that the Hyena will come and get me later tonight. That he was upstairs right now, having a drink with Slavros at the bar. I told him that the police would find out one day, and arrest all of them. That they could be on their way to raid them already. Mikhail just laughed at me. Said that they had just beaten the shit out of some loser that had come to look for me. To save me. No idea who that could be?! I think it was a lie. To taunt me even more. Make me lose my mind. He said I was going to die anyway. So he would tell me a secret: There was a good reason why the Hyena has never been caught. Because he wasn't one of us. The Hyena is above us all. Above everything. Above the law. Because the Hyena is a C.O.P.

Thomas rolled up the notebook and stuffed it back in his pocket.

"Hey, man, you okay?" the driver said. "You look like you've seen a ghost."

Thomas did not reply, but he got out of the taxi, drawing glances from the officers standing close by. The last sentence Masja had written didn't make any sense. He walked past the uniformed men and took the stairs to the main door of number 5. Mikhail could have been lying to Masja, filling her head with all sorts of bullshit. *But why would he do that?* What would he have to gain? The fact of the matter was that a killer had been on the loose for the last five years, picking his victims among the prostitutes on the streets of Stockholm, without being caught. Without a single suspect being brought in for questioning. And it was a fact that no one interfered with Slavros's business at Arizona, despite the apparent criminal activity that went on out there. If Mikhail was telling the truth, then how far up in the hierarchy did the corruption in *Rikspolisen* go?

Thomas strode into the entrance hall. A large stairway led off to his right. Laughter and loud voices filtered down from the first floor. The notebook confirmed that as recently as *yesterday* Masja was still alive, and he had literally walked over her grave, while she waited to die in the cellar. From the pit of his stomach, a tendril of hope reached up towards the light. *What if she was still alive? What if he wasn't too late?!*

Thomas took the stairs two at a time and entered the glass doors of the large conference room above. Just inside the door about ten policemen were gathered around tall standing tables, and a handful of waitresses were clearing away abandoned drinks. Raucous laughter came from a large table at the far end of the room, where six middle-aged men, too drunk to actually clink glasses in all their grand paraphernalia, were raising a toast to one another. Two empty bottles of cognac stood on the table in front of them.

Over a veritable sea of blue-and-yellow national flags, Thomas scanned the room for Karl Luger but couldn't see him anywhere. He turned to the police officers near the door and asked if they had seen him.

"Luger? It's been a while since I've seen him," one of the men replied.

"Yes, but I don't think he's gone home yet. He must be here somewhere," said another.

Thomas thanked them and kept looking. He noticed the framed photographs that hung all along the wall to his left, summer field trips, days of celebration for the Academy's members, all of which was displayed behind glass and hailed for posterity. Karl Luger appeared in one of them: in his shirtsleeves, together with a group of stern-looking men in front of a hunting lodge. A copper plate imprinted on the frame read: *Rikspolisen Academy Management Team 2007.*

"Jönsson, are you the bastard who invited the fucking radicals?" yelled a corpulent officer, slapping Thomas on the back with his grizzly paw.

The policemen around the nearest table looked up at Thomas and laughed.

"He looks like a guy from the Drug Squad," said one of them. "Jesus Christ, Ivar, you better put away your cola lest he book you, haha."

Another eruption of raucous laughter around the table.

"Do you want to join us for a glass?" asked the grizzly man behind him, swinging another, as yet unopened, bottle of cognac in his hand.

"No, thanks," said Thomas. "I'm looking for Karl Luger. Have any of you guys seen him?"

"Nope, he disappeared with the strippers," said Jönsson, making the men snort with laughter again.

"Afraid not," said the grizzly, taking a seat with the cognac bottle and his mates.

Thomas squeezed past the table and made for the office door at the far end of the conference room. The door was ajar, and he pushed it open. The office was apparently being used as a wardrobe, and apart from the pile of winter coats on the desk, the room was empty. He heard voices coming from outside. Thomas went over to the window and looked out. About five men were gathered in the circular courtyard below, but it was too dark for him to identify anyone. Thomas hurried back through the conference room and made his way down the stairway again. At the other end of the hall, he found the door to the rear entrance.

The cold air hit him in the face the moment he stepped into the courtyard. Brantingtorget reminded him of the Neoclassical style of the Copenhagen Police headquarters, but it was dead quiet. Whoever had been here moments before must have retreated via one of the narrow passages that led to the surrounding streets. His gaze settled on the fountain and statuette displayed on a pedestal in the middle of the courtyard. It portrayed a naked woman down on one knee. Thomas walked over to the statue. It seemed to glow in the dark. The woman had shoulder-length hair and her gaze was directed over the courtyard. Her gaze had a striking similarity to that of the chalk-white dead women on the scrapyard, almost as if the perpetrator had been inspired by it. *His second home*, Susan had said.

Thomas turned his head and looked up at the first floor. Four or five officers stood talking to each other by the lighted windows. Had Karl sat up there all these years, staring at the statue of the kneeling woman in the courtyard? Had he become obsessed with her? Had she become an ideal that he wished to recreate? Thomas rejected the fantasy. It was just too far-fetched, he thought, as he slipped through the passage that led to Myntgatan.

"Are you the guy who was looking for Chief Commissioner Luger?"

Thomas spun on his heel and looked at the man who had just come out of the foyer. He was putting his coat on and was obviously ready to leave. Thomas recognised the man as one of the officers who had been standing nearest the door in the conference hall.

"Yes, have you seen him?" asked Thomas.

"You just missed him," the officer said, nodding goodbye to Thomas in passing.

Thomas peered around frantically for a taxi on Myntgatan. It was imperative that he get hold of Karl Luger—*tonight*—even if he had to drag the Chief Commissioner out of bed himself.

58

Thomas waited five minutes that felt like an eternity before a taxi arrived. He jumped the queue of drunken police officers and climbed into the front passenger seat.

"Where to?" the dark-skinned driver yelled above the hip-hop music that was booming from his radio speakers.

"I'll tell you as soon as you've turned down that racket," said Thomas, searching for Karl's home address on his phone.

The young taxi driver grinned and turned down the music a little. "This too loud for you, gramps?"

"Ugglemossvägen number five."

"*Mälarhöjden?* Where all the snobs live?"

"I wouldn't know. But I need you to get me there *fast*."

"How fast?"

Thomas took out his wallet and peeked inside. He had eight 100-krona bills left. He gave the driver six of them.

"All right, best you buckle up, gramps," said the driver, then he put his foot down.

The taxi lurched forward and accelerated rapidly. The traffic on the main road to Mälarhöjden was intense, and to Thomas's mind it felt as if every car in Stockholm was headed out of the city on their motorway. His driver was unperturbed, however, keeping the needle close to 170 kilometres per hour and using all the lanes at his disposal. Instinctively,

Thomas braced his feet against the floor under the glove compartment, one hand gripped to the passenger seat armrest, the other clutched onto his seatbelt. If Sweden were looking for a Formula 1 driver to take over from Ronnie Peterson, his driver would be a good contender.

Ronnie-wannabe glanced at Thomas. "That's not going to do you any good if we crash," he said with a fat grin. "Are you sure your heart can take this?"

"Let me worry about my heart. You just concentrate on your driving."

"No sweat, gramps, I got this. Just a quiet little cruise along the freeway," he said. Taking his speed up a notch, he changed into the innermost lane and slipped past two cars in the centre lane with inches to spare.

Nine and a half minutes later, the taxi was cruising down Ugglemossvägen in the Mälarhöjden Quarter.

"What number did you say?" asked the driver, squinting at the villas as they drove past.

"Five."

"Shit. We just passed number ninety. This is a looong street, man," he said, and pumped on the accelerator.

All the houses were set back from the road, behind low white picket fences that seemed to go on for eternity. After about five minutes' driving, a pair of red tail lights appeared in front of them. To his utter surprise, as they came closer to the car, Thomas recognised the form of a black Mercedes SEL.

"You reckon that Mercedes could be a model from the 1970s?" Thomas asked.

"Sure is. Vintage SEL. My brother-in-law used to have one of those. V8 engine that never quits."

The driver put on his indicator to overtake, but Thomas stopped him.

"Stay behind it," he said.

"I thought you said you were in a hurry."

"Not anymore."

Thomas scratched his beard thoughtfully. The car in front of them appeared to be the same model that Masja described in her diary. It seemed absurd, but there it was. He leaned forward and tried to discern who was driving, but the rear shield was toned dark, and it was impossible to see inside. He made a note of the number plate instead.

"Fall back a bit," he said.

"You know that guy?" asked the driver.

"Possibly. How far do we have to go?"

The driver took a sidelong glance through his window pane. "I think we just passed number fifty-two. You'd rather that guy didn't see us, huh?"

"Something like that."

"Cool," said the driver with a grin. He took his foot off the accelerator and let the Mercedes glide ahead of them, as if giving a fish on a hook more line.

When the taxi came to the last few houses on the road, the red tail lights of the Mercedes glowed in the dark ahead.

"Pull over here," Thomas said.

The driver did as he was told.

"Kill the headlights."

"Does this guy owe you money?"

Thomas raised a hand, signalling to the driver that he should be quiet. The black Mercedes had stopped just outside Karl's house. This could only mean one thing: Karl Luger was the Hyena.

Thomas's mind reeled. As the Chief Commissioner of *Rikspolisen*, Karl Luger had had every opportunity to derail a proper investigation into the murders. As for his motive, Thomas knew that the world was full of psychopaths—why should this be any different in the well-to-do suburbs of Stockholm? Thomas ran a hand through his hair anxiously. Who the hell could he turn to now? And could Masja still be alive?!

"You look stressed, gramps. Everything okay?"

Thomas gave the driver a curt nod. "All good, thanks."

"I don't want to get into any trouble. You understand that, right?"

"There isn't going to be any trouble."

The passenger door of the Mercedes opened. A man in uniform stumbled out of the car, turned round and slammed the door shut.

"Fuck me, a shit-faced policeman." The driver laughed.

Thomas recognised the drunken officer under the street lights: It was Karl Luger. He waved at the driver of the Mercedes, who replied with a hoot. Karl weaved up to the front door.

The Mercedes pulled back into the road and picked up speed. There was no time to waste.

"Drive!" yelled Thomas.

"Hey, you're scaring me, gramps. What the hell is going on?" he asked.

Thomas unzipped his hoodie and showed the driver his police badge.

"*Wallah*," said the driver. "Don't tell me I'm helping a fucking Danish cop! If word gets out about this, I'll be stoned to death."

"This *is* a matter of life and death, but not yours," said Thomas.

The driver shrugged, unimpressed. "Well, I saw that you have two more hundreds in your wallet. And I'm very interested in those."

"The money is yours if you start driving—right now!"

The driver relented and set after the black Mercedes SEL.

59

For the next ten minutes, the taxi followed the black Mercedes SEL at a safe distance through Mälarhöjden. It seemed as though the houses became bigger, the cars in the driveway more exclusive, the closer they came to the waterfront.

"Where the hell did he go?!" Thomas said as they came around the next corner without any sign of the Mercedes.

The taxi driver shook his head. "I have no idea, man. Shall I take the next right?" he said, pointing to a dark side road just ahead.

"No, keep going," said Thomas instinctively.

They continued along the road for about 300 metres till they came to the next crossroads.

"Let's take this one," Thomas said, pointing to the blind alley that led down to the lake.

When the taxi had almost reached the end, Thomas spotted the black Mercedes in the driveway in front of a redbrick villa. The house was enormous. It had an impressive entrance with massive wooden doors and black wrought-iron trimmings that lent an air of a castle from the Middle Ages. Suddenly, the radio squealed with an incoming call from the taxi exchange, making the driver jump in fright and fumble with the dial to turn the noise down. "Is this . . . where you're getting out?"

Thomas gave him the last two 100-krona notes in his wallet.

"Could you wait for me?" he said, and got out of the taxi.

"I've got other clients, gramps. Good luck," the driver said, swiftly leaning over the passenger seat and smacking the door closed before Thomas could protest. He shrugged apologetically, turned the car around and sped away.

After the taxi disappeared, it was completely quiet on the deserted road. Thomas looked up at the façade of the dark villa. He walked up the driveway and glanced through the driver's seat window of the Mercedes. Apart from a grey flat cap on the passenger seat, there was no sign of the owner. He went over to the green postbox that was placed by the garden path. He looked for a name, any kind of identification of the owners of the house, but there was none. He pried his fingers through the slot to check if there were any letters that might give him a clue to who lived here, but the postbox seemed to be empty. He continued to the main entrance, but there was no name tag here either, not that he could see. He tried the handle, but of course the door was locked. Thomas walked back down the snow-covered garden path and went around to the back of the house.

The rear garden was beautifully landscaped, almost like a park, down to the bank of the lake where he could see the outlines of a small boat-house. The garden had a stunning view of Lake Mälar, where lanterns on the passing ships glowed in the dark night. Whoever lived here would have paid dearly for this view. He turned his head and looked up at the first floor. The blinds were down, but he could see light coming from one of the rooms.

Thomas continued along the back of the house and as he came past the kitchen, he found a tipped window. He rummaged in his pocket for a pen and worked it in under the frame. After two failed attempts, he managed to lift the hook and open it. He crawled through the narrow opening, slithered over the kitchen sink and dove headlong onto the tiled floor. He rolled over onto his back for a moment to catch his breath, listening for any sounds in the house. It was still as the grave. He got to his feet slowly and took a look around.

The kitchen was large and opened onto a spacious dining area. The jacket and cap of a police uniform were discarded on the solid-oak dining table. Thomas picked up the jacket and searched the pockets, but they were empty, so he put it down where he had found it. He continued into the hallway. There was a series of plaques bearing impressive deer antlers along the left wall. The first door led into adjoining living rooms, which were very cold, but a smell of burnt coals emanated from the open fireplace. A huge elk head was mounted above the mantelpiece, its glass eyes staring sombrely over the living rooms. In the dim light, Thomas identified antique Louis XVI furniture. A grandfather clock in the corner emitted a constant and melancholy tick-tock into the room. He walked over to a sideboard that displayed a series of silver-framed photographs. All of them were black-and-white family pictures: a wedding photograph, a man in an officer's uniform, a couple and a little boy standing beside the black Mercedes.

Thomas picked up the picture and studied the man's face. There was nothing familiar about him. He put the photograph down and went back into the entrance hall. The soft tones of what sounded like an old-fashioned jingle were coming from the first floor. Thomas ascended the stairway, his footsteps muffled by its thick carpet. When he reached the landing, he noticed a crack of blue light in the open door of the room at the end of the corridor. He approached silently and carefully pushed open the door.

Inside, an elderly gentleman with thick-rimmed glasses was sitting in an armchair, watching TV. In front of him on a small round table stood a glass of milk, into which he was dipping what appeared to be an oatmeal cookie. Thomas recognised the man from the framed pictures downstairs. The old man hadn't noticed Thomas yet, and he was afraid he might get a heart attack when he did. Thomas took out his police badge and knocked on the door, putting what he hoped was a friendly smile on his face.

It took a few seconds before the man turned his head away from the screen. He gave Thomas a brief and indifferent glance before returning his attention to the TV. Then he took a bite of his soggy warm cookie. Thomas stepped into the room and looked at the screen. What looked to be an old black-and-white cowboy film was playing.

"What are you watching?" asked Thomas.

The man finished chewing his cookie and swallowed before he replied. "*Hopalong Cassidy* . . . episode six."

"What is your name?"

"*Hopalong Cassidy* . . . episode six."

Thomas nodded. "Is there anyone else in the house?"

"*Hopalong Cassidy* . . ."

"Episode six, I understand," said Thomas in a friendly tone, resting a hand on the old man's shoulder.

Thomas retreated from the room and left the man in peace. He searched the first floor without finding anyone else. He surmised that whoever had taken off his jacket and brought the old man a hot cup of milk was no longer in the house.

Thomas took a moment to study the tableau of a squirrel that stood on the bureau in the entrance hall. It was holding a hazelnut, which it appeared to be eating. The squirrel looked quite peaceful, but Thomas could not help thinking about the pictures of the hideously preserved and limewashed women that Karl had showed him. He considered searching the boathouse he had seen in the garden but was interrupted by a sharp metallic sound. It seemed to be coming from under the floorboards. He looked around but could see no door to a cellar in the hallway, so he returned to the kitchen. The metallic sound grew louder, so he continued towards the utility room. Next to the door to the utility, Thomas found a steep wooden stairway. A pale light rose up to meet him as he descended into the cellar.

Thomas skirted the large zinc tub that was filled with a milky liquid and continued deeper into the cellar. There was a strong smell of formaldehyde, and it was difficult to breathe down here. He let his gaze wander through the low-ceilinged room, which was divided by a row of metal shelves with crates and cardboard boxes that were filled with dusty glass jugs, stuffed birds and various other mammals. At the far end of the cellar stood a man in a white lab coat with his back turned, manoeuvring an old hoist and chain that was suspended from the ceiling.

Thomas approached cautiously. To his surprise he realised that the man was not alone. A pallet was leaned up against the wall, and the arms and legs of a naked girl were tied to it with broad leather straps. Thomas looked around quickly for a weapon and grabbed a small screwdriver from the nearest shelf. When he was just three or four metres away from the man in the lab coat, he paused, hiding behind the crates on the shelves. There was little likeness between the girl in the picture that Nadja had given him and the haggard girl strapped to the pallet, but he knew that he had found Masja. Thomas noticed the thick needle that was inserted in her groin, and it was connected to a rubber tube that led to an apparatus that stood on a trolley in front of her. More rubber tubing connected the apparatus to a series of glass lab jars below, which were filled with various liquid solutions. The man turned around suddenly, and Thomas ducked instinctively.

"I have great expectations for you," the man said in a whisper.

He was wearing a large black respirator that covered the better part of his face.

"Just . . . let me die," Masja said almost inaudibly.

"That is exactly the right attitude," the man said cheerfully. "The other girls were so tearful. I think their pathetic attitude actually had an effect on the process. Too many negative thoughts."

"So why did you . . . display the others?"

"One never destroys a good sketch. If you do, you will never learn from your mistakes. Irrespective of how painful your mistakes may be, you must confront them."

"You're sick."

The man shrugged. "No. I think *dedicated* is the right word. *Purposeful* and *dedicated*, that's what I am."

"Dedicated to . . . what?"

"My mission in life. My dear father was a master of the art. When I was a boy, I used to look up to him. He taught me how to preserve the wild animals and birds that he and his friend had hunted down and killed. I cannot count the number of partridges that I learned to preserve in this way. Taxidermy was his great hobby. Papa always used to say that it was here, in his cellar, where he could relax and forget all his troubles. And I couldn't agree with my dear father more. Here you can feel at peace, don't you think?"

He paused to check the display of the apparatus and punch in a combination of figures on the keypad.

"When I grew a little older and became more experienced at the craft, I realised that my father was a mere amateur. A skilled one, of course, but he was no master. I caught him taking shortcuts with the filling, sewing, and, God forbid, the actual tanning process. I'm not sure you can understand how disappointed I was to discover that my idol was tarnished. But Papa did teach me the basics of the technique. And for that I will always be grateful."

The man bent down and unscrewed the lid of one of the jars under the apparatus.

"So you could prepare . . . your corpses?"

"Good Lord, no, my dear. You make me sound like some sort of undertaker."

Masja closed her eyes in exhaustion. "But isn't that exactly what you are?"

"No, far from it. An undertaker's task is to make the dead look as attractive as possible. The undertaker creates an illusion that there is something beautiful about death. He distracts the bereaved from the inevitable process of decomposition. What I aim to do, on the other hand, is *capture* life. I *create* the immaculate female subject that will show no signs of the aging process—she will shine with vitality for a thousand years to come."

"So why me? I'm not beautiful or anything."

"An artist needs a lesser canvas before he begins with his masterpiece. Luckily, there is plenty of material like you that I can use to try out my techniques. Did you know that a low BMI improves the effect of the chloride in my solution?" he said excitedly, pointing to one of the jars below the apparatus. "Similarly, if the subject—you, that is—takes a morphine solution regularly, it has a substantial preservative effect. However, stress hormones, which are released during withdrawal symptoms for example, have a destructive effect on the process. And this means that I constantly have to take new challenges into consideration. In the good old days when people did not stuff themselves with junk food and all sorts of medication, the task at hand was easier. Embalmers from the turn of the century were not faced with the same problems that I have to deal with today."

The man shook his head slightly. Then he took a test tube out of his pocket, unscrewed the cap and poured the substance it contained into the first jar. The liquid in the jar changed from clear to green. He returned the cap. "If it works this time, I promise I will conserve your body and give you pride of place," he said, and pointed to the shelves of stuffed animals. "Then I won't just skin, flesh and wire you, but preserve your body from the inside. I will create an immaculate woman."

"Fuck you," Masja said.

The man approached her and removed his respirator. He dabbed the pearls of sweat that had gathered on his face and mouth.

Thomas watched him from behind the cardboard boxes and recognised the deputy investigator at once. It was Lindgren. Karl's trusted assistant, his right-hand man. Lindgren was the Hyena—the man who had been intimately involved in the investigation of the murders that he had committed himself. A combination of factors—Lindgren's official police status, his incompetent boss and the efficiency of Slavros's organisation—had played into his murderous hands. And he could continue his heinous acts for years to come if he wasn't stopped now.

"There is no reason to be vulgar," Lindgren said, fondling one of Masja's breasts with his rubber-gloved hand. "You are not ugly, not as imperfect as the other girls were. I can see that you must have been beautiful once. I'll bet you used to make men weak. That is what you women have the power to do: make men worship you like a goddess. Women suck the marrow out of our bones to satisfy their insatiable need for validation. To this extent all women are simple. So unbelievably predictable," he said, stroking Masja's hair.

"Women like you are truly most beautiful, most complete in the state of eternal death . . . Goodbye, my dear."

Lindgren turned around to the apparatus and reached for the keypad.

Thomas tightened his grip on the screwdriver. The distance between himself and Lindgren was too great for him to intervene in time, so Thomas hurled the screwdriver to the other end of the cellar where it clanged against the zinc tub.

Lindgren turned around and stared. "Papa, is that you?"

When he received no answer, Lindgren walked towards the tub to investigate. "Papa? You know that you are not supposed to be down here."

Thomas took the gap to sneak over to Masja. She looked wide-eyed at him but didn't make a sound.

Thomas quickly removed the syringe from her groin. Suddenly, he felt a blow to the back of his head, and he fell to the ground.

When he looked up, Lindgren was standing over him. "What the hell? If it isn't the pesky Dane. Can one *never* get rid of you?" Lindgren said. He kicked Thomas in the stomach, knocking the breath out of him. Then he reached inside his lab coat, unclipped his holster and pointed his pistol at Thomas. "You should have stayed in Denmark. You're a goddamn nuisance. No one needs you here. Don't you get that?! You're disturbing the process," Lindgren said, and unclipped the safety on his pistol.

Thomas caught sight of the syringe on the floor. He threw himself forwards and jabbed it into Lindgren's thigh. The deputy stumbled backwards. Thomas got to his knees, lunged at the apparatus, slapped his hand down on the keypad, and the pump activated immediately. Lindgren fired his weapon. The bullet hit the floor and ricocheted about in the cellar. Moments after the toxic substance pumped through the rubber tubing and penetrated his blood, Lindgren screamed in pain. He aimed and fired again. Again, the bullet ricocheted, shattering jars on the shelves and perforating the zinc tub, which started to leak from a hole in the side.

Lindgren thudded onto the cellar floor, his eyes bulging and bloodshot. The pistol fell out of his hand and froth bubbled out of his mouth. He tried to remove the needle from his thigh, but he could not control his hand. At last, he keeled over and remained still.

Thomas got to his feet and loosened the leather straps that tied Masja to the pallet. Then he took off his jacket and put it around her shoulders. "Can you walk?" he asked.

Masja nodded. "Who . . . are you?" she asked through chattering teeth.

"My name is Thomas. I know your mother. She asked me to look for you."

"She did?"

Thomas nodded.

"Is . . . is he dead?"

Thomas knelt down and checked for a pulse. Lindgren's face was sallow, and his lips curled back, exposing his teeth in a silent scream. "Yes. He's stone dead."

"Was . . . was he a cop?"

Thomas nodded and pulled his phone out of his pocket.

"Who are you calling?"

"An ambulance."

"Forget it," said Masja, shaking her head. "I just want to go home."

"We need to get a doctor to take a look at you."

"I'm okay. Can't we just go, please?"

"To be honest, you don't look particularly well."

"You don't look particularly well yourself," she said.

"I mean it. You need help. And I'm sure that the police would like to have a word with you."

Masja shook her head firmly. "Forget it. I am NOT talking to the cops."

"Don't you want to lay charges against Slavros?"

"What good would that do? Slavros is untouchable."

Thomas shrugged. "Perhaps. But what about the other girls? The ones in the cellar?"

"I don't know." Masja started to sob, and her entire body was trembling. "Can't you just take me home now? Please?"

"Okay," Thomas said, putting an arm around her shoulders.

"Thank you," Masja said, taking a step back, clearly uncomfortable about being touched. "How did you find me?"

Thomas showed her the notebook. "I read your diary."

60

Sweden

The frost-white sun was low between the trees, casting its golden rays over the old Mercedes on the country road. Masja was dozing in the passenger seat with her feet up on the dashboard, her head resting on Thomas's shoulder. They had found her bag in Lindgren's cellar, and she was wearing her pastel-blue jumpsuit. She was so frail and sickeningly thin that the large leather seat practically swallowed her whole. As soon as they were back in Denmark, Thomas resolved, he would make sure that she received proper medical care. If he couldn't persuade her to be examined, he would get her mother to insist that she go to a hospital. They had already covered 300 kilometres and there were at least as many ahead on the road before they reached Christianshavn.

Thomas looked at his watch. It was six thirty in the morning. So it would be a while before Karl Luger woke up from his hangover and called him back. But he had no intention of calling Karl before they had crossed the Øresund Bridge and were safely home on the other side. He knew that the moment Karl realised the magnitude of the case against Slavros, he would move heaven and earth to get hold of Thomas. *Rikspolisen*'s forensics team would have a field day in Lindgren's cellar, where they could find ample evidence of the deputy's perpetration of the murders. To this extent, it was almost a blessing that his father was senile, shielding him from the knowledge of his son's actions. Thomas guessed that the old man would probably spend the rest of his days in a retirement home, in blissful ignorance of the horror that had occurred in his home. Karl Luger, on the other hand, would have a hard time surviving the political storm in Sweden. Management, politicians, and not least the media would grill him alive when it became public that Sweden's most wanted murderer was one of their own.

For Karl's sake, Thomas hoped that the "nightcap" at the Academy had been a good one because his hangover was going to last well into the future.

61

Christianshavn, 2013

Eduardo dashed into The Sea Otter with a doe-eyed brunette for whom he gallantly held open the door. The lovebirds were both soaked by the rain that was coming down in buckets on the canal.

A bottle of Hof on the counter before him, Thomas was propping up one end of the bar. Victoria was propping up the other with her glass of vermouth. Curled up under Thomas's stool, Møffe wagged his tail when he caught sight of Eduardo.

"Johnson?" Eduardo called, taking off his fogged-up glasses. "You don't happen to have a towel for me and my *señorita*?"

Johnson appeared in the doorway of the storeroom behind the bar. "What do you think this is? A bloody hotel?" he said gruffly. Then he grabbed a handful of clean dishcloths from under the counter and flung them at Eduardo.

"*Gracias*, my friend," Eduardo said with a smile as he caught the dishcloths in the air.

Eduardo and the girl rubbed their heads with the dishcloths, dripping rainwater all over the place. Møffe grumbled, smacked his chops and crept a little deeper under the bar for cover.

Eduardo ordered two beers, unzipped his jacket and produced a stack of Swedish newspapers, which he slapped down on the counter.

"Where did you get those?" asked Johnson.

"At Magasin du Nord on Kongens Nytorv."

Johnson snorted. "I had no idea that an old-school communist like yourself would shop in a fancy store like that," he said.

"Whatever it takes for my good comrade here," Eduardo said, clapping Thomas on the back.

Johnson picked up the *Express*, which was on the top of the pile. The front page displayed a large picture of Erik Lindgren. The headline was printed in red caps: PSYCHOPATH POLICEMAN. The other papers were no less dramatic with their front-page stories.

"This case has caused shockwaves in Sweden. Strangely enough, there's not a single mention of your role in all this," said Eduardo with a note of indignation.

"But it was Thomas who stopped the bastard," said Victoria. "What do they write about that?"

"They say that the police are 'still investigating the cause of death,'" replied Eduardo.

"That shouldn't be too difficult to determine," said Thomas, "considering the fact that I left him on the floor with a toxic syringe planted in his thigh."

Johnson looked up from the article that he was skimming. "Well, at least they mention that the perpetrator was caught with the assistance of the Danish police."

"Ravn, we are in the middle of a series of articles about this case," said Eduardo, looking at Thomas. "I think we should write them from the angle that you were instrumental in—"

"No thanks," Thomas interrupted. "I don't want to be in the papers."

Eduardo put on his glasses again, even though they were still foggy. "But the public has a right to know the truth. His capture was entirely to your credit."

"I don't care what the public is entitled to."

"Come on, Ravn, this is hardly the time for false modesty," said Victoria. "I, for one, would love to read all about how we beat the Swedes for a change."

"The most important thing is that Masja is home. That concludes the case," Thomas said, raising his Hof in a toast.

"How is she doing?" asked Johnson. "I haven't been able to get hold of Nadja."

"Masja is still in hospital for observation. They're taking all kinds of tests. But she's in relatively good spirits. The nurses at Amager Hospital are taking good care of her."

"It's hard to imagine that she will ever recover from this ordeal," said Johnson.

"I'd be mega-terrified the rest of my life if I had run into such a psycho," the brunette chipped in.

"Yeah. You already look a bit like you've been caught in the headlights," Victoria remarked drily as she blew another cloud of smoke up to the ceiling.

"Has Masja said anything . . . about what happened to her?" Johnson intervened evenly.

Thomas shook his head. "No. I think that, more than anything else, Masja would just like to forget what happened and put it all behind her."

"That's understandable," said Johnson, pushing the newspaper away from him. He took a sip from his coffee cup thoughtfully. "You did a great job, Ravn."

Thomas shrugged. "I was just lucky that I found her."

"It was more than luck; it was an excellent piece of police work!"

"You don't know what you're talking about, Johnson," Thomas muttered in embarrassment, fixing his gaze on the countertop.

"I mean it," said Johnson. "I don't know anyone who is as determined as you are to see things through. When it's important to you, that is." He took the Jim Beam bottle from the shelf and put a shot glass in front of Thomas.

Thomas put his hand over the glass before Johnson could fill it. "Thanks, old friend, but it's a little too early for me."

Johnson shrugged and shelved the Jim Beam. "But it's got to feel good, right?"

"It feels . . . unreal," said Thomas.

Johnson gave him a puzzled look. "So what now? When are you going back to work?"

Thomas shook his head. "I'm not sure that I am."

"But Station City would be *more* than happy to have you back."

"I'm saying I'm not sure I *want* to go back."

"What's not to be sure about?" said Johnson. "You've just accomplished more than the entire Swedish police corps put together!"

Thomas sighed deeply. He didn't know how to explain it, so he just kept his mouth shut.

"Stop bugging Ravn already," said Victoria. "Of course the man has doubts; he's just been to Sweden, doubt's homeland. A trip over the Øresund Bridge could confuse anyone."

Johnson gave Victoria a cool stare over the rim of his glasses. "Since when are you an expert on Swedish affairs, Victoria?" he said, wiping the counter energetically. "As I recall, you've never crossed the bridge yourself."

Victoria narrowed her eyes. "You know damn well that I don't use that scandalous bridge out of principle. That contraption was built over the Øresund for one reason only: so Volvo can drive their shit cars to the rest of Europe."

Thomas got up from his barstool. The conversation had taken a turn that was beginning to bore him.

Johnson sighed. "How long are you going to sing the same old song, Victoria? Just because you accidently put diesel in your Volvo Amazon."

Laughter erupted from the other guests.

"It's a PV, not an Amazon. And how many times do I have to say that the tanks weren't properly labelled?" Victoria said, taking a sip of her vermouth. "What about that old Mercedes SEL, Ravn, are you going to keep it?"

"It was picked up by the boys from Forensics. They're going to send it back to Stockholm."

"Pity. It's a nice car."

"Yes, if you don't dwell on what has been in the trunk," he said.

Victoria put down her glass. "Good point."

Thomas rummaged in his pocket for some money to pay for his beer.

Johnson shook his head. "This round is on the house, Ravn. Where are you going? It's still pissing down rain outside."

"Station City. I've been called in for a meeting. Management is keen to hear an explanation for what the hell I was doing in Stockholm."

"Well, I still think they ought to give you a medal," said Johnson.

"I'll be lucky if I get away with a slap on the wrist and a lecture," Thomas said. He slid onto his feet and bent down to hook the leash onto Møffe's collar.

Møffe grunted and reluctantly rose from his warm spot under the barstool.

62

Thomas was dripping wet when he entered the Crime Ops Division of Station City. He wiped his face with his hand and looked around the office for someone he knew. But as far as he could tell, there was nothing but a sea of unfamiliar faces. Møffe shook out his coat, sending a cascade of water in all directions.

"Ravn!" Mikkel yelled, waving him over to his desk. Thomas nodded and crossed the room slowly.

As Thomas approached, Mikkel gave him a round of applause. "If you weren't so fucking drenched, I'd give you . . ."

"A hug, I know, thank you," said Thomas, putting his arms around his pal, who hugged him back, despite his sodden state.

"Bloody hell, you both look like drowned rats." Mikkel stepped back and looked down at the wet stains on his white shirt. "Great job with that Swedish case, my friend. I thought you were on leave." He smiled.

Thomas returned it sheepishly. "An exaggeration, apparently."

"They say that cellar in Mälarhöjden was full of dead whores," said Melby in greeting.

Thomas reluctantly shook Melby's hand. "It wasn't quite as bad as that."

"But he was a horny psychopath, am I right?"

"I have no idea what his motives were."

Mikkel sat down on the edge of his desk. "So you just waltzed in there, without your service pistol or a radio, without jack shit for back-up?"

"Well, unfortunately my Glock was in my safe in Christianshavn at the time," Thomas said with a smile.

Mikkel clapped him hard on the shoulder. "Jesus, Ravn. You're like bloody Rambo."

"Yes, I admit that it's not the best decision I've ever made."

"Well, it's great to have you back," Mikkel said. He turned to the table next to him where a young officer with blond hair was sitting. "Tim, you can pack your things and move over to Allan's desk, your new best friend."

Tim looked up from his computer in surprise. "But . . . but *this* is my desk?"

"No, Tim, I think you've misunderstood the situation. You were borrowing that desk until Ravn came back. Just be grateful that you were able to sit with the grown-ups for such a long time. Chop-chop, pack your things," Mikkel said with a wave of his hand.

Tim made a motion to get to his feet.

"Please, keep your seat," said Thomas. "I'm just visiting."

Mikkel shot Thomas a look. "What do you mean?"

"Brask called me in."

"Sure he did. But after you've spoken to him . . . ?"

Thomas made no reply. Instead, he bent down and tied Møffe's leash around a leg of Melby's desk.

"That has got to be the fattest police dog the world has ever seen," said Melby, glancing down at Møffe.

"Possibly, but he has a four-tonne bite on him, so you shouldn't get on his nerves when you're within his reach."

Melby looked down at Møffe and pedalled his office chair back half a metre.

When Thomas entered Klaus Brask's corner office a short while later, he found the Chief of Police standing by the window, staring out over Halmtorvet, which was desolate in the pouring rain.

"No matter where you look, there are people breaking the law," Brask said, shaking his head in disgust. "Right in front of our noses. It's like being held up in the last bastion with bloodthirsty Indians closing in on you."

Brask turned to face Thomas. "But that's none of *your* concern, is it, because you're still on leave?"

Thomas made no reply. He pulled up a chair and sat down in front of Brask's desk instead.

"Do have a seat," Brask said sarcastically. Then he came over to his desk and sat down heavily in his chair. "Sweden is furious," he said.

"The country, or just the police force?"

Brask narrowed his eyes. "Cut the crap, Ravn. I'm not in the mood for your wisecracks today."

"Sorry."

"I've had one inspector after the other yelling at me in Swedish on the phone. And I can't understand half of what they're saying."

"They ought to be happy that they've got one less case on their desks."

"I can promise you that they're not smiling when one of their own has been killed."

Thomas frowned. "Erik Lindgren could hardly be considered 'one of their own.' The man was a serial killer. I would've thought they'd be eager to distance themselves from him."

"Not with the same speed as you did. *You* chose to flee from the scene of the crime—with the killer's car, not to mention the key witness in the passenger seat."

Thomas shrugged. "I did everything in my power to get the Swedish police to act in this case. Time was of the essence, and I called up Lindgren's superior repeatedly on the night in question, but due to a party at the Academy, the Chief Commissioner was . . . indisposed."

Thomas chose not to bring any more shame on Karl's head by mentioning that in his drunken state he had actually hitched a ride home with Lindgren.

Brask rested his elbows on his desk and regarded Thomas evenly. "I know your style, Ravn. So I'm perfectly aware of what a pain in the arse you have been to *Rikspolisen*—just as you've always been a pain in mine."

"I'm sorry if that's the way my efforts were received. I would be more than happy to go back to Stockholm and explain. I acted in self-defence against Lindgren; the forensics team will be able to confirm this. The man was armed and fired two shots at me."

"No one at *Rikspolisen* wants you back in Sweden, believe me."

"So what's the problem?"

"The girl."

"The girl? You mean Masja?"

"Bingo" said Brask, snapping his fingers.

"She can't tell them any more about Lindgren than I can."

"What about the people who collaborated with Lindgren?"

Thomas shifted in his chair. His wet jeans were beginning to stick to the plastic covering of the seat. "Lindgren was working alone. But he was protecting Vladimir Slavros and his men. If only the Swedish police could pull their fingers out and organise a raid of Arizona Market, they would obtain ample material to lay charges against Slavros."

Brask picked up the file that was within reach on his desk. He opened it up on the first page and skimmed the contents. "*Rikspolisen* have already raided the area north of Hjulsta, where they confiscated fifteen kilograms of cocaine and eight kilos of heroin. As well as twenty luxury cars and contraband with a preliminary street value estimated at three million Swedish krona."

"There was also a brothel out there. What happened to the girls?"

Brask returned his attention to the file and ran his finger down the margin. "A total of thirty-five individuals of various nationalities were arrested during the raid. Most of them will be deported, pending detention. Naturally, the same goes for the girls, if, as you say, they engaged in prostitution."

"Naturally," Thomas repeated sarcastically. "But then the Swedes have already got what they want?"

"Not quite," said Brask, looking up from the page. "Unfortunately, Vladimir Slavros was not among the men who were arrested. Accordingly, he is now wanted all over Europe. The Swedish police would like to talk to the girl in order to find out where they should start looking."

"I understand, but I doubt that Masja has any idea where he is. She was being held prisoner in the cellar with all the other girls."

"Yes, which also makes her a key witness in any potential legal proceedings against Slavros, so the Swedes would very much like to talk to her."

"Then they should do so."

"The problem is that she won't talk to anybody, not even us," Brask said, folding his hands on his desk in front of him. "To be honest, it's starting to look as if she's protecting Slavros."

"When did you try to talk to her?"

"Melby went out to the hospital to talk to her last night."

"Melby? Seriously?" Thomas snorted. "I wouldn't talk to that guy either, even if my life depended on it. He's a complete arsehole without a modicum of empathy. Masja needs to recover. Gain a little distance from the whole ordeal."

"Has she said anything to you?"

"Not a word." Thomas looked over to the window. He briefly considered whether he ought to hand over her diary to Brask, for the sole purpose of winning her some time to recover. But it wouldn't be fair to just hand it over without her consent. Ultimately, it was *her* choice if she wanted to assist the investigation or not.

"You're hedging your bets, Ravn, which is never a good idea. What are you hiding?"

"Nothing."

"You and the girl have had a *special* relationship, right?" he said. The way he emphasised the word made Thomas's hackles rise.

"Not to my knowledge."

"Come off it, Ravn. You saved the girl's life. Obviously, that creates a 'special' bond between the two of you."

"If you say so."

"The girl is grateful that you saved her life. Perhaps she even feels a need to pay you back. It's pop psychology."

"With all due respect, it is pure speculation," Thomas said with a stiff smile. "Masja definitely doesn't owe me a thing."

Brask leaned back in his chair and folded his hands over his chest. "Either way, you could still have a chat with her, persuade her to talk to us, as well as the Swedes."

"I've already told her that I think she should lay charges against Slavros. If she does not feel up to that right now, it's her choice. I think you should give her time to rest. Perhaps she will feel differently once she has recovered somewhat and gained some distance."

"Distance my arse. I don't understand why you are being so stubborn about this. Has this got something to do with your own case? Am I to understand your reluctance as some kind of personal revenge against our department?!"

"I'm not sure I understand where . . ."

Brask was no longer listening. "Believe me when I say that we have done *everything* we could to find out who was responsible for the break-in and . . . and what happened to Eva."

Thomas gripped the plastic armrests of his chair with both hands. "I . . . I'm not connecting one case with the other."

Brask rose to his feet and looked down at Thomas. "Well, perhaps it's about time that you did."

"What do you mean?"

"Ninety percent of all break-ins are committed by the Baltic Mafia. They are relatively organised. Perhaps a man like Slavros has the right kind of connections with them. Perhaps he knows things that we don't. Something he can bargain with."

Thomas made no reply.

"Who knows . . . if we catch Slavros, we might be able to gain information that leads us directly to Eva's killer," Brask said, smiling at Thomas ingratiatingly.

Thomas got to his feet. He was fighting the urge to strangle Brask with the grease-stained tie he had around his neck. The bullshit theory he had just dished out was obviously a complete fabrication with the sole purpose of putting pressure on him to cooperate. Thomas glared at Brask. "Before I came in here today, I was of two minds as to whether I should return to Crime Ops. Mostly, because I really love this job. Many of the guys in this division are like family to me," he said, pointing his thumb over his shoulder in the direction of the office outside Brask's door. "You know, I think you're right about one thing: Our division *is* the last bastion. Crime Ops is the last resort for everyone out there," he said, pointing to the window.

"I don't believe that's what I was saying," Brask replied with a frosty smile.

Thomas shrugged. "Whatever. The point is that you've made the decision easy for me." Thomas stuck out his hand and Brask took it in surprise. "Not that I'll ever thank you for it. Goodbye, Brask."

The Chief of Police stared after him in bewilderment as Thomas and made for the door.

"Ravn? Ravn, for fuck's sake," Brask said, banging on his desk, "we're not done in here . . ."

But Thomas had walked out the door without looking back.

63

The rain had stopped, and a group of boys were playing football in the street in front of the residential block on Dronningensgade. The ball rolled over to Thomas, who came sauntering along with shopping bags in both hands and Møffe on a leash. He kicked the ball back to the boys, who greeted him briefly before continuing their game. Thomas went on his way again. It was great being back in the neighbourhood. He felt as though he was a sailor returned from a long journey at sea, which only made him more depressed about putting *Bianca* up for sale. But now that he was officially unemployed, he had no choice but to sell the boat. He would probably lose money on the deal, but saving on expenses like harbour dues and the essential upkeep of *Bianca* could salvage his dire financial situation.

Thomas put his shopping bags down on the steps and retrieved his house keys from his pocket. He glanced at the name tag next to the buzzer. The little scrap of paper had now disintegrated almost completely, and their names were unreadable. It was high time he replaced it. He opened the door and dragged his shopping up to the top floor. As he entered his ice-cold flat, he cast a glance at the stack of advertisements and post piled on the doormat. He continued down the corridor and dumped the shopping bags on the kitchen counter. It reminded him of before, when he and Eva had done their weekly shop on Sundays. Eva had always made lists as long as her arm. For his part, he simply hauled what he thought they needed off the shelves and popped it in the trolley.

When he had packed away the shopping, he went into the living room and turned up the radiators. It was getting dark outside, so he put on the lights. It was the first time since Eva's death that he had been in the flat sober, which didn't make his return any easier. Perhaps things would change if he renovated the place a little? He could paint the walls and fix up the bathroom, just like they had wanted to, but never did anything about. He went back to the entrance. Møffe had plonked himself down on the stack of post, his eyes fixed on the door.

"Spare yourself the trouble, Møffe. We're not going anywhere."

Møffe lowered his head and licked his chops without any sign of budging from the spot.

Thomas went into the bedroom and started ripping the cover off the duvet and pillows. He found clean linen in the top of the cupboard and started changing the bedding. He had always hated this chore, and Eva had been the one who had taken care of it. His eyes lingered on her clothing in the cupboard. Sooner or later, he would have to get rid of it. The thought made him feel sick and gave him a guilty conscience. Perhaps he would just pack everything into a cardboard box and stow it in the storeroom in the cellar. When he was done with the bed, he went back to the kitchen and made himself two sandwiches. Then he filled the dog's bowls with food and water. For his part, Møffe obviously had no intention of abandoning his sit-in by the door.

All at once, the silence in the flat was deafening.

Thomas put on the TV and sat down on the sofa to eat his dinner. The evening news brought a brief report from Stockholm: *Rikspolisen*'s forensics investigation of the Lindgren residence had confirmed that Erik Lindgren was the perpetrator of all six murders. It was also reported that an earlier case involving the death of Lindgren's mother would be reopened. Karl Luger was interviewed in front of the residence. The Chief Commissioner looked utterly exhausted, and Thomas felt for the man. He could imagine how he would feel if someone in his own department was found guilty of murder. If Mikkel or anyone else at Ops had done something similar, it would shake the foundation of his ability to distinguish the good guys from the bad.

He was done with his dinner, so he went into the bathroom. One glance in the mirror confirmed that he looked like shit. The swelling had abated somewhat, but the split eyebrow would not heal. It looked like a black slug stuck above his eye socket.

Thomas took off his clothes, got into the shower, and turned on the hot water. The dog-bite wound on his leg oozed an opaque puss. He cursed himself for not asking a doctor to check it out when he was at the hospital to visit Masja. After his shower, he got into bed. The clean bedding felt good. He called for Møffe and tried to coax him into the bedroom, but he was unrelenting. Thomas gave up and closed his eyes.

Sleep hit him almost immediately, like a hammer planted in his forehead. He dreamt about Sweden, about Masja and about Eva. About the naked statue of the kneeling woman in the courtyard of Brantingtorget. He saw Mother Tove in her gold attire like an angel, serving soup to all the girls from the brothel at Arizona Market. He saw Lindgren with froth around his mouth rising up from the floor with a gun in his hand. He aimed and fired at Thomas, and this time he didn't miss. He felt the bullet penetrate his chest and he flew backwards. He landed in the chalky-white water in the zinc tub and slid to the bottom as the lime solution rushed into his mouth and filled his nose and throat.

Thomas started upright and gasped for breath. His T-shirt was drenched in sweat, and he peeled it up over his head. On the bedside table his mobile phone was vibrating next to the alarm clock that showed that the time was just before half-past five. He had no idea who would call him at this hour of the morning. He took the call.

"Good morning, Danish-Pig. Did I wake you?" a voice said with a thick Russian accent.

"Who . . . who am I talking to?"

"Slavros . . . Vladimir Slavros."

"Is this a joke?"

"I've lost my sense of humour, Danish-Pig. The police have closed my business and ransacked my house in the middle of the night, terrifying my family and forcing me to flee for my life. So I can assure you that this call is dead serious."

"It sounds to me as though you've finally got what you deserved," said Thomas evenly. "How does it feel to be on the run? Are you afraid?"

"I think we should keep feelings out of this conversation."

"Sure. Even though I don't understand why you are calling me. You ought to turn yourself in and get it over with. You're going to be detained sooner or later."

"Only if that is what I want. There are many places to hide."

Thomas yawned and scratched his beard. "In that case it will be without your family because the Swedish police will be watching them until you are safely behind bars. That has got to hurt. Kinda put a damper on the whole hide-and-seek routine."

"You're quite a smart man for a cop, Danish-Pig. I don't mind admitting that I have become somewhat of a 'Svensson' with a house in the suburbs and a Volvo in the driveway. It's not a bad life. Safe and secure. Very *lugnt*, a quiet existence, as the Swedes say."

"An existence that you can wave goodbye to for the next . . . sixteen years?"

"Perhaps. Unless the case goes away."

Thomas let out a laugh. "I don't think you should be too optimistic about that. They've got too much evidence against you already. You're going to end up sharing a cell with Arkan in Halldalan. Then you guys can be a couple and play house. I'm sure he'd like that. You should have given up Lindgren when you had a chance, then at least you would have something to bargain with."

"What makes you think that I don't?"

"I can't imagine that you have much to offer."

"You disappoint me, Ravn. Where is your intuition? Perhaps you're not as smart as I thought."

"It's very early in the morning, so why don't you spell it out for me?"

"Sure," said Slavros.

There was a brief period of static on the other end of the line. "Thomas . . . ?" It was Masja's voice. "Help me . . . please, Thomas . . ."

Thomas felt his heart hammering in his chest. "Where are you?"

Masja didn't get a chance to reply because Slavros was back on the line. "I've taken the liberty of discharging Masja from the hospital. Now it's up to you whether she survives or not."

"What do you want me to do?"

"Do I detect a different tone now? Not nearly as smug? A tad more respectful?"

"What do you want?"

Slavros let out a sigh. "Imagine my disappointment. There I was, thinking that this whole business could disappear together with the key witness. But just as we were standing on the roof of the hospital and Masja was on her way over the edge, she tells me that she's written everything down. And suddenly everything became complicated—too many loose ends. I hate loose ends. The question is whether I should believe her or take the chance and throw her off the roof."

"She's telling the truth."

"Really? According to Masja, you have important material on you . . . something which she gave to you."

"I have her diary. It's written in the notebook that you gave her to account for her work."

Slavros laughed. "Okay, I believe you. It sounds like she has told me the truth. Do I need to say that I would really like to have that notebook?"

"Where shall we meet?"

"On . . . Yderlandsvej there is a run-down warehouse. Large blue gates up front. You can't miss it. Be there in twenty minutes with her diary. Come alone."

"Slavros . . . ?"

There was a click on the line. Slavros had ended the call.

Thomas threw down the phone and ran his hands through his hair. This was going to be tricky. As soon as Slavros had received Masja's diary, he would kill them both, that was for sure. This was Slavros's only option to get off the hook. He considered calling Mikkel and involving Crime Ops, but he didn't dare. If Slavros got as much as a hint that cops were on the scene, he'd kill Masja and make a run for it.

Thomas got out of bed and retrieved the diary that lay under his jacket on the chair. He considered taking pictures of the whole book with his phone. He could send the pictures either to Mikkel or Johnson, but it wouldn't help. In order to get the case against Slavros to stick, the prosecutor needed the key witness as well as Masja's original recording of events. And right now, both parts were in Slavros's hands.

Thomas weighed his possibilities. There had to be a solution—a checkmate move he could make.

While he pulled on his clothes, a plan slowly formed in his head. He had no idea if it would work. Any number of pieces of the puzzle could fail along the way, but it was the best plan he could come up with on the spur of the moment, a faint hope to secure Masja and close this case for good.

64

The tall blue gates protested on their hinges when Thomas flung them aside and entered the abandoned warehouse on Yderlandsvej. It reeked nauseatingly of oil. Near the grease pit, which was lit by the only fluorescent light, Slavros was smoking a cigar. Mikhail stood to his right.

Slavros looked up when Thomas approached. "I said twenty minutes. You're late," he said, blowing a cloud of smoke into the air. Thomas stuck his hands in his pockets and walked towards them.

"The traffic was hell."

"At this time of the morning? Bullshit."

"Where is Masja?" said Thomas, looking around without seeing any sign of her.

"Where is the book, Thomas Ravns . . . holdt?" Slavros extended his hand.

When Thomas made no effort to accept the invitation, never mind remove his hands from his pockets, Slavros puffed vigorously on his cigar. "Ravn . . . ? Interesting surname. In the old days, ravens were used as hunting birds akin to falcons and eagles," he said, and tapped the ash of his cigar. "The raven is particularly gruesome. It blinds its victims by pecking out their eyes, before going for the vital organs."

"Let's skip the biology lesson, shall we? Where is Masja?"

Slavros ignored him. "But in the Middle Ages, ravens were regarded as an evil omen. Vermin. You know what we do with vermin, right?"

"We exterminate them," Mikhail answered for his boss.

"I'm here to collect Masja. Where is she?"

Slavros took a step to the side and pointed to the grease pit.

Thomas squinted into the sharp light, and glimpsed Masja at the far end, where she stood shivering in the cold.

"Masja? Are you all right?"

She did not reply and Slavros stepped in front of him, blocking his view. "Imagine being named after vermin," he said, shaking his head. "A thieving and winged vermin, nothing but a scavenger that lives off the dead. Do you have the book with you?"

"You'll get it as soon as I have Masja."

Slavros flicked the cigar hard at Thomas, and a cascade of glowing embers burst over his chest. "You don't give the orders around here; I do! I want that notebook—right now!"

Thomas didn't flinch. "Do you think that I'm stupid enough to have it on me?"

"Do you think I'm so weak that I can't beat a proper answer out of you?"

Thomas shrugged. "This would all go a lot faster if you'd stick to your own terms."

The corners of Slavros's mouth curled into a smile. Then he signalled to Mikhail.

Mikhail went into the pit and helped Masja up the steep stairs.

"Are you okay?" Thomas asked.

"The whore is fine! Now give me the book!"

Thomas turned his head and whistled. The next moment the outside door opened, and Eduardo entered the workshop. He tripped over the cables on the ground and almost fell flat on his face.

"Who the hell is this clown?" Slavros spat. "I said you should come alone."

"I needed a lift."

Eduardo came over and slipped Thomas the book. Then he took Masja's hand. "This way, *señorita.*"

Slavros blocked their path. "Not so fast, clown."

Thomas tossed the book just short of Slavros's feet. When he bent down to pick it up, Eduardo brought Masja behind Thomas.

Slavros opened the book. *Niels Lyhne* was printed on the first page with a stamp underneath: *Victoria's Antikvariat*, followed by an address and telephone number.

"What the hell is this?! This is not the whore's diary!" yelled Slavros, flinging the book at Thomas.

In that moment, the lights went out. Rapid footsteps approached in the dark. Slavros lunged forwards, swinging his arms blindly. "I'm going to kill you!"

Thomas smacked his fist into Slavros's face. "As you said, the raven always blinds his victims first."

Slavros reeled backwards. He punched the air a few times without making contact.

"Slavros? What's happening?" Mikhail stood at the edge of the grease pit, holding his fists in front of his face, till a mallet hit him in the stomach and he doubled over. The next blow smacked him on the jaw and Mikhail staggered backwards. He teetered on the edge of the pit a moment before a shove on the chest sent him crashing into the pit. Johnson emerged from the dark and glared down at Mikhail, satisfying himself that the bloke wasn't getting up again.

Slavros pulled a knife out of his boot. "Danish-Pig, where are you?" he yelled into the dark, shifting the knife from one hand to the other.

A rumbling sound came from the distance. Too late, Slavros sensed rather than saw the motor block in the tackle that came hurtling towards him. With a final shove from Thomas, the block rammed into Slavros and sent him flying. He hit the ground hard and didn't get up again. Thomas kicked the knife out of his reach.

Suddenly, the lights came on again. Johnson came up to Thomas.

"Thanks for your help," Thomas said.

"You're welcome," said Johnson, rubbing his swollen fist.

"Are you okay?" Thomas asked.

"Yes, of course, it's nothing," said Johnson, hiding his hand behind his back.

Victoria came up alongside them. "Did you get the bastards?"

"Where is Masja?" asked Thomas.

"She's outside with Eduardo," said Victoria.

Thomas nodded and took out his phone.

Half an hour later, the parking lot in front of the warehouse was teeming with police vehicles from Station City. It had started to rain again. Two uniformed policemen brought out Slavros and Mikhail in handcuffs and escorted them into the back seat of a police car.

Masja came over to Thomas. The ambulance team had given her a blanket that she had wrapped around her shoulders. "I can't thank you enough."

Thomas smiled at her. "Don't give it another thought."

Masja looked down. "I want to do the right thing. It's time that I did. I've made so many stupid mistakes."

"Stop blaming yourself, Masja. You've been through enough."

As Slavros came past in the patrol car, for a moment, their eyes met through the windshield. She turned towards Thomas. "I'd like to give a statement to the police."

"Are you sure?"

"Well, most of all I'm terrified. But yes, I'm sure I want to testify. I don't want Slavros to hurt any more people."

The rain came down over their heads, and Thomas smiled.

65

The winter cold blew in from the north, as if a delayed greeting from Stockholm. Despite the biting cold, Thomas was standing on the aft deck of *Bianca* in his shirtsleeves, pumping the bilge of rainwater that had collected in a murky sludge in the bottom of the rearmost storage hold. He was sweating and had discarded his jacket from the strenuous work. Møffe was keeping indoors and minding his own business, making short shrift of the old army boot that Thomas had found for him.

"Ravn?" A voice from the quay above interrupted his work.

Thomas twisted his head and caught sight of a pair of white tennis socks stuffed into heelless black clogs. "What can I do for you, Preben?" he said to the quay master, without breaking his stride with the pump.

Preben had his hands in his pockets and lifted his trousers, involuntarily flashing his tennis socks again. "Have you fixed the electrical wiring?" he asked.

"At least to the extent that she won't short-circuit the fuse box up there," Thomas said. "So if you've received complaints, it wasn't me."

"No complaints," replied Preben, looking at the boat critically. "Eduardo tells me that you've put her up for sale."

"Yes, and?"

"What do you want for her?"

Thomas stopped his work with the pump and straightened up.

"You are interested in buying her?"

"Perhaps," Preben said with a shrug. "For the right price."

Thomas could not help laughing. "Didn't you call her a floating environmental catastrophe the last time you came by?"

"Yes. Naturally, it will take quite a bit of time and money to get her in shape, so I can't offer you the world, but I'd like to help, take her off your hands."

"Thanks, Preben, that's kind of you, but I think I'll keep her after all."

Preben goggled at Thomas. Then a sour expression came over his face. "I see. Well, it's your choice, of course. I just wanted to do you a favour more than anything else."

Thomas nodded in Preben's general direction and resumed his pumping action.

"Your boat is still leaking oil, Ravnsholdt. You ought to do something about that."

Thomas kept scooping water out of the storage hold. Declined to make any further reply. Soon after, he heard Preben's clogs clattering over the cobblestones.

Later that afternoon, Eduardo came past. He stuck his head through the cabin door just as Thomas was preparing himself a coffee in the kitchenette. "What's this I hear?"

"I don't know. Want to join me for a coffee?"

"*Sí, gracias.* You don't want to sell the boat after all?"

Thomas smiled. "Rumours spread quickly along Christianshavn quay."

"As always. Preben's over at The Sea Otter as we speak, waxing lyrical about harbour dues to anyone who will listen."

The corners of Thomas's mouth curled into a smile again. "Preben is probably the last person in the world I would sell *Bianca* to," he said, pouring hot water into their mugs.

"So what's the plan? Can you afford to keep the boat now you don't have a job?"

"Nah." Thomas took a seat in the captain's chair and sipped his steaming mug of coffee. "Unless I sell the flat."

Eduardo put his mug down on the counter. "Are you seriously considering that option?"

"Yes, I think so. The flat will never be a home for me again, I don't think."

"But it's an amazing flat."

"Without a doubt. And I reckon I could get a pretty good deal on it."

"But don't you think you'll regret it?"

"Honestly, I'm not entirely sure. But right now, all I know is that I need to move on. I need to get away from everything . . . you understand?" Thomas's eyes dropped to the deck.

"Do you think they'll ever find Eva's murderer?"

"There is of course *a* chance, but no, I don't think they ever will." Thomas slipped off the chair. "Besides, Møffe loves being on board the boat."

Eduardo looked down at the dog dozing by the cabin stairs. "So now the dog gets to decide?"

Thomas shrugged. "I guess he always has."

"But if you sell the flat, will you and Møffe move in to *Bianca*?"

"Yes. At least until I've found another place to live."

Eduardo glanced around. "It could get pretty cold on the boat."

"Nonsense, it has a heating system."

"Yeah, but does it work?"

Thomas shook his head. "Nah, not yet. But it will. Just you wait, this is going to be a damn fine little yacht once I'm done with her." He winked at Eduardo. "The finest *señorita* in Christianshavn canal."

ABOUT THE AUTHOR

Michael Katz Krefeld (b. 1966) is one of the most-read Danish crime authors, and his critically acclaimed books have been awarded several fiction prizes. He is best known for his bestselling crime series featuring Detective Ravn, which has thrilled readers across the globe. Having begun his career as a screenwriter, Krefeld tends toward fast-paced and highly unpredictable thrillers. The fight against evil and personal sacrifices made for the greater good are typical recurring elements of his work.